THE CROWN OF LIFE

Other novels by George Gissing also published by Harvester

THE NETHER WORLD
Edited and with an introduction by John Goode

THYRZA
Edited and with an introduction by Jacob Korg

DEMOS: A STORY OF ENGLISH SOCIALISM
Edited and with an introduction by Pierre Coustillas

SLEEPING FIRES
Edited and with an introduction by Pierre Coustillas

ISABEL CLARENDON
Edited and with an introduction by Pierre Coustillas

IN THE YEAR OF JUBILEE
Edited by P. F. Kropholler, and with an introduction by Gillian Tindall

THE UNCLASSED
Edited and with an introduction by Jacob Korg

THE WHIRLPOOL
Edited and with an introduction by Patrick Parrinder

THE EMANCIPATED
Edited and with an introduction by Pierre Coustillas

DENZIL QUARRIER
Edited and with an introduction by John Halperin

OUR FRIEND THE CHARLATAN
Edited and with an introduction by Pierre Coustillas

BORN IN EXILE
Edited and with an introduction by Pierre Coustillas

Forthcoming:
WILL WARBURTON
Edited and with an introduction by Colin Partridge

THE PAYING GUEST
Edited and with an introduction by Ian Fletcher

THE TOWN TRAVELLER
Edited and with an introduction by Pierre Coustillas

THE CROWN OF LIFE

George Gissing

Edited and with an introduction by
Michel Ballard
Lecturer, Centre for Victorian Studies
University of Lille

THE HARVESTER PRESS

This edition first published by
THE HARVESTER PRESS·LIMITED
Publisher: John Spiers
2 Stanford Terrace, Hassocks, Sussex

©New editorial material, Michel Ballard, 1978

British Library Cataloguing in Publication Data
Gissing, George
 The crown of life.
 I. Title II. Ballard, Michel
 823'.8   PR4716.C/

ISBN 0-85527-692-4

Printed and bound in Great Britain by
REDWOOD BURN LIMITED
Trowbridge & Esher

Contents

Bibliographical Note

The Crown of Life was first published at six shillings by Methuen & Co. in late October 1899, shortly before the outbreak of the Boer War. The first edition consisted of 4,500 copies, which exist in a number of states, all in red cloth gilt but with or without publishers' advertisements with dates ranging from 1899 to 1914. The novel was issued simultaneously in Methuen's Colonial Library in blue-green cloth. In Canada W. J. Gage & Co. produced an edition of the book from American plates, also in the autumn of 1899. Methuen published a sixpenny edition of the novel in pictorial covers in June 1905, this being no. 65 in the Novelist Series; then, at a time when many of Gissing's books were reissued, a 3s. 6d. pocket edition in red cloth appeared in June 1927. Part of this edition was issued in stiff wrappers at a later date. The new edition by Methuen, listed in the *English Catalogue* (1943), did not achieve publication.

The first American edition of *The Crown of Life* was brought out by Stokes in October 1899 in dark green and in red cloth gilt. An undated reissue in light-green cloth with silver titling is also on record. The AMS Press reprinted the first American edition in 1969, the three volumes bound in one.

The original handwritten manuscript is held by the Huntington Library, San Marino, California.

Acknowledgements

I wish to express my thanks to Professor Coustillas for his help and advice, as well as to Mr. Kropholler for his generous assistance with the notes to the text.

Introduction

There are often strong personal strains in Gissing's novels. In this respect *The Crown of Life* undoubtedly holds a special position inasmuch as it not only expresses the writer's long frustration in love but also his more recent hopes of having at last found the ideal companion he had always thought himself debarred from approaching.

After returning from Italy in April 1898, Gissing settled in Dorking and tried to keep his retreat secret from his second wife, Edith. She eventually found him in September, and after a last scene accepted an informal separation but refused a divorce. Quite independently of the state reached by their relationship, Gissing had good reasons for desiring a dissolution of their marriage. On 23 June he had received a letter from a young French woman, asking his permission to translate *New Grub Street*. He first met her in the company of the Wellses, and she came to Dorking on 26 July, promising another visit in October. She had made a deep impression on him, and their correspondence shows the gradual development of their friendship into love. It was on 15 July, 1898 that Gissing entered in his diary: 'Made a beginning of *The Crown of Life*', and it seems that Gabrielle Fleury's one-week stay in early October stimulated further his creative powers. Having made a fresh start of the novel on 18 October, he recorded its completion on 16 January, 1899.

The Crown of Life is a love story written by a man in love, but it is also an anti-imperialist pamphlet written by a convinced pacifist. The novel did not turn out to be a success, although this was partly the result of delays in publication. Reviews, on the whole, were unfavourable. Nevertheless the criteria of compliments as well as of criticisms are somewhat astonishing; they bear no relation to the novel as a work of art. Gissing, for instance, was commended for his greater optimism and grossly attacked for his lack of patriotism. Subsequent assessments offer the same fragmentary or derogatory approaches.

To a modern reader, for whom free love, eroticism and pornography have become commonplaces, the final scene of *The Crown of Life,* which shows Piers Otway enraptured by his first kiss from Irene Derwent after an exile of eight years, will no doubt appear singularly old-fashioned, unreal, or even laughable. Moreover the oddity of the situation is reinforced when one considers the apparent reason for his banishment: Piers being slightly flushed and tipsy on a visit to Irene, who remarked that he had better disappear. Such a statement of the subject matter of the love story would seem to justify Wells's scathing judgment: 'Love in a frock-coat'. There may be some truth in this view but, like all caricatures, it tends to exaggerate one feature at the expense of the whole. It does not make room for the specific qualities of the novel and the author's intentions; and above all it gives the wrong impression that love in its more physical or sensual aspects is absent from the book.

Gissing asserts the force of love by making it a need which dies only with man. This appears in the continued interests of the previous generation: the frustrated Mrs. Hannaford craves for love and flings herself into the arms of the unscrupulous Daniel Otway, 'for *life meant love*'. The sixty-year-old MP John Jacks has just married a young woman of twenty-five. Jerome Otway, the hero's father, significantly, has had three female companions in his life. The sensuality of the two old friends is underlined by their marrying again wives much younger than themselves. And finally there is the figure of Dr Derwent worshipping his wife's memory beyond death. The younger generation is not deficient in that field either. Alexander Otway speaks highly of his wife, as if she were a rare collector's item. Olga Hannaford is devoured by her passion for Piers. In her turn she is pursued by Florio's possessive devotion. Her friend Miss Bonnicastle seems to be leading a rather free bohemian life. And Kite does not hide the fact that sensuality is a major problem for him.

For the young hero himself, the force of love finds expression at first in sensuality and sexual instinct. Morley Roberts rightly pointed out that 'almost alone among modern writers he (Gissing) has dared to delineate the tortures of the undebauched celibate.' [1] The Piers Otway described in the beginning of the novel, and especially in Chapter XIII, calls to mind the tantalizing desires of other young bachelors such as Harold Biffen and Godwin Peak (see p. 98). The scene in which Piers watches Irene basking in the sun is certainly as erotic as proprieties would allow it at the time (see p. 41). *Love and Mr Lewisham* (1900) will offer no better treatment of the conflict arising between studies and the effects of budding love on a young male sexuality.

Gissing even overdoes Pier's capacity for love, so as to show that he is a mere toy in the hands of instinct. In Chapter XXVII he nearly proposes to Olga Hannaford because he misunderstands one of her gestures. The incident is strongly reminiscent of the scene which Clara Hewett plays for Sidney Kirkwood in *The Nether World.* In both cases a love-like stimulus engenders an amorous response. Piers at times is like a vast antenna of love ready to turn to any object apparently fit for his purpose: pictures of beautiful women, Mrs. John Jacks, Irene or even Olga. Obviously in this so-called optimistic novel, the eternal Gissing remains lurking, ready to point out, not without scepticism, the comparative indifference of the object when love is based on sexual impulse alone. But it is on this very scepticism and on the scarcity of successful unions that he bases his optimism: 'Only to the elect is it granted' thinks Jerome Otway of true love. And this is partly the meaning of the sort of Pilgrim's Progress which takes place during the two lovers' separation.

Unfortunately those two 'elects' make a rather poor impression when love as a feeling is concerned. And this is perhaps where the trouble lies with this love story: there is a certain lack of credibility and aesthetic unity. It begins and ends with human characters placed in normal emotional situations, while in between takes place a long theoretical process tending to demonstrate that the Gissingian ideal is possible. The strange thing of course is that the two young people reach the stature of a couple by living separately, hardly seeing each other except under formal circumstances. There is too much of platonic romance. Sensuality for Piers remains a solitary, morbid and frustrating experience. Yet if one is to make something out of these contradictions one must turn to the author's intentions: they are stamped as it were on the first page in the form of the opening scene.

The description of Piers Otway gazing at the three pictures of women displayed in a Haymarket shopwindow is a static prologue on love. It is an artistic projection of the hero's frame of mind, his conception of love and a clue to the general pattern of this theme within the novel. Beauty and sensuousness, education and culture, nature and serenity constitute the ingredients required of a true Gissingian passion. They determine, together with social considerations, the successive phases of the present love story. Irritating or artificial as it may appear to some readers, it is the description of a slow process of civilization, refinement and personal adjustment. Most of Gissing's early love stories follow a ritualistic pattern into which the religious notions of fall, sin, worship and redemption enter. His own experience is not without having shaped the arrangement of his fictional universe. It is significant that it is his earlier novels, *Workers in the Dawn* and *The Unclassed,* which offer this sort of composition at its purest. It is no less remarkable that he should revert to this pattern when he feels regenerated by his liaison with Gabrielle Fleury. This disposition of mind may account for a number of the improbabilities of the present story.

In an earlier novel Piers's fall would have been caused by a prostitute; here it is his connection with his brother Alexander and his being slightly drunk that amounts to the sin of vulgarity. It is an incident similar to the coming of Peak's uncle near Whitelaw College: popular origins emerging in broad daylight. But Gissing draws too much on the device of social differences: Piers is not as inferior as all that to Irene. He may be a natural child, but his father has a certain fame and recommends him to his friend, the MP John Jacks. Besides, Irene's father, Dr Derwent himself, is of humble origins and has known poverty. Obviously the author wanted to establish a social gap and a separation between hero and heroine but he did it by straining the elements he had in his hands. The final stigma on Piers's character is his sensuality. The author's attitude is not far from being ambiguous: while extolling his hero's sensuality and asserting the rights of the body in love, Gissing continually diverts them from their natural out come and tries to justify them from an aesthetic point of view. There may be some concession to Victorian proprieties here but undoubtedly it is part of the worshipping attitude typical of Gissingian lovers. It is no accident that, from the first page, love is connected with pictures. Art speaks to the senses but also to other emotions. Playing on the imagination it conveniently diverts desire towards the fields of dream. The inhuman nature of artistic representations reproduces the distance existing between lover and beloved. They delight in a sort of semi-masochistic, semi-hedonistic voyeurism: thus in *Workers in the Dawn* Arthur Golding watches Helen Norman from behind a pillar in a church and she, in her turn, months later, peeps at him through a door ajar without revealing her presence. Here Piers begins by examining Irene from his bedroom window. This feature may be interesting as temperamental curiosity, but it tends to become awkward because of the readiness with which characters accept long separations. In *Born in Exile* Gissing had shown, with the adventures of Christian Moxey and Malkin, that he had grown aware of the comic effects which might be drawn from those life-long lovers, but the freshness of his own passion rendered him particularly uncritical. Finally Piers's redemption, if one looks at it carefully, is not particularly romantic: it consists of making money. It is a change from the behaviour pattern of the usual Gissingian hero and the sign of a realistic adjustment to the world.

The case of Irene Derwent is a strange one. She is supposed to represent 'the lady' and she offers the same coldness and aloofness as Sidwell Warricombe. During their separation, Piers's love lives on sensuality and genuine feeling, she on her side does not love him at first. In fact, rather than *falling* in love, one should speak of her *growing* in love. Moreover ones does not get the impression that she is in love with Piers Otway personally but rather with what he stands for. Her attachment is closer to the infatuation that a young middle-class girl might develop for a hippie, an anarchist or a communist, because he represents a life style entirely opposed to that of her environment. In case purists might find such a comparison anachronistic let us say that Irene turns to Piers in the same way as Amy Reardon turns to Jasper Milvain. To some readers this may not be convincing as a love story but it is undoubtedly a remarkable study in evolution— an exercise in which Gissing excels.

In the first section of the novel she is an illustration of the combined influences of inherited tendencies and above all of environment. This provides a meaning for her accepting Arnold Jacks as her fiancé. When she contemplates marriage it is with Victorian coldness and propriety. It is her body that reacts to this unnatural view of love. As in the case of Thyrza, in the novel of the same name, it is a number of psychosomatic disorders which bring her to listen to her real self: vapours and irritability

(Chapter XIX), insomnia (Chapter XXV). All this, added to a number of observations concerning her official fiancé, brings about the breaking of her engagement. In itself this act is a challenge to public opinion and proprieties. Her conscious evolution is an indictment of Victorian society in so far as its conventions prevent the development of true love and breed only frustration. In discovering that she needed love as a real sentiment and not simply as social camouflage, Irene has felt the need for certain qualities existing in Piers. The Irene who asserts her right to love and be happy in defiance of proprieties is no longer the same woman as at the beginning. In several ways she foreshadows the character of Helen in *Howards End*, especially in Chapter XXVII: her interview with Arnold Jacks amounts to the confrontation of two members from different communities who do not speak the same language. The completeness of her transformation is underlined by her growing awareness of the ugliness of London as a reflection of modern civilization. Her flight abroad completes, in a tangible form, this escape from conventions. From another point of view her attitude is an assertion of the right of the individual to be happy in defiance of morals and especially of the notion of duty. In Gissing's first novels, lovers (for instance Golding, Casti, Waymark, Kirkwood) feel obliged to persevere to the end of an unhappy affair because they are bound by a promise or some sense of duty, whereas Irene Derwent, like Everard Barfoot or Godwin Peak, refuses the traditional notions of honour. Piers on the other hand escapes this fate thanks only to Olga's honesty.

The next phase in Irene's transformation illustrates for Gissing the importance of effort, education and culture in any process of human evolution. Her first step was negative, the second is positive. Turning to Piers Otway for human love, Irene gradually enters the mental world he is living in. The fact that she learns Russian in order to read his articles has often been presented as rather laughable. The notion is not as absurd as that: the wish to share the same culture may well naturally breed such a desire. On another level her friend Mrs Borisoff says: 'It's a mental and moral advance her new love of music. I notice that she talks much less about science, much more about the things one really likes' (p. 282). Finally her condemnation of war and shooting shows that she has adopted Piers's pacifist views.

In the end, love blooms in the natural setting evoked by the third picture of woman from the first chapter. Actually, nature has never been absent from the novel. It was at first associated with the retreats of Jerome Otway and Irene's aunts. Piers has always enjoyed nature for the peace it might procure him. It is frequent for Gissing to place his main love scenes in natural settings (think of *Demos* or *In the Year of Jubilee*) probably because of the notions of privacy and sensuousness connected with nature, but in the present case the effect is particularly successful. The last chapter opens with the beautiful image of the two lovers walking towards each other over the grass near a brook. The general movement of the scene and the gaily sensuous touches suggests the plenitude, the light spirit and elation of a pastoral symphony.

The novel begins with a scattered projection of love into artistic but remote and geometric pictures— it was an ideal, mental theoretical image. The book closes on a live picture of union in which all the elements are harmoniously blended.

The Crown of Life was disliked because Gissing's indictment of a worldwide imperialism and budding militarism went against the grain of public opinion. Not only in Britain but in several continental nations also, imperialism and colonialism were practised and politically acceptable to the majority. The strength of this current found expression in the creation of such societies as The Imperial Federation League and The Primrose League. The movement had its poet, Rudyard Kipling, and its theoretician, John Seeley, whose *Expansion of England* echoes Charles Dilke's *Greater Britain.* One must bear both this and the legitimate pride of an expanding nation in mind to understand that many an Englishman did not question his own outlook on such matters. *The Crown of Life,* therefore, must have seemed particularly irrelevant, at worst the work of a traitor, at best that of a dreamer. As a matter of fact both aspects coexist, they are part of Gissing's constant approach to any problem: the critical intellectual and the generous idealist. But what his disparagers failed to see was that his criticism was not aimed at England but at a certain trend of thought identifiable in other European nations as well. For him the choice was not between being a patriot or not— for he was a patriot— but among a number of values that could shape the future of man and involved him deeply. In this resides Gissing's classicism: his concern for man, and his belief that everything, and above all good and evil, are in man himself.

His theory of humanity, influenced by reading Schopenhauer and Darwin, makes constant reference to the will to live and dominate. In this book he seeks to bring out the difference between temperamental aggressiveness and gentleness. The vigorous practical Milvain and the sickly unpractical Reardon of *New Grub Street* are the archetypes presiding over the opposition between imperialists and pacifists.

Piers Otway is not the first mild sensitive idealist portrayed by Gissing. Arthur Golding in *Workers in the Dawn* reflected his own flirtation with radicalism. It is significant of his rejuvenation by love that he should have conjured up that association and placed it in the background in the person of Jerome Otway. A similar, but weaker, evocation of it is to be found in *Born in Exile* with Peak's father. It is part of Gissing's contradictions that, while being alarmed at democratization, he never entirely gives up his ideas about radicalism and, above all, anarchy. Besides his connection with the international names of socialism Jerome Otway is a Christ-like figure, an unobtrusive martyr who dies through violence. This, and repeated references to Christianity and Christian virtues, are further evidence of Gissing's reverting to the frame of mind characteristic of his first novel. Technically too the idealism and didacticism of the book is brought to a climax in Jerome Otway's fable of War and Peace. Some will criticize it on the ground of its childishness, but one must remember, on the one hand, that this is a literary genre, on the other that most generous ideas at the start sound utopian. One could certainly attack with the same weapons a book like *News from Nowhere*. Jerome Otway's stature and ideas make a Blakian figure of him. Unlike his father, Piers does not belong to a party, he rather appears as a member of an enlightened community of individualists whose passwords are lucidity, culture and generosity. Later embodiments of the type, such as Lord Dymchurch in *Our Friend The Charlatan* or the hermit of the *Ryecroft Papers*, will be more discreet in their defence of pacifism and content to live in retirement. Piers, on the contrary, does not seek isolation; he is always ready to speak out for his ideals and to struggle in his own mild way to promote them. It is a fight which might be carried out by an honest man in everyday life. His absence of links with a group reflects Gissing's own distrust of organizations. This characteristic, on the other hand, is clearly a weakness in face of the imperialists, who definitely give the impression of forming a better organized body. The opposition is of the same nature and nearly as clear-cut as that of the two groups of children in William Golding's *Lord of the Flies*. The parting line between the two types of men thus contrasted goes through love, sensibility, culture. Just as Piers is a born lover, Arnold Jacks and Lee Hannaford are born haters. Their political line is an extension of their capacity or incapacity to love. For them love is merely an individual social function devoid of feeling, and Lee Hannaford is shown to spread misery in his domestic environment. Their main imperfection is to lack the Christian virtues of charity, humility and love for their fellow creatures. Such a biased portrayal of characters is of course questionable. It obviously derives from the too overt commitment of the book. All imperialists, colonialists or militarists were not monsters—far from it—and one can regret that a writer capable of creating such a complex personality as Godwin Peak contented himself with a black and white division in this instance. Obviously his desire to unify his novel around the theme of love. contributed to the flaw. The only concession he makes to the imperialists is to grant them intelligence, but a debased one according to Gissingian standards, operative in practical matters only: they are blind to culture and its civilizing influence.

And yet the relevance of this contrasted distinction, based on simple but vital human qualities, appears throughout the book when Gissing questions the neutrality of language and the media. In the same way as Alexander Otway believes in the power of the Press and words to spread hatred and violence, John Jacks believes in their power to spread peace. The same words are constantly used for different purposes by the two opposite camps. Both speak in the name of civilization but not with the same views in mind. For Arnold Jacks 'his religion was the British Empire' (p. 11). Piers says to Irene: 'It seems to me that this is the world's only hope—Peace made a religion' (p. 289). There seems to be a language beyond language. Ambiguity, a key notion in Gissingian characterization, is here projected into language as if to stress the inadequacy of words in themselves as a medium to truth, and our dependence on man's good will and honesty to fill them with their noblest meaning.

What characterizes Gissing's vision of evil as an active force in the world is its organic unity, its coherence. He sees it as the forces of hatred, self-interest, egoism, aggressiveness, domination developing inconcentric circles wider and wider as they contaminate vaster fields of human activity: from commerce to fierce competition; from competition inland to competition abroad; from commerce to colonialism; from personal domination and violence to imperialism and international warfare. Individual history illuminates world history with particular consistency and comprehensiveness.

Commerce is not really criticized as such, except insofar as, diverted — from its original purpose— the exchange of goods it comes to mean merely making money, and can have a corrupting influence on man and culture. Although he is 'savagely set on making money' for love, Piers strives to keep his integrity and, while acquiring some of the solid qualities of the business man, he retains the air of a scholar and of a gentleman. He, together with his friend Moncharmont and John Jacks himself, belongs to a series of human and cultured business men which began with Egremont in *Thyrza,* and continued with Mr Athel in *A Life's Morning,* Mr Doran and Mr Spence in *The Emancipated,* and Basil Morton in *The Whirlpool.* Commerce is represented as displaying its aggressiveness and vulgarity at home in advertising. The mania is here embodied in Florio who considers it as 'the triumph of our century, the supreme outcome of civilization' (p. 261). Miss Bonnicastle and, to a lesser extent, Olga and Kite stand for the artists who gradually place themselves in the service of commerce for money. Gissing's criticism is partly based on the sacredness of art; the notion is particularly clear when, in front of a beautiful picture, Miss Bonnicastle feels that she is about to commit a sacrilege by turning it into an advertisement for a shampoo. Gissing's concern for the future of culture and civilization places him in the line of such authors as Aldous Huxley, George Duhamel, George Orwell and Jean-Louis Curtis.

While turning Darwinian theories into artistic material, Gissing had hitherto been an observer of the struggle for life within British society, opposing the practical, shrewd character generally bent on business to the mild, weak man of letters destined to fail and die. With *The Crown of Life* he gives both greater stamina to his typical hero and wider scope to his study in aggressiveness by enlarging the scene to the world itself. The protagonists of the struggle for life become the nations themselves and violence assumes a cruder aspect.

The basic elements of the situation were of two kinds: economic and political. In the last quarter of the nineteenth century, although Britain still seemed the most major of world powers, there were signs that its leadership was on the way to be questioned. The growing competition of such countries as Germany and United States, the development of local industries closed a number of markets to British goods. As a consequence and as a reaction the conquest of new markets became a vital matter. On the other hand the system of alliances prevailing in Europe caused France and

Russia to appear as Britain's greatest enemies; all the more so as the latter feared Russian expansion in the Mediterranean. Both elements enter the fabric of the novel.

The views of commercial imperialism, the necessity of competition between Britain and Russia are set forth straightforwardly in Chapter XXIX by the merchant Piers meets in a Liverpool hotel. The link with commerce is established more lastingly in the novel through Arnold Jacks, the official theoretician and champion of the movement being Trafford Romaine. But imperialism does not always set forth its creed so crudely. Usually it tries to justify its existence by citing higher motives such as the civilizing influence of commerce. Throughout the novel runs a mythology of racial superiority based on cultural superiority as advocated by Alexander Otway and Arnold Jacks. Besides the irony with which their assertions are treated Gissing humorously depicts their impact abroad on such snobbish foreigners as Florio, who are naively ready to give up their nationality.

Gissing had perceived that modern warfare would no longer be limited to the mere brutal conflict between two armies and that it would have extensions and help from a corrupted form of culture: the Press. He had shown in other works such as *New Grub Street* and *Born in Exile* the poor opinion he had of that medium, which, is represented here in action as a potent agent of war and propaganda. The approach is the same as with commerce: it is not the Press as such which is being attacked but the wrong use which can be made of it— because of mercantile interests on the one hand and the lack of education of the masses on the other.

Both attitudes are placed in historical and geographical perspective. In their Ryecroft-like retirement, Irene's old aunts, with the help of their culture, proceed to a mild but effective ironical debunking of Trafford Romaine and his ideas, describing him as 'an old type under new conditions . . . I admire Sir Walter Raleigh, but I should be sorry to see him, just as he was, playing an active part in our time' (p. 80). In other words, imperialism is a thing of the past. Pacifism on the contrary belongs to a more recent past: it is the cause for which John Jacks and Jerome Otway started to campaign in their youth; it is the hope of the future. Moreover the connection of the old men with the great European names of revolution and emancipation lends the movement an internationalism which is contrasted with the narrowly British field of Arnold Jacks and Trafford Romaine's patriotism. In that respect, many may have failed to grasp the poise of Piers's vision. He is not blind to the defects of Russian society, or Germany's rampant militarism [2] but he does not systematically look down on these nations as do the supporters of imperialism who flaunt their contempt of the poor barbarians. Piers strikes up a personal friendship with a Russian, proclaims the intellectual contribution of Slavonic thinkers, and does not conceal his admiration for the non-violent doctrine of the Dukhobortsi. [3] It is intended as a significant sign of the greater realism of the hero that, unlike so many other figures in Gissing's universe, he does not turn to 'foreign countries' for escape but for exchange and coexistence.

Thus pacifism and militarism are made to appear as the international forms of two more general outlooks on life: violence and non-violence. Speaking of Gissing, Morley Roberts states: 'I do not suppose that he was physically a coward, but a dread of scenes and physical violence lay deep in his organisation.' [4] More widely he insists on the respect due to life by contrasting the uses of science made by Dr Derwent and Lee Hannaford. The sacredness of life, in all its forms, is proclaimed by Dr Derwent's rejection of vivisection, Irene's criticism of shooting and Piers's plea against the death penalty.

Gissing's anti militarism and pacifism did not start with *The Crown of Life,* nor did they cease with it. Already visible in *Isabel Clarendon, New Grub Street* and *The Whirlpool,* they are present also in *Henry Ryecroft* and various other writings,[5] but nowhere do the ideas receive such extensive treatment as in the present novel. The extent to which the problem of war lay deep in his heart can be measured by what he wrote in a letter to his son Walter after the publication of *The Crown of Life:* 'You must understand. . . that *War* is a horrible thing which ought to be left to savages— a thing to be ashamed of and not to glory in . . . . What we ought to be proud of is peace and kindness— not fighting and hatred.' [6] Walter was eight years old at the time and was to be killed on the Somme during the First World War!

In most of Gissing's previous novels the opposition between good and evil had mainly taken the shape of an antagonism between spiritual and material values, culture and the world. His concern for the more human aspect of the notion was never absent. But suffering and doing good to others remained isolated experiences, situations which were tolerated, acts which were performed with a rather resigned sense of destiny. In *The Crown of Life* Gissing temporarily discards the solution of retirement to turn to the problem of reaching satisfactory and enduring human relationships, and eventually enlarges it to a world-wide dimension. Dealing more specifically with the question, he integrates his individualistic and intellectual system of values within a more gregarious and explicit code of morals. *The Crown of Life,* as a love story, offers an epitome of Gissing's views on the subject. It is a political book of a special nature inasmuch as it gives prominence to human respect and love, the contribution of an artist trying to strike a balance between life and culture, the intelligence 'of the brain and that of the heart'.[7]

THE CROWN OF LIFE

CHAPTER I

AMID the throng of suburban arrivals volleyed forth from Waterloo Station on a May morning in the year '86, moved a slim, dark, absent-looking young man of one-and-twenty, whose name was Piers Otway. In regard to costume —blameless silk hat, and dark morning coat with lighter trousers—the City would not have disowned him, but he had not the City countenance. The rush for omnibus seats left him unconcerned; clear of the railway station, he walked at a moderate pace, his eyes mostly on the ground; he crossed the foot-bridge to Charing Cross, and steadily made his way into the Haymarket, where his progress was arrested by a picture shop.

A window hung with engravings, mostly after pictures of the day; some of them very large, and attractive to a passing glance. One or two admirable landscapes offered solace to the street-wearied imagination, but upon these Piers Otway did not fix his eye; it was drawn irresistibly to the faces and forms of beautiful women set forth with varied allurement. Some great lady of the passing time lounged in exquisite array amid luxurious furniture lightly suggested; the faint smile of her flattered loveliness hovered about the gazer; the subtle perfume of her presence touched his nerves; the greys of her complexion transmuted themselves through the current of his blood into life's carnation; whilst he dreamed upon her lips, his breath was caught, as though of a sudden she had smiled for him, and for him alone. Near to her was a maiden of Hellas, resting upon a marble seat, her eyes bent towards some Ægean isle; the translucent robe clung about her

I

perfect body; her breast was warm against the white stone; the mazes of her woven hair shone with unguent. The gazer lost himself in memories of epic and idyll, warming through worship to desire. Then his look strayed to the next engraving; a peasant girl, consummate in grace and strength, supreme in chaste pride, cheek and neck soft-glowing from the sunny field, eyes revealing the heart at one with nature. Others there were, women of many worlds, only less beautiful; but by these three the young man was held bound. He could not satisfy himself with looking and musing; he could not pluck himself away. An old experience; he always lingered by the print shops of the Haymarket, and always went on with troubled blood, with mind rapt above familiar circumstance, dreaming passionately, making wild forecast of his fate.

At this hour of the morning not many passers had leisure to stand and gaze; one, however, came to a pause beside Piers Otway, and viewed the engravings. He was a man considerably older; not so well dressed, but still, on the strength of externals, entitled to the style of gentleman; his brown, hard felt hat was entirely respectable, as were his tan gloves and his boots, but the cut-away coat began to hint at release from service, and the trousers owed a superficial smartness merely to being tightly strapped. This man had a not quite agreeable face; inasmuch as it was smoothly shaven, and exhibited a peculiar mobility, it might have denoted him an actor; but the actor is wont to twinkle a good-natured mood which did not appear upon this visage. The contour was good, and spoke intelligence; the eyes must once have been charming. It was a face which had lost by the advance of years; which had hardened where it was soft, and seemed likely to grow harder yet; for about the lips, as he stood examining these pictures, came a suggestion of the vice in blood which tends to cruelty. The nostrils began to expand and to tremble a little; the eyes seemed to project themselves; the long throat grew longer. Presently, he turned a glance upon the young man standing near to him, and in that moment his expression entirely altered.

"Why," he exclaimed, "Piers!"

The other gave a start of astonishment, and at once smiled recognition.

"Daniel! I hadn't looked—I had no idea"—

They shook hands, with graceful cordiality on the elder

man's part, with a slightly embarrassed goodwill on that of the younger. Daniel Otway, whose age was about eight-and-thirty, stood in the relation of half-brotherhood to Piers, a relation suggested by no single trait of their visages. Piers had a dark complexion, a face of the square, emphatic type, and an eye of shy vivacity; Daniel, with the long, smooth curves of his countenance and his chestnut hair, was, in the common sense, better looking, and managed his expression with a skill which concealed the characteristics visible a few moments ago; he bore himself like a suave man of the world, whereas his brother still betrayed something of the boy in tone and gesture, something, too, of the student accustomed to seclusion. Daniel's accent had nothing at all in keeping with a shabby coat; that of the younger man was less markedly refined, with much more of individuality.

" You live in London ? " inquired Daniel, reading the other's look as if affectionately.

" No. Out at Ewell—in Surrey."

" Oh yes, I know Ewell. Reading ? "

" Yes, for the Civil Service. I've come up to lunch with a man who knows father—Mr. Jacks."

" John Jacks, the M.P. ? "

Piers nodded nervously, and the other regarded him with a smile of new interest.

" But you're very early. Any other engagements ? "

" None," said Piers. It being so fine a morning, he had purposed a long ramble about London streets before making for his destination in the West End.

" Then you must come to my club," returned Daniel. " I shall be glad of a talk with you, very glad, my dear boy. Why, it must be four years since we saw each other. And, by the bye, you are just of age, I think ? "

" Three days ago."

" To be sure. Heard anything from father ?—No ?—You're looking very well, Piers—take my arm. I understood you were going into business. Altered your mind ? And how is the dear old man ? "

They walked for a quarter of an hour, turning at last into a quiet, genteel byway westward of Regent Street, and so into a club house of respectable appearance. Daniel wrote his brother's name, and led up to the smoking-room, which they found unoccupied.

"You smoke?—I am very glad to hear it. I began far too young, and have suffered. It's too early to drink—and perhaps you don't do that either?—Really? Vegetarian also, perhaps? —Why, you are the model son of your father. And the régime seems to suit you. *Per Bacco!* I couldn't follow it myself: but I, like our fat friend, am little better than one of the wicked.—So you are one-and-twenty. You have entered upon your inheritance, I presume?"

Piers answered with a look of puzzled inquiry.

"Haven't you heard about it? The little capital due to you."

"Not a word!"

"That's odd. *Was soll es bedeuten?*—By the bye, I suppose you speak German well?"

"Tolerably."

"And French?"

"Moderately."

"*Benissimo!*" Daniel had just lit a cigar; he lounged gracefully, observing his brother with an eye of veiled keenness. "Well, I think there is no harm in telling you that you are entitled to something—your mother's money, you know."

"I had no idea of it," replied Piers, whom the news had in some degree excited.

"Apropos, why don't you live with father? Couldn't you read as well down there?"

"Not quite, I think, and—the truth is, the stepmother doesn't much like me. She's rather difficult to get on with, you know."

"I imagined it. So you're just in lodgings?"

"I am with some people called Hannaford. I got to know them at Geneva—they're not very well off; I have a room and they board me."

"I must look you up there.—Piers, my dear boy, I suppose you know your mother's history?"

It was asked with an affected carelessness, with a look suggestive of delicacy in approaching the subject. More and more perturbed, Piers abruptly declared his ignorance; he sat in an awkward attitude, bending forward; his brows were knit, his dark eyes had a solemn intensity, and his square jaw asserted itself more than usual.

"Well, between brothers, I don't see why you shouldn't. In fact, I am a good deal surprised that the worthy old man has held his peace about that legacy, and I don't think I shall scruple to tell you all I know. You are aware, at all events, that our interesting parent has been a little unfortunate in his matrimonial ventures. His first wife—not to pick one's phrase —quarrelled furiously with him. His second, you inform me, is somewhat difficult to live with."

" His *third*," interrupted Piers.

" No, my dear boy," said the other gravely, sympathetically. " That intermediate connection was not legal."

" Not—? My mother was not—? "

" Don't worry about it," proceeded Daniel in a kind tone. " These are the merest prejudices, you know. She could not become Mrs. Otway, being already Mrs. Somebody-else. Her death, I fear, was a great misfortune to our parent. I have gathered that they suited each other—fate, you know, plays these little tricks. Your mother, I am sure, was a most charming and admirable woman—I remember her portrait. "*A l'heure qu'il est*, no doubt, it has to be kept out of sight. She had, I am given to understand, a trifling capital of her own, and this was to become yours."

Piers stared at vacancy. When he recovered himself he said with decision :

"Of course I shall hear about it. There's no hurry. Father knows I don't want it just now. Why, of course he will tell me. The exam. comes off in autumn, and no doubt he keeps the news back as a sort of reward when I get my place. I think that would be just like him, you know."

" Or as a solatium, if you fail," remarked the other genially.

" Fail ? Oh, I'm not going to fail," cried Piers in a voice of half-resentful confidence.

" Bravo ! " laughed the other ; " I like that spirit. — So you're going to lunch with John Jacks. I don't exactly know him, but I know friends of his very well. Known him long ? "

Piers explained that as yet he had no personal acquaintance with Mr. Jacks ; that he had, to his surprise, received a written invitation a few days ago.

" It may be useful," Daniel remarked reflectively. " But, if you'll permit the liberty, Piers, I am sorry you didn't pay a little more attention to costume. It should have been a frock coat—really it should."

" I haven't such a thing," exclaimed the younger brother,

with some annoyance and confusion. "And what can it matter? You know very well how father would go."

"Yes, yes; but Jerome Otway the democratic prophet and young Mr. Piers Otway his promising son, are very different persons. Never mind, but take care to get a frock coat; you'll find it indispensable if you are going into that world. Where does Jacks live?"

"Queen's Gate."

Daniel Otway meditated, half closing his eyes as he seemed to watch the smoke from his cigar. Dropping them upon his brother, he found that the young man wore a look of troubled thoughtfulness.

"Daniel," began Piers suddenly, "are you quite sure about all you have told me?"

"Quite. I am astonished it's news to you."

Piers was no longer able to converse, and very soon he found it difficult to sit still. Observant of his face and movements, the elder brother proposed that they should resume their walk together, and forth they went. But both were now taciturn, and they did not walk far in company.

"I shall look you up at Ewell," said Daniel, taking leave. "Address me at that club; I have no permanent quarters just now. We must see more of each other."

And Piers went his way with shadowed countenance.

CHAPTER II

STRAYING about Kensington Gardens in the pleasant
sunshine, his mind occupied with Daniel's information,
Piers Otway lost count of time, and at last had to hurry to
keep his engagement. As he entered the house in Queen's
Gate, a mirrored image of himself made him uneasy about his
costume. But for Daniel, such a point would never have
troubled him. It was with an unfamiliar sense of irritation
and misgiving that he moved into the drawing-room.

A man of sixty or so, well preserved, with a warm complexion,
broad homely countenance, and genial smile, stepped forward
to receive him. Mr. Jacks was member for the Penistone
Division of the West Riding; new to Parliament, having
entered with the triumphant Liberals in the January of this
year 1886. His friends believed, and it seemed credible,
that he had sought election to please the lady whom, as a
widower of twenty years' endurance, he had wedded only a
short time before; politics interested him but moderately,
and the greater part of his life had been devoted to the
manufacturing business which brought him wealth and local
influence. Not many people remembered that in the days of
his youth John Jacks had been something of a Revolutionist,
that he had supported the People's Charter; that he had
written, nay had published, verses of democratic tenor, earning
thereby dark reputation in the respectable society of his native
town. The turning-point was his early marriage. For a while
he still wrote verses—of another kind, but he ceased to talk
about liberty, ceased to attend public meetings, and led an
entirely private life until, years later, his name became
reputably connected with municipal affairs. Observing Mr.
Jacks' face, one saw the possibility of that early enthusiasm;
he had fine eyes full of subdued tenderness, and something
youthful, impulsive, in his expression when he uttered a
thought. Good-humoured, often merry, abounding in kind-

ness and generosity, he passed for a man as happy as he was prosperous; yet those who talked intimately with him obtained now and then a glimpse of something not quite in harmony with these characteristics, a touch of what would be called fancifulness, of uncertain spirits. Men of his world knew that he was not particularly shrewd in commerce; the great business to which his name was attached had been established by his father, and was kept flourishing mainly by the energy of his younger brother. As an occasional lecturer before his towns-folk, he gave evidence of wide reading and literary aptitudes. Of three children of his first marriage, two had died; his profound grief at their loss, and the inclination for domestic life which always appeared in the man, made it matter for surprise that he had waited so long before taking another wife. It would not have occurred to most of those who knew him that his extreme devotion to women made him shy, diffident, all but timorous in their presence. But Piers Otway, for all his mental disturbance at this moment, remarked the singular deference, the tone and look of admiring gentleness, with which Mr. Jacks turned to his wife as he presented their guest.

Mrs. Jacks was well fitted to inspire homage. Her age appeared to be less than five-and-twenty; she was of that tall and gracefully commanding height which has become the English ideal in the last quarter of our century—her portrait appears on every page illustrated by Du Maurier. She had a brilliant complexion, a perfect profile; her smile, though perhaps a little mechanical, was the last expression of im-mutable sweetness, of impeccable self-control; her voice never slipped from the just note of unexaggerated suavity. Con-summate as an ornament of the drawing-room, she would be no less admirably at ease on the tennis lawn, in the boat, on horseback, or walking by the seashore. Beyond criticism her breeding; excellent her education. There appeared, too, in her ordinary speech, her common look, a real amiability of disposition; one could not imagine her behaving harshly or with conscious injustice. Her manners—within the recognised limits—were frank, spontaneous; she had for the most part a liberal tone in conversation, and was evidently quite in-capable of bitter feeling on any everyday subject. Piers Otway bent before her with unfeigned reverence; she dazzled him, she delighted and confused his senses. As often as he dared look at her, his eye discovered some new elegance in her attitude, some marvel of delicate beauty in the details of her person. A spectator might have observed that this worship was manifest to Mr. Jacks, and that it by no means displeased him.

"You are very like your father, Mr. Otway," was the host's first remark after a moment of ceremony. "Very like what he was forty years ago." He laughed, not quite naturally, glancing at his wife. "At that time he and I were much together. But he went to London; I stayed in the North; and so we lost sight of each other for many a long year. Somewhere about 1870 we met by chance, on a Channel steamer; yes, it was just before the war; I remember your father prophesied it, and foretold its course very accurately. Then we didn't see each other again until a month ago—I had run down into Yorkshire for a couple of days and stood waiting for a train at Northallerton. Someone came towards me, and looked me in the face, then held out his hand without speaking; and it was my old friend. He has become a man of few words."

"Yes, he talks very little," said Piers. "I've known him silent for two or three days together."

"And what does he do with himself there among the moors? You don't know Hawes," he remarked to the graciously attentive Mrs. Jacks. "A little stony town at the wild end of Wensleydale. Delightful for a few months, but very grim all the rest of the year. Has he any society there?"

"None outside his home, I think. He sits by the fire and reads Dante."

"Dante?"

"Yes, Dante; he seems to care for hardly anything else. It has been so for two or three years. Editions of Dante and books about Dante crowd his room—they are constantly coming. I asked him once if he was going to write on the subject, but he shook his head."

"It must be a very engrossing study," remarked Mrs. Jacks, with her most intelligent air. "Dante opens such a world!"

"Strange!" murmured her husband, with his kindly smile. "The last thing I should have imagined."

They were summoned to luncheon. As they entered the dining-room, there appeared a young man whom Mr. Jacks greeted warmly.

"Hullo, Arnold! I am so glad you lunch here to-day. Here is the son of my old friend Jerome Otway."

Arnold Jacks pressed the visitor's hand and spoke a few courteous words in a remarkably pleasant voice. In physique he was quite unlike his father; tall, well but slenderly built, with a small finely-shaped head, large grey-blue eyes and brown hair. The delicacy of his complexion and the lines of his figure did not suggest strength, yet he walked with a very firm step, and his whole bearing betokened habits of healthy activity. In early years he had seemed to inherit a very feeble constitution; the death of his brother and sister, followed by that of their mother at an untimely age, left little hope that he would reach manhood; now, in his thirtieth year, he was rarely troubled on the score of health, and few men relieved from the necessity of earning money found fuller occupation for their time. Some portion of each day he spent at the offices of a certain Company, which held rule in a British colony of considerable importance. His interest in this colony had originated at the time when he was gaining vigour and enlarging his experience in world-wide travel; he enjoyed the sense of power, and his voice did not lack weight at the Board of the Company in question. He had all manner of talents and pursuits. Knowledge—the only kind of knowledge he cared for, that of practical things, things alive in the world of to-day—seemed to come to him without any effort on his part. A new invention concealed no mysteries from him; he looked into it; understood, calculated its scope. A strange piece of news from any part of the world found him unsurprised, explanatory. He liked mathematics, and was wont to say jocosely that an abstract computation had a fine moral effect, favouring unselfishness. Music was one of his foibles; he learnt an instrument with wonderful facility, and, up to a certain point, played well. For poetry, though as a rule he disguised the fact, he had a strong distaste; once, when aged about twenty, he startled his father by observing that "In Memoriam" seemed to him a shocking instance of wasted energy; he would undertake to compress the whole significance of each section, with its laborious rhymings, into two or three lines of good clear prose. Naturally the young man had undergone no sentimental troubles; he had not yet talked of marrying, and cared only for the society of mature women who took common-sense views of life. His religion was the British Empire; his saints, the men who had made it; his prophets, the politicians and publicists who held most firmly the Imperial tone.

Where Arnold Jacks was in company, there could be no dulness. Alone with his host and hostess, Otway would have found the occasion rather solemn, and have wished it over, but Arnold's melodious voice, his sprightly discussion and anecdotage, his frequent laughter, charmed the guest into self-oblivion.

"You are no doubt a Home Ruler, Mr. Otway," observed Arnold, soon after they were seated.

"Yes, I am," answered Piers cheerily. "You too, I hope?"

"Why, yes. I would grant Home Rule of the completest description, and I would let it run its natural course for—shall we say five years? When the state of Ireland had become intolerable to herself and dangerous to this adjacent island, I would send over dragoons. And," he added quietly, crumbling his bread, "the question would not rise again."

"Arnold," remarked Mr. Jacks, with good humour, "you are quite incapable of understanding this question. We shall see. Mr. Gladstone's Bill"—

"Mr. Gladstone's *little* Bill—do say his *little* Bill."

"Arnold, you are too absurd!" exclaimed the hostess mirthfully.

"What does your father think?" Mr. Jacks inquired of their guest. "Has he broken silence on the subject?"

"I think not. He never says a word about politics."

"The little Bill hasn't a chance," cried Arnold. "Your majority is melting away. You, of course, will stand by the old man, but that is chivalry, not politics. You don't know what a picturesque figure you make, sir; you help me to realise Horatius Cocles, and that kind of thing."

John Jacks laughed heartily at his own expense, but his wife seemed to think the jest unmannerly. Home Rule did not in the least commend itself to her sedate, practical mind, but she would never have committed such an error in taste as to proclaim divergence from her husband's views.

"It is a most difficult and complicated question," she said, addressing herself to Otway. "The character of the people makes it so; the Irish are so sentimental."

Upon the young man's ear this utterance fell strangely; it gave him a little shock, and he could only murmur some commonplace of assent.   With men, Piers had plenty of moral courage, but women daunted him.

"I heard a capital idea last night," resumed Arnold Jacks, "from a man I was dining with—interesting fellow called Hannaford.   He suggested that Ireland should be made into a military and naval depôt—used solely for that purpose. The details of his scheme were really very ingenious.   He didn't propose to exterminate the natives"—

John Jacks interrupted with hilarity, which his son affected to resent : the look exchanged by the two making pleasant proof of how little their natural affection was disturbed by political and other differences.   At the name of Hannaford, Otway had looked keenly towards the speaker.

"Is that Lee Hannaford?" he asked.   "Oh, I know him. In fact, I'm living in his house just now."

Arnold was interested.   He had only the slightest acquaintance with Hannaford, and would like to hear more of him.

"Not long ago," Piers responded, "he was a teacher of chemistry at Geneva—I got to know him there.   He seems to speak half a dozen languages in perfection ; I believe he was born in Switzerland.   His house down in Surrey is a museum of modern weapons—a regular armoury.   He has invented some new gun."

"So I gathered.   And a new explosive, I'm told."

"I hope he doesn't store it in his house?" said Mr. Jacks, looking with concern at Piers.

"I've had a moment's uneasiness about that, now and then," Otway replied, laughing, "especially after hearing him talk."

"A tremendous fellow!" Arnold exclaimed admiringly. "He showed me, by sketch diagrams, how many men he could kill within a given space."

"If this gentleman were not your friend, Mr. Otway," began the host, "I should say"—

"Oh, pray say whatever you like!   He isn't my friend at all, and I detest his inventions."

"Shocking!" fell sweetly from the lady at the head of the table.

"As usual, I must beg leave to differ," put in Arnold. "What would become of us if we left all that kind of thing to the other countries?   Hannaford is a patriot.   He struck me as quite disinterested ; personal gain is nothing to him. He loves his country, and is using his genius in her service."

John Jacks nodded.

"Well, yes, yes. But I wish your father were here, Mr. Otway, to give his estimate of such genius; at all events if he thinks as he did years ago. Get him on that topic, and he was one of the most eloquent men living. I am convinced that he only wanted a little more self-confidence to become a real power in public life—a genuine orator, such, perhaps, as England has never had."

"Nor ever will have," Arnold interrupted. "We act instead of talking."

"My dear boy," said his father weightily, "we talk very much, and very badly; in pulpit, and Parliament, and press. We want the man who has something new to say, and knows how to say it. For my own part, I don't think, when he comes, that he will glorify explosives. I want to hear someone talk about Peace—and *not* from the commercial point of view. The slaughterers shan't have it all their own way, Arnold; civilisation will be too strong for them, and if Old England doesn't lead in that direction, it will be her shame to the end of history."

Arnold smiled, but kept silence. Mrs. Jacks looked and murmured her approval.

"I wish Hannaford could hear you," said Piers Otway.

When they rose from the table, John Jacks invited the young man to come with him into his study for a little private talk.

"I haven't many books here," he said, noticing Otway's glance at the shelves. "My library is down in Yorkshire, at the old home; where I shall be very glad indeed to see you, whenever you come North in vacation-time.—Well now, let us make friends; tell me something about yourself. You are reading for the Civil Service, I understand?"

Piers liked Mr. Jacks, and was soon chatting freely. He told how his education had begun at a private school in London, how he had then gone to school at Geneva, and, when seventeen years old, had entered an office of London merchants, dealing with Russia.

"It wasn't my own choice. My father talked to me, and seemed so anxious for me to go into business that I made no objection. I didn't understand him then, but I think I do now. You know"—he added in a lower tone—"that I have two elder brothers?"

"Yes, I know. And a word that fell from your father at Northallerton the other day—I think I understand."

"Both went in for professions," Otway pursued, "and I suppose he wasn't very well satisfied with the results. However, after I had been two years in the office, I felt I couldn't stand it, and I began privately to read law. Then one day I wrote to my father, and asked whether he would allow me to be articled to a solicitor. He replied that he would, if, at the age of twenty, I had gone steadily on with the distasteful office work, and had continued to read law in my leisure. Well, I accepted this, of course, and in a year's time found how right he had been; already I had got sick of the law books, and didn't care for the idea of being articled. I told father that, and he asked me to wait six months more, and then to let him know my mind again. I hadn't got to like business any better, and one day it seemed to me that I would try for a place in a Government office. When the time came, I suggested this, and my father ultimately agreed. I lived with him at Hawes for a month or two, then came into Surrey, to work on for the examination.—We shall see what I get."

The young man spoke with a curious blending of modesty and self-confidence, of sobriety beyond his years and the glow of a fervid temperament. He seemed to hold himself consciously in restraint, but, as if to compensate for subdued language, he used more gesticulation than is common with Englishmen. Mr. Jacks watched him very closely, and, when he ceased, reflected for a moment.

"True; we shall see. You are working steadily?"

"About fourteen hours a day."

"Too much! too much!—All at the Civil Service subjects?"

"No; I manage a few other things. For instance, I'm trying to learn Russian. Father says he made the attempt long ago, but was beaten. I don't think I shall give in."

"Your father knew Herzen and Bakounine, in the old days. Well, don't overdo it; don't neglect the body. We must have another talk before long."

Again Mr. Jacks looked thoughtfully at the keen young face, and his countenance betrayed a troublous mood.

"How you remind me of my old friend, forty years ago—forty years ago!"

CHAPTER III

A LITTLE apart from the village of Ewell, within sight of the noble trees and broad herbage of Nonsuch Park, and looking southward to the tilth and pasture of the Downs, stood the house occupied by Mr. Lee Hannaford. It was just too large to be called a cottage; not quite old enough to be picturesque; a pleasant enough dwelling, amid its green garden plot, sheltered on the north side by a dark hedge of yew, and shut from the quiet road by privet topped with lilac and laburnum. This day of early summer, fresh after rains, with a clear sky and the sun wide-gleaming over young leaf and bright blossom, with Nature's perfume wafted along every alley, about every field and lane, showed the spot at its best. But it was with no eye to natural beauty that Mr. Hannaford had chosen this abode; such considerations left him untouched. He wanted a cheap house not far from London, where his wife's uncertain health might receive benefit, and where the simplicity of the surroundings would offer no temptations to casual expense. For his own part, he was a good deal from home, coming and going as it suited him; a very small income from capital, and occasional earnings by contribution to scientific journalism, left slender resources to Mrs. Hannaford and her daughter after the husband's needs were supplied. Thus it came about that they gladly ceded a spare room to Piers Otway, who, having boarded with them during his student time at Geneva, had at long intervals kept up a correspondence with Mrs. Hannaford, a lady he admired.

The rooms were indifferently furnished; in part, owing to poverty, and partly because neither of the ladies cared much for things domestic. Mr. Hannaford's sanctum alone had character; it was hung about with lethal weapons of many kinds and many epochs, including a memento of every important war waged in Europe since the date of Waterloo.

A smoke-grimed rifle from some battlefield was in Hannaford's view a thing greatly precious; still more, a bayonet with stain of blood; these relics appealed to his emotions. Under glass were ranged minutiæ such as bullets, fragments of shells, bits of gore-drenched cloth or linen, a splinter of human bone— all ticketed with neat inscription. A bookcase contained volumes of military history, works on firearms, treatises on (chiefly explosive) chemistry; several great portfolios were packed with maps and diagrams of warfare. Upstairs, a long garret served as laboratory, and here were ranged less valuable possessions; weapons to which some doubt attached, unbloody scraps of accoutrements, also a few models of cannon and the like.

In society, Hannaford was an entertaining, sometimes a charming, man, with a flow of well-informed talk, of agreeable anecdote; his friends liked to have him at the dinner-table; he could never be at a loss for a day or two's board and lodging when his home wearied him. Under his own roof he seldom spoke save to find fault, rarely showed anything but an acrid countenance. He and his wife were completely alienated; but for their child, they would long ago have parted. It had been a love match, and the daughter's name, Olga, still testified to the romance of their honeymoon; but that was nearly twenty years gone by, and of these at least fifteen had been spent in discord, concealed or flagrant. Mrs. Hannaford was something of an artist; her husband spoke of all art with contempt—except the great art of human slaughter. She liked the society of foreigners; he, though a remarkable linguist, at heart distrusted and despised all but English-speaking folk. As a girl in her teens, she had been charmed by the man's virile accomplishments, his soldierly bearing and gay talk of martial things, though Hannaford was only a teacher of science. Nowadays she thought with dreary wonder of that fascination, and had come to loathe every trapping and habiliment of war. She knew him profoundly selfish, and recognised the other faults which had hindered so clever a man from success in life; indolent habits, moral untrustworthiness, and a conceit which at times menaced insanity. He hated her, she was well aware, because of her cold criticism; she returned his hate with interest.

Save in suicide, of which she had sometimes thought, Mrs. Hannaford saw but one hope of release. A sister of hers had married a rich American, and was now a widow in failing health. That sister's death might perchance endow her with the means of liberty; she hung upon every message from across the Atlantic.

She had a brother, too; a distinguished, but not a wealthy, man. Dr. Derwent would gladly have seen more of her, gladly have helped to cheer her life, but a hearty antipathy held him aloof from Lee Hannaford. Communication between the two families was chiefly maintained through Dr. Derwent's daughter Irene, now in her nineteenth year. The girl had visited her aunt at Geneva, and since then had occasionally been a guest at Ewell. Having just returned from a winter abroad with her father, and no house being ready for her reception in London, Irene was even now about to pass a week with her relatives. They expected her to-day. The prospect of Irene's arrival enabled Mrs. Hannaford and Olga to find pleasure in the sunshine, which otherwise brought them little solace.

Neither was in sound health. The mother had an interesting face; the daughter had a touch of beauty; but something morbid appeared on the countenance of each. They lived a strange life, lonely, silent; the stillness of the house unbroken by a note of music, unrelieved by a sound of laughter. In the neighbourhood they had no friends; only at long intervals did a London acquaintance come thus far to call upon them. But for the presence of Piers Otway at meals, and sometimes in the afternoon or evening, they would hardly have known conversation. For when Hannaford was at home, his sour muteness discouraged any kind of talk; in his absence, mother and daughter soon exhausted all they had to say to each other, and read or brooded or nursed their headaches apart.

With the coming of Irene, gloom vanished. It had always been so, since the beginning of her girlhood; the name of Irene Derwent signified miseries forgotten, mirthful hours, the revival of health and hope. Unable to resist her influence, Hannaford always kept as much as possible out of the way when she was under his roof; the conflict between inclination to unbend and stubborn coldness towards his family made him too uncomfortable. Vivaciously tactful in this as in all things, Irene had invented a pleasant fiction which enabled her to meet Mr. Hannaford without embarrassment; she always asked him "How is your neuralgia?" And the man, according as he felt, made answer that it was better or worse. That neuralgia was often a subject of bitter jest between Mrs. Hannaford and Olga, but it had entered into the life of the family, and at times seemed to be believed in even by the imagined sufferer.

Nothing could have been more characteristic of Irene. Wit at the service of good feeling expressed her nature.

Her visit this time would be specially interesting, for she had passed the winter in Finland, amid the intellectual society of Helsingfors. Letters had given a foretaste of what she would have to tell, but Irene was no great letter-writer. She had an impatience of remaining seated at a desk. She did not even read very much. Her delight was in conversation, in movement, in active life. For several years her father had made her his companion, as often as possible, in holiday travel and on the journeys prompted by scientific study. Though successful as a medical man, Dr. Derwent no longer practised; he devoted himself to pathological research, and was making a name in the world of science. His wife, who had died young, left him two children; the elder, Eustace, was an amiable and intelligent young man, but had small place in his father's life compared with that held by Irene.

She was to arrive at Ewell in time for luncheon. Her brother would bring her, and return to London in the afternoon.

Olga walked to the station to meet them. Mrs. Hannaford, having paid unusual attention to her dress—she had long since ceased to care how she looked, save on very exceptional occasions—moved impatiently, nervously, about the house and the garden. Her age was not yet forty, but a life of disappointment and unrest had dulled her complexion, made her movements languid, and was beginning to touch with grey her soft, wavy hair. Under happier circumstances she would have been a most attractive woman; her natural graces were many, her emotions were vivid and linked with a bright intelligence, her natural temper inclined to the nobler modes of life. Unfortunately, little care had been given to her education; her best possibilities lay undeveloped; thrown upon her inadequate resources, she nourished the weaknesses instead of the virtues of her nature. She was always saying to herself that life had gone by, and was wasted; for life meant love, and love in her experience had been a flitting folly, an error of crude years, which should, in all justice, have been thrown aside and forgotten, allowing her a second chance. Too late, now. Often she lay through the long nights shedding tears of misery. Too late; her beauty blurred, her heart worn with suffering, often poisoned with bitterness. Yet there came moments of revolt, when she rose and looked at herself in the mirror, and asked— But for Olga, she would have tried to shape her own destiny.

To-day she could look up at the sunshine. Irene was coming.

A sound of young voices in the quiet road; then the shimmer of a bright costume, the gleam of a face all health and charm and merriment. Irene came into the garden, followed by her brother, and behind them Olga.

Her voice woke the dull house; of a sudden it was alive, responding to the cheerful mood of its inhabitants. The rooms had a new appearance; sunlight seemed to penetrate to every shadowed corner; colours were brighter, too familiar objects became interesting. The dining-room table, commonly so uninviting, gleamed as for a festival. Irene's eyes fell on everything, and diffused her own happy spirit. Irene had an excellent appetite; everyone enjoyed the meal. This girl could not but bestow something of herself on all with whom she came together; where she felt liking, her influence was incalculable.

"How much better you look than when I last saw you," she said to her aunt. "Ewell evidently suits you."

And at once Mrs. Hannaford felt that she was stronger, younger, than she had thought. Yes, she felt better than for a long time, and Ewell was exactly suited to her health.

"Is that pastel yours, Olga? Admirable! The best thing of yours I ever saw."

And Olga, who had thought her pastel worthless, saw all at once that it really was not bad; she glowed with gratification.

The cousins were almost of an age, of much the same stature; but Olga had a pallid tint, tawny hair, and bluish eyes, whilst Irene's was a warm complexion, her hair of dark-brown, and her eyes of hazel. As efficient human beings, there could be no comparison between them; Olga looked frail, despondent, inclined to sullenness, whilst Irene impressed one as in perfect health, abounding in gay vitality, infinite in helpful resource. Straight as an arrow, her shoulders the perfect curve, bosom and hips full-moulded to the ideal of ripe girlhood, she could not make a gesture which was not graceful, nor change her position without revealing a new excellence of form. Yet a

certain taste would have leant towards Miss Hannaford, whose
traits had more mystery; as an uncommon type, she gained
by this juxtaposition. Miss Derwent, despite her larger experience of the world, her vastly better education, was a much
younger person than Olga; she had an occasional naïveté
unknown to her cousin; her sex was far less developed. To
the average man, Olga's proximity would have been troubling,
whereas Irene's would simply have given delight.

During the excitement of the arrival, and through the
cheerful meal which followed, Eustace Derwent maintained a
certain reserve, was always rather in the background. This
implied no defect of decent sentiment; the young man—he
was four-and-twenty—could not regard his aunt and cousin
with any fond emotion, but he did not dislike them, and was
willing to credit them with all the excellent qualities perceived
by Irene, wondering merely how his father's sister, a member
of the Derwent family, could have married such a "doubtful
customer" as Lee Hannaford. Eustace never became demon-
strative; he had in perfection the repose of a self-conscious,
delicately bred, and highly trained Englishman. In a day of
democratisation, he supported the ancient fame of the
University which fostered gentlemen. Balliol was his College.
His respect for that name, and his reverence for the great
Master who ruled there, were not inconsistent with a private
feeling that, whatever he might owe to Balliol, Balliol in turn
lay under a certain obligation to him. His academic record
had no brilliancy; he aimed at nothing of the kind, knowing
his limitations—or rather his distinctions; but he was quietly
conscious that no graduate of his year better understood the
niceties of decorum, more creditably represented the tone of
that famous school of manners.

Eustace Derwent was in fact a thoroughly clear-minded and
well-meaning young man; sensitive as to his honour; ambitious
of such social advancement as would illustrate his name;
unaffectedly attached to those of his own blood, and anxious
to fulfil with entire propriety all the recognised duties of life.
He was intelligent, with originality; he was good-natured,
without shadow of boisterous impulse. In countenance he
strongly resembled his mother, who had been a very handsome
woman (Irene had more of her father's features), and of course
he well knew that the eyes of ladies rested upon him with
peculiar interest; but no vulgar vanity appeared in his

demeanour. As a matter of routine, he dressed well, but he abhorred the hint of foppishness. In athletics he had kept the golden mean, as in all else; he exercised his body for health, not for the pride of emulation. As to his career, he was at present reading for the Bar. In meditative moments it seemed to him that he was perhaps best fitted for the diplomatic service.

Not till this gentleman had taken his leave, which he did (to catch a train) soon after lunch, was there any mention of the fact that the Hannafords had a stranger residing under their roof: in coarse English, a lodger.

To Eustace, as his aunt knew, the subject would necessarily have been painful; and not only in the snobbish sense; it would really have distressed him to learn that his kinsfolk were glad of such a supplement to their income. But soon after his retirement, Mrs. Hannaford spoke of the matter, and no sooner had she mentioned Piers Otway's name than Irene flashed upon her a look of attentive interest.

"Is he related to Jerome Otway, the agitator?—His son? How delightful! Oh, I know all about him; I mean, about the old man. One of our friends at Helsingfors was an old French revolutionist, who has lived a great deal in England; he was always talking about his English friends of long ago, and Jerome Otway often came in. He didn't know whether he was still alive. Oh, I must write and tell him."

The ladies gave what information they could (it amounted to very little) about the recluse of Wensleydale; then they talked of the young man.

"We knew him at Geneva, first of all," said Mrs. Hannaford. "Indeed, he lived with us there for a time; he was only a boy then, and such a nice boy! He has changed a good deal— don't you think so, Olga? I don't mean for the worse; not at all; but he is not so talkative and companionable. You'll find him shy at first, I fancy."

"He works terrifically," put in Olga. "It's certain he must be injuring his health."

"Then," exclaimed Irene, "why do you let him?"

"Let him? We have no right to interfere with a young man of one-and-twenty."

"Surely you have, if he's behaving foolishly, to his own harm. But what do you call terrific work?"

"All day long, and goodness knows how much of the night.

Somebody told us his light had been seen burning once at nearly three o'clock."

"Is he at it now?" asked Irene, with a comical look towards the ceiling.

They explained Otway's absence.

"Oh, he lunches with Members of Parliament, does he?"

"It's a very exceptional thing for him to leave home," said Mrs. Hannaford. "He only goes out to breathe the air for half an hour or so in an afternoon."

"You astonish me, aunt! You oughtn't to allow it—*I* shan't allow it, I assure you."

The listeners laughed gaily.

"My dear Irene," said her aunt, "Mr. Otway will be much flattered, I'm sure. But his examination comes on very soon, and he was telling us only yesterday that he didn't want to lose an hour if he could help it."

"He'll lose a good many hours before long, at this rate. Silly fellow! That's not the way to do well at an exam! I must counsel him for his soul's good, I must indeed.—Will he dine here to-night?"

"No doubt."

"And make all haste to get away when dinner is over," said Olga, with a smile.

"Then we won't let him. He shall tell us all about the Member of Parliament; and then all about his famous father. I undertake to keep him talking till ten."

"Then, poor fellow, he'll have to work all night to make it up."

"Indeed, no! I shall expressly forbid it.—What a shocking thing if he died here, and it got into the papers! Aunt, do consider; they would call you his *landlady*!"

Mrs. Hannaford reddened whilst laughing, and the girl saw that her joke was not entirely relished, but she could never resist the temptation to make fun of certain prejudices.

"And when you give your evidence," she went on, "the coroner will remark that if the influence of a lady so obviously sweet and right-feeling and intelligent could not avail to save the poor youth, he was plainly destined to a premature end."

At which Mrs. Hannaford again laughed and reddened, but this time with gratification.

If Irene sometimes made a mistake, no one could have perceived it more quickly, and more charmingly have redeemed the slip.

CHAPTER IV

WHEN Piers Otway got back to Ewell, about four o'clock, he felt the beginning of a headache. The day of excitement might have accounted for it, but in the last few weeks it had been too common an experience with him, a warning, naturally, against his mode of life, and of course unheeded. On reaching the house, he saw and heard no one; the door stood open, and he went straight up to his room.

He had only one, which served him for study and bedchamber. In front of the window stood a large table, covered with his books and papers, and there, on the blotting pad, lay a letter which had arrived for him since his departure this morning. It came, he saw, from his father. He took it up eagerly, and was tearing the envelope when his eye fell on something that stayed his hand.

The wide-open window offered a view over the garden at the back of the house, and on the lawn he saw a little group of ladies. Seated in basket chairs, Mrs. Hannaford and her daughter were conversing with a third person whom Piers did not know, a tall, fair-faced girl who stood before them and seemed at this moment to be narrating some lively story. Even had her features been hidden, the attitude of this stranger, her admirable form and rapid graceful gestures, must have held the young man's attention; seeing her with the light full on her countenance, he gazed and gazed, in sudden complete forgetfulness of his half-opened letter. Just so had he stood before the print shop in London this morning, with the same wide eyes, the same hurried breathing; rapt, self-oblivious.

He remembered. The Hannafords' relative, Miss Derwent, was expected to-day; and Miss Derwent, doubtless, he beheld.

The next moment it occurred to him that his observation, within earshot of the group, was a sort of eavesdropping; he closed his window and turned away. The sound must have drawn attention, for very soon there came a knock at the door, and the servant inquired of him whether he would have tea, as usual, in his room, or join the ladies below.

"Bring it here, please," he replied. "And—yes, tell Mrs. Hannaford that I shall not come down to dinner—you can bring me anything you like—just a mouthful of something."

Now there went, obscurely, no less than three reasons to the quick shaping of this decision. In the first place, Piers had glanced over his father's letter, and saw in it matter for long reflection. Secondly, his headache was declared, and he would be better alone for the evening. Thirdly, he shrank from meeting Miss Derwent. And this last was the pre-dominant motive. Letter and headache notwithstanding, he would have joined the ladies at dinner but for the presence of their guest. An inexplicable irritation all at once possessed him ; a grotesque resentment of Miss Derwent's arrival.

Why should she have come just when he wanted to work harder than ever? That was how things happened — the perversity of circumstance ! She would be at every meal for at least a week ; he must needs talk with her, look at her, think about her. His annoyance became so acute that he tramped nervously about the floor, muttering maledictions.

It passed. A cup of tea brought him to his right mind, and he no longer saw the event in such exaggerated colours. But he was glad of his decision to spend the evening alone.

His father's letter had come at the right moment; in some degree it allayed the worry caused by his brother Daniel's talk this morning. Jerome Otway wrote, as usual, briefly, on the large letter-paper he always used ; his bold hand, full of a certain character, demanded space. He began by congratulat-ing Piers on the completion of his one-and-twentieth year. "I am late, but had not forgotten the day; it costs me an effort to put pen to paper, as you know." Proceeding, he informed his son that a sum of money, a few hundred pounds, had become payable to him on the attainment of his majority. "It was your mother's, and she wished you to have it. A man of law will communicate with you about the matter. Speak of it to me, or not, as you prefer. If you wish it, I will advise ; if you wish it not, I will keep silence." There followed a few words about the beauty of spring in the moorland ; then: "Your ordeal approaches. An absurdity, I fear, but the wisdom of our day will have it thus. I wish you success.

If you fall short of your hopes, come to me and we will talk once more. Befall what may, I am to the end your father who wishes you well." The signature was very large, and might have drawn censure of affectation from the unsympathetic. As indeed might the whole epistle: very significant of the mind and temper of Jerome Otway.

To Piers the style was too familiar to suggest reflections: besides, he had a loyal mind towards his father, and never criticised the old man's dealings with him. The confirmation of Daniel's report about the legacy concerned him little in itself; he had no immediate need of money, and so small a sum could not affect the course of his life; but, this being true, it seemed probable that Daniel's other piece of information was equally well founded. If so, what matter? Already he had asked himself why the story about his mother should have caused him a shock. His father, in all likelihood, would now never speak of that; and indeed why should he? The story no longer affected either of them, and to worry oneself about it was mere "philistinism," a favourite term with Piers at that day.

In replying, which he did this same night, he decided to make no mention of Daniel. The name would give his father no pleasure.

When he rang to have his tea-things taken away, Mrs. Hannaford presented herself. She was anxious about him. Why would he not dine? She wished him to make the acquaintance of Miss Derwent, whose talk was sure to interest him. Piers pleaded his headache, causing the lady more solicitude. She entreated. As he could not work, it would be much better for him to spend an hour or two in company. Would he not? to please her?

Mrs. Hannaford spoke in a soft, caressing voice, and Piers returned her look of kindness; but he was firm. An affection had grown up between these two; their intercourse, though they seldom talked long together, was much like that of mother and son.

"You are injuring your health," said Mrs. Hannaford gravely, "and it is unkind to those who care for you."

"Wait a few weeks," he replied cheerily, "and I'll make up the health account."

"You refuse to come down to please me, this once?"

"I must be alone—indeed I must," Piers replied, with

unusual abruptness. And Mrs. Hannaford, a little hurt, left
the room without speaking.

He all but hastened after her, to apologise ; but the irritable
impulse overcame him again, and he had to pace the room till
his nerves grew steady.

Very soon after it was dark he gave up the effort to read,
and went to bed. A good night's sleep restored him. He
rose with the sun, felt the old appetite for work, and when the
breakfast bell rang had redeemed more than three good hours.
He was able now to face Miss Derwent, or anyone else.
Indeed, that young lady hardly came into his mind before he
met her downstairs. At the introduction he behaved with his
natural reserve, which had nothing, as a rule, of awkwardness.
Irene was equally formal, though a smile at the corner of her
lips half betrayed a mischievous thought. They barely spoke
to each other, and at table Irene took no heed of him.

But with the others she talked as brightly as usual, managing,
none the less, to do full justice to the meal. Miss Derwent's
vigour of mind and body was not sustained on air, and she
never affected a delicate appetite. There was still something
of the healthy schoolgirl in her manner. Otway glanced at
her once or twice, but immediately averted his eyes—with a
slight frown, as if the light had dazzled him.

She was talking of Finland, and mentioned the name of her
father's man-servant Thibaut. It entered several times into the
narrative and always with an approving epithet, the excellent
Thibaut, the brave Thibaut.

"Oh !" exclaimed Mrs. Hannaford presently, "do tell Mr.
Otway the story of Thibaut."

"Yes, do !" urged Olga.

Piers raised his eyes to the last speaker, and moved them
timidly towards Irene. She smiled, meeting his look with a
sort of merry satisfaction.

"Mr. Otway is occupied with serious thoughts," was her
good-humoured remark.

"I should much like to hear the story of Thibaut," said
Piers, bending forward a little.

"Would you? You shall—Thibaut Rossignol; delightful
name, isn't it? And one of the most delightful of men,
though only a servant, and the son of a village shopkeeper.
It begins fifteen years ago, just after the Franco-Prussian
War. My father was taking a holiday in eastern France, and

he came one day to a village where an epidemic of typhoid was raging. *Tant mieux!* Something to do; some help to be given. If you knew my father—but you will understand. He offered his services to the overworked couple of doctors, and was welcomed. He fought the typhoid day and night— if you knew my father! Well, there was a bad case in a family named Rossignol: a boy of twelve. What made it worse was that two elder brothers had been killed in the war, and the parents sat in despair by the bedside of their only remaining child. The father was old and very shaky; the mother much younger, but she had suffered dreadfully from the death of her two boys—you should hear my father tell it! I make a hash of it; when *he* tells it people cry. Madame Rossignol was the sweetest little woman—you know that kind of Frenchwoman, don't you? Soft-voiced, tender, intelligent, using the most delightful phrases; a jewel of a woman. My father settled himself by the bedside and fought; Madame Rossignol watching him with eyes he did not dare to meet—until a certain moment. Then—*then* the soft voice for once was loud. '*Il est sauvé!*' My father shed tears; everybody shed tears—except Thibaut himself."

Piers hung on the speaker's lips. No music had ever held him so rapt. When she ceased he gazed at her.

"No, of course that's not all," Irene proceeded, with the mischievous smile again; and she spoke much as she might have done to an eagerly listening child. "Six years pass by. My father is again in the east of France, and he goes to the old village. He is received with enthusiasm; his name has become a proverb. Rossignol *père*, alas, is dead, long since. Dear Madame Rossignol lives, but my father sees at a glance that she will not live long. The excitement of meeting him was almost too much for her — pale, sweet little woman. Thibaut was keeping shop with her, but he seemed out of place there; a fine lad of eighteen; very intelligent, wonderfully good-humoured, and his poor mother had no peace night or day for the thought of what would become of him after her death; he had no male kinsfolk, and certainly would not stick to a dull little trade. My father thought, and after thinking spoke. 'Madame, will you let me take your son to England, and find something for him to do?' She screamed with delight. 'But will Thibaut consent?' Thibaut had his patriotic scruples; but when he saw and heard his poor mother, he consented. Madame Rossignol had a sister near by, with whom she could live. And so on the spot it was settled."

Piers hung on the speaker's lips; no tale had ever so engrossed him. Indeed, it was charmingly told; with so much girlish sincerity, so much womanly feeling.

"No, that's not all. My father went to his inn for the night. Early in the morning he was hastily summoned; he must come at once to the house of the Rossignols; something was wrong. He went, and there, in her bed, lay the little woman, just as if asleep, and a smile on her face—but she was dead."

Piers had a lump in his throat; he straightened himself, and tried to command his features. Irene, smiling, looked steadily at him.

"From that day," she added, "Thibaut has been my father's servant. He wouldn't be anything else. This, he always says, would best have pleased his mother. He will never leave Dr. Derwent. The good Thibaut!"

All were silent for a minute; then Piers pushed back his chair.

"Work?" said Mrs. Hannaford, with a little note of allusion to last evening.

"Work!" Piers replied grimly, his eyes down.

"Well, now," exclaimed Irene, turning to her cousin, "what shall we do this splendid morning? Where can we go?"

Piers left the room as the words were spoken. He went upstairs with slower step than usual, head bent. On entering his room (it was always made ready for him while he was at breakfast), he walked to the window, and stared out at the fleecy clouds in the summer blue, at the trees and the lawn. He was thinking of the story of Thibaut. What a fine fellow Dr. Derwent must be! He would like to know him.

To work! He meant to give an hour or two to his Russian, with which he had already made fair progress. By the bye, he must tell his father that; the old man would be pleased,

An hour later, he again stood at his window, staring at the clouds and the blue. Russian was against the grain, somehow, this morning. He wondered whether Miss Derwent had learnt any during her winter at Helsingfors.

What a long day was before him! He kept looking at his watch. And instead of getting on with his work, he thought and thought again of the story of Thibaut.

CHAPTER V

A T lunch Piers was as silent as at breakfast; he hardly
spoke, save in answer to a chance question from Mrs.
Hannaford. His face had an unwonted expression, a shade
of sullenness, mood rarely seen in him. Miss Derwent, whose
animation more than made up for this muteness in one of
the company, glanced occasionally at Otway, but did not
address him.

As his habit was, he went out for an afternoon walk, and
returned with no brighter countenance. On the first landing
of the staircase, as he stole softly to his room, he came face
to face with Miss Derwent, descending.

"We are going to have tea in the garden," she exclaimed,
with the friendliest look and tone.

"Are you? It will be enjoyable — it's so warm and
sunny."

"You will come, of course?"

"I'm sorry—I have too much to do."

He blundered out the words with hot embarrassment, and
would have passed on. Irene did not permit it.

"But you have been working all the morning?"

"Oh yes"—

"Since when?"

"Since about—oh, five o'clock"—

"Then you have already worked something like eight hours,
Mr. Otway. How many more do you think of working?"

"Five or six, I hope," Piers answered, finding courage to
look into her face, and trying to smile.

"Mr. Otway," she rejoined, with an air of self-possession
which made him feel like a rebuked schoolboy, "I prophesy
that you will come to grief over your examination."

"I don't think so, Miss Derwent," he said, with the firm-
ness of desperation, as he felt his face grow red under her
gaze.

"I am the daughter of a medical man. Prescriptions are in my blood. Allow me to tell you that you have worked enough for one day, and that it is your plain duty to come and have tea in the garden."

So serious was the note of interest which blended with her natural gaiety as she spoke these words that Piers felt his nerves thrill with delight. He was able to meet her eyes, and to respond in becoming terms.

"You are right. Certainly I will come, and gladly."

Irene nodded, smiled approval, and moved past him.

In his room he walked hither and thither aimlessly, still holding his hat and stick. A throbbing of the heart, a quickening of the senses, seemed to give him a new consciousness of life. His mood of five minutes ago had completely vanished. He remembered his dreary ramble about the lanes as if it had taken place last week. Miss Derwent was still speaking to him; his mind echoed again and again every word she had said, perfectly reproducing her voice, her intonation; he saw her bright, beautiful face, its changing lights, its infinite subtleties of expression. The arch of her eyebrows and the lovely hazel eyes beneath; the small and exquisitely shaped mouth; the little chin, so delicately round and firm; all were engraved on his memory, once and for ever.

He sat down and was lost in a dream. His arms hung idly; all his muscles were relaxed. His eyes dwelt on a point of the carpet, which he did not see.

Then, with a sudden start of activity, he went to the looking-glass and surveyed himself. His tie was the worse for wear. He exchanged it for another. He brushed his hair violently, and smoothed his moustache. Never had he felt such dissatisfaction with his appearance. Never had it struck him so disagreeably before that he was hard-featured, sallow, anything but a handsome man. Yet, he had good teeth, very white and regular; that was something, perhaps. Observing them, he grinned at himself grotesquely—and at once was so disgusted that he turned with a shudder away.

Ordinarily he would have awaited the summons of the bell for tea. But, after making himself ready, he gazed from the window and saw Miss Derwent walking alone in the garden; he hastened down.

She gave him a look of intelligence, but took his arrival as a matter of course, and spoke to him about a flowering shrub which pleased her. Otway's heart sank. What had he expected? He neither knew nor asked himself; he stood beside her, seeing nothing, hearing only a voice and wishing it would speak on for ever. He was no longer a reflecting, reasoning young man, with a tolerably firm will and fixed purposes, but a mere embodied emotion, and that of the vaguest, swaying in dependence on another's personality.

Olga Hannaford joined them. Olga, for all the various charms of her face, had never thus affected him. But then he had known her a few years ago, when, as something between child and woman, she had little power to interest an imaginative boy, whose ideal was some actress seen only in a photograph, or some great lady on her travels glimpsed as he strayed about Geneva. She, in turn, regarded him with the coolest friendliness, her own imagination busy with far other figures than that of a would-be Government clerk.

Just as tea was being served, there sounded a voice welcome to no one present, that of Lee Hannaford. He came forward with his wonted air of preoccupation; a well-built man, in the prime of life; carefully dressed, his lips close-set, his eyes seemingly vacant, but in reality very attentive; a pinched ironical smile meant for cordiality. After greetings, he stood before Miss Derwent's chair conversing with her; a cup of tea in his steady hand, his body just bent, his forehead curiously wrinkled—a habit of his when he talked for civility's sake and nothing else. Hannaford could never be at ease in the presence of his wife and daughter if others were there to observe him; he avoided speaking to them, or, if obliged, did so with awkward formality. Indeed, he was not fond of the society of women, and grew less so every year. His tone with regard to them was marked with an almost puritanical coldness; he visited any feminine breach of the proprieties with angry censure. Yet, before his marriage he had lived if anything more laxly than the average man, and to his wife he had confessed (strange memory nowadays) that he owed to her a moral redemption. His morality, in fact, no one doubted; the suspicions Mrs. Hannaford had once entertained when his coldness to her began, she now knew to be baseless. Absorbed in meditations upon bloodshed and havoc, he held high the ideal of chastity, and, in company agreeable to him, could allude to it as the safeguard of civil life.

When he withdrew into the house, Mrs. Hannaford followed him. Olga, always nervous when her father was near, sat silent. Piers Otway, with a new reluctance, was rising to return to his studies, when Miss Derwent checked him with a look.

"What a perfect afternoon!"

"It is, indeed," he murmured, his eyes falling.

"Olga, are you too tired for another walk?"

"I? Oh no! I should enjoy it."

"Do you think"—Irene looked roguishly at her cousin— "Mr. Otway would forgive us if we begged him to come too?"

Olga smiled, and glanced at the young man with certainty that he would excuse himself.

"We can but ask," she said.

And Piers, to her astonishment, at once assented. He did so with sudden colour in his cheeks, avoiding Olga's look.

So they set forth together; and little by little Piers grew remarkably talkative. Miss Derwent mentioned his father, declared an interest in Jerome Otway, and this was a subject on which Piers could always discourse to friendly hearers. This evening he did so with exceptional fervour, abounded in reminiscences, rose at moments to enthusiasm. His companions were impressed; to Irene it was an unexpected revelation of character. She had imagined young Otway dry and rather conventional, perhaps conceited; she found him impassioned and an idealist, full of hero-worship, devoted to his father's name and fame.

"And he lives all the year round in that out-of-the-way place?" she asked. "I must make a pilgrimage to Hawes. Would he be annoyed? I could tell him about his old friends at Helsingfors"—

"He would be delighted to see you!" cried Piers, his face glowing. "Let me know before—let me write"—

"Is he quite alone?"

"No, his wife—my stepmother—is living."

Irene's quick perception interpreted the change of note.

"It would really be very interesting—if I can manage to get so far," she said, less impulsively.

They walked the length of the great avenue at Nonsuch, and back again in the golden light of the west. Piers Otway disregarded the beauty of earth and sky, he had eyes for nothing but the face and form beside him. At dinner, made dull by Hannaford's presence, he lived still in the dream of his delight, listening only when Irene spoke, speaking only when she addressed him, which she did several times. The meal over, he sought an excuse for spending the next hour in the drawing-room; but Mrs. Hannaford, unconscious of any change in his habits, offered no invitation, and he stole silently away.

He did not light his lamp, but sat in the dim afterglow till it faded through dusk into dark. He sat without movement, in an enchanted reverie. And when night had fallen, he suddenly threw off his clothes and got into bed, where for hours he lay dreaming in wakefulness.

He rose at eight the next morning, and would, under ordinary circumstances, have taken a book till breakfast. But no book could hold him, for he had already looked from the window, and in the garden below had seen Irene. Panting with the haste he had made to finish his toilet, he stepped towards her.

"Three hours' work already, I suppose," she said, as they shook hands.

"Unfortunately, not one. I overslept myself."

"Come, that's reasonable! There's hope of you. Tell me about this examination. What are the subjects?"

He expounded the matter as they walked up and down. It led to a question regarding the possibilities of such a career as he had in view.

"To tell the truth, I haven't thought much about that," said Piers, with wandering look. "My idea was, I fancy, to get a means of earning my living which would leave me a good deal of time for private work."

"What, literary work?"

"No; I didn't think of writing. I like study for its own sake."

"Then you have no ambitions, of the common kind?"

"Well, perhaps not. I suppose I have been influenced by my father's talk about that kind of thing."

"To be sure."

He noticed a shrinking movement in Miss Derwent and saw that Hannaford was approaching. This dislike of the man, involuntarily betrayed, gave Piers an exquisite pleasure. Not only because it showed they had a strong feeling in common; it would have delighted him in any case, for he was jealous of any human being who approached Irene.

3

Hannaford made known at breakfast that he was leaving home again that afternoon, and might be absent for several days. A sensitive person must have felt the secret satisfaction caused all round the table by this announcement; Hannaford, whether he noticed it or not, was completely indifferent; certain letters he had received took most of his attention during the meal. One of them related to an appointment in London which he was trying to obtain; the news was favourable, and it cheered him.

An hour later, as he sat writing in his study, Mrs. Hannaford brought in a parcel which had just arrived for him.

"Ah, what's that?" he asked, looking up with interest.

"I'm sure I don't know," answered his wife. "Something with blood on it, I daresay."

Hannaford uttered a crowing laugh of scorn and amusement.

Through the afternoon Piers Otway sat in the garden with the ladies. After tea he again went for a walk with Olga and Irene. After dinner, he lingered so significantly, that Mrs. Hannaford invited him to the drawing-room, and with unconcealed pleasure he followed her thither. When at length he had taken his leave for the night, there was a short silence, Mrs. Hannaford glancing from her daughter to Irene, and smiling reflectively.

"Mr. Otway seems to be taking a holiday," she said at length.

"Yes, so it seemed to me," fell from Olga, who caught her mother's eye.

"It'll do him good," was Miss Derwent's remark. She exchanged no glance with the others, and seemed to be thinking of something else.

Next morning, though the sun shone brilliantly, she did not appear in the garden before breakfast. From a window above, eyes were watching, watching in vain. At the meal Irene was her wonted self, but she did not enter into conversation with Otway. The young man had grown silent again.

Heavily he went up to his room. Mechanically he seated himself at the table. But, instead of opening books, he propped his head upon his hands, and so sat for a long, long time.

When thoughts began to shape themselves (at first he did not think, but lived in a mere tumult of emotions) he recalled Irene's question: what career had he really in view? A dull, respectable clerkship, with two or three hundred a year, and

the chance of dreary progress by seniority, till it was time to
retire on a decent pension? That he knew was what the
Civil Service meant. The far, faint possibility of some
assistant secretaryship to some statesman in office; really
nothing else. His inquiries had apprised him of this delightful state of things, but he had not cared. Now he did care.
He was beginning to understand himself better.

In truth, he had never looked forward beyond a year or
two. Ambition, desires, he possessed in no common degree,
but as a vague, unexamined impulse. He had dreamt of love,
but timidly, tremulously; that was for the time to come. He
had dreamt of distinction; that also must be patiently awaited.
In the meantime, labour. He enjoyed intellectual effort; he
gloried in the amassing of mental riches.

> "To follow Knowledge like a sinking star,
> Beyond the utmost bound of human thought"—

these lines were frequently in his mind, and helped to shape
his enthusiasm. Consciously he subdued a great part of
himself, binding his daily life in asceticism. He would not
live in London because he dreaded its temptations. Gladly
he adhered to his father's principles in the matter of food and
drink; this helped him to subdue his body, or at least he
thought so. He was happiest when, throwing himself into
bed after some fourteen hours of hard reading, he felt the
stupor of utter weariness creep upon him, with certainty of
oblivion until the next sunrise.

He did not much reflect upon the course of his life hitherto,
with its false starts, its wavering; he had not experience enough
to understand their significance. Of course his father was
mainly responsible for what had so far happened. Jerome
Otway, whilst deciding that this youngest son of his should be
set in the sober way of commerce, to advance himself, if fate
pleased, through recognised grades of social respectability, was
by no means careful to hide from the lad his own rooted
contempt of such ideals. Nothing could have been more
inconsistent than the old agitator's behaviour in attempting to
discharge this practical duty. That he meant well was all
one could say of him; for it was not permissible to suppose
Jerome Otway defective in intelligence. Perhaps the outcome
of solicitude in the case of his two elder sons had so far
discouraged him, that, on the first symptoms of instability,
he ceased to regard Piers as within his influence.

Piers, this morning, had a terrible sense of loneliness, of abandonment. The one certainty by which he had lived, his delight in books, his resolve to become erudite, now of a sudden vanished. He did not know himself; he was in a strange world, and bewildered. Nay, he was suffering anguish.

Why had Miss Derwent disregarded him at breakfast? He must have offended her last night. And that could only be in one way, by neglecting his work to loiter about the drawing-room. She had respected him at all events; now, no doubt, she fancied he had not deserved her respect.

This magnificent piece of self-torturing logic sufficed to occupy him all the morning.

At luncheon-time he was careful not to come down before the bell rang. As he prepared himself, the glass showed a drawn visage, heavy eyes; he thought he was uglier than ever.

Descending, he heard no voices. With tremors he stepped into the dining-room, and there sat Mrs. Hannaford alone.

"They have gone off for the day," she said, with a kind look. "To Dorking, and Leith Hill, and I don't know where."

Piers felt a stab through the heart. He stammered something about a hope that they would enjoy themselves. The meal passed very silently, for Mrs. Hannaford was meditative. She paid unusual attention to Piers, trying to tempt his appetite; but with difficulty he swallowed a mouthful. And, the meal over, he returned at once to his room.

About four o'clock—he was lying on the bed, staring at the ceiling—a knock aroused him. The servant opened the door.

"A gentleman wanting to see you, sir—Mr. Daniel Otway."

Piers was glad. He would have welcomed any visitor. When Daniel—who was better dressed than the other day— came into the room, Piers shook hands warmly with him.

"Delightful spot!" exclaimed the elder, with more than his accustomed suavity. "Charming little house!—I hope I shan't be wasting your time?"

"Of course not. We shall have some tea presently. How glad I am to see you! — I must introduce you to Mrs. Hannaford."

"Delighted, my dear boy! How well you look!—stop, though; you are *not* looking very well"—

Piers broke into extravagant gaiety.

CHAPTER VI

THERE had only been time to satisfy Daniel's profound and touching interest in his brother's work for the examination when the tea bell rang, and they went down to the drawing-room. Piers noticed that Mrs. Hannaford had made a special toilet; so rarely did a new acquaintance enter the house that she was a little fluttered in receiving Daniel Otway, whose manners evidently impressed and pleased her. Had he known his brother well, Piers would have understood that this exhibition of fine courtesy meant a peculiar interest on Daniel's part. Such interest was not difficult to excite; there needed only an agreeable woman's face of a type not familiar to him, in circumstances which offered the chance of intimacy. And Mrs. Hannaford, as it happened, made peculiar appeal to Daniel's sensibilities. As they conversed, her thin cheeks grew warm, her eyes gathered light; she unfolded a charm of personality barely to be divined in her usual despondent mood.

Daniel's talk was animated, varied, full of cleverness and character. No wonder if his hostess thought that she had never met so delightful a man. Incidentally, in quite the permissible way, he made known that he was a connoisseur of art; he spoke of his travels on the track of this or that old master, of being consulted by directors of great Galleries, by wealthy amateurs. He was gracefully anecdotic; he allowed one to perceive a fine enthusiasm. And Piers listened quite as attentively as Mrs. Hannaford, for he had no idea how Daniel made his living. The kernel of truth in this fascinating representation was that Daniel Otway, among other things, collected *bric-à-brac* for a certain dealer, and at times himself disposed of it to persons with more money than knowledge or taste. At the age of thirty-eight this was the point he had reached in a career which once promised brilliant things. In whatever profession he had

37

steadily pursued, Daniel would have come to the front; but precisely that steady pursuit was the thing impossible to him. His special weakness, originally amiable, had become an enthralling vice; the soul of goodness in the man was corrupted, and had turned poisonous.

The conversation was still unflagging, when Olga and her cousin returned from their day's ramble. Daniel was presented to them. Olga at once noticed her mother's strange vivacity, and, sitting silent, closely observed Mr. Otway. Irene, also, studied him with her keen eyes; not, one would have guessed, with very satisfactory results. As time was drawing on, Mrs. Hannaford presently asked Daniel if he could give them the pleasure of staying to dine; and Daniel accepted without a moment's hesitation. When the ladies retired to dress, he went up to Piers' room, where a little dialogue of some importance passed between the brothers.

"Have you heard anything about that matter I spoke of?" Daniel began by asking, confidentially.

Piers answered in the affirmative, and gave details, much to the elder's satisfaction. Thereupon, Daniel began talking in a strain of yet closer confidence, sitting knee to knee with Piers, and tapping him occasionally in a fraternal way. It might interest Piers to know that he was writing a book—a book which would revolutionise opinion with regard to certain matters, and certain periods of art. The work was all but finished. Unfortunately, no publisher could be found to bear the entire expense of this publication, which of course appealed to a very small circle of readers. The illustrations made it costly, and — in short, Daniel found himself pressingly in need of a certain sum to complete this undertaking, which could not but establish his fame as a connoisseur, and in all likelihood would secure his appointment as Director of a certain Gallery which he must not name. The money could be had for the asking from twenty persons—a mere bagatelle of a hundred and fifty pounds or so; but how much pleasanter it would be if this little loan could be arranged between brothers! Daniel would engage to return the sum on publication of the book, probably some six months hence. Of course, he merely threw out the suggestion—

"I shall be only too glad to help," exclaimed Piers at once. "You shall have the money as soon as I get it."

"That's really noble of you, my dear boy.—By the bye,

let all this be very strictly *entre nous*. To tell you the truth,
I want to give the dear old philosopher of Wensleydale
a pleasant surprise. I'm afraid he misjudges me; we have
not been on the terms of perfect confidence which I should
desire. But this book will delight him, I know. Let it
come as a surprise."

Piers undertook to say nothing; and Daniel, after washing
his hands and face, and smoothing his thin hair, was radiant
with gratification.

"Charming girl, Miss Derwent — eh, Piers? I seem to
know the name—Dr. Derwent? Why, to be sure! Capital
acquaintance for you. Lucky rascal, to have got into this
house. Miss Hannaford, too, has points. Nothing so good
at your age, my dear boy, as the habit of associating with
intelligent girls and women. *Emollit mores*, and something
more than that. An excellent influence, every way. I'm no
preacher, Piers, but I hold by morality; it's the salt of life—
the salt of life!"

At dinner, Daniel surpassed himself. He told admirable
stories, he started just the right topics, and dealt with them
in the right way; he seemed to know intuitively the habits
of thought of each person he addressed. The hostess was
radiant; Olga looked almost happy; Irene, after a seeming
struggle with herself, which an unkind observer might have
attributed to displeasure at being rivalled in talk, yielded to
the cheery influence, and held her own against the visitor
in wit and merriment. Not till half-past ten did Daniel
resolve to tear himself away. His thanks to Mrs. Hannaford
for "an enjoyable evening" were spoken with impressive
sincerity, and the lady's expression of hope that they might
meet again made his face shine.

Piers accompanied him to the station. After humming to
himself for a few moments, as they walked along the dark
lane, Daniel slipped a hand through his brother's arm and
spoke affectionately.

"You don't know how glad I am that we have met, old
boy! Now don't let us lose sight of each other.—By the bye,
do you ever hear of Alec?"

Alexander, Jerome Otway's second son, had not com-
municated with his father for a good many years. His
reputation was that of a good-natured wastrel. Piers replied
that he knew nothing whatever of him.

"He is in London," pursued Daniel, "and he is rather anxious to meet *you*. Now let me give you a word of warning. Alec isn't at all a bad sort. I confess I like him, for all his faults—and unfortunately he has plenty of them; but to you, Piers, he would be dangerous. Dangerous, first of all, because of his want of principle—you know my feelings on that point. Then, I'm afraid he knows of your little inheritance, and he *might*—I don't say he would—but he might be tempted to presume upon your good-nature. You understand?"

"What is he doing?" Piers inquired.

"Nothing worth speaking of, I fear. Alec has no stability —so unlike you and me in that. You and I inherit the brave old man's love of work; Alec was born an idler. If I thought you might influence him for good—but no, it is too risky. One doesn't like to speak so of a brother, Piers, but I feel it my duty to warn you against poor Alec. *Basta!*"

That night Piers did not close his eyes. The evening's excitement and the unusual warmth of the weather enhanced the feverishness due to his passionate thoughts. Before daybreak he rose and tried to read, but no book would hold his attention. Again he flung himself on to the bed, and lay till sunrise vainly groaning for sleep.

With the new day came a light rain, which threatened to continue. Dulness ruled at breakfast. The cousins spoke fitfully of what they might do if the rain ceased

"A good time for work," said Irene to Piers. "But perhaps it's all the same to you, rain or shine?"

"Much the same," Piers answered mechanically.

He passed a strange morning. Though to begin with he had seated himself resolutely, the attempt to study was ridiculous; the sight of his books and papers moved him to loathing. He watched the sky, hoping to see it broken. He stood by his door, listening, listening, if perchance he might hear the movements of the girls, or hear a word in Irene's voice. Once he did hear her; she called to Olga, laughingly; and at the sound he quivered, his breath stopped.

The clouds parted; a fresh breeze unveiled the summer blue. Piers stood at the window, watching; and at length he had his reward; the cousins came out and walked along the garden paths, conversing intimately. At one moment, Olga gave a glance up at his window, and he darted back, fearful of having been detected. Were they talking of him? How would Miss Derwent speak of him? Did he interest her in the least?

He peeped again. Irene was standing with her hands linked at the back of her head, seeming to gaze at a lovely cloud above the great elm tree. This attitude showed her to perfection. Piers felt sick and dizzy as his eyes fed upon her form.

At an impulse as sudden as irresistible, he pushed up the sash.

"Miss Hannaford! It's going to be fine, you see."

The girls turned to him with surprise.

"Shall you have a walk after lunch?" he continued.

"Certainly," replied Olga. "We were just talking about it."

A moment's pause—then:

"Would you let me go with you?"

"Of course—if you can really spare the time."

"Thank you."

He shut down the window, turned away, stood in an agony of shame. Why had he done this absurd thing? Was it not as good as telling them that he had been spying? Irene's absolute silence meant disapproval, perhaps annoyance. And Olga's remark about his ability to spare time had hinted the same thing: her tone was not quite natural; she averted her look in speaking. Idiot that he was! He had forced his company upon them, when, more likely than not, they much preferred to be alone. Oh, tactless idiot! Now they would never be able to walk in the garden without a suspicion that he was observing them.

He all but resolved to pack a travelling-bag and leave home at once. It seemed impossible to face Irene at luncheon.

When the bell rang, he stole, slunk, downstairs. Scarcely had he entered the dining-room, when he began an apology; after all, he could not go this afternoon; he must work; the sky had tempted him, but—

"Mr. Otway," said Irene, regarding him with mock sternness, "we don't allow that kind of thing. It is shameful vacillation—I love a long word—What's the other word I was trying for?—still longer—I mean, tergiversation! It comes from *tergum* and *verso*, and means turning the back. It is rude to turn your back on ladies."

Piers would have liked to fall at her feet, in his voiceless gratitude. She had rescued him from his shame, had put an end to all awkwardness, and, instead of merely permitting, had invited his company.

"That decides it, Miss Derwent. Of course I shall come. Forgive me for being so uncivil."

At lunch and during their long walk afterwards, Irene was very gracious to him. She had never talked with him in such a tone of entire friendliness; all at once they seemed to have become intimate. Yet there was another change less pleasing to the young man; Irene talked as though either she had become older, or he younger. She counselled him with serious kindness, urged him to make rational rules about study and recreation.

"You're overdoing it, you know. To-day you don't look very well."

"I had no sleep last night," he replied abruptly, shunning her gaze.

"That's bad. You weren't so foolish as to try to make up for lost time?"

"No, no! I *couldn't* sleep."

He reddened, hung his head. Miss Derwent grew almost maternal. This, she pointed out, was the natural result of nerves overstrained. He must really use common sense. Come now, would he promise?

"I will promise you anything!"

Olga glanced quickly at him from one side; Irene, on the other, looked away with a slight smile.

"No," she said, "you shall promise Miss Hannaford. She will have you under observation; whereas you might play tricks with me, after I'm gone. Olga, be strict with this young gentleman. He is well-meaning, but he vacillates; at times he even tergiversates—a shocking thing."

There was laughter, but Piers suffered. He felt humiliated. Had he been alone with Miss Derwent, he might have asserted his manhood, and it would have been *her* turn to blush, to be confused. He had a couple of years more than she. The trouble was that he could not feel this superiority of age; she treated him like a schoolboy, and to himself he seemed one. Even more than Irene's, he avoided Olga's look, and walked on shamefaced.

The remaining days, until Miss Derwent departed, were to him a mere blank of misery. Impossible to open a book, and sleep came only with uttermost exhaustion. How he passed the hours, he knew not. Spying at windows, listening for voices, creeping hither and thither in torment of multiform ignominy, forcing speech when he longed to be silent, not daring to break silence when his heart seemed bursting with desire to utter itself—a terrible time. And Irene persevered in her elder-sister attitude; she was kindness itself, but never seemed to remark a strangeness in his look and manner. Once he found courage to say that he would like to know Dr. Derwent; sne replied that her father was a very busy man, but that no doubt some opportunity for their meeting would arise—and that was all. When the moment came for leave-taking, Piers tried to put all his soul into a look; but he failed, his eyes dropped, even as his tongue faltered. And Irene Derwent was gone.

If, in the night that followed, a wish could have put an end to his existence, Piers would have died. He saw no hope in living, and the burden seemed intolerable. Love-anguish of one-and-twenty; we smile at it, but it is anguish all the same, and may break or mould a life.

CHAPTER VII

A WEEK went by, and Piers was as far as ever from re-
suming his regular laborious life. One day he spent in
London. His father's solicitor had desired to see him, in the
matter of the legacy; Piers received his money, and on the
same day made over one hundred and fifty pounds to Daniel
Otway, whom he met by appointment; in exchange, Daniel
handed him a beautifully written I.O.U., which the younger
brother would pocket only with protest.

Another week passed. Piers no longer pretended to keep
his usual times; he wandered forth whenever home grew
intolerable, and sometimes snatched his only sleep in the
four-and-twenty hours under the hawthorn blossom of some
remote meadow. His mood had passed into bitterness. "I
was well before; why did she interfere with me? She did it
knowing what would happen; it promised her amusement. I
should have kept to myself, and have been safe. She
waylaid me. That first meeting on the stairs"—

He raged against her and against all women.

One evening, towards sunset, he came home dusty and
weary and with a hang-dog air, for he had done something
which made him ashamed. Miles away from Ewell thirst and
misery had brought him to a wayside inn, where—the first
time for years—he drank strong liquor. He drank more
than he needed, and afterwards fell asleep in a lane, and woke
to new wretchedness.

As he entered the house and was about to ascend the
stairs, a voice called to him. It was Mrs. Hannaford's;
she bade him come to her in the drawing-room. Reluctantly
he moved thither. The lady was sitting idle and alone; she
looked at him for a moment without speaking, then beckoned
him forward.

"Your brother has been here," she said, in a low voice not
quite her own.

" Daniel ? "

" Yes. He called very soon after you had gone out. He wouldn't—couldn't stay. He'll let you know when he is coming next time."

" Oh, all right."

" Come and sit down." She pointed to a chair next hers. " How tired you look ! "

Her tone was very soft, and, as he seated himself, she touched his arm gently. The room was scented with roses. A blind half-drawn on the open window broke the warm western rays ; upon a tree near by, a garden warbler was piping evensong.

" What is it ? " she asked, with a timid kindness. " What has happened ? Won't you tell me ? "

" You know—I am sure you know "—

His voice was choked into silence.

" But you will get over it — oh yes, you will ! Your work "—

" I can't work ! " he broke out vehemently—" I shall never work again. She has changed all my life. I must find something else to do—I don't care what. I can't go in for that examination."

Then abruptly he turned to her with a look of eagerness.

" Would it be any use ? Suppose I got a place in one of the offices ? Would there be any hope for me ? "

Mrs. Hannaford's eyes dropped.

" Don't think of her," she answered. " She has such brilliant prospects—it is so unlikely. You think me unsympathetic—oh, I'm not ! " Again she let her fingers rest on his arm. " I feel so much with you that I daren't offer imaginary hopes. She belongs to such a different world, try, try to forget her."

" Of course I know she cares and thinks nothing about me now. But if I made my way "—

" She will marry very early, and someone "—

With an upward movement of her hand, the speaker was sufficiently explicit. Otway, he knew not why, tried to laugh, and frightened himself with the sound.

" She is not the only girl, good and beautiful," Mrs. Hannaford continued, pleading with him.

" For me she is," he replied, in a hard voice. " And I believe she will be always."

For a minute or two, the little warbler sang in silence, then Piers of a sudden stood up, and strode hastily away.

Mrs. Hannaford fell into reverie. Her daughter was in London to-day, her husband absent somewhere else. But she had not been solitary, for Daniel Otway, failing to meet his brother, lingered a couple of hours in the drawing-room. As she sat dreaming under the soft light, her face relieved for the moment of its weariness and discontent, had a beauty more touching than that of youth.

Upstairs Piers found a letter awaiting him. He did not know the writing, and found with surprise that it came from his brother Alexander, who had addressed it to him through their father's solicitor. Alexander wrote from the neighbourhood of Bloomsbury Square; it was an odd letter, beginning formally, almost paternally, and running off into chirruping facetiousness, as if the writer had tried in vain to subdue his natural gaiety. There were extraordinary phrases. "I congratulate you on being gazetted major in the regiment of Old Time." "For my own part I am just beginning my thirty-fifth round with knuckly life, and I rejoice to say that I have come up smiling. Floorers I have suffered, not a few, in the rounds preceding, but I am harder for it, harder and gamer." "Shall we not crack a bottle together on this side of the circumfluent Oceanus?" And so on, to the effect that Alexander much wished for a meeting with his brother, and urged him to come to Theobald's Road as soon as possible, at his own convenience.

It gave Piers—what he needed badly—something new to think about. From what he remembered of Alexander, he did not dislike him, and this letter made, on the whole, an agreeable impression; but he remembered Daniel's warning. In any case there could be no harm in calling on his brother; it made an excuse for a day in London, the country stillness having driven him all but to frenzy. So he replied at once, saying that he would call on the following afternoon.

Alexander occupied the top floor of a great old house in Theobald's Road. Whether he was married or not, Piers had not heard; the appearance of the place suggested bachelor quarters, but, as he knocked at what seemed the likely door, there sounded from within an infantine wail, which became alarmingly shrill when the door was thrown open by a dirty little girl. At sight of Piers this young person, evidently a servant, drew back smiling, and said with a strong Irish accent :

"Plase to come in. They're expecting of you."

He passed into a large room, magnificently lighted by the sunshine, but very simply furnished. A small round table, two or three chairs and a piano were lost on the great floor, which had no carpeting, only a small Indian rug being displayed as a thing of beauty, in the very middle. There were no pictures, but here and there, to break the surface of the wall, strips of bright-coloured material were hung from the cornice. At the table, next the window, sat a man writing, also as his lips showed whistling a tune ; and on the bare boards beside him sat a young woman with her baby on her lap, another child, of two or three years old, amusing itself by pulling her dishevelled hair.

"Here's your brother, Mr. Otw'y," yelled the little servant. "Give that baby to me, mum. I know what'll quoiet him, bless his little heart."

Alexander sprang up, waving his arm in welcome. He was a stoutish man of middle height, with thick curly auburn hair and a full beard ; geniality beamed from his blue eyes.

"Is it yourself, Piers ?" he shouted, with utterance suggestive of the Emerald Isle, though the man was so loudly English. "It does me good to set eyes on you, upon my soul it does ! I knew you'd come. Didn't I say he'd come, Biddy?—Piers, this is my wife, Bridget ; the best wife living in all the four quarters of the world !"

Mrs. Otway had risen, and stood smiling, the picture of cordiality. She was not a beauty, though the black hair broadflung over her shoulders made no common adornment ; but her round healthy face, with its merry eyes and gleaming teeth, had an honest attractiveness, and her soft Irish tongue went to the heart. It never occurred to her to apologise for the disorderly state of things. Having got rid of her fractious baby—not without a kiss—she took the other child by the hand and with pride presented "My daughter Leonora"—a name which gave Piers a little shock of astonishment.

"Sit down, Piers," shouted her husband. "First we'll have tea and talk ; then we'll have talk and tobacco ; then we'll have dinner and talk again, and after that whatever the gods please to send us. My day's work is done—*ecce signum !*"

He pointed to the slips of manuscript from which he had

risen. Alexander had begun life as a medical student, but
never got so far as a diploma. In many capacities, often
humble but never disgraceful, he had wandered over Broader
Britain — drifting at length, as he was bound to do, into
irregular journalism.

"And how's the old man at home?" he asked, whilst Mrs.
Otway busied herself in getting tea. "Piers, it's the sorrow
of my life that he hasn't a good opinion of me. I don't say
I deserve it, but, as I live, I've always meant to! And I
admire him, Piers. I've written about him; and I sent him
the article, but he didn't acknowledge it. How does he bear
his years, the old Trojan? And how does his wife use him?
Ah, that was a mistake, Piers; that was a mistake. In
marriage—and remember this, Piers, for your time 'll come—
it must be the best, or none at all. I acted upon that, though
Heaven knows the trials and temptations I went through. I
said to myself, The best or none! And I found her, Piers;
I found her sitting at a cottage door by Enniscorthy, County
Wexford, where for a time I had the honour of acting as tutor
to a young gentleman of promise, cut short, alas!—'the blind
Fury with the abhorred shears'! I wrote an elegy on him,
which I'll show you. His father admired it, had it printed,
and gave me twenty pounds, like the gentleman he was!"

There appeared a handsome tea-service; the only objection
to it being that every piece was chipped or cracked, and not
one thoroughly clean. Leonora, a well-behaved little creature
who gave earnest of a striking face, sat on her mother's lap,
watching the visitor and plainly afraid of him.

"Well," exclaimed Mrs. Otway, "I should never have taken
you two for brothers—no, not even the half of it!"

"He has an intellectual face, Biddy," observed her husband.
"Pale just now, but it's 'the pale cast of thought.' What are
you aiming at, Piers?"

"I don't know," was the reply, absently spoken.

"Ah, but I'm sorry to hear that. You should have concentrated yourself by now, indeed you should. If I had to
begin over again, I should go in for commerce."

Piers gave him a look of interest.

"Indeed? You mean that?"

"I do. I would apply myself to the science and art of
money-making in the only hopeful way—honest buying and
selling. There's something so satisfying about it. I envy

even the little shopkeeper, who reckons up his profits every Saturday night, and sees his business growing. But you must begin early; you must learn money-making like anything else. If I had made money, Piers, I should be at this moment the most virtuous and meritorious citizen of the British Empire!"

Alexander was vexed to find that his brother did not smoke. He lit his pipe after tea, and for a couple of hours talked ceaselessly, relating the course of his adventurous life; an entertaining story, told with abundant vigour, with humorous originality. Though he had in his possession scarce a dozen volumes, Alexander was really a bookish man and something of a scholar; his quotations, which were frequent, ranged from Homer to Horace, from Chaucer to Tennyson. He recited a few of his own poetical compositions, and they might have been worse; Piers made him glow and sparkle with a little praise.

Meanwhile, Bridget was putting the children to bed and cooking the evening meal—styled dinner for this occasion. Both proceedings were rather tumultuous, but, amid the clamour they necessitated, no word of ill-temper could be heard; screams of laughter, on the other hand, were frequent. With manifest pride the little servant came in to lay the table; she only broke one glass in the operation, and her "Sure now, who'd have thought it!" as she looked at the fragments, delighted Alexander beyond measure. The chief dish was a stewed rabbit, smothered in onions; after it appeared an immense gooseberry tart, the pastry hardly to be attacked with an ordinary table knife. Compromising for the nonce with his teetotalism as well as his vegetarianism—not to pain the hosts—Piers drank bottled ale. It was an uproarious meal. The little servant, whilst in attendance, took her full share of the conversation, and joined shrilly in the laughter. Mrs. Otway had arrayed herself in a scarlet gown, and her hair was picturesquely braided; she ceased not from hospitable cares, and set a brave example in eating and drinking. Yet she was never vulgar, as an untaught London woman in her circumstances would have been, and many a delightful phrase fell from her lips in the mellow language of County Wexford.

When the remnants of dinner were removed, a bottle of Irish whisky came forth, with the due appurtenances. Then it was that Alexander, with pride in his eye, made known Bridget's one accomplishment; she had a voice, and would

presently use it for their guest's delectation. She was trying
to learn the piano, as yet with small success; but Alexander,
who had studied music concurrently with medicine, and to
better result, was able to furnish accompaniments. The
concert began, and Piers, who had felt misgivings, was most
agreeably surprised. Not only had Bridget a voice, a very
sweet mezzo-contralto, but she sang with remarkable feeling.
More than once the listener had much ado to keep tears out
of his eyes; they were at his throat all the time, and his heart
swelled with the passionate emotion which had lurked there
to the ruin of his peace. But music, the blessed, the peace-
maker (for music called martial is but a blustering bastard),
changed his torments to ecstasy; his love, however hopeless,
became an inestimable possession, and he seemed to himself
capable of such great, such noble things as had never entered
into the thought of man.

The crying of her baby obliged Bridget to withdraw for a
little. Alexander, who had already made gallant inroad on
the whisky bottle, looked almost fiercely at his brother, and
exclaimed:

"What do you say to *that*? Isn't that a woman? Isn't
that a wife to be proud of?"

Piers replied with enthusiasm.

"Not long ago," proceeded the other, "when we were really
hard up, she wanted me to let her try to earn money with her
voice. She could, you know! But do you think I'd allow
it? Sooner I'll fry the soles of my boots and make believe
they're beefsteak!—Look at her, and remember her when
you're seeking for a wife of your own. Never mind if you
have to wait; it's worth it. When it comes to wives, the best
or none! That's my motto."

In his emotional mood, Piers had an impulse. He bent
forward, and asked quietly:

"Are things all right now? About money, I mean."

"Oh, we get on. We could do with a little more furniture,
but all in good time."

Piers again listened to his impulse. He spoke hurriedly of
the money he had received, and hinted, suggested, made an
embarrassed offer. Impossible not to remark the gleam of
joy that came into Alexander's eyes; though he vehemently,
almost angrily, declared such a thing impossible, it was plain
he quivered to accept. And in the end accept he did—a

round fifty pounds. A loan, strictly a loan, of course; the most binding legal instrument should be given in acknowledgment of the debt; interest should be paid at the rate of three and a half per cent. per annum—not a doit less! And just when this was settled, Bridget came back again, the sleepless baby at her breast.

"He wants to have his share of the good company," she exclaimed. "And why shouldn't he, bless um!"

Alexander grew glorious. It was one of his peculiarities that, when he had drunk more than enough, he broke into noisy patriotism.

"Piers, have you ever felt grateful enough for being born an Englishman? I've seen the world, and I know; the Englishman is the top of creation. When I say English, I mean all of us, English, Irish, or Scotch. Give me an Englishman and an Irishwoman, and let all the rest of the world go hang!—I've travelled, Piers, my boy. I've seen what the great British race is doing the world round; and I'm that proud of it I can't find words to express myself."

"I've seen something of other races," interposed Piers, lifting his glass with unsteady hand, "and I don't think we've any right to despise them."

"I don't exactly despise them, but I say, What are they compared with us? A poor lot! A shabby lot!—I'm a journalist, Piers, and let me tell you that we English newspaper men have the destiny of the world in our hands. It makes me proud when I think of it. We guard the national honour. Let any confounded foreigner insult England, and he has to reckon with *us*. A word from *us*, and it means war, Piers, glorious war, with triumphs for the race and for civilisation! England means civilisation; the other nations don't count."

"Oh, come"—

"I tell you they don't count!" roared Alexander, his hair wild and his beard ferocious. "You're not one of the muffs who want to keep England little and tame, are you?"

"I think pretty much with father about these things."

"The old man! Oh, I'd forgotten the old man. But he's not of our time, Piers; he's old-fashioned, though a good old man, I admit. No, no; we must be armed and triple-armed; we must be so strong that not all the confounded foreigners leagued together can touch us. It's the cause of civilisation, Piers. I preach it whenever I get the chance ; I wish I got it oftener. I stand for England's honour, England's supremacy on sea and land. I st-tand "—

He tried to do so, to reach the bottle, which proved to be empty.

"Send for another, Biddy—the right Irish, my lass ! Another bottle to the glory of the British Empire ! Piers, we'll make a night of it. I haven't a bed to offer you, but Biddy 'll give you a shake-down here on the floor. You're the right sort, Piers. You're a noble-minded, generous-hearted Englishman."

Mrs. Otway, with a glance at the visitor, only made pretence of sending for more whisky, and Piers, after looking at his watch, insisted on taking leave. Alexander would have gone with him to the station, but Bridget forbade this. The patriot had to be content with promises of another such evening, and Piers, saying significantly "You will hear from me," hastened to catch his train.

CHAPTER VIII

WHEN he awoke next morning from a heavy sleep, Piers suffered the half-recollection of some reproachful dream. His musty palate and dull brain reminded him of Alexander's whisky; matter, that, for self-reproach; but in the background was something more. He had dreamt of his father, and seemed to have discharged in sleep a duty still in reality neglected; that, namely, of responding to the old man's offer of advice respecting the use he should make of his money. Out of four hundred pounds, two hundred were already given away,—for he had no serious expectation that his brothers would repay the so-called loans. Plainly it behoved him to be frank on this subject. Affectionate loyalty to his father had ever been a guiding principle in Piers Otway's life; he was uneasy under the sense that he had begun to slip towards neglectfulness, towards careless independence.

He would have written this morning, but, after all, it was better to wait until he had settled the doubt which made havoc of his days. At heart he knew that he would not present himself for the Civil Service examination; but he durst not yet put the resolve into words. It seemed a sort of madness, after so many months of laborious preparation, and the fixity of purpose which had grown with his studious habit. And what a return for the patient kindness with which his father had counselled and assisted him! He thought of Daniel and Alexander. Was he, too, going to drift in life, instead of following a steadfast, manly course? The perception and fear of such a danger were something new to him. Piers had seen himself as an example of moral and intellectual vigour. His abandonment of commerce had shown as a strong step in practical wisdom; the fourteen hours of daily reading had flattered his pride. Thereupon came this sudden collapse of the whole scheme. He could no longer endure the prospects for which he had toiled so strenuously.

But for shame, he would have bundled together all the books that lay on his table, and have flung them out of sight.

In the afternoon, he sought a private conversation with Mrs. Hannaford. It was not easily managed, as Hannaford and Olga were both at home; but, by watching and waiting, he caught a moment when the lady stood alone in the garden.

"Do you think," he asked, with tremulous, sudden speech, "that I might call at Dr. Derwent's?"

"Why not?" was the answer, but given with troubled countenance. "You mean"—she smiled—"call upon Miss Derwent. There would be no harm; she is the lady of the house, at present."

"Would she be annoyed?"

"I don't see why. But of course I can't answer for another person in such things."

Their eyes met. Mrs. Hannaford gazed at him sadly for an instant, shook her head, and turned away. Piers went back to lonely misery.

Early next day he stole from the house, and went to London. His business was at the tailor's; he ordered a suit of ceremony—the frock coat on which his brother Daniel had so pathetically insisted—and begged that it might be ready at the earliest possible moment. Next he made certain purchases in haberdashery. Through it all, he had a most oppressive feeling of self-contempt, which—Piers was but one-and-twenty—he did not try to analyse. Every shop-mirror which reflected him seemed to present a malicious caricature; he hurried away on to the pavement, small, ignoble, silly. His heart did battle, and at moments assailed him in a triumph of heroic desire; but then again came the sinking moments, the sense of a grovelling fellowship with people he despised.

It was raining. His shopping done, he entered an omnibus, which took him as far as the Marble Arch; thence, beneath his umbrella, he walked in search of Bryanston Square. Here was Dr. Derwent's house. Very much like a burglar, a beginner at the business, making survey of his field, he moved timidly into the Square, and sought the number; having found it with unexpected suddenness, he hurried past. To be detected here would be dreadful; he durst not go to the opposite side, lest Irene should perchance be at a window; yet he wanted to observe the house, and did, from behind his umbrella, when a few doors away.

Never had he known what it was to feel such an insignificant mortal. Standing here in the rain, he saw no distinction between himself and the ragged, muddy crossing-sweeper; alike, they were lost in the huge welter of common London. On the other hand, there in the hard-fronted, exclusive-looking house sat Irene Derwent, a pearl of women, the prize of wealth, distinction, and high manliness. What was this wild dream he had been harbouring? Like a chill wind, reality smote him in the face; he turned away, saying to himself that he was cured of folly.

On the journey home, he shaped a project. He would seek an interview with the head of the City house in which he had spent so much time and worked so conscientiously, a quite approachable man as he knew from experience, and would ask if he might be allowed to re-enter their service; not, however, in London, but in their place of business at Odessa. He had made a good beginning with Russian, and living in Russia, might hope soon to master the language. If necessary, he would support himself at Odessa for a time, until he was capable of serving the firm in some position of trust. Yes, this was what he would do; it gave him a new hope. For Alexander, foolish fellow as he might be in some respects, had spoken the truth on the subject of money-making; the best and surest way was by honourable commerce. Money he must have; a substantial position; a prospect of social advance. Not for their own sake, these things, but as steps to the only end he felt worth living for—an ideal marriage.

He marvelled that the end of life should have been so obscure to him hitherto. Knowledge! What satisfaction was there in that? Fame! What profit in that by itself? Yet he had thought these aims predominant; had been willing to toil day and night in such pursuits. His eyes were opened. His first torturing love might be for ever frustrate, but it had revealed him to himself. He looked forth upon the world, its activities, its glories, and behold there was for him but one prize worth winning, the love of the ideal woman.

He found a letter at Ewell. It contained a card of invitation; Mrs. John Jacks graciously announced to him that she would be at home on an evening a week hence, at nine o'clock.

How came he to have forgotten the Jacks family? Not once had he mentioned to Miss Derwent that he was on friendly terms with these most respectable people. What a foolish omission! It would at once have given him a better standing in her sight, have smoothed their social relations.

Instantly, his plan of exile was forgotten. He would accept this invitation, and on the same day, in the afternoon, he would boldly call at the Derwents'. Why not?—as Mrs. Hannaford said. John Jacks, M.P., was undoubtedly the social superior of Dr. Derwent; admitted to the house at Queen's Gate, one might surely with all confidence present oneself in Bryanston Square. Was he not an educated man, by birth a gentleman? If he had no position, why, who had at one-and-twenty? How needlessly he had been humiliating and discouraging himself! In the highest spirits he went down into the garden to talk with Mrs. Hannaford and Olga. They gazed at him, astonished; he was a new creature; he joked and laughed and could hardly contain his exuberance of joy. When there fell from him a casual mention of Mrs. Jacks' card, no one could have imagined that this was the explanation of his altered mood. Mrs. Hannaford felt sure that he had been to see Irene, and had received, or fancied, some sort of encouragement. Olga thought so too, and felt sorry to see him in a fool's paradise.

That very evening he sat down and resolved to work. He had an appetite for it once more. He worked till long after midnight, and on the morrow kept his old hours. Moreover, he wrote a long letter to Hawes, a good, frank letter, giving his father a full account of the meetings with Daniel and Alexander, and telling all about the pecuniary transactions :—" I hope you will not think I behaved very foolishly. Indeed, it has given me pleasure to share with them. My trouble is lest you should think I acted in complete disregard of you ; but, if I am glad to do a good turn, remember, dear father, that it is to you I owe this habit of mind. And I shall not need money. I feel it practically certain that I shall get my office, and then it will go smoothly. The examination draws near, and I am working like a Trojan ! "

" I cannot carp at you," wrote Jerome Otway in reply, " but tighten the purse-strings after this, and be not overmuch familiar with Alexander the Little or Daniel the Purblind. Their ways are not mine ; let them not be yours."

He had to run up to town for the trying-on of his new garments, and this time the business gave him satisfaction. In future he would be seeing much more society; he must have a decent regard for appearances.

His spirits faltered not; they were in harmony with the June weather. Never had he laboured to such purpose. Everything seemed easy; he strode with giant strides into the field of knowledge. Papers such as would be set him at the examination were matter for his mirth, mere schoolboy tests. Now and then he rose from study with a troublesome dizziness, and of a morning his head generally ached a little; but these were trifles. *Frisch zu !*—as a German friend of his at Geneva used to say.

Even on the morning of the great day, he worked; it was to prove his will-power, his worthiness. After lunch, clad in the garb of respectability, he went up by a quick train. His evening suit he had previously despatched to Alexander's abode, where he was to dine and dress.

At four o'clock he was in Bryanston Square, tremulous but sanguine, a different man from him who had sneaked about here under the umbrella. He knocked. The servant civilly informed him that Miss Derwent was not at home, asked his name, and bowed him away.

It was a shock. This possibility had not entered his mind, so engrossed was he in forecasting, in dramatising, the details of the interview. Looking like one who has received some dreadful news, he turned slowly from the door and walked away with head down. Probably no event in all his life had given him such a sense of desolating frustration. At once the sky was overcast, the ways were woebegone; he shrank within his new garments, and endured once more the feeling of personal paltriness.

Though the time before him was so long, he had no choice but to go at once to Theobald's Road, where at all events friendly faces would greet him. The streets of London are terrible to one who is both lonely and unhappy; the indifference of their hard egotism becomes fierce hostility; instead of merely disregarding, they crush. As soon as he could command his thoughts, Piers made for the shortest way, and hurried on.

Mrs. Otway admitted him; Alexander, she said, was away on business, but would soon return. On entering the large room, Piers was startled at the change in its appearance. The well-carpeted floor, the numerous chairs of inviting depth and

softness, the centre-table, the handsome bureau, the numerous
pictures, and a multitude of knick-knacks not to be taken in
at one glance, made it plain that most of the money he had
lent his brother had been expended at once in this direction.
Bridget stood watching his face, and at the first glimmer of a
smile broke into jubilation. What did he think? How did
he like it? Wasn't it a room to be pr-roud of? She knew it
would do his kind heart good to see such splendours! Let
him sit down—after selecting his chair—and take it all in
whilst she got some tea. No wonder it took away his breath!
She herself had hardly yet done gazing in mute ecstasy.

"It's been such a feast for my eyes, Mr. Piers, that I've
scarcely wanted to put a bit in my mouth since the room was
finished!"

When Alexander arrived, he greeted his brother as though
with rapturous congratulation; one would have thought some
great good fortune had befallen the younger man.

"Biddy!" he shouted, "I've a grand idea! We'll celebrate
the occasion with a dinner out; we'll go to a restaurant.
Hanged if you shall have the trouble of cooking on such a
day as this! Get ready; make yourself beautiful—though
you're always that. We'll dine early, as Piers has to leave us
at nine o'clock."

Outcries and gesticulations confirmed the happy thought.
Tea over, Piers was dismissed to the bedroom (very bare and
uncomfortable, this) to don his evening suit, and by six o'clock
the trio set forth. They drove in a cab to festive regions, and,
as one to the manner born, Alexander made speedy arrangements for their banquet. An odd-looking party; the young
man's ceremonious garb and not ungraceful figure contrasting
with his brother's aspect of Bohemian carelessness and jollity,
whilst Bridget, adorned in striking colours, would have passed
for anything you like but a legitimate and devoted spouse.
Once again did Piers stifle his conscience in face of the
exhilarating bottle; indeed, he drank deliberately to drown
his troubles, and before the second course had already to
some extent succeeded.

Alexander talked of his journalistic prospects. Whether
there was any special reason for hopefulness, Piers could not
discover; it seemed probable that here also the windfall of
fifty pounds had changed the aspect of the world. To hear
him, one might have supposed that the struggling casual

contributor had suddenly been offered some brilliant appointment on a great journal; but he discoursed with magnificent vagueness, and could not be brought to answer direct questions. His attention to the wine was unremittent; he kept his brother's glass full, nor was Bridget allowed to shirk her convivial duty. At dessert appeared a third bottle; by this time, Piers was drinking without heed to results; jovially, mechanically, glass after glass, talking, too, in a strain of nebulous imaginativeness. There could be little doubt, he hinted, that *one* of his Parliamentary friends (John Jacks had been insensibly multiplied) would give him a friendly lift. A secretaryship was sure to come pretty quickly, and then, who knew what opening might present itself! He wouldn't mind a consulship, for a year or two, at some agreeable place. But eventually—who could doubt it ?—he would enter the House. Why, of course! cried Alexander; the outline of his career was plain beyond discussion. And let him go in strong for Home Rule. That would be the great question for the next few years, until it was triumphantly settled. Private information —from a source only to be hinted at—assured him that Mr. Gladstone (after the recent defeat) was already hard at work preparing another Bill. Come now, they must drink Home Rule—"Justice to Ireland, and the world-supremacy of the British Empire!"—that was his toast. They interrupted their sipping of green Chartreuse to drink it in brimming glasses of claret.

"We'll drive you to Queen's Gate!" said Alexander, when Piers began to look at his watch. "No hurry, my boy! The night is young! 'And'"—he broke into lyric quotation— "'haply the Queen Moon is on her throne, clustered around with all her starry fays.'—I shall never forget this dinner; shall you, Biddy? We'll have a song when we get home."

One little matter had to be attended to, the paying of the bill. Having glanced carelessly at the total, Alexander began to search his pockets.

"Why, hang it!" he exclaimed. "What a fellow I am! Piers, it's really too absurd, but I shall have to ask you to lend me a sovereign; I can't make up enough—stupid carelessness! Biddy, why didn't you ask me if I'd got money?—No, no; just a sovereign, Piers; I have the rest. I'll pay you back to-morrow morning."

With laughter at such a capital joke, Piers disbursed the

coin. Quaint, comical fellow, this brother of his! He liked him, and was beginning to like Biddy too.

A cab bore them all to Queen's Gate, Alexander and his wife making the journey just for the fun of the thing. Piers would have paid for the vehicle back to Theobald's Road, but this his brother declined; he and Mrs. Otway preferred the top of a 'bus this warm night. They parted at Mr. Jacks' door, where carriages and cabs were stopping every minute or two.

"I'll sit up for you, Piers," roared Alexander genially. "You'll want a whisky-and-soda after this job. Come along, Biddy!"

In another frame of mind, Piers would have felt the impropriety of these loud remarks at such a moment. Even as it was, he would doubtless have regretted the incident had he turned his head to observe the two persons who had just alighted and were moving up the steps close behind him. A young, slim, perfectly equipped man, with features expressive of the most becoming sentiment; a lady—or girl—of admirable figure, with bright, intelligent, handsome face. These two exchanged a look; they exchanged a discreet murmur; and were careful not to overtake Piers Otway in the hall.

He, hat and overcoat surrendered, moved up the gleaming staircase. A sound of soft music fluttered his happy temper. Seeing his form in a mirror, he did not at once recognise himself; for his face had a high colour, with the result of making him far more comely than at ordinary times. He stepped firmly on, delighted to be here, eager to perceive his hostess. Mrs. Jacks, for a moment, failed to remember him; but needless to say that this did not appear in her greeting, which, as she recollected, dropped upon a tone of special friendliness. To her, Piers Otway was the least interesting of young men; but her husband had spoken of him very favourably, and Mrs. Jacks had a fine sense of her duty on such points. Piers was dazzled by the lady's personal charm; her brilliantly pure complexion, her faultless shoulders and soft white arms, her pose of consummate dignity and courtesy. Happily, his instincts and his breeding held their own against perilous circumstance; excited as he was, nothing of the cause appeared in his brief colloquy with the hostess, and he acquitted himself very creditably. A little farther on, John Jacks advanced to him with cordial welcome,

"So glad you could come. By the bye"—he lowered his voice—"if you have any trouble about trains back to Ewell, do let us put you up for the night. Just stay or not, as you like. Delighted if you do."

Piers replied that he was staying at his brother's. Whereupon John Jacks became suddenly thoughtful, said, "Ah, I see," and with a pleasant smile turned to someone else. Only when it was too late did Piers remember that Mr. Jacks possibly had a private opinion about Jerome Otway's elder sons. He wished, above all things, that he could have accepted the invitation. But doubtless it would be repeated some other time.

As he looked about him at the gathering guests, he recalled his depression this afternoon in Bryanston Square, and it seemed to him so ridiculous that he could have laughed aloud. As if he would not have other chances of calling upon Irene Derwent! Ah, but, to be sure, he must provide himself with visiting-cards. A trifling point, but he had since reflected on it with some annoyance.

A hand was extended to him, a pink, delicate, but shapely hand, which his eyes fell upon as he stood in half-reverie. He exchanged civilities with Arnold Jacks.

"I think some particular friends of yours are here," said Arnold. "The Derwents"—

"Indeed! Are they? Miss Derwent?"

Piers' vivacity caused the other to examine him curiously.

"I only learned a day or two ago," Arnold pursued, "that you knew each other."

"I knew Miss Derwent. I haven't met Dr. Derwent or her brother. Are they here yet? I wish you would introduce me."

Again Arnold, smiling discreetly, scrutinised the young man's countenance, and for an instant seemed to reflect as he glanced around.

"The Doctor perhaps hasn't come. But I see Eustace Derwent. Shall we go and speak to him?"

They walked towards Irene's brother, Piers gazing this way and that in eager hope of perceiving Irene herself. He was wild with delight. Could Fortune have been kinder? Under what more favourable circumstance could he possibly have renewed his relations with Miss Derwent? Eustace, turning at the right moment, stood face to face with Arnold Jacks, who presented his companion, then moved away. Had he lingered, John Jacks' critical son would have found hints for amused speculation in the scene that followed. For Eustace Derwent, remembering, as always, what he owed to himself and to society, behaved with entire politeness; only, like certain beverages downstairs, it was iced. Otway did not immediately become aware of this.

"I think we missed each other only by an hour or two, when you brought Miss Derwent to Ewell. That very day, curiously, I was lunching here."

"Indeed?" said Eustace, with a marble smile.

"Miss Derwent is here, I hope?" pursued Piers; not with any offensive presumption, but speaking as he thought, rather impetuously.

"I believe Miss Derwent is in the room," was the answer, uttered with singular gravity and accompanied with a particularly freezing look.

This time, Piers could not but feel that Eustace Derwent was speaking oddly. In his peculiar condition, however, he thought it only an amusing characteristic of the young man. He smiled, and was about to continue the dialogue, when, with a slight, quick bow, the other turned away.

"Disagreeable fellow, that!" said Piers to himself. "I hope the Doctor isn't like him. Who could imagine him Irene's brother?"

His spirits were not in the least affected; indeed, every moment they grew more exuberant, as the wine he had drunk wrought progressively upon his brain. Only he could have wished that his cheeks and ears did not burn so; seeing himself again in a glass, he decided that he was really too high-coloured. It would pass, no doubt. Meanwhile, his eyes kept seeking Miss Derwent. The longer she escaped him, the more vehement grew his agitation. Ah, there! She was seated, and had been hidden by a little group standing in front. At this moment, Eustace Derwent was bending to speak to her; she gave a nod in reply to what he said. As soon as the objectionable brother moved from her side, Piers stepped quickly forward.

"How delightful to meet you here! It seems too good to be true. I called this afternoon at your house—called to see you—but you were not at home. I little imagined I should see you this evening."

Irene raised her eyes, and let them fall back upon her fan; raised them again, and observed the speaker attentively.

"I was told you had called, Mr. Otway."

How her voice thrilled him! What music like that voice! It made him live through his agonies again, which by contrast heightened the rapture of this hour.

"May I sit down by you?"

"Pray do."

He remarked nothing of her coldness; he was conscious only of her presence, of the perfume which breathed from her and made his heart faint with longing.

Irene again glanced at him, and her countenance was troubled. She looked to left and right, sure that they were not overheard, and addressed him with quick directness.

"Where did you dine, Mr. Otway?"

"Dine?—Oh, at a restaurant, with one of my brothers and his wife."

"Did your brother and his wife accompany you to this house?"

Piers was startled. He gazed into her face, and Irene allowed him to meet her eyes, which reminded him most unpleasantly of the look he had seen in those of Eustace.

"Why do you ask that, Miss Derwent?" he faltered.

"I will tell you. I happened to be just behind you as you entered, and couldn't help hearing the words shouted to you by your brother. Will you forgive me for mentioning such a thing? And, as your friend, will you let me say that I think it would be unfortunate if you were introduced to my father this evening? He is not here yet, but he will be.—I have taken a great liberty, Mr. Otway; but it seemed to me that I had no choice. When an unpleasant thing *has* to be done, I always try to do it quickly."

Piers was no longer red of face. A terrible sobriety had fallen upon him; his lips quivered; cold currents ran down his spine. He looked at Irene with the eyes of a dog entreating mercy.

"Had I"— his dry throat forced him to begin again—"had I better go now?"

"That is as you think fit."

Piers stood up, bowed before her, gave her one humble, imploring look, and walked away.

He went down, as though to the supper-room; in a few minutes, he had left the house. He walked to Waterloo Station, and by the last train returned to Ewell.

CHAPTER IX

AT the head of Wensleydale, where rolling moor grows mountainous toward the marches of Yorkshire and Westmorland, stands the little market-town named Hawes. One winding street of houses and shops, grey, hard-featured, stout against the weather; with little byways climbing to the height above, on which rises the rugged church, stern even in sunshine; its tower, like a stronghold, looking out upon the brooding-place of storms. Like its inhabitants, the place is harsh of aspect, warm at heart; scornful of graces, its honest solidity speaks the people that built it for their home. This way and that go forth the well-kept roads, leading to other towns; their sharp tracks shine over the dark moorland, climbing by wind-swept hamlets, by many a lonely farm; dipping into sudden hollows, where streams become cascades, and guiding the wayfarers by high, rocky passes from dale to dale. A country always impressive by the severe beauty of its outlines; sometimes speaking to the heart in radiant stillness, its moments of repose; mirthful sometimes, inspiring joyous life, with the gleams of its vast sky, the sweet, keen breath of its heaths and pastures; but for the most part shadowed, melancholy, an austere nurse of the striving spirit of man, with menace in its mountain-rack, in the rushing voice of its winds and torrents.

Here, in a small, plain cottage, stone-walled, stone-roofed, looking over the wide and deep hollow of a stream—a beck in the local language—which at this point makes a sounding cataract on its course from the great moor above, lived Jerome Otway. It had been his home for some ten years. He lived as a man of small but sufficient means, amid very plain household furniture, and with no sort of social pretence. With him dwelt his wife, and one maid-servant.

On an evening of midsummer, still and sunny, the old man sat among his books; open before him the great poem of

Dante. His much-lined face, austere in habitual expression, yet with infinite possibilities of radiance in the dark eyes, of tenderness on the mobile lips, was crowned with hair which had turned iron-grey but remained wonderfully thick and strong; the moustache and beard, only a slight growth, were perfectly white. He had once been of more than average stature; now his bent shoulders and meagre limbs gave him an appearance of shortness, whilst he suffered on the score of dignity by an excessive disregard of his clothing. He sat in a round-backed wooden chair at an ordinary table, on which were several volumes ranked on end, a large blotter, and an inkstand. The room was exclusively his, two book-cases and a few portraits on the walls being almost the only other furniture; but at this moment it was shared by Mrs. Otway, who, having some sort of woman's work on her lap, sat using her fingers and her tongue with steady diligence. She looked about forty, had a colourless but healthy face, not remarkable for charm, and was dressed as a sober, self-respecting gentlewoman. In her accents sounded nothing harsh, nothing vehement; she talked quietly, without varied inflections, as if thoughtfully expounding an agreeable theme; such talk might well have inclined a disinterested hearer to somnolence. But her husband's visage, and his movements, betokened no such peaceful tendency; every moment he grew more fidgety, betrayed a stronger irritation.

"I suppose," Mrs. Otway was saying, "there are persons who live without any religious conscience. It seems very strange; one would think that no soul could be at rest in utter disregard of its Maker, in complete neglect of the plainest duties of a creature endowed with human intelligence —which means, of course, power to perceive spiritual truths. Yet such persons seem capable of going through a long life without once feeling the impulse to worship, to render thanks and praise to the Supreme Being. I suppose they very early deaden their spiritual faculties; perhaps by loose habits of life, or by the indulgence of excessive self-esteem, or by"—

Jerome made a quick gesture with his hands, as if defending himself against a blow; then he turned to his wife, and regarded her fixedly.

"Will it take you much longer," he asked, with obvious struggle for self-command, but speaking courteously, "to exhaust this theme?"

5

"It annoys you?" said the lady, very coldly, straightening herself to an offended attitude.

"I confess it does. Or rather, it worries me. If I may beg"—

"I understood you to invite me to your room."

"I did. And the fact of my having done so ought, I should think, to have withheld you from assailing me with your acrid tedium."

"Thank you," said Mrs. Otway, as she rose to her full height. "I will leave you to your own tedium, which must be acrid enough, I imagine, to judge from the face you generally wear."

And she haughtily withdrew.

A scene of this kind—never more violent, always checked at the right moment—occurred between them about once every month. During the rest of their time they lived without mutual aggression; seldom conversing, but maintaining the externals of ordinary domestic intercourse. Nor was either of them acutely unhappy. The old man (Jerome Otway was sixty-five, but might have been taken for seventy) did not, as a rule, wear a sour countenance; he seldom smiled, but his grave air had no cast of gloominess; it was profoundly meditative, tending often to the rapture of high vision. The lady had her own sufficient pursuits, chief among them a rigid attention to matters ecclesiastical, local and national. That her husband held notably aloof from such interests was the subject of Mrs. Otway's avowed grief, and her peculiar method of assailing his position brought about the periodical disturbance which seemed on the whole an agreeable feature of her existence.

He lived much in the past, brooding upon his years of activity as author, journalist, lecturer, conspirator, between 1846 and 1870. He talked in his long days of silence with men whose names are written in history, men whom he had familiarly known, with whom he had struggled and hoped for the Better Time. Mazzini and Herzen, Kossuth and Ledru-Rollin, Bakounine, Louis Blanc, and a crowd of less eminent fighters in the everlasting war of human emancipation. The war that aims at Peace: the strife that assails tyranny, and militarism, and international hatred. Beginning with Chartism (and narrowly escaping the fierce penalties suffered by some of his comrades), he grew to wider activities, and for a moment seemed likely to achieve a bright position among the liberators of mankind; but Jerome Otway had more zeal than power, and such powers as he commanded were scattered over too wide a field of enthusiastic endeavour. He succeeded neither as man of thought nor as man of action. His verses were not quite poetry; his prose was not quite literature; personally, he interested and exalted, but without inspiring confidence such as is given to the born leader. And in this year 1886, when two or three letters on the Irish Question appeared over his signature, few readers attached any meaning to the name. Jerome Otway had fought his fight, and was forgotten.

He married, for the first time, at one-and-twenty, his choice being the daughter of an impoverished "county" family, a girl neither handsome nor sweet-natured, but, as it seemed, much in sympathy with his humanitarian views. Properly speaking, he did not choose her; the men who choose, who deliberately select, a wife are very few, and Jerome Otway could never have been one of them. He was ardent and impulsive; marriage becoming a necessity, he clutched at the first chance which in any way addressed his imagination; and the result was calamitous. In a year or two his wife repented the thoughtlessness with which she had sacrificed the possibilities of her birth and breeding for marriage with a man of no wealth. Narrow of soul, with a certain frothy intelligence, she quickly outgrew the mood of social rebellion which had originated in personal discontent, and thenceforward she had nothing but angry scorn for the husband who allowed her to live in poverty. Two sons were born to them; the elder named Daniel (after O'Connell), the second called Alexander (after the Russian Herzen). For twelve years they lived in suppressed or flagrant hostility; then Mrs. Otway died of cholera. To add to the bitterness of her fate, she had just received, from one of her "county" relatives, a legacy of a couple of thousand pounds.

This money, which became his own, Otway invested in a newspaper then being started by certain of his friends; a paper, as it seemed, little likely to have commercial success, but which, after many changes of editorship, ultimately became an established organ of Liberalism. The agitator retained an interest in this venture, and the small income it still continued to yield him was more than enough for his personal needs; it enabled him to set a little aside, year after year, thus forming a fund which, latterly, he always thought of as destined to benefit his youngest son—the child of his second marriage.

For he did not long remain solitary, and his next adventure was somewhat in keeping with the character he had earned in public estimate. Living for a time in Switzerland, he there met with a young Englishwoman, married, but parted from her husband, who was maintaining herself at Geneva as a teacher of languages; Jerome was drawn to her, wooed her, and won her love. The husband, a Catholic, refused her legal release, but the irregular union was a true marriage. It had lasted for about four years when their only child was born. In another twelvemonth, Jerome was again a widower. A small sum of money which had belonged to the dead woman, Jerome, at her wish, put out at interest for their boy, if he should attain manhood. The child's name was Piers; for Jerome happened at that time to be studying old Langland's "Vision," with delight in the brave singer, who so long ago cried for social justice—one of the few in Christendom who held by the spirit of Christ.

He was now forty-five years old; he mourned the loss of his comrade, a gentle, loving woman, whom, though she seldom understood his views of life, his moods and his aims, he had held in affection and esteem. For eight years he went his way alone; then, chancing to be at a seaside place in the north of England, he made the acquaintance of a mother and daughter who kept a circulating library, and in less than six months the daughter became Mrs. Otway. Aged not quite thirty, tall, graceful, with a long, pale face, distinguished by its air of meditative refinement, this lady probably never made quite clear to herself her motives in accepting the wooer of fifty-three, whose life had passed in labours and experiences with which she could feel nothing like true sympathy. Perhaps it was that she had never before received offer of marriage.; possibly Jerome's eloquent dark eyes, of which the gleam was not yet dulled, seconded the emotional language of his lips, and stirred her for the moment to genuine feeling. For a few months they seemed tolerably mated, then the inevitable divergence began to show itself. Jerome withdrew into his reveries, became taciturn, absorbed himself at length in the study of Dante; Mrs. Otway, resenting this desertion, grew critical, condemnatory, and, as if to atone for her union with a man who stood outside all the creeds, developed her mild orthodoxy into a peculiarly virulent form of Anglican puritanism. The only thing that kept them together was their common inclination for a retired existence, and their love of the northern moorland.

Looking back upon his marriages, the old man wondered sadly. Why had he not—he who worshipped the idea of womanhood—sought patiently for his perfect wife? Somewhere in the world he would have found her, could he but have subdued himself to the high seriousness of the quest. In a youthful poem, he had sung of Love as "the crown of life," believing it fervently; he believed it now with a fervour more intense, because more spiritual. That crown he had missed, even as did the multitude of mankind. Only to the elect is it granted—the few chosen, where all are called. To some it falls as if by the pure grace of Heaven, meeting them as they walk in the common way. Some, the fewest, attain it by merit of patient hope, climbing resolute until, on the heights of noble life, a face shines before them, the face of one who murmurs " *Guardami ben !*"

He thought much, too, about his offspring. The two children of his first marriage he had educated on the approved English model, making them "gentlemen." Partly because he knew not well how else to train them, for Jerome was far too weak on the practical side to have shaped a working system of his own—a system he durst rely upon; and partly, too, because they seemed to him to inherit many characteristics from their mother, and so to be naturally fitted for some conventional upper-class career. The result was grievous failure. In the case of Piers, he decided to disregard the boy's seeming qualifications, and, after having him schooled abroad for the sake of modern languages, to put him early into commerce. If Piers were marked out for better things, this discipline could do him no harm. And to all appearances, the course had been a wise one. Piers had as yet given no cause for complaint. In wearying of trade, in aiming at something more liberal, he claimed no more than his rights. With silent satisfaction, Jerome watched the boy's endeavours, his heart warming when he received one of those well-worded and dutiful, yet by no means commonplace letters, which came from Geneva and from London. On Piers he put the hope of his latter day; and it gladdened him to think that this, his only promising child, was the offspring of the union which he could recall with tenderness.

When Mrs. Otway had withdrawn with her sour dignity, the old man sighed and lost himself in melancholy musing. The house was, as usual, very still, and from without the only sound was that of the beck, leaping down over its stony ledges. Jerome loved this sound. It tuned his thoughts; it saved him from many a fit of ill-humour. It harmonised with the melody of Dante's verses, fit accompaniment to many a passage of profound feeling, of noble imagery. Even now he had been brooding the anguish of Maëstro Adamo who hears for ever

> "Li ruscelletti che de' verdi colli
> Del Casentin discendon giuso in Arno"—

and the music of the Tuscan fountains blended with the voice of this moorland stream.

There was a knock at the door; the maid-servant handed him a letter; it came from Piers. The father read it, and, after a few lines, with grave visage. Piers began by saying that, a day or two ago, he had all but resolved to run down to Hawes, for he had something very serious to speak about; on the whole, it seemed better to make the communication in writing.

"I have abandoned the examination, and all thought of the Civil Service. If I invented reasons for this, you would not believe them, and you would think ill of me. The best way is to tell you the plain truth, and run the risk of being thought a simpleton, or something worse. I have been in great trouble, have gone through a bad time. Some weeks ago there came to stay here a girl of eighteen or nineteen, the daughter of Dr. Lowndes Derwent (whose name perhaps you know). She is very beautiful, and I was unlucky enough— if I ought to use such a phrase—to fall in love with her. I won't try to explain what this meant to me; you wouldn't have patience to read it; but it stopped my studies, utterly overthrew my work. I was all but ill; I suffered horribly. It was my first such experience; I hope it may be the last— in that form. Indeed, I believe it will, for I can't imagine that I shall ever feel towards anyone else in the same way, and—you will smile, no doubt—I have a conviction that Irene Derwent will remain my ideal as long as I live.

" Enough of that. It being quite clear to me that I simply could not go in for the examination, I hit upon another scheme; one, it seemed to me, which might not altogether displease you. I went to see Mr. Tadworth, and told him that I had decided to go back into business; could he, I asked, think of giving me a place in their office at Odessa ? If necessary, I would work without salary till I had thoroughly learnt Russian, and could substantially serve them. Well, Mr. Tadworth was very kind, and, after a little questioning, promised to send me out to Odessa in some capacity or other, still to be determined. I am to go in about ten days.

" This, father, is my final decision. I shall give myself to the business, heartily and energetically. I think there is no harm in telling you that I hope to make money. If I do so, it will be done, I think, honourably, as the result of hard work. I had better not see you; I should be ashamed. But I beg you will write to me soon. I hope I shall not have overtried your patience. Bear with me, if you can, and give me the encouragement I value."

Jerome pondered long. He looked anything but displeased : there was tenderness in his smile, and sympathy, something too of pride. Very much against his usual practice, he wrote a reply the same day.

" So be it, my dear lad ! I have no fault to find, no criticism to offer. Your letter is an honest one, and it has much moved me. Let me just say this : you rightly doubt whether you should call yourself unlucky. If, as I can imagine, the daughter of Dr. Derwent is a girl worth your homage, nothing better could have befallen you than this discovery of your 'ideal.' Whether you will be faithful to it, the gods alone know. If you *can* be, even for a few years of youth, so much the happier and nobler your lot !

" Work at money-making, then. And, as I catch a glimmer of your meaning in this resolve, I will tell you something for your comfort. If you hold on at commerce, and verily make way, and otherwise approve yourself what I think you, I promise that you shall not lack advancement. Plainly, I have a little matter of money put by, for sundry uses ; and, if the day comes when something of capital would stead you (after due trial, as I premise), it shall be at your disposal.

" Write to me with a free heart. I have lived my life ;

perchance I can help you to live yours better. The will, assuredly, is not wanting.

"Courage, then! Pursue your purpose—

> 'Con l'animo che vince ogni battaglia,
>   Se col suo grave corpo non s'accascia.'

"And believe me that you could have no better intimate for leisure hours than the old Florentine, who knew so many things; among them, your own particular complaint."

CHAPTER X

CLAD for a long railway journey on a hot day; a grey figure of fluent lines, of composedly decisive movements; a little felt hat close-fitting to the spirited head, leaving full and frank the soft rounded face, with its quietly observant eyes, its lips of contained humour — Irene Derwent stepped from a cab at Euston Station and went forward into the booking-office. From the box-seat of the same vehicle descended a brisk, cheerful little man, looking rather like a courier than an ordinary servant, who paid the cabman, saw to the luggage, and, at a respectful distance, followed Miss Derwent along the platform; it was Thibaut Rossignol.

Grey-clad also, with air no less calm and sufficient, a gentleman carrying newspapers in Britannic abundance moved towards the train which was about to start. Surveying for a moment, with distant curiosity, the travellers about him, his eye fell upon that maiden of the sunny countenance just as she was entering a carriage; he stopped, insensibly drew himself together, subdued a smile, and advanced for recognition.

"I am going to Liverpool, Miss Derwent. May I have the pleasure—?"

"If you will promise not to talk politics, Mr. Jacks."

"I can't promise that. I want to talk politics."

"From here to Crewe?"

"As far as Rugby, let us say. After that—morphology, or some other of your light topics."

It seemed possible that they might have the compartment to themselves, for it was mid-August, and the tumult of northward migration had ceased. Arnold Jacks, had he known a moment sooner, would have settled it with the guard. He looked forbiddingly at a man who approached; who, in his turn, stared haughtily and turned away.

Irene beckoned to Thibaut, and from the window gave him a trivial message for her father, speaking in French; Thibaut,

happy to serve her, put a world of chivalrous respect into his
"Bien, Mademoiselle!" Arnold Jacks averted his face and
smiled. Was she girlish enough, then, to find pleasure in
speaking French before him? A charming trait!

The train started, and Mr. Jacks began to talk. It was not
the first time that they had merrily skirmished on political and
other grounds; they amused each other, and, as it seemed, in
a perfectly harmless way; the English way of mirth between
man and maid, candid, inallusive, without self-consciousness.
Arnold made the most of his thirty years, spoke with a tone
something paternal. He was wholly sure of himself, knew so
well his own mind, his scheme of existence, that Irene's beauty
and her charm were nothing more to him than an æsthetic
perception. That she should feel an interest in him, a little
awe of him, was to be hoped and enjoyed : he had not the least
thought of engaging deeper emotion—would, indeed, have held
himself reprobate had such purpose entered his head. Nor is
it natural to an Englishman of this type to imagine that girls
may fall in love with him. Love has such a restricted place in
their lives, is so consistently kept out of sight in their familiar
converse. They do not entirely believe in it; it ill accords
with their practical philosophy. Marriage—that is another
thing. The approaches to wedlock are a subject of honourable
convention, not to be confused with the trivialities of romance.

"I'm going down to Liverpool," he said presently, "to meet
Trafford Romaine."

It gratified him to see the gleam in Miss Derwent's eyes;
the announcement had its hoped-for effect. Trafford Romaine,
the Atlas of our Colonial world; the much-debated, the
universally interesting champion of Greater British interests!
She knew, of course, that Arnold Jacks was his friend; no one
could talk with Mr. Jacks for half an hour without learning
that; but the off-hand mention of their being about to meet
this very day had an impressiveness for Irene.

"I saw that he was coming to England."

"From the States—yes. He has been over there on a
holiday—merely a holiday. Of course the papers have tried
to find a meaning in it. That kind of thing amuses him
vastly. He says in his last letter to me"—

Carelessly, the letter was drawn from an inner pocket. Only
a page and a half; Arnold read it out. A bluff and rather
slangy epistolary style.

"May I see his hand?" asked Irene, trying to make fun of her wish.

He gave her the letter, and watched her amusedly as she gazed at the first page. On receiving it back again, he took his penknife, carefully cut out the great man's signature, and offered it for Irene's acceptance.

"Thank you. But you know, of course, that I regard it as a mere curiosity."

"Oh yes! Why not? So do I the theory of Evolution."

By a leading question or two, Miss Derwent set her companion talking at large of Trafford Romaine, his views and policies. The greatest man in the Empire! he declared. The only man, in fact, who held the true Imperial conception, and had genius to inspire multitudes with his own zeal. Arnold's fervour of admiration betrayed him into no excessive vivacity, no exuberance in phrase or unusual gesture such as could conflict with "good form"; he talked like the typical public schoolboy, with a veneering of wisdom current in circles of higher officialdom. Enthusiasm was never the term for his state of mind; instinctively he shrank from that, as a thing Gallic, "foreign." But the spirit of practical determination could go no further. He followed Trafford Romaine as at school he had given allegiance to his cricket captain; impossible to detect a hint that he felt the life of peoples in any way more serious than the sports of his boyhood; yet equally impossible to perceive how he could have been more profoundly in earnest. This made the attractiveness of the man; he compelled confidence; it was felt that he never exaggerated in the suggestion of force concealed beneath his careless, mirthful manner. Irene, in spite of her humorous observation, hung upon his speech. Involuntarily, she glanced at his delicate complexion, at the whiteness and softness of his ungloved hand, and felt in a subtle way this combination of the physically fine with the morally hard, trenchant, tenacious. Close your eyes, and Arnold Jacks was a high-bred bull-dog endowed with speech; not otherwise would a game animal of that species, advanced to a world polity, utter his convictions.

"You take for granted," she remarked, "that our race is the finest fruit of civilisation."

"Certainly. Don't you?"

"It's having a pretty good conceit of ourselves. Is every

foreigner who contests it a poor deluded creature? Take the best type of Frenchman, for instance. Is he necessarily fatuous in his criticism of us?"

"Why, of course he is. He doesn't understand us. He doesn't understand the world. He has his place, to be sure, but that isn't in international politics. We are the political people; we are the ultimate rulers. Our language"—

"There's a quotation from Virgil"—

"I know. We are very like the Romans. But there are no new races to overthrow us."

He began to sketch the future extension of Britannic lordship and influence. Kingdoms were overthrown with a joke, continents were annexed in a boyish phrase; Armageddon transacted itself in sheer lightness of heart. Laughing, he waded through the blood of nations, and in the end seated himself with crossed legs upon the throne of the universe.

"Do you know what it makes me wish?" said Irene, looking wicked.

"That you may live to see it?"

"No. That someone would give us a good licking, for the benefit of our souls."

Having spoken it, she was ashamed, and her lip quivered a little. But the train had slackened speed; they entered a station.

"Rugby!" she exclaimed, with relief. "Have you any views about treatment of the phylloxera?"

"Odd that you should mention that. Why?"

"Only because my father has been thinking about it: we have a friend from Avignon staying with us—all but ruined in his vineyards."

Jacks had again taken out his letter-case. He selected a folded sheet of paper, and showed what looked like a dry blade of grass. The wheat, he said, on certain farms in his Company's territory had begun to suffer from a strange disease; here was an example of the parasite-eaten growth; no one yet had recognised the disease or discovered a check for it.

"Let my father have it," said Irene. "He is interested in all that kind of thing."

"Really? Seriously?"

"Quite seriously. He would much like to see it."

"Then I will either call on him, or write to him, when I get back."

Miss Derwent had not yet spoken of her destination. She mentioned, now, that she was going to spend a week or two with relations at a country place in Cheshire. She must change trains at Crewe. This gave a lighter turn to the conversation. Arnold Jacks launched into frank gaiety, and Irene met him with spirit. Not a little remarkable was the absence of the note of sex from their merry gossip in the narrow seclusion of a little railway compartment. Irene was as safe with this world-conquering young man as with her own brother; would have been so, probably, on a desert island. They were not man and woman, but English gentleman and lady, and, from one point of view, very brilliant specimens of their kind.

At Crewe both alighted, Arnold to stretch his legs for a moment.

"By the bye," he said, as Miss Derwent, having seen to her luggage, was bidding him farewell, "I'm sorry to hear that young Otway has been very ill."

"Ill?—I had no knowledge of it.—In Russia?"

"Yes. My father was speaking of it yesterday. He had heard it from his friend, old Mr. Otway. A fever of some kind. He's all right again, I believe."

"We have heard nothing of it.—There's your whistle. Good-bye!"

Jacks leapt into his train, waved a hand from the window, and was whirled away.

For the rest of her journey, Irene seemed occupied with an alternation of grave and amusing thoughts. At moments she looked seriously troubled. This passed, and the arrival found her bright as ever; the pink of modern maidenhood, fancy free.

The relatives she was visiting were two elderly ladies, cousins of her mother; representatives of a family native to this locality for hundreds of years. One of the two had been married, but husband and child were long since dead; the other, devoted to sisterly affection, had shared in the brief happiness of the wife and remained the solace of the widow's latter years. They were in circumstances of simple security, living as honoured gentlewomen, without display as without embarrassment; fulfilling cheerfully the natural duties of their position, but seeking no influence beyond the homely limits; their life a humanising example, a centre of charity and peace. The house they dwelt in came to them from their yeoman ancestors of long ago; it was held on a lease of one thousand years from near the end of the sixteenth century, "at a quit-rent of one shilling," and certain pieces of furniture still in use were contemporary with the beginning of the tenure. No corner of England more safely rural; beyond sound of railway whistle, bosomed in great old elms, amid wide meadows and generous tillage; sloping westward to the river Dee, and from its soft green hills descrying the mountains of Wales.

Here in the old churchyard lay Irene's mother. She died in London, but Dr. Derwent wished her to rest by the home of her childhood, where Irene, too, as a little maid, had spent many a summer holiday. Over the grave stood a simple slab of marble, white as the soul of her it commemorated, graven thereon a name, parentage, dates of birth and death—no more. Irene's father cared not to tell the world how that bereavement left him.

Round about were many kindred tombs, the most noticeable that of Mrs. Derwent's grandfather, a ripe old scholar, who rested from his mellow meditations just before our century began.

> " GULIELMI W ——
>
> Pii, docti, integri,
> Reliquiæ seu potius exuviæ."

It was the first Latin Irene learnt, and its quaint phrasing to this day influenced her thoughts of mortality. Standing by her mother's grave, she often repeated to herself "seu potius exuviæ," and wondered whether her father's faith in science excluded the hope of that old-world reasoning. She would not have dared to ask him, for all the frank tenderness of their companionship. On that subject Dr. Derwent had no word to say, no hint to let fall. She knew only that, in speaking of her they had lost, his voice would still falter; she knew that he always came into this churchyard alone, and was silent, troubled, for hours after the visit. Instinctively, too, she understood that, though her father might almost be called a young man, and had abounding vitality, no second wife would ever obscure to him that sacred memory. It was one of the many grounds she had for admiring as much as she loved him. His loyalty stirrred her heart, coloured her view of life.

The ladies had some little apprehension that their young relative, fresh from contact with a many-sided world, might feel a dulness in their life and their interests ; but nothing of the sort entered Irene's mind. She was intelligent enough to appreciate the superiority of these quiet sisters to all but the very best of the acquaintances she had made in London or abroad, and modest enough to see in their entire refinement a correction of the excessive *sans-gêne* to which society tempted her. They were behind the times only in the sense of escaping, by seclusion, those modern tendencies which vulgarise. An excellent library of their own supplied them with the essentials of culture, and one or two periodicals kept them acquainted with all that was worth knowing in the activity of the day. They belonged to the very small class of persons who still read, who have mind and leisure to find companionship in books. Their knowledge of languages passed the common ; in earlier years they had travelled, and their reminiscences fostered the liberality which was the natural tone of their minds. To converse familiarly with them was to discover their grasp of historical principles, their insight into philosophic systems, their large apprehension of world-problems. At the same time, they nurtured jealously their intellectual preferences, differing on such points from each other as they did from the common world. One of them would betray an intimate knowledge of some French or Italian poet scarce known by name to ordinary educated people ; something in him had appealed to her mind at a certain time, and her memory held him in gratitude. The other would be found to have informed herself exhaustively concerning the history of some neglected people, dear to her for some subtle reason of affinity or association. But in their table-talk appeared no pedantry ; things merely human were as interesting to them as to the babbler of any drawing-room, and their inexhaustible kindliness sweetened every word they spoke.

Nothing more salutary for Irene Derwent than this sojourn with persons whom she in every way respected,—with whom there was not the least temptation to exhibit her mere dexterities. In London, during this past season, she had sometimes talked as a young, clever, and admired girl is prone to do ;

always to the mockery of her sager self when looking back on such easy triumphs. How very easy it was to shine in London drawing-rooms, no one knew better. Here in the country stillness, in this beautiful old house sacred to sincerity of heart and mind, to aim at "smartness" would indeed have been to condemn oneself. Instead of phrasing, she was content, as became her years, to listen; she enjoyed the feeling of natural youthfulness, of spontaneity without misgiving. The things of life and intellect appeared in their true proportions; she saw the virtue of repose.

When she had been here a day or two, the conversation chanced to take a turn which led to her showing the autograph of Trafford Romaine; she said merely that a friend had given it to her.

"An interesting man, I should think," remarked the elder of the two sisters, without emphasis.

"An Englishman of a new type, wouldn't you say?" fell from the other.

"So far as I understand him. Or perhaps of an old type under new conditions."

Irene, paying close attention, was not sure that she understood all that these words implied.

"He is immensely admired by some of our friends," she said with restraint. "They compare him to the fighting heroes of our history."

"Indeed?" rejoined the elder lady. "But the question is: Are those the qualities that we want nowadays? I admire Sir Walter Raleigh, but I should be sorry to see him, just as he was, playing an active part in our time."

"They say," ventured Irene, with a smile, "that, but for such men, we may really become a mere nation of shopkeepers."

"Do they? But may we not fear that their ideal is simply a shopkeeper ready to shoot anyone who rivals him in trade? The finer qualities I admit; but one distrusts the objects they serve."

"We are told," said Irene, "that England *must* expand."

"Probably. But the mere necessity of the case must not become our law. It won't do for a great people to say, 'Make room for us, and we promise to set you a fine example of civilisation; refuse to make room, and we'll blow your brains out!' One doubts the quality of the civilisation promised."

Irene laughed, delighted with the vigour underlying the old lady's calm and gentle habit of speech. Yet she was not convinced, though she wished to be. A good many times, she had heard in thought the suavely virile utterances of Arnold Jacks; his voice had something that pleased her, and his way of looking at things touched her imagination. She wished these ladies knew Arnold Jacks, that she might ask their opinion of him.

And yet, she felt she would rather not have asked it.

CHAPTER XI

FROM this retreat, Irene wrote to her cousin Olga Hannaford, and in the course of the letter made inquiry whether anything was known at Ewell about a severe illness that had befallen young Mr. Otway. Olga replied that she had heard of no such event; that they had received no news at all of Mr. Otway since his leaving England. This did not allay an uneasiness which, in various forms, had troubled Irene ever since she heard that her studious acquaintance had abandoned his ambitions and gone back to commerce. A few weeks more elapsed, and—being now in Scotland—she received a confirmation of what Arnold Jacks had reported. Immediately on reaching Odessa, Piers Otway had fallen ill, and for a time was in danger. Irene mused. She would have preferred not to think of Otway at all, but often did so, and could not help it. A certain reproach of conscience connected itself with his name. But as time went on, and it appeared that the young man was settled to his mercantile career in Russia, she succeeded in dismissing him from her mind.

For the next three years she lived with her father in London; a life pretty evenly divided between studies and the amusements of her world.

Dr. Derwent pursued his quiet activity. In a certain sphere he had reputation; the world at large knew little or nothing of him. All he aimed at was the diminution of human suffering; whether men thanked him for his life's labour did not seem to him a point worth considering. He knew that only his scientific brethren could gauge the advance in knowledge, and consequent power over disease, due to his patient toil; it was a question of minute discoveries, of investigations unintelligible to the layman. Some of his colleagues held that he foolishly restricted himself in declining to experimentalise *in corpore vili*, whenever such experiments were attended with pain; he was spoken of in some quarters as a "sentimentalist," a man who might go far but for his "fads.". One great pathologist held that the whole idea of pursuing science for mitigation of human ills was nothing but a sentimentality and a fad. A debate between this personage and Dr. Derwent was brought to a close by the latter's inextinguishable mirth. He was, indeed, a man who laughed heartily, and laughter often served him where another would have waxed choleric.

"Only a dog!" he exclaimed once to Irene, apropos of this subject, and being in his graver mood.—"Why, what assurance have I that any given man is of more importance to the world than any given dog? How can I know what is important and what is not, when it comes to the ultimate mystery of life? Create me a dog—just a poor little mongrel puppy—and you shall torture him; then, and not till then. And in that event I reserve my opinion of the"— He checked himself on the point of a remark which seemed of too wide bearing for the girl's ears. But Irene supplied the hiatus for herself, as she was beginning to do pretty often when listening to her father.

Dr. Derwent was in a sense a self-made man; in youth he had gone through a hard struggle, and but for his academic successes he could not have completed the course of medical training. Twenty years of very successful practice had made him independent, and a mechanical invention—which he had patented—an ingenuity of which he thought nothing till some friend insisted on its value—raised his independence to moderate wealth. For his children's sake he was glad of this comfort; like every educated man who has known poverty at the outset of life, he feared it more than he cared to say.

His wife had brought him nothing—save her beauty and her noble heart. She wedded him when it was still doubtful whether he would hold his own in the fierce fight for a living; she died before the days of his victory. Now and then, a friend who heard him speak of his wife's family smiled with the thought that he only just escaped being something of a snob. Which merely signified that a man of science attached value to descent. Dr. Derwent knew the properties of such blood as ran in his wife's veins, and it rejoiced him to mark the characteristics which Irene inherited from her mother.

He often suffered anxiety on behalf of his sister, Mrs.

Hannaford, whom he knew to be pinched in circumstances, but whom it was impossible to help. Lee Hannaford he disliked and distrusted; the men were poles apart in character and purpose. The family had now left Ewell, and lived in a poor house in London. Olga was trying to earn money by her drawing, not, it seemed, with much success. Hannaford was always said to be on the point of selling some explosive invention to the British Government, whence would result a fortune; but the Government had not yet come to terms.

"What a shame it is," quoth Dr. Derwent, "that an honest man who facilitates murder on so great a scale should be kept waiting for his reward!"

Hannaford pursued his slight acquaintance with Arnold Jacks, who, in ignorance of any relationship, once spoke of him to Miss Derwent.

"An ingenious fellow. I should like to make some use of him, but I don't quite know how."

"I am sorry to say he belongs by marriage to our family," replied Irene.

"Indeed? Why sorry?"

"I detest his character. He is neither a gentleman, nor anything else that one can respect."

It closed a conversation in which they had differed more sharply than usual, with—on Irene's part—something less than the wonted gaiety of humour. They did not see each other very often, but always seemed glad to meet, and always talked in a tone of peculiar intimacy, as if conscious of mutual understanding. Yet no two acquaintances could have been in greater doubt as to each other's mind and character. Irene was often mentally occupied with Mr. Jacks, and one of the questions she found most uncertain was whether he in turn ever thought of her with like interest. Now she seemed to have proof that he sought an opportunity of meeting; now, again, he appeared to have forgotten her existence. He interested her in his personality, he interested her in his work. She would have liked to speak of him with her father; but Dr. Derwent never broached the subject, and she could not herself lead up to it. Whenever she saw his name in the paper—where it often stood in reports of public festivities or in items of social news—her eye dwelt upon it, and her fancy was stirred. Curiosity, perhaps, had the greater part in her feeling. Arnold Jacks seemed to live so "largely," in contact with such great affairs and such eminent people. One day, at length, a little paragraph in an evening journal announced that he was engaged to be married, and to a lady much in the light, the widowed daughter of a Conservative statesman. It was only an hour or two after reading this news that Irene met him at dinner, and spoke with him of Hannaford; neither to Arnold himself nor to anyone else did she allude to the rumoured engagement; but that night she was not herself.

About lunch-time on the next day she received a note from Jacks. His attention had been drawn—he wrote—to an absurd bit of gossip connecting his name with that of a lady whose friend he was and absolutely nothing more. Would Miss Derwent, if occasion arose, do him the kindness to contradict this story in her circle? He would be greatly obliged to her.

Irene was something more than surprised. It struck her as odd that Arnold Jacks should request her services in such a matter as this. In an obscure way she half resented the brief, off-hand missive. And she paid no further attention to it.

A month later, she, her father and brother, were on their way to Switzerland. Stepping into the boat at Dover, she saw in front of her Arnold Jacks. It was a perfectly smooth passage, and they talked all the way; for part of the time, alone.

"I think," said Arnold, at the first opportunity, looking her in the face, "you never replied to a letter of mine last month about a certain private affair?"

"A letter? Oh yes. I didn't think it required an answer."

"Don't you generally answer letters from your friends?"

Irene, in turn, gave him a steady look.

"Generally, yes. But not when I have the choice between silence and being disagreeable."

"You were both silent *and* disagreeable," said Arnold, smiling. "Do you mind being disagreeable again, and telling me what your answer would have been?"

"Simply that I never, if I can help it, talk about weddings and rumours of weddings, and that I couldn't make an exception in your case."

Arnold laughed in the old way.

"A most original rule, Miss Derwent, and admirable. If

all kept to it I shouldn't have been annoyed by that silly chatter. It occurs to me that I perhaps ought not to have sent you that note. I did it in a moment of irritation— wanting to have the stupid thing contradicted right and left, as fast as possible. I won't do it again."

They were on excellent terms once more. Irene felt a singular pleasure in his having apologised ; it was one of the very rare occasions of his yielding to her on any point whatever. Never had she felt so kindly disposed to him.

Arnold was going to Paris, and on business ; he hinted at something pending between his Company and a French Syndicate.

"You are a sort of informal diplomatist," said Irene, her interest keen.

"Now and then, yes. And "—he added with the frankness which was one of his more amiable points—" I rather like it."

"One sees that you do. Better, I suppose, than the thought of going into Parliament."

"That may come some day," he answered, glancing at a gull that hovered above the ship. "Not whilst my father sits there."

"You would be on different sides, I suppose."

Arnold smiled, and went on to say that he was uneasy about his father's health. John Jacks had fallen of late into a habit of worry about things great and small, as though age were suddenly telling upon him. He fretted over public affairs ; he suffered from the death of old friends, especially that of John Bright, whom he had held in affectionate regard for a lifetime. Irene was glad to hear this expression of anxiety. For it sometimes seemed to her that Arnold Jacks had little if any domestic feeling.

She wished they could have travelled further together. Their talks were always broken off too soon, just when she began to get a glimpse of characteristics still unknown to her. On the journey she thought constantly of him ; not with any sort of tender emotion, but with much curiosity. It would have gratified her to know what degree of truth there was in that rumour of his engagement a month ago ; some, undoubtedly, for she had noticed a peculiar smile on the faces of persons who alluded to it. His apparent coldness towards women in general might be natural, or might conceal mysteries. So difficult a man to know! And so impossible to decide whether he was really worth knowing!

Among intimates of her own sex Irene had a reputation for a certain chaste severity becoming at moments all but prudery. It did not altogether harmonise with the tone of highly taught young women who rather prided themselves on freedom of thought, and to some extent of utterance. Singular in one so far from cold-blooded, so abounding in vitality. Towards men, her attitude seemed purely intellectual; no one had ever so much as suspected a warmer interest. A hint of things forbidden with regard to any male acquaintance caused her to turn away, silent, austere. That such things not seldom came to her hearing was a motive of troubled reflection, common enough in all intelligent girls who live in touch with the wider world. Men puzzled her, and Irene did not like to be puzzled. As free from unwholesome inquisitiveness as a girl can possibly be, she often wished to know, once for all, whatever was to be learnt about the concealed life of men; to know it and to have done with it; to settle her mind on that point, as on any other that affected the life of a reasonable being. Yet she shrank from all such inquiry, with a sense of womanly pride, doing her best to believe that there *was* no concealment in the case of any man with whom she could have friendly relations. She scorned the female cynic; she disliked the carelessly liberal in moral judgment. Profoundly mysterious to her was everything covered by the word "passion"—a word she detested.

Her way of seeing life on the amusing side aided, of course, her maidenly severity against trouble of sense and sentiment. This she had from her father, a man of quips and jokes on the surface of his seriousness. As she grew older, it threatened a decline of intimacy between her and her cousin Olga, who, never naturally buoyant, was becoming so cheerless, so turbid of temper, that Irene found it difficult to talk with her for long together. Domestic miseries might greatly account for the girl's mood, but Irene had insight enough to perceive that this was not all. And she felt uncomfortably helpless. To jest seemed unfeeling; sympathy of the sentimental sort she could not give. She feared that Olga was beginning to shrink from her.

Since the Hannafords' removal to London, they had not

been able to see much of each other. Irene understood
that she was not very welcome in the little house at
Hammersmith, even before her aunt wrote to ask her not
to come. Lee Hannaford's aloofness from his wife's relatives
had turned to hostility; he spoke of them with increasing
bitterness, threw contempt on Dr. Derwent's scientific work,
and condemned Irene as a butterfly of fashion. Olga ceased
to visit the house in Bryanston Square, and the cousins only
corresponded. It was Dr. Derwent's opinion that Hannaford
could not be quite sane; he was much troubled on his
sister's account, and had often pondered extreme measures
for her rescue from an intolerable position.

At length there came to pass the event to which Mrs.
Hannaford had looked as her only hope. The widowed sister
in America died, and, out of her abundance, her children all
provided for, left to the unhappy wife in England a substantial
bequest. News of this came first to Dr. Derwent, who was
appointed trustee.

But before he had time to communicate with Mrs.
Hannaford, a letter from her occasioned him new anxiety.
His sister wrote that Olga was bent on making a most
undesirable marriage, having fallen in love with a penniless
nondescript who called himself an artist; a man given, it
was suspected, to drink, and without any decent connection
that one could hear of. A wretched, squalid affair ! Would
the Doctor come at once and see Olga ? Her father was away,
as usual; of course the girl would not be influenced by *him*,
in any case; she was altogether in a strange, wild, headstrong
state, and one could not be sure how soon the marriage might
come about.

With wrinkled brows, the vexed pathologist set forth for
Hammersmith.

CHAPTER XII

A SEMI-DETACHED dwelling in a part of Hammersmith just being invaded by the social class below that for which it was built; where, in consequence, rents had slightly fallen, and notices of "apartments" were beginning to rise; where itinerant vendors, finding a new market, strained their voices with special discord; where hired pianos vied with each other through parti-walls; where the earth was always very dusty or very muddy, and the sky above in all seasons had a discouraging hue. The house itself furnished half-heartedly, as if it was felt to be a mere encampment; no comfort in any chamber, no air of home. Hannaford had not cared to distribute his mementoes of battle and death in the room called his own; they remained in packing-cases. Each member of the family, unhappy trio, knew that their state was transitional, and waited rather than lived.

With the surprise of a woman long bitter against destiny, Mrs. Hannaford learnt that something *had* happened, and that it was a piece of good, not ill, fortune. When her brother left the house (having waited two hours in vain for Olga's return), she made a change of garb, arranged her hair with something of the old grace, and moved restlessly from room to room. A light had touched her countenance, dispelling years of premature age; she was still a handsome woman; she could still find in her heart the courage for a strong decision.

There was no maid—Mrs. Hannaford herself laid upon the table what was to serve for an evening meal; and she had just done so when her daughter came in. Olga had changed considerably in the past three years; at one-and-twenty she would have passed for several years older; her complexion was fatigued, her mouth had a nervous mobility which told of suppressed suffering, her movements were impatient, irritable. But at this moment she did not wear a look of unhappiness;

there was a glow in her fine eyes, a tremor of resolve on all her features. On entering the room where her mother stood, she at once noticed a change. Their looks met: they gazed excitedly at each other.

"What is it? Why have you dressed?"

"Because I am a free woman. My sister is dead, and has left me a lot of money."

They rushed into each other's arms; they caressed with tears and sobs; it was minutes before they could utter more than broken phrases and exclamations.

"What shall you do?" the girl asked at length, holding her mother's hand against her heart. Of late there had been unwonted conflict between them, and in the reaction of joy they became all tenderness.

".What I ought to have done long ago—go and live away"—

"Will it be possible, dear?"

"It shall be!" exclaimed the mother vehemently. "I am not a slave—I am not a wife! I ought to have had courage to go away years since. It was wrong, wrong to live as I have done. —The money is my own, and I will be free. He shall have a third of it every year, if he leaves me free. One-third is yours, one mine."

"No, no!" said Olga, drawing back. "For me, none of it!"

"Yes, you will live with me—you will, Olga! This makes everything different. You will see that you cannot do what you thought of! Don't speak of it now :—think—wait"—

The girl moved apart. Her face lost its brightness; hardened in passionate determination.

"I can't begin all that again," she said, with an accent of weariness.

"No! I won't speak of it now, Olga. But will you do one thing for me? Will you put it off for a short time? I'll tell you what I have planned; your uncle and I talked it all over. I must leave this house before *he* comes back, to-morrow morning. I can't go to your uncle's house, as he asked me; you see why it is better not, don't you? The best will be to go into lodgings for a time, and not to let *him* know where I am, till I hear whether he will accept the terms I offer. Look, I have enough money for the present." She showed gold that had been left with her by Dr. Derwent. "But am I to go alone? Will you desert me in my struggle? I want you, dear; I need your help. Oh, it would be cruel to leave me just now! Will you put it off for a few weeks, until I know what my life is going to be? You won't refuse me this one thing, Olga, after all we have gone through together?"

"For a few weeks: of course I will do that," replied the girl, still in an attitude of resistance. "But you mustn't deceive yourself, mother. My mind is made up; *nothing* will change it. Money is nothing to me; we shall be able to live"—

"I can count on you till the struggle is over?"

"I won't leave you until it is settled. And perhaps there will be no struggle at all. I should think it will be enough for you to say what you have decided"—

"Perhaps. But I can't feel sure. He has got to be such a tyrant, and it will enrage him—But perhaps the money— Yes, he will be glad of the money."

Presently they sat down to make a pretence of eating; it was over in a few minutes. Mrs. Hannaford made known in detail what she had rapidly decided with her brother. To-night she would pack her clothing and Olga's; she would leave a letter for her husband; and early in the morning they would leave London. Not for any distant hiding-place; it was better to be within easy reach of Dr. Derwent, and a retreat in Surrey would best suit their purposes, some place where lodgings could be at once obtained. The subject of difference put aside, they talked again freely and affectionately of this sudden escape from a life which in any case Mrs. Hannaford could not have endured much longer. About nine o'clock, the quiet of the house was broken by a postman's knock; Olga ran to take the letter, and exclaimed on seeing the address—

"Why, it's from Mr. Otway, and an English stamp!"

Mrs. Hannaford found a note of a few lines. Piers Otway had reached London that morning, and would be in town for a day or two only, before going on into Yorkshire. Could he see his old friends to-morrow? He would call in the afternoon.

"Better reply to-night," said Olga, "and save him the trouble of coming here."

The letter in her hand, Mrs. Hannaford stood thinking, a half-smile about her lips.

"Yes; I must write," she said slowly. "But perhaps he could come and see us in the country. I'll tell him where we are going."

They talked of possible retreats, and decided upon Epsom, which was not far from their old home at Ewell; then Mrs. Hannaford replied to Otway. Through the past three years she had often heard from him, and she knew that he was purposing a visit to England, but no date had been mentioned. After writing, she was silent, thoughtful. Olga, too, having been out to post the letter, sat absorbed in her own meditations. They did some hasty packing before bedtime, but talked little. They were to rise early, and flee at once from the hated house.

A sunny morning—it was July—saw them start on their journey, tremulous, but rejoicing. Long before midday they had found lodgings that suited them, and had made themselves at home. The sense of liberty gave everything a delightful aspect; their little sitting-room was perfection; the trees and fields had an ideal beauty after Hammersmith, and they promised themselves breezy walks on the Downs above. Not a word of the trouble between them. The mother held to a hope that the great change of circumstance would insensibly turn Olga's thoughts from her reckless purpose; and, for the moment, Olga herself seemed happy in self-forgetfulness.

The man to whom she had plighted herself was named Kite. He did not look like a bird of prey; his countenance, his speech, were anything but sinister; but for his unlucky position, Mrs. Hannaford would probably have rather taken to him. Olga's announcement came with startling suddenness. For a twelvemonth she had been trying to make money by artistic work, and to a small extent had succeeded, managing to sell a few drawings to weekly papers, and even to get a poor little commission for the illustrating of a poor little book. In this way she had made a few acquaintances in the so-called Bohemian world, but she spoke seldom of them, and Mrs. Hannaford suspected no special intimacy with anyone whose name was mentioned to her. One evening (a week ago) Olga said quietly that she was going to be married.

Mr. Kite was summoned to Hammersmith. A lank, loose-limbed, indolent-looking man of thirty or so, with a long, thin face, tangled hair, gentle eyes. The clothes he wore were decent, but suggested the idea that they had been purchased at second-hand; they did not fit him well; perhaps he was the kind of man whose clothes never do fit. Unless Mrs.

Hannaford was mistaken, his breath wafted an alcoholic odour; but Mr. Kite had every appearance of present sobriety. He seemed chronically tired; sat down with a little sigh of satisfaction; stretched his legs, and let his arms fall at full length. To the maternal eye, a singular, problematic being, anything but likely to inspire confidence. Yet he talked agreeably, if oddly; his incomplete sentences were full of good feeling; above all, he evidently meant to be frank, put his poverty in the baldest aspect, set forth his hopes with extreme moderation. "We seem to suit each other," was his quiet remark, with a glance at Olga; and Mrs. Hannaford could not doubt that he meant well. But what a match! Scarcely had he gone, when the mother began her dissuasions, and from that moment there was misery.

For Olga, Mrs. Hannaford had always been ambitious. The girl was clever, warm-hearted, and in her way handsome. But for the disastrous father, she would have had every chance of marrying "well." Mrs. Hannaford was not a worldly woman, and all her secret inclinations were to romance, but it is hard for a mother to dissociate the thought of marriage from that of wealth and respectability. Mr. Kite, well-meaning as he might be, would never do.

To-day there was truce. They talked much of Piers Otway, and in the afternoon, as had been arranged by letter, both went to the railway station, to meet the train by which it was hoped he would come.—Piers arrived.

"How much improved!" was the thought of both. He was larger, manlier, and though still of pale complexion had no longer the bloodless look of years ago. Walking, he bore himself well; he was self-possessed in manner, courteous in not quite the English way; brief, at first, in his sentences, but his face lit with cordiality. On the way to the ladies' lodgings, he stole frequent glances at one and the other; plainly he saw change in them, and perhaps not for the better.

Mrs. Hannaford kept mentally comparing him with the scarecrow Kite. A tremor of speculation took hold upon her; a flush was on her cheeks, she talked nervously, laughed much.

Nothing was to be said about the flight from home; they were at Epsom for change of air. But Mrs. Hannaford could not keep silence concerning her good fortune; she had revealed it, in a few nervous words, before they reached the house.

"You will live in London?" asked Otway.

"That isn't settled. It would be nice to go abroad again. We liked Geneva."

"I must tell you about a Swiss friend of mine," Piers resumed. "A man you would like; the best, jolliest, most amusing fellow I ever met; his name is Moncharmont. He is in business at Odessa. There was talk of his coming to England with me, but we put it off; another time. He's a man who does me good; but for him, I shouldn't have held on."

"Then you don't like it, after all?" asked Mrs. Hannaford.

"Like it? No. But I have stuck to it—partly for very shame, as you know. I've stuck to it hard, and it's getting too late to think of anything else. I have plans; I'll tell you."

These plans were laid open when tea had been served in the little sitting-room. Piers had it in mind to start an independent business, together with his friend Moncharmont; one of them to live in Russia, one in London.

"My father has promised the money. He promised it three years ago. I might have had it when I liked; but I should have been ashamed to ask till a reasonable time had gone by. It won't be a large capital, but Moncharmont has some, and putting it together, we shall manage to start, I think."

He paused, watching the effect of his announcement. Mrs. Hannaford was radiant with pleasure; Olga looked amused.

"Why do you laugh?" Piers asked, turning to the girl.

"I didn't exactly laugh. But it seems odd. I can't quite think of you as a merchant."

"To tell you the truth, I can't quite think of myself in that light either. I'm only a bungler at commerce, but I've worked hard, and I have a certain amount of knowledge. For one thing, I've got hold of the language; this last year, I've travelled a good deal in Russia for our firm, and it often struck me that I might just as well be doing the business on my own account. I dreamt once of a partnership, with our people; but there's no chance of that. They're very close; besides, they don't make any serious account of me; I'm not the type that gains English confidence. Strange that I get on so much better with almost any other nationality—with men, that is to say."

He smiled, reddened, turned it off with a laugh. For the moment, he was his old self, and his wandering eyes kept a look such as had often been seen in them during that month of torture three years ago.

"You are quite sure," said Mrs. Hannaford, "that it wouldn't be better to use your capital in some other way?"

"Don't, don't!" Piers exclaimed, tossing his arm in exaggerated dread. "Don't set me adrift again. I've thought about it; it's settled. This is the only way of making money, that I can see."

"You are so set on making money?" said Olga, looking at him in surprise.

"Savagely set on it!"

"You have really come to see that as the end of life?" Olga asked, regarding him curiously.

"The end? Oh, dear no! The means of life, only the means!"

Olga was about to put another question, but she met her mother's eye, and kept silence. All were silent for a space, and meditative.

They went out to walk together. Looking over the wide prospect from the top of the Downs, the soft English landscape, homely, peaceful, Otway talked of Russia. It was a country, he said, which interested him more, the more he knew of it. He hoped to know it very well, and perhaps— here he grew dreamy—to impart his knowledge to others. Not many Englishmen mastered the language, or indeed knew anything of it; that huge empire was a mere blank to be filled up by the imaginings of prejudice and hostility. Was it not a task worth setting before oneself, worth pursuing for a lifetime, that of trying to make known to English folk their bugbear of the East?

"Then this," said Olga, "is to be the end of your life?"

"The end? No, not even that."

On their return, he found himself alone with Mrs. Hannaford for a few minutes. He spoke abruptly, with an effort.

"Do you see much of the Derwents?"

"Not much. Our lives are so different, you know."

"Will you tell me frankly? If I called there—when I come South again—should I be welcome?"

"Oh, why not?" replied the lady, veiling embarrassment.

"I see." Otway's face darkened. "You think it better I shouldn't. I understand."

Olga reappeared, and the young man turned to her with

resolute cheerfulness. When at length he took leave of his friends, they saw nothing but good spirits and healthful energy. He would certainly see them again before leaving England, and before long would let them know all his projects in detail. So he went his way into the summer night, back to the roaring world of London; one man in the multitude who knew his heart's desire, and saw all else in the light thereof.

For three days, Mrs. Hannaford and her daughter lived expectant; then arrived an answer to the letter left behind at Hammersmith. It came through Dr. Derwent's solicitor, whose address Mrs. Hannaford had given for this purpose. A curt, dry communication, saying simply that the fugitive might do as she chose, and would never be interfered with. Parting was, under the circumstances, evidently the wise course; but it must be definite, legalised; the writer had no wish ever to see his wife again. As to her suggestion about money, in that too she would please herself; it relieved him to know her independent, and he was glad to be equally so.

For all that, Lee Hannaford made no objection to receiving the portion of his wife's income which she offered. He took it without thanks, keeping his reflections to himself. And therewith was practically dissolved one, at least, of the innumerable mock marriages which burden the lives of mankind. Mrs. Hannaford's only bitterness was that in law she remained wedded. It soothed her but moderately to reflect that she was a martyr to national morality.

She was pressed to come and stay for a while in Bryanston Square, but Olga would not accept that invitation. Her mother's affairs being satisfactorily settled, the girl returned to her fixed purpose; she would hear of no further postponement of her marriage. Thereupon Mrs. Hannaford took a step she feared to be useless, but which was the only hope remaining to her. She wrote to Kite; she explained to him her circumstances; she asked him whether, out of justice to Olga, who might repent a hasty union, he would join her (Mrs. Hannaford) in a decision to put off the marriage for one year. If, in a twelvemonth, Olga were still of the same mind, all opposition should be abandoned, and, more than that, pecuniary help would be given to the couple. She appealed to his manhood, to his generosity, to his good sense.

And, much to her surprise, the appeal was successful. Kite wrote the oddest letter in reply, all disjointed philosophising, with the gist that perhaps Mrs. Hannaford was right. No harm in waiting a year; perhaps much good. Life was a mystery; love was uncertain. He would get on with his art, the only stable thing from his point of view.

From her next meeting with her lover, Olga came back pale and wretched.

"I must go and live alone, mother," she said. "I must go to London and work. This life would be impossible to me, now."

She would hear of nothing else. Her marriage was postponed; they need say no more about it. If her mother would let her have a little money, till she could support herself, she would be grateful; but she must live apart. And so, after many tears, it was decided. Olga went by herself into lodgings, and Mrs. Hannaford accepted her brother's invitation to Bryanston Square.

CHAPTER XIII

PIERS OTWAY spent ten days in Yorkshire. His father was well, but more than ever silent, sunk in prophetic brooding; Mrs. Otway kept the wonted tenor of her life, apprehensive for the purity of the Anglican Church (assailed by insidious papistry), and monologising at large to her inattentive husband upon the godlessness of his impenitent old age.

"Piers," said the father one day, with a twinkle in his eye, "I find myself growing a little deaf. Your stepmother is fond of saying that Providence sends blessings in disguise, and for once she seems to have hit upon a truth."

On a glorious night of stars, he walked with his son up to the open moor. A summer breeze whispered fitfully between the dark-blue vault and the grey earth; there was a sound of water that leapt from the bosom of the hills; deep answering to deep, infinite to infinite. After standing silent for a while, Jerome Otway laid a hand on his companion's shoulder, and muttered, "The creeds—the dogmas!"

They had two or three long conversations. Most of his time Piers spent in rambling alone about the moorland, for health and for weariness. When unoccupied, he durst not be physically idle; the passions that ever lurked to frenzy him could only be baffled at such times by vigorous exercise. His cold bath in the early morning was followed by play of dumb-bells. He had made a cult of physical soundness; he looked anxiously at his lithe, well-moulded limbs; feebleness, disease, were the menaces of a supreme hope. Ideal love dwells not in the soul alone, but in every vein and nerve and muscle of a frame strung to perfect service. Would he win his heart's desire?—let him be worthy of it in body as in mind. He pursued to excess the point of cleanliness. With no touch of personal conceit, he excelled the perfumed exquisite in care for minute perfections. Not in costume; on that score he was indifferent, once the conditions of health fulfilled. His

inherited tone was far from perfect; with rage he looked back
upon those insensate years of study, which had weakened him
just when he should have been carefully fortifying his constitution.   Only by conflict daily renewed did he keep in the way
of safety; a natural indolence had ever to be combated; there
was always the fear of relapse, such as had befallen him now
and again during his years in Russia; a relapse not alone in
physical training, but from the ideal of chastity. He had
cursed the temper of his blood; he had raved at himself for
vulgar gratifications; and once more the struggle was renewed.
Asceticism in diet had failed him doubly; it reduced his
power of wholesome exertion, and caused a mental languor
treacherous to his chief purpose. Nowadays he ate and
drank like any other of the sons of men, on the whole to his
plain advantage.

A day or two after receiving a letter from Mrs. Hannaford,
in which she told him of her removal to Dr. Derwent's house,
he bade farewell to his father.

To his hotel in London, that night, came a note he had
expected. Mrs. Hannaford asked him to call in Bryanston
Square at eleven the next morning.

As he approached the house, memories shamed him. How
he had slunk about the Square under his umbrella; how he
had turned away in black despair after that "Not at home";
his foolish long-tailed coat, his glistening stove-pipe! To-day,
with scarce a thought for his dress, he looked merely what he
was: an educated man, of average physique, of intelligent
visage, of easy bearing. For all that, his heart throbbed as he
stood at the door, and with catching breath he followed the
servant upstairs.

Before Mrs. Hannaford appeared, he had time to glance
round the drawing-room, which was simpler in array than is
common in such houses. His eye fell upon a portrait, a large
crayon drawing, hung in a place of honour; he knew it must
represent Irene's mother; there was a resemblance to the face
which haunted him, with more of sweetness, with a riper
humanity. Whilst his wife still lived, Dr. Derwent had not
been able to afford a painting of her: this drawing was done,
and well done, in the after days from photographs. On the
wall beneath it was a little bracket, supporting a little glass
vessel which held a rose. The year round, this tiny altar
never lacked its flower.

Mrs. Hannaford entered. Her smile of greeting was not untroubled, but, seeing her for the first time somewhat ornately clad, and with suitable background, Piers was struck by the air of youth that animated her features. He had always admired Mrs. Hannaford, had always liked her, and as she took his hand in both her own, he felt a warm response to her unfeigned kindliness.

"Well, is it settled?"

"It is settled. I go back to Odessa, remain with the firm for another six months, then make the great launch!"

They laughed together, both nervously. Piers' eyes wandered, and Mrs. Hannaford, as she sat down, made an obvious effort to compose herself.

"I didn't ask you, the other day," she began, as if on a sudden thought, "whether you had seen either of your brothers."

Piers shook his head, smiling.

"No. Alexander, I hear, is somewhere in the North, doing provincial journalism. Daniel—I believe he is in London, but I'm not very likely to meet him."

"Don't you wish to?" asked the other lightly.

"Oh, I'm not very anxious. Daniel and I haven't a great interest in each other, I'm afraid. You haven't seen him lately?"

"No, no," Mrs. Hannaford answered, with an absent air. "No—not for a long time. I have hoped to see an announcement of his book."

"His book?—Ah, I remember. I fear we shall wait long for that."

"But he really was working at it," said Mrs. Hannaford, bending forward with a peculiar earnestness. "When he last spoke to me about it, he said the material grew so on his hands. And then, there is the expense of publication. Such a volume, really well illustrated, must cost much to produce, and the author would have to bear"—

Piers was smiling oddly; she broke off, and observed him, as if the smile pained her.

"Let us have faith," said Otway. "Daniel is a clever man, no doubt, and may do something yet."

Mrs. Hannaford abruptly changed the subject, returning to Piers' prospects. They talked for half an hour, the lady's eyes occasionally turning towards the door, and Otway sometimes losing himself as he glanced at the crayon portrait. He was thinking of a reluctant withdrawal, when the door opened. He heard a soft rustle, turned his head, and rose.

It was Irene! Irene in all the grace of her earlier day, and with maturer beauty; Irene with her light step, her bravely balanced head, her smile of admirable courtesy, her golden voice. Otway knew not what she said to him; something frank, cordial, welcoming. For an instant he had held her hand, and felt its coolness thrill him to his heart of hearts; he had bent before her, mutely worshipping. His brain was on fire with the old passion newly kindled. He spoke, he was beginning to converse; the room grew real again; he was aware once more of Mrs. Hannaford's presence, of a look she had fixed upon him. A look half amused, half compassionate; he answered it with a courageous smile.

Miss Derwent was in her happiest mood; impossible to be kinder and friendlier in that merry way of hers. Scarce having expected to meet her, still keeping in his mind the anguish of that calamitous and shameful night three years ago when he fled before her grave reproof, Piers beheld her and listened to her with such a sense of passionate gratitude that he feared lest some crazy word should escape him. That Irene remembered, no look or word of hers suggested; unless, indeed, the perfection of her kindness aimed at assuring him that the past was wholly past. She made inquiry about his father's health; she spoke of his life at Odessa, and was full of interest when he sketched his projects. To crown all, she said, with her eyes smiling upon him:

"My father would so like to know you; could you dine with us one evening before you go?"

Piers declared his absolute freedom for a week to come.

"Suppose, then, we say Thursday? An old friend of ours will be with us, whom you may like to meet."

She spoke a name which surprised and delighted him; that of a scientific man known the world over. Piers went his way with raptures and high resolves singing at his heart.

For the rest of daytime it was enough to walk about the streets in sun and shower, seeing a glorified London, one exquisite presence obscuring every mean thing and throwing light upon all that was beautiful. He did not reason with himself about Irene's friendliness; it had cast a spell upon him, and he knew only his joy, his worship. Three years of laborious exile were trifling in the balance; had they been passed in sufferings ten times as great, her smile would have paid for all.

Fortunately, he had a little business to transact in London; on the two mornings that followed he was at his firm's house in the City, making reports, answering inquiries — mainly about wool and hemp. Piers was erudite concerning Russian wool and hemp. He talked about it not like the ordinary business man, but as a scholar might who had very thoroughly got up the subject. His firm did not altogether approve this attitude of mind; they thought it *queer*, and would have smiled caustically had they known Otway's purpose of starting as a merchant on his own account. That, he had not yet announced, and would not do so until he had seen his Swiss friend at Odessa again.

The evening of the dinner arrived, and again Piers was rapt above himself. Nothing could have been more cordial than Dr. Derwent's reception of him, and he had but to look into the Doctor's face to recognise a man worthy of reverence; a man of genial wisdom, of the largest humanity, of the sanest mirth. Eustace Derwent was present; he behaved with exemplary good-breeding, remarking suavely that they had met before, and betraying in no corner of his pleasant smile that that meeting had been other than delightful to both. Three guests arrived, besides Otway, one of them the distinguished person whose name had impressed him; a grizzled gentleman, of bland brows, and the simplest, softest manner.

At table there was general conversation — the mode of civilised beings. His mind in a whirl at first, Otway presently found himself quite capable of taking part in the talk. Someone had told a story illustrative of superstition in English peasant folk, and Piers had only to draw upon his Russian experiences for pursuit of the subject. He told how, in a time of great drought, he had known a corpse dug up from its grave by peasantry, and thrown into a muddy pond—a vigorous measure for the calling down of rain; also, how he had seen a priest submit to be dragged on his back across a turnip-field, that thereby a great crop might be secured. These things interested the great man, who sat opposite; he beamed upon Otway, and sought from him further information regarding Russia. Piers saw that Irene had turned to him; he held himself in command, he spoke neither too much nor too little, and as the things he knew were worth knowing, his share in the talk made a very favourable impression. In truth, these three years had intellectually much advanced him. It was at this time that he began to use the brief, decisive turn of speech which afterwards became his habit; a mode of utterance suggesting both mental resources and force of character.

Later in the evening, he found himself beside Mrs. Hannaford in a corner of the drawing-room. He had hoped to speak a little with Miss Derwent, in semi-privacy, but of that there seemed no chance; enough that he had her so long before his eyes. Nor did he venture to speak of her to her aunt, though with difficulty subduing the desire. He knew that Mrs. Hannaford understood what was in his mind, and he felt pleased to have her for a silent confidante. She, not altogether at ease in this company, was glad to talk to Otway of everyday things; she mentioned her daughter, who was understood to be living elsewhere for the convenience of artistic studies.

"I hope you will be able to meet Olga before you go. She shuts herself up from us a great deal—something like you used to do at Ewell, you remember."

"I do, only too well. Why mayn't I go and call on her?"

Mrs. Hannaford shook her head, vaguely, trying to smile.

"She must have her own way, like all artists. If she succeeds, she will come amongst us again."

"I know that spirit," said Piers, "and perhaps it's the right one. Give her my good wishes—they will do no harm."

The image of Olga Hannaford was distinct before his mind's eye, but did not touch his emotions. He thought with little interest of her embarking on an artist's career, and had small belief in her chances of success. Under the spell of Irene, he felt coldly critical towards all other women; every image of feminine charm paled and grew remote when hers was actually before him, and it would have cost a great effort of mind to assure himself that he had not felt precisely thus ever since the days at Ewell. The truth was, of course, that though imagination could always restore Irene's supremacy, and constantly did so, though his intellectual being never failed from allegiance to her, his blood had been at the mercy of any face sufficiently alluring. So it would be again, little as he could now believe it.

Before he departed, he had his wish of a few minutes' talk

with her. The words exchanged were insignificant. Piers had
nothing ready to his tongue but commonplace, and Miss
Derwent answered as became her. As he left the room he
suffered a flush of anger, the natural revolt of every being who
lives by emotion against the restraints of polite intercourse. At
such moments one *feels* the bonds wrought for themselves by
civilised mankind; commonly accepted without consciousness
of voluntary or involuntary restraint. In revolt, he broke
through these trammels of self-subduing nature, saw himself
free man before her free woman, in some sphere of the unem-
barrassed impulse, and uttered what was in him, pleaded with
all his life, conquered by vital energy. Only when he had
walked back to the hotel was he capable of remembering that
Irene, in taking leave, had spoken the kindest wishes for his
future, assuredly with more than the common hostess-note.
Dr. Derwent, too, had held his hand with a pleasant grip, saying
good things. It was better than nothing, and he felt humanly
grateful amid the fire that tortured him.

In his room, the sight of pen, ink and paper was a sore
temptation. At Odessa he had from time to time written
what he thought poetry (it was not quite that, yet as verse not
contemptible), and now, recalling to memory some favourite
lines, he asked himself whether he might venture to write them
out and send them to Miss Derwent. Could he leave England,
this time, without confessing himself to her? Faint heart—
he mused over the proverb. The thought of a laboured letter
repelled him, and perhaps her reply—if she replied at all—
would be a blow scarce endurable. In the offer of a copy of
verses there is no undue presumption; it is a consecrated
form of homage; it demands no immediate response. But
were they good enough, these rhymes of his?—He would
decide to-morrow, his last day.

And, as was his habit, he read a little before sleeping, in one
of the half-dozen volumes which he had chosen for this
journey. It was *Les Chants du Crépuscule*, and thus the page
sang:

> " Laisse-toi donc aimer ! Car l'amour, c'est la vie,
> C'est tout ce qu'on regrette et tout ce qu'on envie
> Quand on voit sa jeunesse au couchant décliner.
> Sans lui rien n'est complet, sans lui rien ne rayonne.
> La beauté c'est le front, l'amour c'est la couronne.
> Laisse-toi couronner ! "

His own lines sounded a sad jingle; he grew ashamed of them, and in the weariness of his passions he fell asleep.

He had left till to-morrow the visit he owed to John Jacks. It was not pleasant, the thought of calling at the house at Queen's Gate; Mrs. Jacks might have heard strange things about him on that mad evening three years ago. Yet in decency he must go; perhaps, too, in self-interest. And at the wonted hour he went.

Fortunately; for John Jacks seemed unfeignedly glad to see him, and talked with him in private for half an hour after the observances of the drawing-room, where Mrs. Jacks had been very sweetly proper and properly sweet. In the library, much more at his ease, Otway told what he had before him, all the details of his commercial project.

"It occurs to me," said John Jacks—who was looking far from well, and at times spoke with an effort—"that I may be able to be of some use in this matter. I'll think about it, and —leave me your address—I shall probably write to you. And now tell me all about your father. He is hale and hearty?"

"In excellent health, I think," Piers replied cheerfully. "Dante suffices him still."

"Odd that you should have come to-day. I don't know why, I was thinking of your father all last night,—I don't sleep very well just now. I thought of the old days, a lifetime ago; and I said to myself that I would write him a letter. So I will, to-day. And in a month or two I shall see him. I'm a walking copybook-line; procrastination—nothing but putting off pleasures and duties these last years; I don't know how it is. But certainly I will go over to Hawes when I'm in Yorkshire. And I'll write to-day, tell him I've seen you."

Much better in spirits, Piers returned to the hotel. Yes, after all, he would copy out those verses of his, and send them to Miss Derwent. They were not bad; they came from his heart, and they might speak to hers. Just his name at the end; no address. If she desired to write to him, she could easily learn his address from Mrs. Hannaford. He would send them!

"A telegram for you, sir," said the porter, as he entered.

Wondering, he opened it.

"Your father has suddenly died.   Hope this will reach you in time.   EMMA OTWAY."

For a minute or two, the message was meaningless.   He stood reading and re-reading the figures which indicated hour of despatch and of delivery.   Presently he asked for a railway-guide, and with shaking hands, with agony of mental confusion, sought out the next train northwards.   There was just time to catch it; not time to pack his bag.   He rushed out to the cab.

CHAPTER XIV

"THE circumstances are these. On the day after I said good-bye to him, my father went for his usual morning walk, and was absent for two hours. He returned looking very pale and disturbed, and with some difficulty was persuaded (you know how he disliked speaking of himself) to tell what had happened. It seems that, somewhere on the lonely road, he came across two men, honest-looking country folk, engaged in a violent quarrel; their language made it clear that one accused the other of some sort of slander, a very trivial affair. Just as my father came up to them, they began fighting. He interfered, tried to separate them—as he would have done, I am sure, had they been armed with pistols, for the sight of fighting was intolerable to him, it put him beside himself with a sort of passionate disgust. They were great strong fellows, and one of them, whether intentionally or not, dealt him a fierce blow in the chest, knocking him down. That put an end to the fight. My father had to sit by the roadside for a time before he could go home.

"The next day he did not look well, but spent his time as usual, and on the morning after, he seemed to be all right again. The next day again he went for his walk, and did not return. When his absence became alarming, messengers were sent to look for him, and by one of these he was found lying on the moorside, dead. The post-mortem showed that the blow he had received affected the heart, which was already diseased (he did not know that). Of course the man who struck him cannot be discovered, and I don't know that it matters. My father would no doubt have been glad to foresee such a death as this. It was sudden (for that he always hoped), and it came of a protest against the thing he most hated, brutal violence."

So Piers Otway wrote in a letter to John Jacks. He did not add that his father had died intestate, but of that he was aware before any inquiries had been set on foot; in one of their last talks, Jerome had expressly told his son that he would shortly make a will, not having hitherto been able to decide how his possessions should be distributed. This intestacy meant (if Daniel Otway had spoken truth) that Piers would have no fruit whatever of his father's promises; that his recent hopes and schemes would straightway fall to the ground.

And so it was. A telegram from Piers brought down into Yorkshire the solicitor who had for many years been Jerome Otway's friend and adviser; he answered the young man's inquiries with full and decisive information. Mrs. Otway already knew the fact; whence her habitual coldness to Piers, and the silent acerbity with which she behaved to him at this juncture.

"Mrs. Otway," said Piers to her, on the day of the inquest, "I shall stay for my father's funeral, and to avoid gossip I still ask your hospitality. I do it with reluctance, but you will very soon see the last of me."

"You are of course welcome to stay in the house," replied the lady. "There is no need to say that we shall in future be strangers, and I only hope that the example of this shockingly sudden death in the midst of"—

His blood boiling, Piers left the room before the sentence was finished.

Had he obeyed his conscience, he would have followed the coffin in the clothes he was wearing, for many a time he had heard his father speak with dislike of the black trappings which made a burial hideous; but enforced regard for public opinion, that which makes cowards of good men and hampers the world's progress, sent him to the outfitter's, where he was duly disguised. With the secret tears he shed, there mingled a bitterness at being unable to show respect to his father's memory in such small matters. That Jerome Otway should be buried as a son of the Church, to which he had never belonged, was a ground of indignation, but neither in this could any effective protest be made. Mute in his sorrow, Piers marvelled with a young man's freshness of feeling at the forms and insincerities which rule the world. He had a miserable sense of his helplessness amid forces which he despised.

On the day of the inquest arrived Daniel Otway, Piers having telegraphed to the club where he had seen his brother three years ago. Before leaving London, Daniel had provided himself with solemn black, of the latest cut; Hawes people remarked him with curiosity, saying what a gentleman he looked, but whispering at the same time rumours and doubts; for the little town had long gossiped about Jerome, a man not much to its mind. A day later came Alexander. With him there had been no means of communicating, and a newspaper paragraph informed him of his father's death. Appearing in rough tweeds, with a felt hat, he inspired more curiosity than respect. Both brothers greeted Piers cordially; both were curt and formal with the widow, but, for appearances' sake, accepted a cramped lodging in the cottage. Piers kept very much to himself until the funeral was over; he was then invited by Daniel to join a conference in what had been his father's room. Here the man of law (Jerome's name for him) expounded the posture of things; with all professional, and some personal, tact and delicacy. Will there was certainly none; Daniel, in the course of things, would apply for letters of administration. The estate, it might be said, consisted of certain shares in a prosperous newspaper, an investment which could be easily realised, and of a small capital in consols; to the best of the speaker's judgment, the shares were worth about six thousand pounds, the consols amounted to nearly fifteen hundred. This capital sum, the widow and the sons would divide in legal proportion. Followed technicalities, with conversation. Mrs. Otway kept dignified silence; Piers, in the background, sat with eyes sunk.

"I think," remarked the solicitor gravely and firmly, "that, assembled as we are in privacy, I am only doing my duty in making known that the deceased had in view (as I know from hints in his correspondence) to assist his youngest son substantially, as soon as that son appeared likely to benefit by such pecuniary aid. I think I am justified in saying that that time had arrived, that death interposed at an unfortunate moment as regards such plans. I wished only to put the point before you, as one within my own knowledge.— Is there any question you would like to ask me at present, Mrs. Otway?"

The widow shook her head (and her funeral trappings). Thereupon sounded Piers Otway's voice.

"I should like to say that as I have no legal claim whatever upon my father's estate, I do not wish to put forward a claim of any other kind. Let that be understood at once."

There was silence. They heard the waters of the beck rushing over its stony channel. For how many thousand years had the beck so murmured? For how many thousand would it murmur still?

"As the eldest son," then observed Daniel, with his Oxford accent, and a sub-note of feeling, "I desire to say that my brother"—he generously emphasised the word—"has expressed himself very well, in the spirit of a gentleman. Perhaps I had better say no more at this moment. We shall have other opportunities of—of considering this point."

"Decidedly," remarked Alexander, who sat with legs crossed. "We'll talk it over."

And he nodded with a good - natured smile in Piers' direction.

Later in the day—a family council having been held at which Piers was not present — Daniel led the young man apart.

"You insist on leaving Hawes to-night? Well, perhaps it is best. But, my dear boy, I can't let you go without saying how deeply I sympathise with your position. You bear it like a man, Piers; indeed you do. I think I have mentioned to you before how strong I am on the side of morals."

"If you please," Piers interrupted, with brow dark.

"No, no, no!" exclaimed the other. "I was far from casting any reflection. *De mortuis*, you know; much more so when one speaks of a father. I think, by the bye, Alec ought to write something about him for publication; don't you? I was going to say, Piers, that, if I remember rightly, I am in your debt for a small sum, which you very generously lent me. Ah, that book! It grows and grows; I *can't* get it into final form. The fact is Continental art critics— But I was going to say that I must really insist on being allowed to pay my debt —indeed I must—as soon as this business is settled."

He paused, watching Piers' face. His own had not waxed more spiritual of late years, nor had his demeanour become more likely to inspire confidence; but he was handsome, in a way, and very fluent, very suave.

"Be it so," replied Piers frankly; "I shall be glad of the money, I confess."

"To be sure! You shall have it with the least possible delay. And, Piers, it has struck us, my dear fellow, that you might like to choose a volume or two of the good old man's

library, as a memento. We beg you will do so. We beg you
will do it at once, before you leave."

"Thank you. I should like the Dante he used to carry in
his pocket."

"A most natural wish, Piers. Take it by all means.
Nothing else, you think?"

"Yes. You once told me that you had seen a portrait of
my mother. Do you think it still exists?"

"I will inquire about it," answered Daniel gravely. "It
was a framed photograph, and at one time—many years ago—
used to stand on his writing-table. I will inquire, my dear
boy."

Next, Alexander sought a private colloquy with his dis-
inherited brother.

"Look here, Piers," he began bluffly, "it's a cursed shame!
I'm hanged if it isn't! If we weren't so solemn, my boy, I
should quote Bumble about the law. Of course it's the grossest
absurdity, and as far as I'm concerned— By Jove, Piers!" he
cried, with sudden change of subject, "if you knew the hard
times Biddy and I have been going through! Eh, but she's
a brick, is Biddy! She sent you her love, old boy, and that's
worth something, I can tell you. But I was going to say that
you mustn't suppose I've forgotten about the debt. You shall
be repaid as soon as ever we realise this property; you shall,
Piers! And, what's more, you shall be repaid with interest;
yes, three per cent. It would be cursed meanness if I
didn't."

"The fifty pounds I shall be glad of," said Piers. "I want
no interest. I'm not a money-lender."

"We won't quarrel about that," rejoined Alexander, with a
merry look. "But come now, why don't you let a fellow hear
from you now and then? What are you doing? Going back
among the Muscovites?"

"Straight back to Odessa, yes."

"I may look you up there some day, if Biddy can spare me
for a few weeks. A glimpse of the bear—it might be useful to
me. Terrible savages, I suppose?"

Piers laughed impatiently, and gave no other answer.

"Well, the one thing I really wanted to say, Piers—you
must let me say it—I, for one, shall take a strong stand about
your moral rights in this business here. Of course your claim
is every bit as good as ours; only a dunder-headed jackass

would see it in any other way. Daniel quite agrees with me. The difficulty will be that woman. A terrible woman! She regards you as sealed for perdition by the mere fact of your birth. But you will hear from us, old boy, be sure of that. Give me your Muscovite address."

Piers carelessly gave it. He was paying hardly any attention to his brother's talk, and would have felt it waste of energy to reassert what he had said in the formal conclave. Weariness had come upon him after these days of grief and indignant tumult; he wanted to be alone.

The portrait for which he had asked was very quickly found. It lay in a drawer, locked away among other mementoes of the past. With a shock of disappointment, Piers saw that the old photograph had faded almost to invisibility. He just discerned the outlines of a pleasant face, the dim suggestion of womanly charm—all he would ever see of the mother who bore him.

"It seems to me," said Daniel, after sympathising with his chagrin, "that there must be a lot of papers, literary work, letters, and that kind of thing, which will have more interest for you than for anyone else. When we get things looked through, shall I send you whatever I think you would care for?"

With gratitude Piers accepted what he could not have brought himself to ask for.

On the southward journey he kept taking from his pocket two letters which had reached him at Hawes. One was from John Jacks, full of the kindliest condolence; a manly letter which it did him good to read. The other came from Mrs. Hannaford, womanly, sincere; it contained a passage to which Piers returned again and again. "My niece is really grieved to hear of your sudden loss; happening at a moment when all seemed going well with you. She begs me to assure you of her very true sympathy, and sends every good wish." Little enough, this, but the recipient tried to make much of it. He had faintly hoped that Irene might send him a line in her own hand. That was denied, and perhaps he was foolish even to have dreamt of it.

He could not address his verses to her, now. He must hurry away from England, and try to forget her.

Of course she would hear, one way or another, about the circumstances of his birth. It would come out that he had no share in the property left by his father, and the reason be made known. He hoped that she might also learn that death had prevented his father's plan for benefiting him. He hoped it; for in that case she might feel compassion. Yet in the same moment he felt that this was a delusive solace. Pity for a man because he had lost money does not incline to warmer emotion. The hope was sheer feebleness of spirit. He spurned it; he desired no one's compassion.

How would Irene regard the fact of his illegitimacy? Not, assuredly, from Mrs. Otway's point of view; she was a century ahead of that. Possibly she was capable of dismissing it as indifferent. But he could not be certain of her freedom from social prejudice. He remembered the singular shock with which he himself had first learnt what he was; a state of mind quite irrational, but only to be dismissed with an effort of the trained intelligence. Irene would undergo the same experience, and it might affect her thought of him for ever.

Not for one instant did he visit these troubles upon the dead man. His loyalty to his father was absolute; no thought, or half-thought, looked towards accusation.

He arrived at his hotel in London late at night, drank a glass of spirits, and went to bed. The sleep he hoped for came immediately, but lasted only a couple of hours. Suddenly he was wide awake, and a horror of great darkness enveloped him. What he now suffered he had known before, but with less intensity. He stared forward into the coming years, and saw nothing that his soul desired. A life of solitude, of bitter frustration. Were it Irene, were it another, the woman for whom he longed would never become his. He had not the power of inspiring love. The mere flesh would constrain him to marriage, a sordid union, a desecration of his ideal, his worship; and in the latter days he would look back upon a futile life. What is life without love? And to him love meant communion with the noblest. Nature had kindled in him this fiery ambition only for his woe.

All the passion of the great hungry world seemed concentrated in his sole being. Images of maddening beauty glowed upon him out of the darkness, glowed and gleamed by he knew not what creative mandate; faces, forms, such as may visit the delirium of a supreme artist. Of him they knew not; they were worlds away, though his own brain bodied them forth. He smothered cries of agony; he flung himself upon his face, and lay as one dead.

For the men capable of passionate love (and they are few)

8

to miss love is to miss everything. Life has but the mockery of consolation for that one gift denied. The heart may be dulled by time ; it is not comforted. Illusion if it be, it is that which crowns all other illusions whereof life is made. The man must prove it, or he is born in vain.

At sunrise, Piers dressed himself, and made ready for his journey. He was worn with fever, had no more strength to hope or to desire. His body was a mechanism which must move and move.

CHAPTER XV

IN the saloon of a homeward-bound steamer, twenty-four
hours from port, and that port Southampton, a lady sat
writing letters. Her age was about thirty; her face was rather
piquant than pretty; she had the air of a person far too
intelligent and spirited to be involved in any life of mere
routine, on whatever plane. Two letters she had written in
French, one in German, and that upon which she was now
engaged was in English, her native tongue; it began "Dearest
Mother."

"All's well. A pleasant and a quick voyage. The one
incident of it which you will care to hear about is that I have
made friends—a real friendship, I think—with a delightful
girl, of respectability which will satisfy even you.—Judge for
yourself; she is the daughter of Dr. Derwent, a distinguished
scientific man, who has been having a glimpse of Colonial
life. When we were a day or two out I found that Miss
Derwent was the object of special interest;—she and her
father had been the guests of no less a personage than Trafford
Romaine, and it was reported that the great man had offered
her marriage! Who started the rumour I don't know, but it
is quite true that Romaine *did* propose to her—and was refused!
I am assured of it by a friend of theirs on board, Mr. Arnold
Jacks, an intimate friend of Romaine; but he declares that he
did not start the story, and was surprised to find it known.
Miss Derwent herself? No, my dear cynical mamma! She
isn't that sort. She likes me as much as I like her, I think,
but in all our talk not a word from her about the great topic
of curiosity. It is just possible, I fear, that she means to marry
Mr. Arnold Jacks, who, by the bye, is a son of a Member of
Parliament, and rather an interesting man, but, I am quite
sure, not the man for *her*. If she will come down into
Hampshire with me, may I bring her? It would so rejoice
your dear soul to be assured that I have made such a

friend, after what you are pleased to call my riff-raff foreign intimacies."

A few words more of affectionate banter, and she signed herself "Helen M. Borisoff."

As she was addressing the envelope, the sound of a book thrown on to the table just in front of her caused her to look up, and she saw Irene Derwent.

"What's the matter? Why are you damaging the ship's literature?" she asked gaily.

"No, I can't stand that!" exclaimed Irene. "It's too imbecile. It really is what our slangy friend calls 'rot,' and very dry rot. Have you read the thing?"

Mrs. Borisoff looked at the title, and answered with a head-shake.

"Imagine! An awful apparatus of mystery; blood-curdling hints about the hero, whose prospects in life are supposed to be utterly blighted. And all because—what do you think? Because his father and mother forgot the marriage ceremony."

The other was amused, and at the same time surprised. It was the first time that Miss Derwent, in their talk, had allowed herself a remark suggestive of what is called "emanci-pation." She would talk with freedom of almost any subject save that specifically forbidden to English girls. Helen Borisoff, whose finger showed a wedding ring, had respected this reticence, but it delighted her to see a new side of her friend's attractive personality.

"I suppose in certain circles"— she began.

"Oh yes! Shopkeepers and clerks and so on. But the book is supposed to deal with civilised people. It really made me angry!"

Mrs. Borisoff regarded her with amused curiosity. Their eyes met. Irene nodded.

"Yes," she continued, as if answering a question, "I know someone in just that position. And all at once it struck me —I had hardly thought of it before—what an idiot I should be if I let it affect my feelings or behaviour!"

"I think no one would have suspected you of such narrowness."

"Indeed, I hope not!—Have you done your letters? Do come up and watch Mrs. Smithson playing at quoits—a sight to rout the brood of cares!"

In the smoking-room on deck sat Dr. Derwent and Arnold

Jacks, conversing gravely, with subdued voices. The Doctor had a smile on his meditative features; his eyes were cast down; he looked a trifle embarrassed.

"Forgive me," Arnold was saying, with some earnestness, "if this course seems to you rather irregular "—

"Not at all! Not at all! But I can only assure you of my honest inability to answer the question. Try, my dear fellow! *Solvitur quærendo!*"

Jacks' behaviour did, in fact, appear to the Doctor a little odd. That the young man should hint at his desire to ask Miss Derwent to marry him, or perhaps ask the parental approval of such a step, was natural enough; the event had been looming since the beginning of the voyage home. But to go beyond this, to ask the girl's father whether he thought success likely, whether he could hold out hopes, was scarcely permissible. It seemed a curious failure of tact in such a man as Arnold Jacks.

The fact was that Arnold, for the first time in his life, had turned coward. Having drifted into a situation which he had always regarded as undesirable, and had felt strong enough to avoid, he lost his head, and clutched rather wildly at the first support within reach. That Irene Derwent should become his wife was not a vital matter; he could contemplate quite coolly the possibility of marrying someone else, or, if it came to that, of not marrying anyone at all. What shook his nerves was the question whether Irene would be sure to accept him.

Six months ago, he had no doubt of it. He viewed Miss Derwent with an eye accustomed to scrutinise, to calculate (in things Imperial and other), and it amused him to reflect that she might be numbered among, say, half a dozen eligible women who would think it an honour to marry him. This was his way of viewing marriage; it was on the woman's side a point of ambition, a gratification of vanity; on the man's, dignified condescension. Arnold conceived himself a brilliant match for any girl below the titled aristocracy; he had grown so accustomed to magnify his place, to regard himself as one of the pillars of the Empire, that he attributed the same estimate to all who knew him. Of personal vanity he had little; purely personal characteristics did not enter, he imagined, into a man's prospects of matrimony. Certain women openly flattered him, and these he despised. His

sense of fitness demanded a woman intelligent enough to
appreciate what he had to offer, and sufficiently well-bred to
conceal her emotions when he approached her. These conditions Miss Derwent fulfilled. Personally she would do him
credit (a wife, of course, must be presentable, though in the
husband appearance did not matter), and her obvious social
qualities would be useful. Yet he had had no serious thought
of proposing to her. For one thing, she was not rich enough.

The change began when he observed the impression made
by her upon Trafford Romaine. This was startling. Romaine,
the administrator of world-wide repute, the man who had but
to choose among Greater Britain's brilliant daughters (or so
his worshipper believed), no sooner looked upon Irene Derwent
than he betrayed his subjugation. No woman had ever
received such honour from him, such homage public and
private. Arnold Jacks was pricked with uneasiness ; Irene
had at once a new value in his eyes, and he feared he had
foolishly neglected his opportunities. If she married Romaine,
it would be mortifying. She refused the great man's offer,
and Arnold was at first astonished, then gratified. For such
refusal there could be only one ground : Miss Derwent's
" heart " was already disposed of. Women have " hearts " ;
they really do grow fond of the men they admire ; a singular
provision of nature.

He would propose during the voyage.

But the voyage was nearly over ; he might have put his
formal little question fifty times ; it was still to be asked—
and he felt afraid. Afraid more than ever, now that he had
committed himself with Dr. Derwent. The Doctor had
received his confession so calmly, whereas Arnold hoped for
some degree of effusiveness. Was he—hideous doubt—preparing for himself an even worse disillusion ?

Undoubtedly the people on board had remarked his atten-
tions ; for all he knew, jokes were being passed, nay, bets
being made. It was a serious thing to proclaim oneself the
wooer of a young lady who had refused Trafford Romaine ;
who was known to have done so, and talked about with envy,
admiration, curiosity. You either carried her off, or you
made yourself fatally ridiculous. Half a dozen of the
passengers would spread this gossip far and wide through
England. There was that problematic Mrs. Borisoff, a frisky
grass widow, who seemed to know crowds of distinguished

people, and who was watching his him day by day with her confounded smile! Who could say what passed between her and
Irene, intimates as they had become? Did they make fun of
him? Did they *dare* to?

Arnold Jacks differed widely from the common type of
fatuous young man. He was himself a merciless critic of
fatuity; he had a faculty of shrewd observation, plenty of
caustic common sense. Yet the position into which he had
drifted threatened him with ridiculous extremes of self-consciousness. Even in his personal carriage, he was not quite
safe against ridicule; and he felt it. This must come to an
end.

He sought his moment, and found it at the hour of dusk.
The sun had gone down gloriously upon a calm sea; the sky
was overspread with clouds still flushed, and the pleasant
coolness of the air foretold to-morrow's breeze on the English
Channel. With pretence of watching a steamer that had
passed, Arnold drew Miss Derwent to a part of the deck
where they would be alone.

"You will feel," he said abruptly, "that you know England
better, now that you have seen something of the England
beyond seas."

"I had imagined it pretty well," replied Irene.

"Yes, one does."

Under common circumstances, Arnold would have scorn-
fully denied the possibility of such imagination. He felt
most unpleasantly tame.

"You wouldn't care to make your home out yonder?"

"Heaven forbid!"

This was better. It sounded like emphatic rejection of
Trafford Romaine, and probably was meant to sound so.

"I myself," he pursued absently, "shall always live in
England. If I know myself, I can be of most service at the
centre of things. Parliament, when the moment arrives"—

"The moment when you can be most mischievous?" said
Irene, with a glance at him.

"That's how you put it. Yes, most mischievous. The
sphere for mischief is growing magnificent."

He talked, without strict command of his tongue, just to
gain time; spoke of expanding Britain, and so on, a dribble
of commonplaces. Irene moved as if to rejoin her company.

"Don't go just yet—I want you—now and always."

Sheer nervousness gave his voice a tremor as if of deep emotion. These simple words, which had burst from him desperately, were the best he could have uttered—Irene stood with her eyes on the darkening horizon.

"We know each other pretty well," he continued, "and the better we know each other, the more we find to talk about. It's a very good sign—don't you think? I can't see how I'm to get along without you, after this journey. I don't like to think of it, and I *won't* think of it! Say there's no need to."

Her silence, her still attitude, had restored his courage. He spoke at length like himself, with quiet assurance, with sincerity; and again it was the best thing he could have done.

"I am not quite sure, Mr. Jacks, that I think about it in the same way."

Her voice was subdued to a very pleasant note, but it did not tremble.

"I can allow for that uncertainty—though I have nothing of it myself. We shall both be in London for a month or so. Let me see you as often as I can, and, before you leave town, let me ask whether the doubt has been overcome."

"I hold myself free," said Irene impulsively.

"Naturally."

"I do you no wrong if it seems to me impossible."

"None whatever."

His eyes were fixed on her face, dimly beautiful in the fading shimmer from sea and sky. Irene met his glance for an instant, and moved away, he following.

Arnold Jacks had never known a mood so jubilant. He was saved from the terror of humiliation. He had comported himself as behoved him, and the result was sure and certain hope. He felt almost grateful, almost tender, towards the woman of his choice.

But Irene, as she lay in her berth, strangely wakeful to the wash of the sea as the breeze freshened, was frightened at the thought of what she had done. Had she not, in the common way of maidenhood, as good as accepted Arnold Jacks' proposal? She did not mean it so; she spoke simply and directly in saying that she was not clear about her own mind; on any other subject she would in fact, or in phrase, have reserved her independence. But an offer of marriage was a thing apart, full of subtle implications, needing to be dealt with according to special rules of conscience and of tact.

Some five or six she had received, and in each case had replied decisively, her mind admitting no doubt. As when, to her astonishment, she heard the frank and large confession of Trafford Romaine; the answer was an inevitable—No! To Arnold Jacks she could not reply thus promptly. Relying on the easy terms of their intercourse, she told him the truth; and now she saw that no form of answer could be less discreet.

For about a year she had thought of Arnold as one who *might* offer her marriage; any girl in her position would have foreseen that possibility. After every opportunity which he allowed to pass, she felt relieved, for she had no reply in readiness. The thought of accepting him was not at all disagreeable; it had even its allurements; but between the speculation and the thing itself was a great gap for the leaping of mind and heart. Her relations with him were very pleasant, and she would have been glad if nothing had ever happened to disturb them.

When her father suggested this long journey in Arnold's company, she hesitated. In deciding to go, she said to herself that if nothing resulted, well and good; if something did, well and good also. She would get to know Arnold better, and on that increase of acquaintance must depend the outcome, as far as she was concerned. She was helped in making up her mind by a little thing that happened. There came to her one day a letter from Odessa; on opening it, she found only a copy of verses, with the signature "P. O." A love poem; not addressed to her, but about her; a pretty poem, she thought, delicately felt and gracefully worded. It surprised her, but only for a moment; thinking, she accepted it as something natural, and was touched by the tribute. She put it carefully away—knowing it by heart.

Impertinence? Surely not. Long ago she had reproached herself with her half-coquetry to Piers Otway, an error of exuberant spirits when she was still very young. There was no obscuring the fact; deliberately she had set herself to draw him away from his studies; she had made it a point of pride to show herself irresistible. Where others failed in their attack upon his austere seclusion, *she* would succeed, and easily. She had succeeded only too well, and it never quite ceased to trouble her conscience. Now, learning that even after four years her victim still remained loyal, she thought of

him with much gentleness, and would have scorned herself
had she felt scorn of his devotion.

No other of her wooers had ever written her a poem; no
other was capable of it. It gave Piers a distinction in her
mind which more than earned her pardon.

But—poor fellow!—he must surely know that she could
never respond to his romantic feeling. It was pure romance,
and charming—if only it did not mean sorrow to him and idle
hopes. Such a love as this, distant, respectful, she would
have liked to keep for years, for a lifetime. If only she could
be sure that romance was as dreamily delightful to her poet
as to her!

The worst of it was that Piers Otway had suffered a sad
wrong, an injustice which, when she heard of it, made her
nobly angry. A month after the death of the old philosopher
at Hawes, Mrs. Hannaford startled her with a strange story.
The form it took was this: That Piers, having for a whispered
reason no share in his father's possessions, had perforce given
up his hopes of commercial enterprise, and returned to his old
subordinate position at Odessa. The two legitimate sons
would gladly have divided with him their lawful due, but
Piers refused this generosity, would not hear of it for a
moment, stood on his pride, and departed. Thus Mrs.
Hannaford, who fully believed what she said; and as she had
her information direct from the eldest son, Daniel Otway,
there could be no doubt as to its correctness. Piers had
behaved well; he could not take alms from his half-brothers.
But what a monstrous thing that accident and the law of the
land left him thus destitute! Feeling strongly about it, Irene
begged her aunt, when next she wrote to Odessa, to give
Piers, from her, a message of friendly encouragement; not,
of course, a message that necessarily implied knowledge of
his story, but one that would help him with the assurance of
his being always kindly remembered by friends in London.

Six months after came the little poem, which Irene, without
purposing it, learnt by heart.

A chapter of pure romance; one which, Irene felt, could
not possibly have any relation to her normal life. And
perhaps because she felt that so strongly, perhaps because
her conscience warned her against the danger of still seeming
to encourage a lover she could not dream of marrying,
perhaps because these airy nothings threw into stronger relief

the circumstances which environed her, she forthwith made up her mind to go on the long journey with her father and Arnold Jacks. Mrs. Hannaford did not fail to acquaint Piers Otway with the occurrence.

And those two months of companionship told in Arnold's favour. Jacks was excellent in travel; he had large experience, and showed to advantage on the highways of the globe. No more entertaining companion during the long days of steamship life; no safer guide in unfamiliar lands. His personality made a striking contrast with the robustious semi-civilisation of the colonists with whom Irene became acquainted; she appreciated all the more his many refinements. Moreover, the respectful reception he met with could not but impress her; it gave reality to what Miss Derwent sometimes laughed at, his claim to be a force in the great world. Then, that eternal word "Empire" gained somewhat of a new meaning. She joked about it, disliking as much as ever its baser significance, but she came to understand better the immense power it represented. On that subject, her father was emphatic.

"If," remarked Dr. Derwent once, "if our politics ever fall into the hands of a stock-jobbing democracy, we shall be the hugest force for evil the poor old world has ever known."

"You think," said Irene, "that one can already see some danger of it?"

"Well, I think so sometimes. But we have good men still, good men."

"Do you mind telling me," Miss Derwent asked, "whether our fellow-traveller seems to you one of them?"

"H'm! On the whole, yes. His faults are balanced, I think, by his aristocratic temper. He is too proud consciously to make dirty bargains. High-handed, of course; but that's the race—the race. Things being as they are, I would as soon see him in power as another."

Irene pondered this. It pleased her.

On the morning after Arnold's proposal, she knew that he and her father had talked. Dr. Derwent, a shy man, rather avoided her look; but he behaved to her with particular kindliness'; as they stood looking towards the coast of England, he drew her hand through his arm, and stroked it once or twice—a thing he had not done on the whole journey.

"The brave old island!" he was murmuring. "I should

be really disturbed if I thought death would find me away
from it. Foolish fancy, but it's strong in me."

Irene was taciturn, and unlike herself. The approach to
port enabled her to avoid gossips, but one person, Helen
Borisoff, guessed what had happened; Irene's grave countenance and Arnold Jacks' meditative smile partly instructed
her. On the railway journey to London, Jacks had the
discretion to keep apart in a smoking-carriage. Dr. Derwent
and his daughter exchanged but few words until they found
themselves in Bryanston Square.

During their absence abroad, Mrs. Hannaford had been
keeping house for them. With brief intervals, spent now and
then in pursuit of health, she had made Bryanston Square her
home since the change in her circumstances two years ago.
Lee Hannaford held no communication with her, content to
draw the modest income she put at his disposal, and Olga, her
mother knew not why, was still unmarried, though declaring
herself still engaged to the man Kite. She lived here and
there in lodgings, at times seeming to maintain herself, at
others accepting help; her existence had an air of mystery
far from reassuring.

On meeting her aunt, Irene found her looking ill and
troubled. Mrs. Hannaford declared that she was much as
usual, and evaded inquiries. She passed from joy at her
relatives' return to a mood of silent depression; her eyes
made one think that she must have often shed tears of late.
In the past twelvemonth she had noticeably aged; her beauty
was vanishing; a nervous tremor often affected her thin hands,
and in her speech there was at times a stammering uncertainty,
such as comes of mental distress. Dr. Derwent, seeing her
after two months' absence, was gravely observant of these
things.

"I wish you could find out what's troubling your aunt," he
said to Irene, next day. "Something is, and something very
serious, though she won't admit it. I'm really uneasy about
her."

Irene tried to win the sufferer's confidence, but without
success. Mrs. Hannaford became irritable, and withdrew as
much as possible from sight.

The girl had her own trouble, and it was one she must
needs keep to herself. She shrank from the next meeting
with Arnold Jacks, which could not long be postponed. It

took place three days after her return, when Arnold and Mrs. Jacks dined in Bryanston Square. John Jacks was to have come, but excused himself on the plea of indisposition. As might have been expected of him, Arnold was absolute discretion; he looked and spoke, perhaps, a trifle more gaily than usual, but to Irene showed no change of demeanour, and conversed with her no more than was necessary. Irene felt grateful, and once more tried to convince herself that she had done nothing irreparable. In fact, as in assertion, she was free. The future depended entirely on her own will and pleasure. That her mind was ceaselessly preoccupied with Arnold could only be deemed natural, for she had to come to a decision within three or four weeks' time. But—if necessary the respite should be prolonged.

Eustace Derwent dined with them, and Irene noticed— what had occurred to her before now—that the young man seemed to have particular pleasure in the society of Mrs. Jacks; he conversed with her more naturally, more variously, than with any other lady of his friends; and Mrs. Jacks, through the unimpeachable correctness of her exterior, almost allowed it to be suspected that she found a special satisfaction in listening to him. Eustace was a frequent guest at the Jackses'; yet there could hardly be much in common between him and the lady's elderly husband, nor was he on terms of much intimacy with Arnold. Of course two such excellent persons, such models of decorum, such examples of the English ideal, masculine and feminine, would naturally see in each other the most desirable of acquaintances; it was an instance of social and personal fitness, which the propriety of our national manners renders as harmless as it is delightful. They talked of art, of literature, discovering an entire unanimity in their preferences, which made for the safely conventional. They chatted of common acquaintances, agreeing that the people they liked were undoubtedly the very nicest people in their circle, and avoiding in the suavest manner any severity regarding those they could not approve. When Eustace apologised for touching on a professional subject (he had just been called to the Bar), Mrs. Jacks declared that nothing could interest her more. If he ventured a jest, she smiled with surpassing sweetness, and was all but moved to laugh. They, at all events, spent a most agreeable evening.

Not so Mrs. Hannaford, who, just before dinner, had

received a letter, which at once she destroyed. The missive ran thus :—

"DEAR MRS. HANNAFORD,—I am distressed to hear that you suffer so in health. Consult your brother; you will find that the only thing to do you good will be a complete change of climate and of habits. You know how often I have urged this; if you had listened to me, you would by now have been both healthy and happy—yes, happy. Is it too late? Don't you value your life? And don't you care at all for the happiness of mine? Meet me to-morrow, I beg, at the Museum, about eleven o'clock, and let us talk it all over once more. Do be sensible; don't wreck your life out of respect for social superstitions. The thing once over, who thinks the worse of you? Not a living creature for whom you need care. You have suffered for years; put an end to it; the remedy is in your hands.—Ever yours,　　　　　　　　　　D. O."

CHAPTER XVI

A FEW days after her return, Irene left home in the morning to make an unceremonious call. She was driven to Great Portland Street, and alighted before a shop, which bore the number of the house she sought. Having found the private entrance—a door that stood wide open—and after ringing once or twice without drawing anyone's attention, she began to ascend the uncarpeted stairs. At that moment there came down a young woman humming an air; a cheery-faced, solidly-built damsel, dressed with attention to broad effect in colours which were then—or recently had been—known as "æsthetic." With some diffidence, for the encounter was not of a kind common in her experience, Irene asked this person for a direction to the rooms occupied by Miss Hannaford.

"Oh, she's my chum," was the genial reply. "Top floor, front. You'll find her there."

With thanks the visitor passed on, but had not climbed half a dozen steps when the clear sounding voice caused her to stop.

"Beg your pardon and all that kind of thing, but would you mind telling her that Tomkins is huffy? I forgot to mention it before I came out. Thanks, awfully."

Puzzled, if not disconcerted, Miss Derwent reached the top floor and knocked. A voice she recognised bade her enter. She found herself in a bare-floored room, furnished with a table, a chair or two, and a divan, on the walls a strange exhibition of designs in glaring colours which seemed to be studies for street posters. At the table, bending over a drawing-board, sat Olga Hannaford, her careless costume and the disorder of her hair suggesting that she had only just got up. She recognised her visitor with some embarrassment.

"Irene—I'm so glad—I really am ashamed—we keep such hours here—please don't mind!"

"Not I, indeed! What is there to mind? I spoke to someone downstairs who gave me a message for you. I was to say that Tomkins was huffy. Do you understand?"

Olga bit her lip in vexation, and to restrain a laugh.

"No, that's too bad! But just like her. That was the girl I live with—Miss Bonnicastle. She's very nice really— not a bit of harm in her; but she will play these silly practical jokes."

"Ah, it was a joke?" said Irene, not altogether pleased with Miss Bonnicastle's facetiousness. But the next moment, good humour coming to her help, she broke into merriment.

"That's what she does," said Olga, pointing to the walls. "She's awfully clever really, and she'll make a great success with that sort of thing before long, I'm sure. Look at that advertisement of Honey's Castor Oil. Isn't the child's face splendid?"

"Very clever indeed," assented Irene, and laughed again, her cousin joining in her mirth. Five minutes ago she had felt anything but hilarious; the impulse to gaiety came she knew not how, and she indulged it with a sense of relief.

"Are you doing the same sort of thing, Olga?"

"Wish I could. I've a little work for a new fashion paper; have to fill in the heads and arms, and so on. It isn't high art, you know, but they pay me."

"Why in the world do you do it? *Why* do you live in a place like this?"

"Oh, I like the life; on the whole. It's freedom; no society nonsense—I beg your pardon, Irene"—

"Please don't. I hope I'm not much in the way of society nonsense. Sit down; I want to talk. When did you see your mother?"

"Not for a long time," answered Olga, her countenance falling. "I sent her the new address when I came here, but she hasn't been yet."

"Why don't you go to her?"

"No! I've broken with that world. I can't make calls in Bryanston Square—or anywhere else. That's all over."

"Nonsense!"

"It isn't nōnsense!" exclaimed Olga, flushing angrily. "Why do you come to interfere with me? What right have you, Irene? I'm old enough to live as I please. I don't come to criticise your life!"

Irene was startled into silence for a moment. She met her cousin's look, and so gravely, so kindly, that Olga turned away in shame.

"You and I used to be friends, and to have confidence in each other," resumed Irene. "Why can't that come over again? Couldn't you tell me what it all means, dear?"

The other shook her head, keeping her eyes averted.

"My first reason for coming," Irene pursued, "was to talk to you about your mother. Do you know that she is very far from well? My father speaks very seriously of her state of health. Something is weighing on her mind, as anyone can see, and we think it can only be *you*—your strange life, and your neglect of her."

Olga shook her head.

"You're mistaken, I know you are."

"You know? Then can you tell us how to be of use to her? To speak plainly, my father fears the worst, if something isn't done."

With elbow on knee, and chin in hand, Olga sat brooding. She had a dishevelled, wild appearance; her cheeks were hollow, her eyes and lips expressed a reckless mood.

"It is not on my account," she let fall, abstractedly.

"Can you help her, Olga?"

"No one can help her," was the reply in the same dreamy tone.

Then followed a long silence. Irene gazed at one of the flaring grotesques on the wall, but did not see it.

"May I ask you a question about your own affairs?" she said at length, very gently. "It isn't for curiosity. I have a deeper interest."

"Of course you may ask, Irene. I'm behaving badly to you, but I don't mean it. I'm miserable—that's what it comes to."

"I can see that, dear. Am I right in thinking that your engagement has been broken off?"

"I'll tell you; you shall know the whole truth. It isn't broken; yet I'm sure it'll never come to anything. I don't think I want it to. He behaves so strangely. You know we were to have been married after the twelvemonth, with mother's consent. When the time drew near, I saw he didn't wish it. He said, that after all he was afraid it would be a miserable marriage for me. The trouble is, he has no character, no will. He cares for me, a great deal; and that's just why he

9

won't marry me. He'll never do anything—in art, I mean. We should have to live on mother's money, and he doesn't like that. If we had been married straight away, as I wanted, two years ago, it would have been all right. It's too late now."

"And this, you feel, is ruining your life?"

"I'm troubled about it, but more on his account than mine. I'll tell you, Irene, I want to break off, for good and all, and I'm afraid. It's a hard thing to do."

"Now I understand you. Do you think"—Irene added in another tone—"that it's well to be what they call in love with the man one marries?"

"Think? Of course I do!"

"Many people doubt it. We are told that French marriages are oftener happier than English, because it is arranged with a practical view, by experienced people."

"It depends," replied Olga, with a half-disdainful smile, "what one calls happiness. I, for one, don't want a respectable, plodding, money-saving married life. I'm not fit for it. Of course some people are."

"Then, you could never bring yourself to marry a man you merely liked—in a friendly way?"

"I think it horrible, hideous!" was the excited reply. "And yet"—her voice dropped—"it may not be so for some women. I judge only by myself."

"I suspect, Olga, that some people are never in love—never could be in that state."

"I daresay, poor things!"

Irene, though much in earnest, was moved to laugh.

"After all, you know," she said, "they have less worry."

"Of course they have, and live more useful lives, if it comes to that."

"A useful life isn't to be despised, you know."

Olga looked at her cousin; so fixedly that Irene had to turn away, and in a moment spoke as though changing the subject.

"Have you heard that Mr. Otway is coming to England again?"

"What!" cried Olga, with sudden astonishment. "You are thinking of *him*—of Piers Otway?"

Irene became the colour of the rose; her eyes flashed with annoyance.

"How extraordinary you are, Olga! As if one couldn't

mention anyone without that sort of meaning! I spoke of
Mr. Otway by pure accident. He had nothing whatever to
do with what I was saying before."

Olga sank into dulness again, murmuring, "I beg your
pardon." When a minute had elapsed in silence, she added,
without looking up, "He was dreadfully in love with you,
poor fellow. I suppose he has got over it."

An uncertain movement, a wandering look, and Miss
Derwent rose. She stood before one of the rough-washed
posters, seeming to admire it; Olga eyed her askance, with
curiosity.

"I know only one thing," Irene exclaimed abruptly, without
turning. "It's better not to think too much about all that."

"How *can* one think too much of it?" said the other.

"Very easily, I'm afraid," rejoined the other, her eyes still
on the picture.

"It's the only thing in life *worth* thinking about!"

"You astonish me. We'll agree to differ.—Olga dear,
come and see us in the old way. Come and dine this evening;
we shall be alone."

But the unkempt girl was not to be persuaded, and Irene
presently took her leave. The conversation had perturbed
her; she went away in a very unwonted frame of mind, beset
with troublesome fancies and misgivings. Olga's state seemed
to her thoroughly unwholesome, to be regarded as a warning;
it was evidently contagious; it affected the imagination with
morbid allurement. Morbid, surely; Irene would not see it
in any other light. She felt the need of protecting herself
against thoughts which had never until now given her a
moment's uneasiness. Happily she was going to lunch with
her friend Mrs. Borisoff, anything but a sentimental person.
She began to discern a possibility of taking Helen Borisoff
into her confidence. With someone she *must* talk freely;
Olga would only harm her; in Helen she might find the tonic
of sound sense which her mood demanded.

Olga Hannaford, meanwhile, finished her toilet, and, having
had no breakfast, went out a little after midday to the restaurant
in Oxford Street where she often lunched. Her walking-dress
showed something of the influence of Miss Bonnicastle; it
was more picturesque, more likely to draw the eye, than her
costume of former days. She walked, too, with an air of liberty
which marked her spiritual progress. Women glanced at her

and looked away with a toss of the head—or its more polite equivalent. Men observed her with a smile of interest; "A fine girl," was their comment, or something to that effect.

Strolling westward after her meal, intending to make a circuit by way of Edgware Road, she was near the Marble Arch when a man who had caught sight of her from the top of an omnibus alighted and hastened in her direction. At the sound of his voice, Olga paused, smiling, and gave him her hand with friendliness. He was an Italian, his name Florio; they had met several times at a house which she visited with Miss Bonnicastle. Mr. Florio had a noticeable visage, very dark of tone, eyes which at one time seemed to glow with noble emotion, and at another betrayed excessive shrewdness; heavy eyebrows and long black lashes; a nose of classical perfection; large mouth with thick and very red lips. He was dressed in approved English fashion, as a man of leisure, wore a massive watchguard across his buff summer waistcoat, and carried a silver-headed cane.

"You are taking a little walk," he said, with a very slight foreign accent. "If you will let me walk with you a little way I shall be honoured. The Park? A delightful day for the Park! Let us walk over the grass, as we may do in this free country. I have something to tell you, Miss Hannaford."

"That's nice of you, Mr. Florio. So few people tell one anything one doesn't know; but yours is sure to be real news."

"It is—I assure you it is. But, first of all, I was thinking on the 'bus—I often ride on the 'bus, it gives one ideas—I was thinking what a pity they do not use the back of the 'bus driver to display advertisements. It is a loss of space. Those men are so beautifully broad, and one looks at their backs, and there is nothing, nothing to see but an ugly coat. I shall mention my little scheme to a friend of mine, a very practical man."

Olga laughed merrily.

"Oh, you are too clever, Mr. Florio!"

"Oh, I have my little ideas. Do you know, I've just come back from Italy."

"I envy you—I mean, I envy you for having been there."

"Ah, that is your mistake, dear Miss Hannaford! That is the mistake of the romantic English young lady. Italy? Yes, there is a blue sky—not always. Yes, there are ruins that interest, if one is educated. And, there is misery, misery! Italy is a poor country, poor, poor, poor, poor." He intoned the words as if speaking his own language. "And poverty is the worst thing in the world. You make an illusion for yourself, Miss Hannaford. For a holiday when one's rich, yes, Italy is not bad—though there is fever, and there are thieves—oh, thieves! Of course! The man who is poor will steal—*ecco!* It amuses me, when the English talk of Italy."

"But you are proud of—of your memories?"

"Memories!" Mr. Florio laughed a whole melody. "One is not proud of former riches when one has become a beggar. It is you, the English, who can be proud of the past, because you can be proud of the present. You have grown free, free, free! Rich, rich, rich, ah!"

Olga laughed.

"I am sorry to say that I have not grown rich."

He bent his gaze upon her, and it glowed with tender amorousness.

"You remind me—I have something to tell you. In Italy, not everybody is quite poor. For example, my grandfather, at Bologna. I have made a visit to my grandfather. He likes me; he admires me because I have intelligence. He will not live very long, that poor grandfather."

Olga glanced at him, and met the queer calculating melancholy of his fine eyes.

"Miss Hannaford, if some day I am rich, I shall of course live in England. In what other country can one live? I shall have a house in the West End; I shall have a carriage; I shall nationalise—you say naturalise?—myself, and be an Englishman, not a beggarly Italian. And that will not be long. The poor old grandfather is weak, weak; he decays, he loses his mind; but he has made his testament, oh yes!"

The girl's look wandered about the grassy space, she was uneasy.

"Shall we turn and walk back, Mr. Florio?"

"If you wish, but slowly, slowly. I am so happy to have met you. Your company is a delight to me, Miss Hannaford. Can we not meet more often?"

"I am always glad to see you," she answered nervously.

"Good!—A thought occurs to me." He pointed to the iron fence they were approaching. "Is not that a waste? Why does not the public authority—what do you call it?—

make money of these railings? Imagine! One attaches
advertisements to the rail, metal plates, of course artistically
designed, not to spoil the Park.   They might swing in the
wind as it blows, and perhaps little bells might ring, to attract
attention.   A good idea, is it not?"

"A splendid idea," Olga answered, with a laugh.

"Ah! England is a great country!   But, Miss Hannaford,
there is one thing in which the Italian is not inferior to the
Englishman.   May I say what that is?"

"There are many things, I am sure"—

"But there is one thing—that is Love!"

Olga walked on, head bent, and Florio enveloped her in
his gaze.

"To-day I say no more, Miss Hannaford.   I had something to tell you, and I have told it.   When I have something
more to tell we shall meet—oh, I am sure we shall meet."

"You are staying in England for some time?" said Olga,
as if in ordinary conversation.

"For a little time; I come, I go.   I have, you know, my
affairs, my business.—How is your friend, the admirable artist,
the charming Miss Bonnicastle?"

"Oh, very well, always well."

"Yes, the English ladies they have wonderful health—I
admire them; but there is one I admire most of all."

A few remarks more, of like tenor, and they drew near
again to the Marble Arch.   With bows and compliments and
significant looks, Mr. Florio walked briskly away in search of
an omnibus.

Olga, her eyes cast down as she turned homeward, was not
aware that someone who had held her in sight for a long time
grew gradually near, until he stepped to her side.   It was Mr.
Kite.   He looked at her with a melancholy smile on his long,
lank face, and, when at length the girl saw him, took off his
shabby hat respectfully.   Olga nodded and walked on without
speaking, Kite accompanying her.

CHAPTER XVII

OLGA was the first to break silence.

"You ought to take your boots to be mended," she said gently. "If it rains, you'll get wet feet, and you know what that means."

"You're very kind to think of it; I will."

"You can pay for them, I hope?"

"Pay? Oh yes, yes! a trifle such as that.—Have you had a long walk?"

"I met a friend. I may as well tell you; it was the Italian, Mr. Florio."

"I saw you together," said Kite absently, but not resentfully. "I half thought of coming up to be introduced to him. But I'm rather shabby, I feared you mightn't like it."

"It wouldn't have mattered a bit, so far as I'm concerned," replied Olga good-naturedly. "But he isn't the kind of man you'd care for. If he had been, I should have got you to meet him before now."

"You like him?"

"Yes, I rather like him. But it's nothing more than that; don't imagine it.—Oh, I had a call from my cousin Irene this morning. We don't quite get on together; she's getting very worldly. Her idea is that one ought to marry cold-bloodedly, just for social advantage, and that kind of thing. No doubt she's going to do it, and then we shall never see each other again, never!—She tells me that Piers Otway is coming to England again."

"Oh, now I should like to know *him*, I really should!" exclaimed Kite, with a mild vivacity.

"So you shall, if he stays in London. Perhaps you would suit each other."

"I'm sure, because you like him so much."

"Do I?" asked Olga doubtfully. "Yes, perhaps so. If he hasn't changed for the worse. But it'll be rather irritating if he talks about nothing but Irene still. Oh, that's impossible! Five years; yes, that's impossible."

"One should think the better of him, in a way," ventured Kite.

"Oh, in a way. But when a thing of that sort is hopeless. I'm afraid Irene looks down upon him, just because—you know. But he's better than most of the men she'll meet in her drawing-rooms, that's certain. Shall I ask him to come to my place?"

"Do. And I hope he'll stay in England, and that you'll see a good deal of him."

"Pray, why?"

"Because that's the right kind of acquaintance for you, he'll do you good."

Olga laughed a little, and said, with compassionate kindness:

"You *are* queer!"

"I meant nothing unpleasant, Olga," was the apologetic rejoinder.

"Of course you didn't. Have you had dinner yet?"

"Dinner? Oh yes—of course, long ago!"

"I know what that means."

"'Sh! 'Sh! May I come home and talk a little?"

Dinner, it might be feared, was no immutable feature of Mr. Kite's day. He had a starved aspect; his long limbs were appallingly meagre; as he strode along, his clothing, thin and disreputable, flapped about him. But his countenance showed nothing whatever of sourness, or of grim endurance. Nor did he appear to be in a feeble state of health; for all his emaciation, his step was firm and he held himself tolerably upright. One thing was obvious, that at Olga's side he forgot his ills. Each time he glanced at her, a strange beautiful smile passed like a light over his hard features, a smile of infinite melancholy, yet of infinite tenderness. The voice in which he addressed her was invariably softened to express something more than homage.

They had the habit of walking side by side, and could keep silence without any feeling of restraint. Kite now and then uttered some word or ejaculation, to which Olga paid no heed; it was only his way, the trick of a man who lived much alone, and who conversed with visions.

On ascending to the room in Great Portland Street, they

found Miss Bonnicastle hard at work on a design of considerable size, which hung against the wall. This young lady, for
all her sportiveness, was never tempted to jest at the expense
of Mr. Kite; removing a charcoal holder from her mouth, she
nodded pleasantly, and stood aside to allow the melancholy
man a view of her work.

"Astonishing vigour!" said Kite, in his soft, sincere voice.
"How I envy you!"

Miss Bonnicastle laughed with self-depreciation. She, no
less than Olga Hannaford, credited Kite with wonderful
artistic powers; in their view, only his constitutional defect
of energy, his incorrigible dreaminess, stood between him and
great achievement. The evidence in support of their faith was
slight enough; a few sketches, a hint in crayon, or a wash in
water-colour, were all he had to show; but Kite belonged to
that strange order of men who, seemingly without effort or
advantage of any kind, awaken the interest and gain the confidence of certain women. Even Mrs. Hannaford, though a
mother's reasons set her against him, had felt this seductive
quality in Olga's lover, and liked though she could not approve
of him. Powers of fascination in a man very often go together
with lax principle, if not with active rascality; Kite was an
instance to the contrary. He had a quixotic sensitiveness, a
morbid instinct of honour. If it is true that virile force, prefer-
ably with a touch of the brutal, has a high place in the natural
woman's heart, none the less does an ideal of male purity, of
the masculine subdued to gentle virtues, make strong appeal
to the imagination in her sex. To the everyday man, Kite
seemed a mere pale grotesque, a creature of flabby foolishness.
But Olga Hannaford was not the only girl who had dreamed
of devoting her life to him. If she could believe his assurance
(and she all but did believe it), for her alone had he felt anything worthy to be called love, to her alone had he spoken
words of tenderness. The high-tide of her passion had long
since ebbed; yet she knew that Kite still had power over her,
power irresistible, if he chose to exercise it, and the strange
fact that he would not, that, still loving her, he did not seem
to be jealous for her love in return, often moved her to
bitterness.

She knew his story. He was the natural son of a spend-
thrift aristocrat, who, after educating him decently, had died
and left a will which seemed to assure Kite a substanial in-

dependence. Unfortunately, the will dealt, for the most part, with property no longer in existence. Kite's income was to be paid by one of the deceased's relatives, who, instead of bene- fiting largely, found that he came in for a mere pittance; and the proportion of that pittance due to the illegitimate son was exactly forty-five pounds, four shillings, and fourpence per annum. It was paid; it kept Kite alive; also, no doubt, it kept him from doing what he might have done, in art or any- thing else. On quarterly pay-day the dreamer always spent two or three pounds on gifts to those of his friends who were least able to make practical return. To Olga, of course, he had offered lordly presents, until the day when she firmly refused to take anything more from him. When his purse was empty he earned something by journeyman work in the studio of a portrait painter, a keen man of business, who gave shillings to this assistant instead of the sovereigns that another would have asked for the same labour.

As usual when he came here, Kite settled himself in a chair, stretched out his legs, let his arms depend, and so watched the two girls at work. There was not much conversation; Kite never began it. Miss Bonnicastle hummed, or whistled, or sang, generally the refrains of the music-hall; if work gave her trouble she swore vigorously — in German, a language with which she was well acquainted; and at the sound of her male- dictions, though he did not understand them, Kite always threw his head back with a silent laugh. Olga naturally had most of his attention; he often fixed his eyes upon her for five minutes at a time, and Olga, being used to this, was not at all disturbed by it.

When five o'clock came, Miss Bonnicastle flung up her arms and yawned.

"Let's have some blooming tea!" she exclaimed. "All right, I'll get it. I've just about ten times the muscle and go of you two put together; it's only right I should do the slavey."

Kite rose, and reached his hat. Whereupon, with soft pressure of her not very delicate hands, Miss Bonnicastle forced him back into his chair.

"Sit still. Do as I tell you. What's the good of you if you can't help us to drink tea?"

And Kite yielded, as always, wishing he could sit there for ever.

Three weeks later, on an afternoon of rain, the trio were

again together in the same way. Someone knocked, and a charwoman at work on the premises handed in a letter for Miss Hannaford.

"I know who this is from," said Olga, looking up at Kite.

"And I can guess," he returned, leaning forward with a look of interest.

She read the note—only a few lines, and handed it to her friend, remarking :

"He'd better come to-morrow."

"Who's that ? " asked Miss Bonnicastle.

"Piers Otway."

The poster artist glanced from one face to the other, with a smile. There had been much talk lately of Otway, who was about to begin business in London ; his partner, André Moncharmont, remaining at Odessa. Olga had heard from her mother that Piers wished to see her, and had allowed Mrs. Hannaford to give him her address ; he now wrote asking if he might call.

"I'll go and send him a wire," she said. "There isn't time to write. To-morrow's Sunday."

When Olga had run out, Kite, as if examining a poster on the wall, turned his back to Miss Bonnicastle. She, after a glance or two in his direction, addressed him by name, and the man looked round.

"You don't mind if I speak plainly ? "

"Of course I don't," he replied, his features distorted, rather than graced, by a smile.

The girl approached him, arms akimbo, but, by virtue of a frank look, suggesting more than usual of womanhood.

"You've got to be either one thing or the other. She doesn't care *that*"—a snap of the fingers—"for this man Otway, and she knows he doesn't care for her. But she's playing him against you, and you must expect more of it. You ought to make up your mind. It isn't fair to her."

"Thank you," murmured Kite, reddening a little. "It's kind of you."

"Well, I hope it is. But she'd be furious if she guessed I'd said such a thing. I only do it because it's for her good as much as yours. Things oughtn't to drag on, you know ; it isn't fair to a girl like that."

Kite thrust his hands into his pockets, and drew himself up to a full five feet eleven.

"I'll go away," he said. "I'll go and live in Paris for a bit."

"That's for *you* to decide. Of course if you feel like that —it's none of my business, I don't pretend to understand *you*; I'm not quite sure I understand *her*. You're a queer couple. All I know is, it's gone on long enough, and it isn't fair to a girl like Olga. She isn't the sort that can doze through a comfortable engagement of ten or twelve years, and surely you know that."

"I'll go away," said Kite again, nodding resolutely.

He turned again to the poster, and Miss Bonnicastle resumed her work. Thus Olga found them when she came back.

"I've asked him to come at three," she said. "You'll be out then, Bonnie. When you come in we'll put the kettle on, and all have tea." She chanted it, to the old nursery tune. "Of course you'll come as well"—she addressed Kite—"say about four. It'll be jolly!"

So, on the following afternoon, Olga sat alone, in readiness for her visitor. She had paid a little more attention than usual to her appearance, but was perfectly self-possessed; a meeting with Piers Otway had never yet quickened her pulse, and would not do so to-day. If anything, she suffered a little from low spirits, conscious of having played a rather disingenuous part before Kite, and not exactly knowing to what purpose she had done so. It still rained; it had been gloomy for several days. Looking at the heavy sky above the gloomy street, Olga had a sense of wasted life. She asked herself whether it would not have been better, on the decline of her love-fever, to go back into the so-called respectable world, share her mother's prosperity, make the most of her personal attractions, and marry as other girls did—if anyone invited her. She was doing no good; all the experience to be had in a life of mild Bohemianism was already tasted, and found rather insipid. An artist she would never become; probably she would never even support herself. To imagine herself really dependent on her own efforts, was to sink into misery and fear. The time had come for a new step, a new beginning, yet all possibilities looked so vague.

A knock at the door. She opened, and saw Piers Otway.

If they had been longing to meet, instead of scarcely ever giving a thought to each other, they could not have clasped hands with more warmth. They gazed eagerly into each other's eyes, and seemed too much overcome for ordinary words of greeting. Then Olga saw that Otway looked nothing like so well as when on his visit to England some couple of years ago. He, in turn, was surprised at the change in Olga's features; the bloom of girlhood had vanished; she was handsome, striking, but might almost have passed for a married woman of thirty.

"A queer place, isn't it?" she said, laughing, as Piers cast a glance round the room.

"Is this your work?" he asked, pointing to the posters.

"No, no! Mine isn't for exhibition. It hides itself—with the modesty of supreme excellence!"

Again they looked at each other; Olga pointed to a chair, herself became seated, and explained the conditions of her life here. Bending forward, his hands folded between his knees, Otway listened with a face on which trouble began to reassert itself after the emotion of their meeting.

"So you have really begun business at last?" said Olga.

"Yes. Rather hopefully, too."

"You don't look hopeful, somehow."

"Oh, that's nothing. Moncharmont has scraped together a fair capital, and as for me, well, a friend has come to my help, I mustn't say who it is. Yes, things look promising enough, for a start. Already I've seen an office in the City, which I think I shall take. I shall decide to-morrow, and then— *avos !*"

"What does that mean?"

"A common word in Russian. It means 'Fire away.'"

"I must remember it," said Olga, laughing. "It'll make a change from English and French slang—*Avos !*"

There was a silence longer than they wished. Olga broke it by asking abruptly:

"Have you seen my mother?"

"Not yet."

"I'm afraid she's not well."

"Then why do you keep away from her?" said Piers, with good-humoured directness. "Is it really necessary for you to live here? She would be much happier if you went back."

"I'm not sure of that."

"But I am, from what she says in her letters, and I should have thought that you, too, would prefer it to this life."

He glanced round the room. Olga looked vexed, and spoke with a note of irony.

"My tastes are unaccountable, I'm afraid. You, no doubt, find it difficult to understand them. So does my cousin Irene. You have heard that she is going to be married?"

Piers, surprised at her change of tone, regarded her fixedly, until she reddened and her eyes fell.

"Is the engagement announced, then?"

"I should think so; but I'm not much in the way of hearing fashionable gossip."

Still Piers regarded her; still her cheeks kept their colour, and her eyes refused to meet his.

"I see I have offended you," he said quietly. "I'm very sorry. Of course I went too far in speaking like that of the life you have chosen. I had no right"—

"Nonsense! If you mustn't tell me what you think, who may?"

Again the change was so sudden, this time from coldness to smiling familiarity, that Piers felt embarrassed.

"The fact is," Olga pursued, with a careless air, "I don't think I shall go on with this much longer. If you said what you have in your mind, that I should never be any good as an artist, you would be quite right. I haven't had the proper training; it'll all come to nothing. And—talking of engagements—I daresay you know that mine is broken off?"

"No, I didn't know that."

"It is. Mr. Kite and I are only friends now. He'll look in presently, I think. I should like you to meet him, if you don't mind."

"Of course I shall be very glad."

"All this, you know," said Olga, with a laugh, "would be monstrously irregular in decent society, but decent society is often foolish, don't you think?"

"To be sure it is," Piers answered genially, "and I never meant to find fault with your preference for a freer way of living. It is only—you say I may speak freely—that I didn't like to think of your going through needless hardships."

"You don't think, then, it has done me good?"

"I am not at all sure of that."

Olga lay back in her chair, as if idly amused.

"You see," she said, "how we have both changed. We are both much more positive, in different directions. To be sure, it makes conversation more interesting. But the change is greatest in me. You always aimed at success in a respectable career."

Otway looked puzzled, a little disconcerted.

"Really, is that how I always struck you? To me it's new light on my own character."

"How did you think of yourself, then?" she asked, looking at him from beneath drooping lids.

"I hardly know; I have thought less on that subject than on most."

Again there came a silence, long enough to be embarrassing. Then Olga took up a sketch that was lying on the table, and held it to her visitor.

"Don't you think that good? It's one of Miss Bonnicastle's. Let us talk about her; she'll be here directly. We don't seem to get on, talking about ourselves."

The sketch showed an elephant sitting upright, imbibing with gusto from a bottle of some much-advertised tonic. Piers broke into a laugh. Other sketches were exhibited, and thus they passed the time until Miss Bonnicastle and Kite arrived together.

CHAPTER XVIII

STRANGERS with whom Piers Otway had business at this time saw in him a young man of considerable energy, though rather nervous and impulsive, capable in all that concerned his special interests, not over-sanguine, inclined to brevity of speech, and scrupulously courteous in a cold way. He seldom smiled; his clean-cut, intelligent features expressed tension of the whole man, ceaseless strain and effort without that joy of combat which compensates physical expenditure. He looked in fair, not robust, health; a shadowed pallor of complexion was natural to him, and made noticeable the very fine texture of his skin, which quickly betrayed in delicate flushes any strong feeling. He shook hands with a short, firm grip which argued more muscle than one might have supposed in him. His walk was rapid; his bearing upright; his glance direct, with something of apprehensive pride. The observant surmised a force more or less at odds with the facts of life. Shrewd men of commerce at once perceived his qualities, but reserved their judgment as to his chances; he was not, in any case, altogether of their world, however well he might have studied its principles and inured himself to its practice.

He took rooms in Guilford Street. Indifferent to locality, asking nothing more than decency in his immediate surroundings, he fell by accident on the better kind of lodging-house, and was at once what is called comfortable; his landlady behaved to him with a peculiar respectfulness, often noticeable in the uneducated who had relations with Otway, and explained perhaps by his quiet air of authority. To those who served him, no man was more considerate, but he never became familiar with them; without a trace of pretentiousness in his demeanour, he was viewed by such persons as one sensibly above them, with some solid right to rule.

In the selection of his place of business, he of course

exercised more care, but here, too, luck favoured him. A Russian merchant moving into more spacious quarters ceded to him a small office in Fenchurch Street, with furniture which he purchased at a very reasonable price. To begin with, he hired only a lad; it would be seen in a month or so whether he had need of more assistance. If business grew, he was ready to take upon himself a double share, for the greater his occupation the less his time for brooding. Labour was what he asked, steady, dogged toil; and his only regret was that he could not work with his hands in the open air, at some day-long employment followed by hunger and weariness and dreamless sleep.

The partner whose name he did not wish to mention was John Jacks. Very soon after learning the result to the young man of Jerome Otway's death (the knowledge came in an indirect way half a year later), Mr. Jacks wrote to Piers, a letter implying what he knew, and made offer of a certain capital towards the proposed business. Piers did not at once accept the offer, for difficulties had arisen on the side of his friend Moncharmont, who, on Otway's announcement of inability to carry out the scheme they had formed together, turned in another direction. A year passed; John Jacks again wrote; and, Moncharmont's other projects having come to nothing, the friends decided at length to revert to their original plan, with the difference that a third partner supplied capital equal to that which Moncharmont himself put into the venture. The arrangement was strictly business-like; John Jacks, for all his kindliness, had no belief in anything else where money was concerned, and Piers Otway would not have listened to any other sort of suggestion. Piers put into the affair only his brains, his vigour, and his experience; he was to reap no reward but that fairly resulting from the exercise of these qualities.

Only a day or two before leaving Odessa he received a letter from Mrs. Hannaford, in which she hinted that Irene Derwent was likely to marry. On reaching London, he found at the hotel her answer to his reply; she now named Miss Derwent's wooer, and spoke as if the marriage were practically a settled thing. This turned to an ordeal for Piers what would otherwise have been a pleasure, his call upon John Jacks. He had to dine at Queen's Gate; he had to converse with Arnold Jacks; and for the first time in his life he knew the meaning of personal jealousy.

The sight of Irene's successful lover made active in him what had for years been only a latent passion. All at once it seemed impossible that he should have lost what hitherto he had scarcely ever felt it possible to win. An unconsciously reared edifice of hope collapsed about him, laid waste his life, left him standing in desolate revolt against fate. Arnold Jacks was the embodiment of a cruel destiny; Piers regarded him, not so much with hate, as with a certain bitter indignation. He had no desire to disparage the man, to caricature his assailable points; rather, in undiminished worship of Irene, he exaggerated the qualities which had won her, the power to which her gallant pride had yielded. These qualities, that power, were so unlike anything in himself, that they gave boundless scope to a jealous imagination. He knew so little of the man, of his pursuits, his society, his prospects or ambitions. But he could not imagine that Irene's love would be given to any man of ordinary type; there must be a nobility in John Jacks' son, and indeed, knowing the father, one could readily believe it. Piers suffered a cruel sense of weakness, of littleness, by comparison.

And Arnold behaved so well to him, with such frank graceful courtesy; to withhold the becoming return was to feel oneself a shrinking creature, basely envious.

It was at Mrs. Hannaford's suggestion that he asked to be allowed to call on Olga. A few days later, having again exchanged letters with Irene's aunt, he sat writing in the office after business hours, his door and that of the ante-room both open. Footsteps on the staircase had become infrequent since the main exodus of clerks; he listened whenever there was a sound, and looked towards the entrance. There, at length, appeared a lady, Mrs. Hannaford herself. Piers went forward, and greeted her without words, motioning her with his hand into the inner office; the outer door he latched.

"So I have tracked you to your lair!" exclaimed the visitor, with a nervous laugh, as she sank in fatigue upon the chair he placed for her. "I looked for your name on the wall downstairs, forgetting that you are Moncharmont & Co."

"It is very, very kind of you to have taken all this trouble!"

He saw in her face the signs of ill-health for which he was prepared, and noticed with pain her tremulousness and shortness of breath after the stair-climbing. The friendship which had existed between them since his boyhood was true and deep as ever; Piers Otway could, as few men can, be the loyal friend of a woman. A reverent tenderness coloured his feeling towards Mrs. Hannaford; it was something like what he would have felt for his mother had she now been living. He did not give much thought to her character or circumstances; she had always been kind to him, and he in turn had always liked her: that was enough. Anything in her service that might fall within his power to do, he would do right gladly.

"So you saw poor Olga?"

"Yes, and the friend she lives with—and Mr. Kite."

"Ah! Mr. Kite!" The speaker's face brightened. "I have news about him; it came this morning. He has gone to Paris, and means to stay there."

"Indeed! I heard no syllable of that the other day."

"But it is true. And Olga's letter to me, in which she mentions it, gives hope that that is the end of their engagement. Naturally, the poor child won't say it in so many words, but it is to be read between the lines. What's more, she is willing to come for her holiday with me! It has made me very happy!—I told you I was going to Malvern; my brother thinks that is most likely to do me good. Irene will go down with me, and stay a day or two, and then I hope to have Olga. It is delightful! I hadn't dared to hope. Perhaps we shall really come together again, after this dreary time!"

Piers was listening, but with a look which had become uneasily preoccupied.

"I am as glad, almost, as you can be," he said. "Malvern, I never was there."

"So healthy, my brother says! And Shakespeare's country, you know; we shall go to Stratford, which I have never seen. I have a feeling that I really shall get better. Everything is more hopeful."

Piers recalled Olga's mysterious hints about her mother. Glancing at the worn face, with its vivid eyes, he could easily conceive that this ill-health had its cause in some grave mental trouble.

"Have you met your brother?" she asked.

"My brother? Oh no!" was the careless reply. Then, on a sudden thought, Piers added, "You don't keep up your acquaintance with him, do you?"

"Oh—I *have* seen him—now and then"—

There was a singular hesitancy in her answer to the abrupt question. Piers, preoccupied as he was, could not but remark Mrs. Hannaford's constraint, almost confusion. At once it struck him that Daniel had been borrowing money of her, and the thought aroused strong indignation. His own hundred and fifty pounds he had never recovered, for all Daniel's fine speeches, and notwithstanding the fact that he had taken suggestive care to let the borrower know his address in Russia. Rapidly he turned in his mind the question whether he ought not to let Mrs. Hannaford know of Daniel's untrustworthiness; but before he could decide, she launched into another subject.

"So this is to be your place of business? Here you will sit day after day. If good wishes could help, how you would flourish! Is it orthodox to pray for a friend's success in business?"

"Why not? Provided you add—so long as he is guilty of no rascality."

"That, *you* will never be."

"Why, to tell you the truth, I shouldn't know how to go about it. Not everyone who wishes becomes a rascal in business. It's difficult enough for me to pursue commerce on the plain, honest track; knavery demands an expertness altogether beyond me. Wherefore, let us give thanks for my honest stupidity!"

They chatted a while of these things. Then Piers, grasping his courage, uttered what was burning within him.

"When is Miss Derwent to be married?"

Mrs. Hannaford's eyes escaped his hard look. She murmured that no date had yet been settled.

"Tell me—I beg you will tell me—is her engagement absolutely certain?"

"I feel sure it is."

"No! I want more than that. Do you *know* that it is?"

"I can only say that her father believes it to be a certain thing. No announcement has yet been made."

"H'm! Then it isn't settled at all."

Piers sat stiffly upon his chair. He held an ivory paper-knife, which he kept bending across his knee, and of a sudden the thing snapped in two. But he paid no attention, merely flinging the handle away. Mrs. Hannaford looked him in the face; he was deeply flushed; his lips and his throat trembled like those of a child on the point of tears.

"Don't! Oh, don't take it so to heart! It seems impossible—after all this time"—

"Impossible or not, it *is*!" he replied impetuously. "Mrs. Hannaford, you will do something for me. You will let me come down to Malvern, whilst she is with you, and see her—speak with her alone."

She drew back, astonished.

"Oh! how can you think of it, Mr. Otway?"

"Why should I not?" he spoke in a low and soft voice, but with vehemence. "Does she know all about me?"

"Everything. It was not I who told her. There has been talk"—

"Of course there has"—he smiled—"and I am glad of it. I wished her to know. Otherwise, I should have told her. Yes, I should have told her! It shocks you, Mrs. Hannaford? But try to understand what this means to me. It is the one thing I greatly desire in all the world; shall I be hindered by a petty consideration of etiquette? A wild desire—you think. Well, the man sentenced to execution clings to life, clings to it with a terrible fierce desire; is it less real because utterly hopeless? Perhaps I am behaving frantically; I can't help myself. As that engagement is still doubtful—you admit it to be doubtful—I shall speak before it is too late. Why not have done so before? Simply, I hadn't the courage. I suppose I was too young. It didn't mean so much to me as it does now. Something tells me to act like a man, before it is too late. I feel I *can* do it. I never could have, till now."

"But listen to me—do listen! Think how extraordinary it will seem to her. She has no suspicion of"—

"She has! She knows! I sent her, a year ago, a poem—some verses of my writing, which told her."

Mrs. Hannaford kept silence with a face of distress.

"Is there any harm," he pursued, "in asking you whether she has ever spoken of me lately—since that time?"

"She has," admitted the other reluctantly, "but not in a way to make one think"—

"No, no! I expected nothing of the kind. She has mentioned me; that is enough. I am not utterly expelled from her thoughts, as a creature outlawed by all decent people"—

"Of course not. She is too reasonable and kind."

"That she is!" exclaimed Piers, with a passionate delight on his visage and in his voice. "And she would *rather* I spoke to her—I feel she would! She, with her fine intelligence and noble heart, she would think it dreadful that a man did not dare to approach her, just because of something not his fault, something that made him no bit the less a man, and capable of honour. I know that thought would shake her with pity and indignation. So far I can read in her. What! You think I know her too little? And the thought of her never out of my mind for these five years! I have got to know her better and better, as time went on. Every word she spoke at Ewell stayed in my memory, and by perpetual repetition has grown into my life. Every sentence has given me its full meaning. I didn't need to be near her, to study her. She was in my mind; I heard her and saw her whenever I wished; as I have grown older and more experienced in life, I have been better able to understand her. I used to think this was enough. I had—you know—that exalted sort of mood; Dante's Beatrice, and all that! It *was* enough for the time, seeing that I lived with it, and through it. But now—no! And there is no single reason why I should be ashamed to stand before her, and tell her that—what I feel."

He checked himself, and gloomed for an instant, then continued in another tone:

"Yet that isn't true. There *are* reasons — I believe no man living could say that when speaking of such a woman as Irene Derwent. I cannot face her without shame—the shame of every man who stands before a pure-hearted girl. We have to bear that, and to hide it as best we can."

The listener bent upon him a wondering gaze, and seemed unable to avert it, till his look answered her.

"You will give me this opportunity, Mrs. Hannaford?" he added pleadingly.

" I have no right whatever to refuse it. Besides, how could I, if I wished ? "

" When shall I come? I must remember that I am not free to wander about. If it could be a Sunday "—

"I have forgotten something I ought to have told you already," said Mrs. Hannaford. "Whilst she was on her travels, Irene had an offer from someone else."

Piers laughed.

" Can that surprise one? Should I wonder if I were told she had had fifty ? "

" Yes, but this was not of the ordinary kind. You know that Mr. Jacks is well acquainted with Trafford Romaine. And it was Trafford Romaine himself."

The news did not fail of its impression. Piers smiled vaguely, and on the smile came a look of troubled pride.

" Well, it is not astonishing, but it gives me a better opinion of the man. I shall always feel a sort of sympathy when I come across his name. Why did you think I ought to know ? "

" For a reason I feel to be rather foolish, now I come to speak of it," replied Mrs. Hannaford. " But—I had a feeling that Irene is by nature rather ambitious ; and if, after such an experience as that, she so soon accepts a man who has done nothing particular, whose position is not brilliant "—

" I understand. She must, you mean, be very strongly drawn to him. But then I needed no such proof of her feeling—if it is *certain* that she is going to marry him. Could I imagine her marrying a man for any reason but one ? Surely you could not ? "

" No—no "—

The denial had a certain lack of emphasis. Otway's eyes flashed.

" You doubt? You speak in that way of Irene Derwent ? "

Gazing into Mrs. Hannaford's face, he saw rising tears. She gave a little laugh, which did not disguise her emotion as she answered him.

" Oh, what an idealist it makes a man !—don't talk of your unworthiness. If some women are good, it is because they try hard to be what the best men think them. No, no, I have no doubts of Irene. And that is why it really grieves me to see you still hoping. She would never have gone so far "—

"But there's the very question!" cried Piers excitedly. "Who knows how far she has gone? It may be the merest conjecture on your part, and her father's. People are so ready to misunderstand a girl who respects herself enough to be free and frank in her association with men.—Let me shame myself by making a confession. Five years ago, when I all but went mad about her, I was contemptible enough to think she had treated me cruelly." He gave a scornful laugh. "You know what I mean. At Ewell, when I lived only for my books, and she drew me away from them. Conceited idiot! And she so bravely honest, so simple and direct, so human! Was it *her* fault if I lost my head?"

"She certainly changed the whole course of your life," said Mrs. Hannaford thoughtfully.

"True, she did. And to my vast advantage! What should I have become? A clerkship at Whitehall — heaven defend us! At best a learned pedant, in my case. She sent me out into the world, where there is always hope. She gave me health and sanity. Above all, she set before me an ideal which has never allowed me to fall hopelessly—never will let me become a contented brute! If she never addresses another word to me, I shall owe her an infinite debt as long as I live. And I want her to hear that from my own lips, if only once."

Mrs. Hannaford held out her hand impulsively.

"Do what you feel you must. You make me feel very strangely. I never knew what"—

Her voice faltered. She rose.

When she had left him, Piers sat for some time communing with his thoughts. Then he went home to the simple meal he called dinner, and afterwards, as the evening was clear, walked for a couple of hours away from the louder streets. His resolve gave him a night of quiet rest.

CHAPTER XIX

AGAIN Irene was going down into Cheshire, to visit the two old ladies, her relatives. It was arranged that she should accompany Mrs. Hannaford to Malvern, and spend a couple of days there. The travellers arrived on a Friday evening. Before leaving town Mrs. Hannaford had written to Piers Otway to give him the address of the house at Malvern in which rooms had been taken for them.

On Saturday morning there was sunshine over the hills. Irene walked, and talked, but it was evident with thoughts elsewhere. When they sat down to rest and to enjoy the landscape before them, the rich heart of England, with its names that echo in history and in song, Irene plucked at the grass beside her, and presently began to strip a stem, after the manner of children playing at a tell-fortune game. She stripped it to the end; her hands fell and she heaved a little sigh. From that moment she grew merry and talked without preoccupation.

After lunch she wrote a short letter, and herself took it to the post. Mrs. Hannaford was lying on the sofa, with eyes closed, but not in sleep; her forehead and lips betraying the restless thoughts which beset her now as always. On returning, Irene took a chair, as if to read; but she gave only an absent glance at the paper in her hands, and smiled to herself in musing.

"I'm sure those thoughts are worth far more than a penny," fell from the lady on the couch, who had observed her for a moment.

"I may as well tell you them," was the gently toned reply, as Irene bent forward. "I have just done something decisive."

Mrs. Hannaford raised herself, a sudden anxiety in her features; she waited.

"You guess, aunt? Yes, that's it, I have written to Mr. Jacks."

" To—to— ? "

" To answer an ultimatum. In the right way, I hope ; any way, it's done."

" You have accepted him ? "

" Even so."

Mrs. Hannaford tried to smile, but could not smooth away the uneasiness which had come into her look. She spoke a few of the natural words, and in doing so looked at the clock.

" There is something I have forgotten," she said, starting to her feet hurriedly. " You reminded me of it — speaking of a letter; I must send a telegram at once—indeed I must. No, no, I will go myself, dear. I had rather ! "

She hastened away, leaving Irene in wonder.

When they were together again, Mrs. Hannaford seemed anxious to atone for her brevity on the all-important subject. She spoke with pleasure of her niece's decision; thought it wise; abounded in happy prophecy; through the rest of the day she had a face which spoke relief, all but contentment. The morning of Sunday saw her nervous. She made an excuse of the slightly clouded sky for lingering within doors; she went often to the window and looked this way and that along the road, as if judging of weather, until Irene, when the church bells had ceased, grew impatient for the open air.

" Yes, we will go," said her aunt. " I think we safely may."

Each went to her room to make ready. At Mrs. Hannaford's door, just as she was about to come forth, there sounded a knock; the servant announced that a gentleman had called to see her—Mr. Otway. Quivering, death-pale, she ran to the sitting-room. Irene had not yet reappeared. Piers Otway stood there alone.

" You didn't get my telegram ? " broke from her lips, in a hurried whisper. " Oh ! I feared it would be too late, and all is too late."

" You mean "—

" The engagement is announced."

She had time to say no more. At that moment Irene entered the room, dressed for walking. At first she did not seem to recognise the visitor, then her face lighted up; she smiled, subdued the slight embarrassment which had succeeded to her perplexity, and stepped quickly forward.

" Mr. Otway ! You are staying here ? "

" A few hours only. I came down yesterday on business—which is finished."

His voice was so steady, his bearing so self-possessed, that Irene found herself relieved from the immediate restraint of the situation. She could not quite understand his presence here ; there was a mystery, in which she saw that her aunt was involved ; the explanation might be forthcoming after their visitor's departure. For the moment, enough to remark that the sun was dispersing the clouds, and that all were ready to enjoy a walk. Mrs. Hannaford, glancing anxiously at Irene before she spoke, hoped that Mr. Otway would return with them to lunch ; Irene added her voice to the invitation ; and Piers at once accepted.

Talk suggested by the locality occupied them until they were away from the houses ; by that time Irene had thoroughly reassured herself, and was as tranquil in mind as in manner. Whatever the meaning of Piers Otway's presence, no difficulty could come about in the few hours he was to spend with them. Involuntarily she found herself listening to the rhythm of certain verses which she had received some months ago, and which she still knew by heart ; but nothing in the author's voice or look indicated a desire to remind her of that romantic passage in their acquaintance. If they were still to meet from time to time—and why not ?—common sense must succeed to vain thoughts in the poet's mind. He was quite capable of the transition, she felt sure. His way of talking, the short and generally pointed sentences in which he spoke on whatever subject, betokened a habit of lucid reflection. Had it been permissible, she would have dwelt with curiosity on the problem of Piers Otway's life and thoughts ; but that she resolutely ignored, strong in the irrevocable choice which she had made only yesterday. He was interesting, but not to her. She knew him on the surface, and cared to know no more.

Business was a safe topic ; at the first noticeable pause, Irene led to it.

Piers laughed with pleasure as he began to describe André Moncharmont. A man of the happiest vivacity, of the sweetest humour, irresistibly amusing, yet never ridiculous — entirely competent in business, yet with a soul as little mercantile as man's could be. Born a French Swiss, he had lived a good deal in Italy, and had all the charm of Italian manners ; but in whatever country, he made himself at home, and by virtue of his sunny temper saw only the best in each nationality. His recreation was music, and he occasionally composed.

"There is a song of Musset's — you know it, perhaps— beginning ' *Quand on perd, par triste occurrence* '—which he has set, to my mind, perfectly. I want him to publish it. If he does I must let you see it."

Irene did not know the verses, and made no remark.

"There are English men of business," pursued Otway, " who would smile with pity at Moncharmont. He is by no means their conception of the merchant. Yet the world would be a vastly better place if its business were often in the hands of such men. He will never make a large fortune, no ; but he will never fall into poverty. He sees commerce from the human point of view, not as the brutal pitiless struggle which justifies every form of ferocity and of low cunning. I never knew him utter an ignoble thought about trade and money-making. An English acquaintance asked me once, ' Is he a gentleman ?' I was obliged to laugh — delicious contrast between what *he* meant by a gentleman and all I see in Moncharmont."

"I picture him," said Irene, smiling, "and I picture the person who made that inquiry."

Piers flashed a look of gratitude. He had, as yet, hardly glanced at her ; he durst not ; his ordeal was to be gone through as became a man. Her voice, at moments, touched him to a sense of faintness ; he saw her without turning his head ; the wave of her dress beside him was like a perfume, was like music ; part of him yielded, languished, part made splendid resistance.

"He is a lesson in civilisation. If trade is not to put an end to human progress, it must be pursued in Moncharmont's spirit. It's only returning to a better time ; our man of business is a creation of our century, and as bad a thing as it has produced. Commerce must be humanised once more. We invented machinery, and it has enslaved us—a rule of iron, the servile belief that money-making is an end in itself, to be attained by hard selfishness."

He checked himself, laughed, and said something about the beauty of the lane along which they were walking.

"Don't you think," fell from Irene's lips, "that Mr. John Jacks is a very human type of the man of business ? "

"Indeed he is ! " replied Piers, with spirit. "An admirable type."

" I have been told that he owed most of his success to his brothers, who are a different sort of men."

" His wealth, perhaps."

" Yes, there's a difference," said Irene, glancing at him. " You may be successful without becoming wealthy; though not of course in the common opinion. But what would have been the history of England these last fifty years, but for our men of iron selfishness? Isn't it a fact that only in this way could we have built up an Empire which ensures the civilisation of the world?"

Piers could not answer with his true thought, for he knew all that was implied in her suggestion of that view. He bent his head and spoke very quietly.

"Some of our best men think so."

An answer which gratified Irene more keenly than he imagined; she showed it in her face.

When they returned to luncheon, and the ladies went upstairs, Mrs. Hannaford stepped into her niece's room.

"What you told me yesterday," she asked, in a nervous undertone, "may it be repeated?"

" Certainly—to anyone."

"Then please not to come down until I have had a few minutes' talk with Mr. Otway. All this shall be explained, dear, when we are alone again."

On entering the sitting-room Irene found it harder to pre- serve a natural demeanour than at her meeting with the visitor a couple of hours ago. Only when she had heard him speak and in just the same voice as during their walk, was she able to turn frankly towards him. His look had not changed. Impossible to divine the thoughts hidden by his smile; he bore himself with perfect control.

At table all was cheerfulness. Speaking of things Russian, Irene recalled her winter in Finland, which she had so greatly enjoyed.

"I remember," said Otway, "you had just returned when I met you for the first time."

It was said with a peculiar intonation, which fell agreeably on the listener's ear; a note familiar, in the permitted degree, yet touchingly respectful; a world of emotion subdued to graceful friendliness. Irene passed over the reminiscence with a light word or two, and went on to gossip merely of trifles.

"Do you like caviare, Mr. Otway?"

"Except perhaps that supplied by the literary censor," was his laughing reply.

"Now I am *intriguée.* Please explain."

"We call caviare the bits blacked out in our newspapers and periodicals."

"Unpalatable enough!" laughed Irene. "How angry that would make me!"

"I got used to it," said Piers, "and thought it rather good fun sometimes. After all, a wise autocrat might well prohibit newspapers altogether, don't you think? They have done good, I suppose, but they are just as likely to do harm. When the next great war comes, newspapers will be the chief cause of it. And for mere profit, that's the worst. There are newspaper proprietors in every country, who would slaughter half mankind for the pennies of the half who were left, without caring a fraction of a penny whether they had preached war for a truth or a lie."

"But doesn't a newspaper simply echo the opinions and feelings of its public?"

"I'm afraid it manufactures opinion, and stirs up feeling. Consider how very few people know or care anything about most subjects of international quarrel. A mere handful at the noisy centre of things who make the quarrel. The business of newspapers, in general, is to give a show of importance to what has no real importance at all—to prevent the world from living quietly—to arouse bitterness when the natural man would be quite·indifferent."

"Oh, surely you paint them too black! We must live, we can't let the world stagnate. Newspapers only express the natural life of peoples, acting and interacting."

"I suppose I quarrel with them," said Piers, once more subduing himself, "because they have such gigantic power and don't make anything like the best use of it."

"That is to say, they are the work of men—I don't mean," Irene added laughingly, "of men instead of women. Though I'm not sure that women wouldn't manage journalism better, if it were left to them."

"A splendid idea! All men to go about their affairs and women to report and comment. Why, it would solve every problem of society! There's the hope of the future, beyond a doubt! Why did I never think of it!"

The next moment Piers was talking about nightingales, how he had heard them sing in Little Russia, where their song is sweeter than in any other part of Europe. And so the meal passed pleasantly, as did the hour or two after it, until it was time for Otway to take leave.

" You travel straight back to London ? " asked Irene.

" Straight back," he answered, his eyes cast down.

" To-morrow," said Mrs. Hannaford, " we think of going to Stratford."

Piers had an impulse which made his hands tremble and his head throb; in spite of himself he had all but asked whether, if he stayed at Malvern overnight, he might accompany them on that expedition. Reason prevailed, but only just in time, and the conquest left him under a gloomy sense of self-pity, which was the worst thing he had suffered all day. Not even Mrs. Hannaford's whispered words on his arrival had been so hard to bear.

He sat in silence, wishing to rise, unable to do so. When at length he stood up, Irene let her eyes fall upon him, and continued to observe him, as if but half consciously, whilst he shook hands with Mrs. Hannaford. He turned to her, and his lips moved, but what he had tried to say went unexpressed. Nor did Irene speak; she could have uttered only a civil commonplace, and the tragic pallor of his countenance in that moment kept her mute. He touched her hand and was gone.

When the house door had closed behind him, the eyes of the two women met. Standing as before, they conversed with low voices, with troubled brows. Mrs. Hannaford rapidly explained her part in what had happened.

" You will forgive me, Irene ? I see now that I ought to have told you about it yesterday."

" Better as it was, perhaps, so far as I am concerned. But he—I'm sorry "—

" He behaved well, don't you think ? "

" Yes," replied Irene thoughtfully, slowly, " he behaved well."

They moved apart, and Irene laid her hand on a book, but did not sit down.

" How old is he ? " she asked of a sudden.

" Six-and-twenty."

" One would take him for more. But of course his ways of thinking show how young he is." She fluttered the pages of her book, and smiled. "It will be interesting to see him in another five years."

That was all. Neither mentioned Otway's name again during the two more days they spent together.

But Irene's mind was busy with the contrast between him and Arnold Jacks. She pursued this track of thought whithersoever it led her, believing it a wholesome exercise in her present mood. Her choice was made, and irrevocable; reason bade her justify it by every means that offered. And she persuaded herself that nothing better could have happened, at such a juncture, than this suggestion of an alternative so widely different.

An interesting boy—six-and-twenty is still a boyish age—with all sorts of vague idealisms; nothing ripe; nothing that convinced; a dreary cosmopolite, little likely to achieve results in any direction. On the other hand, a mature and vigorous man, English to the core, stable in his tested views of life, already an active participant in the affairs of the nation and certain to move victoriously onward; a sure patriot, a sturdy politician. It was humiliating to Piers Otway. Indeed, unfair!

On Monday, when she returned from her visit to Stratford, a telegram awaited her. "Thank you, letter to-morrow, Arnold." That pleased her; the British laconicism; the sensible simplicity of the thing! And when the letter arrived (two pages and a half) it seemed a suitable reply to hers of Saturday, in which she had used only everyday words and phrases. No gushing in Arnold Jacks! He was "happy," he was "grateful"; what more need an honest man say to the woman who has accepted him? She was his "Dearest Irene"; and what more could she ask to be?

A curious thing happened that evening. Mrs. Hannaford and her niece, both tired after the day's excursion, and having already talked over its abundant interests, sat reading, or pretending to read. Suddenly, Irene threw her book aside, with a movement of impatience, and stood up.

"Don't you find it very close?" she said, almost irritably. "I shall go upstairs. Good-night!"

Her aunt gazed at her in surprise.

"You are tired, my dear."

"I suppose I am.—Aunt, there is something I should like to say, if you will let me. You are very kind and good, but that makes you, sometimes, a little indiscreet. Promise me, please, never to make me the subject of conversation with anyone to whom you cannot speak of me quite openly, before all the world."

Mrs. Hannaford was overcome with astonishment, with distress. She tried to reply, but before she could shape a word Irene had swept from the room.

When they met again at breakfast, the girl stepped up to her aunt and kissed her on both cheeks—an unusual greeting. She was her bright self again; talked merrily; read aloud a letter from her father, which proved that at the time of writing he had not seen Arnold Jacks.

"I must write to the Doctor to-morrow," she said, with an air of reflection.

At ten o'clock they drove to the station. While Miss Derwent took her ticket Mrs. Hannaford walked on the platform. On issuing from the booking-office, Irene saw her aunt in conversation with a man, who, in the same moment, turned abruptly and walked away. Neither she nor her aunt spoke of this incident, but Irene noticed that the other was a little flushed.

She took her seat; Mrs. Hannaford stood awaiting the departure of the train. Before it moved, the man Irene had noticed came back along the platform, and passed them without a sign. Irene saw his face, and seemed to recognise it, but could not remember who he was.

Half an hour later, the face came back to her, and with it a name.

"Daniel Otway!" she exclaimed to herself.

It was five years and more since her one meeting with him at Ewell, but the man, on that occasion, had impressed her strongly in a very disagreeable way. She had since heard of him, in relation to Piers Otway's affairs, and knew that her aunt had received a call from him in Bryanston Square. What could be the meaning of this incident on the platform? Irene wondered, and had an unpleasant feeling about it.

CHAPTER XX

ON the journey homeward, and for two or three days after, Piers held argument with his passions, trying to persuade himself that he had in truth lost nothing, inasmuch as his love had never been founded upon a reasonable hope. Irene Derwent was neither more nor less to him now than she had been ever since he first came to know her: a far ideal, the woman he would fain call wife, but only in a dream could think of winning. What audacity had speeded him on that wild expedition? It was well that he had been saved from declaring his folly to Irene herself, who would have shared the pain her answer inflicted. Nay, when the moment came, reason surely would have checked his absurd impulse. In seeing her once more, he saw how wide was the distance between them. No more of that! He had lost nothing but a moment's illusion.

The ideal remained; the worship, the gratitude. How much she had been to him! Rarely a day—very rarely a day—that the thought of Irene did not warm his heart and exalt his ambition. He had yielded to the fleshly impulse, and the measure of his lapse was the sincerity of that nobler desire; he had not the excuse of the ordinary man, nor ever tried to allay his conscience with facile views of life. What times innumerable had he murmured her name, until it was become to him the only woman's name that sounded in truth womanly—all others cold to his imagination. What long evenings had he passed, yonder by the Black Sea, content merely to dream of Irene Derwent; how many a summer night had he wandered in the acacia-planted streets of Odessa, about and about the great square, with its trees, where stands the cathedral; how many a time had his heart throbbed all but to bursting when he listened to the music on the Boulevard, and felt so terribly alone — alone! Irene was England. He knew nothing of the patriotism which is but shouted politics ; from his earliest years of intelligence he had learnt, listening to his father, a contempt for that loud narrowness ; but the tongue which was Irene's, the landscape where shone Irene's figure—these were dear to him for Irene's sake. He believed in his heart of hearts that only the Northern Island could boast the perfect woman—because he had found her there.

Should he talk of loss—he who had gained so unspeakably by an ideal love through the hot years of his youth, who to the end of his life would be made better by it ? That were the basest ingratitude. Irene owed him nothing, yet had enriched him beyond calculation. He did not love her less ; she was the same power in his life. This sinking of the heart, this menace of gloom and rebellion, was treachery to his better self. He fought manfully against it.

Circumstances were unfavourable to such a struggle. Work, absorption in the day's duty, well and good ; but when work and duty led one into the City of London !

At first, he had found excitement in the starting of his business ; so much had to be done, so many points to be debated and decided, so many people to be seen and conversed with, contended with ; it was all an exhilarating effort of mind and body. He felt the joy of combat ; sped to the City like any other man, intent on holding his own amid the furious welter, seeing a delight in the computation of his chances ; at once a fighter and a gambler, like those with whom he rubbed shoulders in the roaring ways. He overtaxed his energy, and in any case there must have come reaction. It came with violence soon after that day at Malvern.

The weather was hot ; one should have been far away from these huge rampart-streets, these stifling burrows of commerce. But here toil and stress went on as usual, and Piers Otway saw it all in a lurid light. These towering edifices with inscriptions numberless, announcing every imaginable form of trade with every corner of the world ; here a vast building, consecrate in all its commercial magnificence, great windows and haughty doorways, the gleam of gilding and of brass, the lustre of polished woods, to a single company or firm ; here a huge structure which housed on its many floors a crowd of enterprises, names by the score signalled at the foot of the gaping staircase ; arrogant suggestions of triumph side by side with desperate beginnings ; titles of world-wide significance meeting the eye at every turn, vulgar names with more weight than those of princes, words in small lettering which ruled the fate of millions of men;—no nightmare was ever so crushing to one in Otway's mood. The brute force of money; the negation of the individual—these, the evils of our time, found their supreme expression in the City of London. Here was opulence at home and superb; here must poverty lurk and shrink, feeling itself alive only on sufferance; the din of highway and byway was a voice of blustering conquest, bidding the weaker to stand aside or be crushed. Here no man was a human being, but each merely a portion of an inconceivably complicated mechanism. The shiny-hatted figure who rushed or sauntered, gloomed by himself at corners or made one of a talking group, might else-where be found a reasonable and kindly person, with traits, peculiarities; here one could see in him nothing but a money-maker of this or that class, ground to a certain pattern. The smooth working of the huge machine made it only the more sinister; one had but to remember what cold tyranny, what elaborate fraud, were served by its manifold ingenuities, only to think of the cries of anguish stifled by its monotonous roar.

Piers had undertaken a task, and would not shirk it; but in spite of all reasonings and idealisms he found life a hard thing during these weeks of August. He lost his sleep, turned from food, and for a moment feared collapse such as he had suffered soon after his first going to Odessa.

By the good offices of John Jacks he had already been elected to a convenient club, and occasionally he passed an evening there; but his habit was to go home to Guilford Street, and sit hour after hour in languid brooding. He feared the streets at night-time; in his loneliness and misery, a gleam upon some wanton face would perchance have lured him, as had happened ere now. Not so much at the bidding of his youthful blood, as out of mere longing for companionship, the common cause of disorder in men condemned to solitude in great cities. A woman's voice, the touch of a soft hand— this is what men so often hunger for, when they are censured for lawless appetite. But Piers Otway knew himself, and chose to sit alone in the dreary lodging-house. Then he thought of Irene, trying to forget what had happened. Now and then successfully; in a waking dream he saw and heard her, and knew again the exalting passion that had been the best of his life, and was saved from ignoble impulse.

When he was at the lowest, there came a letter from Olga Hannaford, the first he had ever received in her writing. Olga had joined her mother at Malvern, and Mrs. Hannaford was so unwell that it seemed likely they would remain there for a few weeks. "When we can move, the best thing will be to take a house in or near London. Mother has decided not to return to Bryanston Square, and I, for my part, shall give up the life you made fun of. You were quite right ; of course it was foolish to go on in that way." She asked him to write to her mother, whom a line from him would cheer. Piers did so ; also replying to his correspondent, and trying to make a humorous picture of the life he led between the City and Guilford Street. It was a sorry jest, but it helped him against his troubles. When, in a week's time, Olga again wrote, he was glad. The letter seemed to him interesting ; it revived their common memories of life at Geneva, whither Olga said she would like to return. "What to do—how to pass the years before me—is the question with me now, as I suppose it is with so many girls of my age. I must find a *mission*. Can you suggest one ? Only don't let it have anything humanitarian about it. That would make me a humbug, which I have never been yet. It must be something entirely for my own pleasure and profit. Do think about it in an idle moment."

With recovery from his physical ill-being came a new mental restlessness ; the return, rather, of a mood which had always assailed him when he lost for a time his ideal hope. He demanded of life the joy natural to his years ; revolted against the barrenness of his lot. A terror fell upon him lest he should be fated never to know the supreme delight of which he was capable, and for which alone he lived. Even now was he not passing his prime, losing the keener faculties of youth ? He trembled at the risks of every day ; what was his assurance against the common ill-hap which might afflict him with disease, blight his life with accident, so that no woman's eye could ever be tempted to rest upon him ? He cursed the restrictions which held him on a strait path of routine, of narrow custom, when a world of possibilities spread about him on either hand, the mirage of his imprisoned spirit. Adventurous projects succeeded each other in his thoughts. He turned to the lands where life was freer, where perchance his happiness awaited him, had he but the courage to set forth. What brought him to London, this squalid blot on the map of the round world? Why did he consume the irrecoverable hours amid its hostile tumult, its menacing gloom?

On the first Sunday in September he aroused himself to travel by an early train, which bore him far into the country. He had taken a ticket at hazard for a place with a pleasant-sounding name, and before village bells had begun to ring he was wandering in deep lanes amid the weald of Sussex. All about him lay the perfect loveliness of that rural landscape which is the old England, the true England, the England dear to the best of her children. Meadow and copse, the yellow rank of new-reaped sheaves, brown roofs of farm and cottage amid shadowing elms, the grassy borders of the road, hedges with their flowered creepers and promise of wild fruit—these things brought him comfort. Mile after mile he wandered, losing himself in simplest enjoyment, forgetting to ask why he was alone. When he felt hungry, an inn supplied him with a meal. Again he rambled on, and in a leafy corner found a spot where he could idle for an hour or two, until it was time to think of the railway station.

He had tired himself ; his mind slipped from the beautiful things around him, and fell into the old reverie. He murmured the haunting name—Irene. As well as for her who bore it, he loved the name for its meaning. Peace ! As a child he had been taught that no word was more beautiful, more solemn ; at this moment, he could hear it in his father's voice, sounding as a note of music, with a tremor of deep feeling. Peace ! Every year that passed gave him a fuller understanding of his father's devotion to that word in all its significance ; he himself knew something of the same fervour, and was glad to foster it in his heart. Peace ! What better could a man pursue? from of old the desire of wisdom, the prayer of the aspiring soul.

And what else was this Love for which he anguished ? Irene herself, the beloved, sought with passion and with worship, what more could she give him, when all was given, than content, repose, peace ?

He had been too ambitious. It was the fault of his character, and, thus far on his life's journey, in recognising the error might he not correct it ? Unbalanced ambition explained his ineffectiveness. At six-and-twenty he had done nothing, and saw no hope of activity correspondent with his pride. In Russia he had at least felt that he was treading an uncrowded path : he had made his own a language familiar to very few western Europeans, and constantly added to his knowledge of a people moving to some unknown greatness ; the position was not ignoble. But here in London he was lost amid the uproar of striving tradesmen. The one thing which would still have justified him, hope of wealth, had all but vanished. He must get rid of his absurd self-estimate, see himself in the light of common day.

Peace ! He could only hope for it in marriage ; but what was marriage without ideal love ? Impossible that he should ever love another woman as he had loved, as he still loved, Irene. The ordinary man seeks a wife just as he takes any other practical step necessary to his welfare ; he marries because he must, not because he has met with the true companion of his life ; he mates to be quiet, to be comfortable, to get on with his work, whatever it be. Love in the high sense between man and woman is of all things the most rare. Few are capable of it ; to fewer still is it granted. " The crown of life ! " said Jerome Otway. A truth, even from the strictly scientific point of view ; for is not a great mutual passion the culminating height of that blind reproductive impulse from which life begins ? Supreme desire ; perfection of union. The purpose of Nature translated into human consciousness, become the glory of the highest soul, uttered in the lyric rapture of noblest speech.

That, he must renounce. But not thereby was he condemned to a foolish or base alliance. Women innumerable might be met, charming, sensible, good, no unfit objects of his wooing : in all modesty he might hope for what the world calls happiness. But, put it at the best, he would be doing as other men do, taking a wife for his solace, for the defeat of his assailing blood. It was the bitterness of his mere humanity that he could not hope to live alone and faithful. Five years ago he might have said to himself, " Irene or no one ! " and have said it with the honesty of youth, of inexperience. No such enthusiasm was possible to him now. For the thing which is common in fable is all but unknown in life : a man, capable of loving ardently, who for the sake of one woman, beyond his hope, sacrifices love altogether. Piers Otway, who read much verse, had not neglected his Browning. He knew the transcendent mood of Browning's ideal lover—the beatific dream of love eternal, world after world, hoping for ever, and finding such hope preferable to every less noble satisfaction. For him, a mood only, passing with a smile and a sigh. To that he was not equal ; these heights heroic were not for his treading. Too insistent were the flesh and blood that composed his earthly being.

He must renounce the best of himself, step consciously to a lower level. Only let it not prove sheer degradation.

In all his struggling against the misery of loss, one thought never tempted him. Never for a fleeting instant did he doubt that his highest love was at the same time highest reason. Men woefully deceive themselves, yearning for women whose image in their minds is a mere illusion, women who scarce for a day could bring them happiness, and whose companionship through life would become a curse. Be it so ; Piers knew it, dwelt upon it as a perilous fact ; it had no application to his love for Irene Derwent. Indeed, Piers was rich in that least common form of intelligence—the intelligence of the heart. Emotional perspicacity, the power of recognising through all forms of desire one's true affinity in the other sex, is bestowed upon one mortal in a vast multitude. Not lack of opportunity alone accounts for the failure of men and women to mate becomingly ; only the elect have eyes to see, even where the field of choice is freely opened to them. But Piers Otway saw and knew, once and for ever. He had the genius of love : where he could not observe, divination came to his help. His knowledge of Irene Derwent surpassed that of the persons most intimate with her, and he could as soon have doubted his own existence as the certainty that Irene was what he thought her, neither more nor less.

But he had erred in dreaming it possible that he might win her love. That he was not all unworthy of it, his pride continued to assure him ; what he had failed to perceive was the impossibility, circumstances being as they were, of urging a direct suit, of making himself known to Irene. His birth, his position, the accidents of his career—all forbade it. This had been forced upon his consciousness from the very first, in hours of despondency or of torment ; but he was too young and too ardent for the fact to have its full weight with him. Hope resisted ; passion refused acquiescence. Nothing short of what had happened could reveal to him the vanity of his imaginings. He looked back on the years of patient confidence with wonder and compassion. Had he really hoped? Yes, for he had lived so long alone.

Paragraphs, morning, evening, and weekly, had long since published Miss Derwent's engagement. Those making simple announcement of the fact were trial enough to him when his eye fell upon them; intolerable were those which commented, as in the case of a society journal which he had idly glanced over at his club. This taught him that Irene had more social importance than he guessed; her marriage would be something of an event. Heaven grant that he might read no journalistic description of the ceremony! Few things more disgusted him than the thought of a fashionable wedding; he could see nothing in it but profanation and indecency. That mattered little, to be sure, in the case of ordinary people, who were born, and lived, and died, in fashionable routine, anxious only to exhibit themselves at any given moment in the way held to be good form; but it was hard to think that custom's tyranny should lay its foul hand on Irene Derwent. Perhaps her future husband meant no such thing, and would arrange it all with quiet becomingness. Certainly her father would not favour the tawdry and the vulgar.

No date was announced. Paragraphs said merely that it would be " before the end of the year."

After all, his day amid the fields was spoilt. He had allowed his mind to stray in the forbidden direction, and the seeming quiet to which he had attained was overthrown once more. Heavily he moved towards the wayside station, and drearily he waited for the train that was to take him back to his meaningless toil and strife.

In the compartment he entered, an empty one, some passenger had left a weekly periodical; Piers seized upon it gladly, and read to distract his thoughts. One article interested him; it was on the subject of national characteristics: cleverly written, what is called "smart" journalism, with grip and epigram, with hint of universal knowledge and the true air of British superiority. Having scanned the writer's comment on the Slavonic peoples, Piers laughed aloud; so evidently it was a report at second or third hand, utterly valueless to one who had any real acquaintance with the Slavs. This moment of spontaneous mirth did him good, helped to restore his self-respect. And as he pondered, old ambitions stirred again in him. Could he not make some use of the knowledge he had gained so laboriously—some use other than that whereby he earned his living? Not so long ago, he had harboured great designs, vague but not irrational. And to-day, even in bidding himself be humble, his intellect was little tuned to humility. He had never, at his point of darkest depression, really believed that life had no shining promise for him. The least boastful of men, he was at heart one of the most aspiring. His moods varied wonderfully. When he alighted at the London terminus, he looked and felt like a man refreshed by some new hope.

Half by accident, he kept the paper he had been reading. It lay on his table in Guilford Street for weeks, for months. Years after, he came upon it one day in turning out the contents of a trunk, and remembered his ramble in the Sussex woodland, and smiled at the chances of life.

On Monday morning he had a characteristic letter from Moncharmont, part English, part French, part Russian. Nothing, or only a passing word, about business; communications of that sort were all addressed to the office, and were as concise, as practical, as any trader could have desired. In his friendly letter, Moncharmont chatted of a certain Polish girl with whom he had newly made acquaintance, whose beauty, according to the good André, was a thing to dream of, not to tell. It meant nothing, as Piers knew. The cosmopolitan Swiss fell in love some dozen times a year, with maidens or women of every nationality and every social station. Be the issue what it might, he was never unhappy. He had a gallery of photographs, and delighted to pore over it, indulging reminiscences or fostering hopes. Once in a twelvemonth or so, he made up his mind to marry, but never went further than the intention. It was doubtful whether he would ever commit himself irrevocably. "It seems such a pity," he often said, with his pensively humorous smile, "to limit the scope of one's emotions—*borner la carrière à ses émotions !*" Then he sighed, and was in the best of spirits.

Not even to Moncharmont—with whom he talked more freely than with any other man—had Piers ever spoken of Irene. André of course suspected some romantic attachment, and was in constant amaze at Piers' fidelity.

"Ah, you English! you English!" he would exclaim. "You are the Stoics of the modern world. I admire; yes, I admire; but, my friend, I do not wish to imitate."

The letter cheered Otway's breakfast; he read it instead of the newspaper, and with vastly more benefit.

Another letter had come to his private address, a note from Mrs. Hannaford. She was regaining strength, and hoped soon to come South again. Her brother had already taken a nice little house for her at Campden Hill, where Olga would have a sort of studio, and, she trusted, would make herself happy. Both looked forward to seeing Piers; they sent him their very kindest remembrances.

CHAPTER XXI

THE passionate temperament is necessarily sanguine. To desire with all one's being is the same thing as to hope. In Piers Otway's case, the temper which defies discouragement existed together with the intellect which ever tends to discourage, with the mind which probes appearances, makes war upon illusions. Hence his oft-varying moods, as the one or the other part of him became ascendant. Hence his fervours of idealism, and the habit of destructive criticism which seemed inconsistent with them. Hence his ardent ambitions, and his appearance of plodding mediocrity in practical life.

Intensely self-conscious, he suffered much from a habit of comparing, contrasting himself with other men, with men who achieved things, who made their way, who played a part in the world. He could not read a newspaper without reflecting, sometimes bitterly, on the careers and position of men whose names were prominent in its columns. So often, he well knew, their success came only of accident—as one uses the word : of favouring circumstance, which had no relation to the man's powers and merits. Piers had no overweening self-esteem ; he judged his abilities more accurately, and more severely, than any observer would have done ; yet it was plain to him that he would be more than capable, so far as endowment went, of filling the high place occupied by this or the other far-shining personage. He frankly envied their success—always for one and the same reason.

Nothing so goaded his imagination as a report of the marriage of some leader in the world's game. He dwelt on these paragraphs, filled up the details, grew faint with realisation of the man's triumphant happiness. At another moment, his reason ridiculed this self-torment. He knew that in all probability such a marriage implied no sense of triumph, involved no high emotions, promised nothing but the commonest domestic satisfaction. Portraits of brides in an illustrated paper sometimes wrought him to intolerable agitation—the mood of his early manhood, as when he stood before the print shop in the Haymarket; now that he had lost Irene, the whole world of beautiful women called again to his senses and his soul. With the cooler moment came a reminder that these lovely faces were for the most part mere masks, tricking out a very ordinary woman, more likely than not unintelligent, unhelpful, as the ordinary human being of either sex is wont to be. What seemed to *him* the crown of a man's career, was, in most cases, a mere incident, deriving its chief importance from social and pecuniary considerations. Even where a sweet countenance told truth about the life behind it, how seldom did the bridegroom appreciate what he had won! For the most part, men who have great good fortune, in marriage, or in anything else, are incapable of tasting their success. It is the imaginative being in the crowd below who marvels and is thrilled.

How was it with Arnold Jacks? Did he understand what had befallen him? If so, on what gleaming heights did he now live and move! What rapture of gratitude must possess the man! What humility! What arrogance!

Piers had not met him since the engagement was made known; he hoped not to meet him for a long time. Happily, in this holiday season, there was no fear of an invitation to Queen's Gate.

Yet the unexpected happened. Early in September, he received a note from John Jacks, asking him to dine. The writer said that he had been at the seaside, and was tired of it, and meant to spend a week or two quietly in London; he was quite alone, so Otway need not dress.

Reassured by the last sentence of the letter, Piers gladly went; for he liked to talk with John Jacks, and had a troubled pleasure in the thought that he might hear something about the approaching marriage. On his arrival, he was shown into the study, where his host lay on a sofa. The greeting was cordial, the voice cheery as ever, but as Mr. Jacks rose he had more of the appearance of old age than Piers had yet seen in him; he seemed to stand with some difficulty, his face betokening a body ill at ease.

"How pleasant London is in September!" he exclaimed, with a laugh. "I've been driving about, as one does in a town abroad, just to see the streets. Strange that one knows Paris and Rome a good deal better than London. Yet it's really very interesting—don't you think?"

The twinkling eye, the humorous accent, which had won Piers' affection, soon allayed his disquietude at being in this house. He spoke of his own recent excursion, confessing that he better appreciated London from a distance.

"Ay, ay! I know all about that," replied Mr. Jacks, his Yorkshire note sounding, as it did occasionally. "But you're young, you're young; what does it matter where you live? To be your age again, I'd live at St. Helens, or Widnes. You have hope, man, always hope. And you may live to see what the world is like half a century from now. It's strange to look at you, and think that!"

John Jacks' presence in London, and alone, at this time of the year had naturally another explanation than that he felt tired of the seaside. In truth, he had come up to see a medical specialist. Carefully he kept from his wife the knowledge of a disease which was taking hold upon him, which —as he had just learnt — threatened rapidly fatal results. From his son, also, he had concealed the serious state of his health, lest it should interfere with Arnold's happy mood in prospect of marriage. He was no coward, but a life hitherto untroubled by sickness had led him to hope that he might pass easily from the world, and a doom of extinction by torture perturbed his philosophy.

He liked to forget himself in contemplation of Piers Otway's youth and soundness. He had pleasure, too, in Piers' talk, which reminded him of Jerome Otway, some half-century ago.

Mrs. Jacks was staying with her own family, and from that house would pass to others, equally decorous, where John had promised to join her. Of course she was uneasy about him; that entered into her rôle of model spouse: but the excellent lady never suspected the true cause of that habit of sadness which had grown upon her husband during the last few years, a melancholy which anticipated his decline in health. John Jacks had made the mistake natural to such a man; wedding at nearly sixty a girl of much less than half his age, he found, of course, that his wife had nothing to give him but duty and respect, and before long he bitterly reproached himself with the sacrifice of which he was guilty.

> "Soar on thy manhood clear of those
>   Whose toothless Winter claws at May,
> And take her as the vein of rose
>   Athwart an evening grey."

These lines met his eye one day in a new volume which bore the name of George Meredith, and they touched him nearly; the poem they closed gave utterance to the manful resignation of one who has passed the age of love, yet is tempted by love's sweetness, and John Jacks took to heart the reproach it seemed to level at himself. Putting aside the point of years, he had not chosen with any discretion; he married a handsome face, a graceful figure, just as any raw boy might have done. His wife, he suspected, was not the woman to suffer greatly in her false position; she had very temperate blood, and a thoroughly English devotion to the proprieties; none the less he had done her wrong, for she belonged to a gentle family in mediocre circumstances, and his prospective "M.P.," his solid wealth, were sore temptations to put before such a girl. He had known—yes, he assuredly knew—that it was nothing but a socially sanctioned purchase. Beauty should have become to him but the "vein of rose," to be regarded with gentle admiration and with reverence, from afar. He yielded to an unworthy temptation, and, being a man of unusual sensitiveness, very soon paid the penalty in self-contempt.

He could not love his wife; he could scarce honour her— for she too must consciously have sinned against the highest law. Her irreproachable behaviour only saddened him. Now that he found himself under sentence of death, his solace was the thought that his widow would still be young enough to redeem her error—if she were capable of redeeming it.

Alone with his guest in the large dining-room, and compelled to make only pretence of eating and drinking, he talked of many things with the old spontaneity, the accustomed liberal kindliness, and dropped at length upon the subject Piers was waiting for.

"You know, I daresay, that Arnold is going to marry?"

"I have heard of it," Piers answered, with the best smile he could command.

"You can imagine it pleases me. I don't see how he could have been luckier. Dr. Derwent is one of the finest men I know, and his daughter is worthy of him."

"She is, I am sure," said Piers, in a balanced voice, which sounded mere civility.

And when silence had lasted rather too long, the host having fallen into reverie, he added:

" Will it take place soon ? "

" Ah—the wedding ? About Christmas, I think. Arnold is looking for a house. By the bye, you know young Derwent —Eustace ? "

Piers answered that he had only the slightest acquaintance with the young man.

" Not brilliant, I think," said Mr. Jacks musingly. " But amiable, straight. I don't know that he'll do much at the Bar."

Again he lost himself for a little, his knitted brows seeming to indicate an anxious thought.

" Now you shall tell me anything you care to, about business," said the host, when they had seated themselves in the library. " And after that I have something to show you— something you'll like to see, I think."

Otway's curiosity was at a loss when presently he saw his host take from a drawer a little packet of papers.

" I had forgotten all about these," said Mr. Jacks. " They are manuscripts of your father ; writings of various kinds which he sent me in the early fifties. Turning out my old papers, I came across them the other day, and thought I would give them to you."

He rustled the faded sheets, glancing over them with a sad smile.

" There's an amusing thing—called ' Historical Fragment.' I remember, oh I remember very well, how it pleased me when I first read it."

He read it aloud now, with many a chuckle, many a pause of sly emphasis.

" ' The Story of the last war between the Asiatic kingdoms of Duroba and Kalaya, though it has reached us in a narrative far too concise, is one of the most interesting chapters in the history of ancient civilisation.

" ' They were bordering states, peopled by races closely akin, whose languages, it appears, were mutually intelligible ; each had developed its own polity, and had advanced to a high degree of refinement in public and private life. Wars between them had been frequent, but at the time with which we are concerned the spirit of hostility was all but forgotten in a happy peace of long duration. Each country was ruled by an aged monarch, beloved of the people, but, under the burden of years, grown of late somewhat less vigilant than was consistent with popular welfare. Thus it came to pass that power fell into the hands of unscrupulous statesmen, who, aided by singular circumstances, succeeded in reviving for a moment the old sanguinary jealousies.

"'We are told that a General in the army of Duroba, having a turn for experimental chemistry, had discovered a substance of terrible explosive power, which, by the exercise of further ingenuity, he had adapted for use in warfare. About the same time, a public official in Kalaya, whose duty it was to convey news to the community by means of a primitive system of manuscript placarding, hit upon a mechanical method whereby news-sheets could be multiplied very rapidly and be sold to readers all over the kingdom. Now the Duroban General felt eager to test his discovery in a campaign, and, happening to have a quarrel with a politician in the neighbouring state, did his utmost to excite hostile feeling against Kalaya. On the other hand, the Kalayan official, his cupidity excited by the profits already arising from his invention, desired nothing better than some stirring event which would lead to still greater demand for the news-sheets he distributed, and so he also was led to the idea of stirring up international strife. To be brief, these intrigues succeeded only too well; war was actually declared, the armies were mustered, and marched to the encounter.

"'They met at a point of the common frontier where only a little brook flowed between the two kingdoms. It was nightfall; each host encamped, to await the great engagement which on the morrow would decide between them.

"'It must be understood that the Durobans and the Kalayans differed markedly in national characteristics. The former people was distinguished by joyous vitality and a keen sense of humour; the latter, by a somewhat meditative disposition inclining to timidity; and doubtless these qualities had become more pronounced during the long peace which would naturally favour them. Now, when night had fallen on the camps, the common soldiers on each side began to discuss, over their evening meal, the position in which they found themselves. The men of Duroba, having drunk well, as their habit was, fell into an odd state of mind. "What!" they exclaimed to one another. "After all these years of tranquillity, are we really going to fight with the Kalayans, and to slaughter them and be ourselves slaughtered! Pray, what is

it all about? Who can tell us?" Not a man could answer,
save with the vaguest generalities. And so, the debate
continuing, the wonder growing from moment to moment, at
length, and all of a sudden, the Duroban camp echoed with
huge peals of laughter. "Why, if we soldiers have no cause of
quarrel, what are we doing here? Shall we be mangled and
killed to please our General with the turn for chemistry? That
were a joke, indeed!" And, as soon as mirth permitted, the
army rose as one man, threw together their belongings, and
with jovial songs trooped off to sleep comfortably in a town a
couple of miles away.

"'The Kalayans, meanwhile, had been occupied with the
very same question. They were anything but martial of mood,
and the soldiery, ill at ease in their camp, grumbled and
protested. "After all, why are we here?" cried one to the
other. "Who wants to injure the Durobans? And what
man among us desires to be blown to pieces by their new
instruments of war? Pray, why should *we* fight? If the
great officials are angry, as the news-sheets tell us, e'en let
them do the fighting themselves." At this moment there
sounded from the enemy's camp a stupendous roar; it was
much like laughter; no doubt the Durobans were jubilant in
anticipation of their victory. Fear seized the Kalayans; they
rose like one man, and incontinently fled far into the sheltering
night!

"'Thus ended the war—the last between these happy
nations, who, not very long after, united to form a noble state
under one ruler. It is interesting to note that the original
instigators of hostility did not go without their deserts. The
Duroban General, having been duly tried for a crime against
his country, was imprisoned in a spacious building, the rooms
of which were hung with great pictures representing every
horror of battle with the ghastliest fidelity; here he was
supplied with materials for chemical experiment, to occupy his
leisure, and very shortly, by accident, blew himself to pieces.
The Kalayan publicist was also convicted of treason against
the state; they banished him to a desert island, where for
many hours daily he had to multiply copies of his news-sheet
—that issue which contained the declaration of war—and at
evening to burn them all. He presently became imbecile,
and so passed away.'"

Piers laughed with delight.

"Whether it ever got into print," said Mr. Jacks, "I don't know. Your father was often careless about his best things. I'm afraid he was never quite convinced that ideals of that kind influence the world. Yet they do, you know, though it's a slow business. It's thought that leads."

"The multitude following in its own fashion," said Piers drily. "Rousseau teaches liberty and fraternity; France learns the lesson, and plunges into '93."

"With Nap to put things straight again. For all that, a step was taken. We are better for Jean Jacques—a little better."

"And for Napoleon, too, I suppose. Napoleon—a wild beast with a genius for arithmetic."

John Jacks let his eyes rest upon the speaker, interested and amused.

"That's how you see him? Not a bad definition. I suppose the truth is, we know nothing about human history. The old view was good for working by—Jehovah holding his balance, smiting on one side, and rewarding on the other. It's our national view to this day. The English are an Old Testament people; they never cared about the New. Do you know that there's a sect who hold that the English are the Lost Tribes—the People of the Promise? I see a great deal to be said for that idea. No other nation has such profound sympathy with the history and the creeds of Israel. Did you ever think of it? That Old Testament religion suits us perfectly—our arrogance and our pugnaciousness; this accounts for its hold on the mind of the people; it couldn't be stronger if the bloodthirsty old Tribes were truly our ancestors. The English seized upon their spiritual inheritance as soon as a translation of the Bible put it before them. In Catholic days we fought because we enjoyed it, and made no pretences; since the Reformation we have fought for Jehovah."

"I suppose," said Piers, "the English are the least Christian of all so-called Christian peoples."

"Undoubtedly. They simply don't know the meaning of the prime Christian virtue—humility. But that's neither here nor there, in talking of progress. You remember Goldsmith—

> 'Pride in their port, defiance in their eye,
> I see the lords of human kind pass by.'

Our pride has been a good thing, on the whole. Whether it

will still be, now that it's so largely the pride of riches, let him say who is alive fifty years hence."

He paused, and added gravely :

"I'm afraid the national character is degenerating. We were always too fond of liquor, and Heaven knows our responsibility for drunkenness all over the world; but worse than that is our gambling. You may drink and be a fine fellow ; but every gambler is a sneak, and possibly a criminal. We're beginning, now, to gamble for slices of the world. We're getting base, too, in our grovelling before the millionaire —who as often as not has got his money vilely. This sort of thing won't do for 'the lords of human kind.' Our pride, if we don't look out, will turn to bluffing and bullying. I'm afraid we govern selfishly where we've conquered. We hear dark things of India, and worse of Africa. And hear the roaring of the Jingoes ! Johnson defined Patriotism, you know, as the last refuge of a scoundrel; it looks as if it might presently be the last refuge of a fool."

"Meanwhile," said Piers, "the real interests of England, real progress in national life, seem to be as good as lost sight of."

"Yes, more and more. They think that material prosperity is progress. So it is—up to a certain point, and who ever stops there ? Look at Germany."

"Once the peaceful home of pure intellect, the land of Goethe."

"Once, yes. And my fear is that our brute, blustering Bismarck may be coming.—But," he suddenly brightened, "croakers be hanged ! The civilisers are at work too, and they have their way in the end. Think of a man like your father, who seemed to pass and be forgotten. Was it really so ? I'll warrant that at this hour Jerome Otway's spirit is working in many of our best minds. There's no calculating the power of the man who speaks from his very heart. His words don't perish, though he himself may lose courage."

Listening, Piers felt a glow pass into all the currents of his life.

"If only," he exclaimed, in a voice that trembled, "I had as much strength as desire to carry on his work ! "

"Why, who knows ? " replied John Jacks, looking with encouragement wherein mingled something of affection. "You have the power of sincerity, I see that. Speak always as you believe, and who knows what opportunity you may find for making yourself heard !"

John Jacks reflected deeply for a few moments.

" I'm going away in a day or two," he said at length, in a measured voice, "and my movements are uncertain—uncertain. But we shall meet again before the end of the year."

When he had left the house, Piers recalled the tone of this remark, and dwelt upon it with disquietude.

CHAPTER XXII

THE night being fair, Piers set out to walk a part of the way home. It was only by thoroughly tiring himself with bodily exercise that he could get sound and long oblivion. Hours of sleeplessness were his dread. However soon he awoke after daybreak, he rose at once and drove his mind to some sort of occupation. To escape from himself was all he lived for in these days. An ascetic of old times, subduing his flesh in cell or cave, battled no harder than this idealist of London City tortured by his solitude.

On the pavement of Piccadilly he saw some yards before him, a man seemingly of the common lounging sort, tall-hatted and frock-coated, who was engaged in the cautious pursuit of a female figure, just in advance. A light and springy and half-stalking step; head jutting a little forward; the cane mechanically swung—a typical woman-hunter, in some doubt as to his quarry. On an impulse of instinct or calculation, the man all at once took a few rapid strides, bringing himself within side-view of the woman's face. Evidently he spoke a word; he received an obviously curt reply; he fell back, paced slowly, turned. And Piers became aware of a countenance he knew—that of his brother Daniel.

It was a disagreeable moment. Daniel's lean, sallow visage had no aptitude for the expression of shame, but his eyes grew very round, and his teeth showed in a hard grin.

"Why, Piers, my boy! Again we meet in a London street—which is rhyme, and sounds like Browning, doesn't it? *Comment ça va-t-il?*"

Piers shook hands very coldly, without pretence of a smile.

"I am walking on," he said. "Yours is the other way, I think."

"What! You wish to cut me? Pray, your exquisite reason?"

"Well, then, I think you have behaved meanly and dis-

honourably to me. I don't wish to discuss the matter, only
to make myself understood."

His ability to use this language, and to command himself
as he did so, was a surprise to Piers. Nothing he disliked
more than personal altercation; he shrank from it at almost
any cost. But the sight of Daniel, the sound of his artificial
voice, moved him deeply with indignation, and for the first
time in his life he spoke out. Having done so, he had a
pleasurable sensation; he felt his assured manhood.

Daniel was astonished, disconcerted, but showed no disposition to close the interview; turning, he walked along by
his brother.

"I suppose I know what you refer to. But let me explain.
I think my explanation will interest you."

"No, I'm afraid it will not," replied Piers quietly.

"In any case, lend me your ears. You are offended by
my failure to pay that debt. Well, my nature is frankness,
and I will plead guilty to a certain procrastination. I meant
to send you the money; I fully meant to do so. But in the
first place, it took much longer than I expected to realise the
good old man's estate, and when at length the money came
into my hands, I delayed and delayed—just as one does, you
know; let us admit these human weaknesses. And I pro-
crastinated till I was really ashamed — you follow the
psychology of the thing? Then I said to myself: Now it is
pretty certain Piers is not in actual want of this sum, or he
would have pressed for it. On the other hand, a day may
come when he will really be glad to remember that I am his
banker for a hundred and fifty pounds. Yes—I said—I will
wait till that moment comes; I will save the money for him,
as becomes his elder brother. Piers is a good fellow, and will
understand. *Voilà!*"

Piers kept silence.

"Tell me, my dear boy," pursued the other. "Alexander
of course paid that little sum he owed you?"

"He too has preferred to remain my banker."

"Now I call that very shameful!" burst out Daniel. "No,
that's too bad!"

"How did you know he owed me money?" inquired Piers.

"How? Why, he told me himself, down at Hawes, after
you went. We were talking of you, of your admirable
qualities, and in his bluff, genial way he threw out how

generously you had behaved to him, at a moment when he was hard up. He wanted to repay you immediately, and asked me to lend him the money for that purpose; unfortunately, I hadn't it to lend. And, to think that, after all, he never paid you! A mere fifty pounds! Why, the thing is unpardonable! In my case the sum was substantial enough to justify me in retaining it for your future benefit. But to owe fifty pounds, and shirk payment—no, I call that really disgraceful. If ever I meet Alexander—!"

Piers was coldly amused. When Daniel sought to draw him into general conversation, with inquiries as to his mode of life, and where he dwelt, the younger brother again spoke with decision. They were not likely, he said, to see more of each other, and he felt as little disposed to give familiar information as to ask it; whereupon Daniel drew himself up with an air of dignified offence, and saying, "I wish you better manners," turned on his heel.

Piers walked on at a rapid pace. Noticing again a well-dressed prowler of the pavement, whose approaches this time were welcomed, a feeling of nausea came upon him. He hailed a passing cab, and drove home.

A week later, he heard from Mrs. Hannaford that she and Olga were established in their own home; she begged him to come and see them soon, mentioning an evening when they would be glad if he could dine with them. And Piers willingly accepted.

The house was at Campden Hill; a house of the kind known to agents as "desirable," larger than the two ladies needed for their comfort, and, as one saw on entering the hall, furnished with tasteful care. The work had been supervised by Dr. Derwent, who thought that his sister and his niece might thus be tempted to live the orderly life so desirable in their unfortunate circumstances. When Piers entered, Mrs. Hannaford sat alone in the drawing-room; she still had the look of an invalid, but wore a gown which showed to advantage the lines of her figure. Otway had been told not to dress, and it caused him some surprise to see his hostess adorned as if for an occasion of ceremony. Her hair was done in a new way, which changed the wonted character of her face, so that she looked younger. A bunch of pale flowers rested against her bosom, and breathed delicate perfume about her.

"It was discussed," she said, in a low, intimate voice,

"whether we should settle in London or abroad. But we didn't like to go away. Our only real friends are in England, and we must hope to make more. Olga is so good, now that she sees that I really need her. She has been so kind and sweet during my illness."

Whilst they were talking, Miss Hannaford silently made her entrance. Piers turned his head, and felt a shock of surprise. Not till now had he seen Olga at her best; he had never imagined her so handsome; it was a wonderful illustration of the effect of apparel. She, too, had reformed the fashion of her hair, and its tawny abundance was much more effective than in the old careless style. She looked taller; she stepped with a more graceful assurance, and in offering her hand, betrayed consciousness of Otway's admiration in a little flush that well became her.

She had subdued her voice, chastened her expressions. The touch of masculinity on which she had prided herself in her later - "Bohemian" days, was quite gone. Wondering as they conversed, Piers had a difficulty in meeting her look; his eyes dropped to the little silk shoe which peeped from beneath her skirt. His senses were gratified; he forgot for the moment his sorrow and unrest.

The talk at dinner was rather formal. Piers, with his indifferent appetite, could do but scanty justice to the dainties offered him, and the sense of luxury added a strangeness to his new relations with Mrs. Hannaford and her daughter. Olga spoke of a Russian novel she had been reading in a French translation, and was anxious to know whether it represented life as Otway knew it in Russia. She evinced a wider interest in several directions, emphasised—perhaps a little too much—her inclination for earnest thought: was altogether a more serious person than hitherto.

Afterwards, when they grouped themselves in the drawing-room, this constraint fell away. Mrs. Hannaford dropped a remark which awakened memories of their life together at Geneva, and Piers turned to her with a bright look.

"You used to play in those days," he said, "and I've never heard you touch a piano since."

There was one in the room. Olga glanced at it, and then smilingly at her mother.

"My playing was so very primitive," said Mrs. Hannaford, with a laugh.

"I liked it."

"Because you were a boy then."

"Let me try to be a boy again. Play something you used to. One of those bits from 'Tell,' which take me back to the lakes and the mountains whenever I hear them."

Mrs. Hannaford rose, laughing as if ashamed; Olga lit the candles on the piano.

"I shall have to play from memory—and a nice mess I shall make of it."

But memory served her for the passages of melody which Piers wished to hear. He listened with deep pleasure, living again in the years when everything he desired seemed a certainty of the future, depending only on the flight of time, on his becoming "a man." He remembered his vivid joy in the pleasures of the moment, the natural happiness now, and for years, unknown to him. So long ago, it seemed; yet Mrs. Hannaford, sitting at the piano, looked younger to him than in those days. And Olga, whom as a girl of fourteen he had not much liked, thinking her both conceited and dull, now was a very different person to him, a woman who seemed to have only just revealed herself, asserting a power of attraction he had never suspected in her. He found himself trying to catch glimpses of her face at different angles, as she sat listening abstractedly to the music.

When it was time to go, he took leave with reluctance. The talk had grown very pleasantly familiar. Mrs. Hannaford said she hoped they would often see him, and the hope had an echo in his own thoughts. This house might offer him the refuge he sought when loneliness weighed too heavily. It was true, he could not accept the idea with a whole heart; some vague warning troubled his imagination; but on the way home he thought persistently of the pleasure he had experienced, and promised himself that it should be soon repeated.

A melody was singing in his mind; becoming conscious of it, he remembered that it was the air to which his friend Moncharmont had set the little song of Alfred de Musset. At Odessa he had been wont to sing it—in a voice which Moncharmont declared to have the quality of a very fair tenor, and only to need training.

> " Quand on perd, par triste occurrence,
>   Son espérance
>   Et sa gaîté,

Le remède au mélancolique
C'est la musique
Et la beauté.

Plus oblige et peut davantage
Un beau visage
Qu'un homme armé,
Et rien n'est meilleur que d'entendre
Air doux et tendre
Jadis aimé !"

It haunted him after he had gone to rest, and for once he did not mind wakefulness.

A week passed. On Friday, Piers said to himself that to-morrow he would go in the afternoon to Campden Hill, on the chance of finding his friends at home. On Saturday morning the post brought him a letter which he saw to be from Mrs. Hannaford, and he opened it with pleasant anticipation; but instead of the friendly lines he expected, he found a note of agitated appeal. The writer entreated him to come and see her exactly at three o'clock; she was in very grave trouble, had the most urgent need of him. Three o'clock; neither sooner or later; if he could possibly find time. If he could not come, would he telegraph an appointment for her at his office?

With perfect punctuality, he arrived at the house, and in the drawing-room found Mrs. Hannaford awaiting him. She came forward with both her hands held out; in her eyes a look almost of terror. Her voice, at first, was in choking whispers, and the words so confusedly hurried as to be barely intelligible.

"I have sent Olga away—I daren't let her know—she will be away for several hours, so we can talk—oh, you will help me—you will do your best"—

Perplexed and alarmed, Piers held her hand as he tried to calm her. She seemed incapable of telling him what had happened, but kept her eyes fixed upon him in a wild entreaty, and uttered broken phrases which conveyed nothing to him; he gathered at length that she was in fear of some person.

"Sit down, and let me hear all about it," he urged.

"Yes, yes—but I'm so ashamed to speak to you about such things. I don't know whether you'll believe me. Oh, the shame—the dreadful shame! It's only because there seems just this hope. How shall I bring myself to tell you?"

"Dear Mrs. Hannaford, we have been friends so long. Trust me to understand you. Of course, of course I shall believe what you say!"

"A dreadful, a shameful thing has happened. How shall I tell you?" Her haggard face flushed scarlet. "My husband has given me notice that he is going to sue for a divorce. He brings a charge against me—a false, cruel charge! It came yesterday. I went to the solicitor whose name was given, and learnt all I could. I have had to hide it from Olga, and oh! what it cost me! At once I thought of you; then it seemed impossible to speak to you; then I felt I must, I must. If only you can believe me! It is—your brother."

Piers was overcome with amazement. He sat looking into the eyes which stared at him with their agony of shame.

"You mean Daniel?" he faltered.

"Yes—Daniel Otway. It is false—it is false! I am not guilty of this! It seems to me like a hateful plot—if one could believe anyone so wicked. I saw him last night—Oh, I must tell you all, else you'll never believe me—I saw him last night. How can anyone behave so to a helpless woman? I never did him anything but kindness. He has me in his power, and he is merciless."

A passion of disgust and hatred took hold on Piers as he remembered the meeting in Piccadilly.

"You mean to say you have put yourself into that fellow's power?" he exclaimed.

"Not willingly! Oh, not willingly! I meant only kindness to him.—Yes, I have been weak, I know, and so foolish! It has gone on so long — You remember when I first saw him, at Ewell? I liked him, just as a friend. Of course I behaved foolishly. It was my miserable life—you know what my life was. But nothing happened—I mean, I never thought of him for a moment as anything but an ordinary friend—until I had my legacy."

The look on the listener's face checked her.

"I begin to understand," said Piers, with bitterness.

"No, no! Don't say that—don't speak like that!"

"It's not you I am thinking of, Mrs. Hannaford. As soon as money comes in— But tell me plainly. I have perfect confidence in what you say, indeed I have."

"It does me good to hear you say that! I can tell you all,

now that I have begun.   It is true, he *did* ask me to go away
with him, again and again.   But he had no right to do that—
I was foolish in showing that I liked him.   Again and again I
forbade him ever to see me ; I tried so hard to break off!   It
was no use.   He always wrote, wherever I was, sending his
letters to Dr. Derwent to be forwarded.   He made me meet
him at all sorts of places—using threats at last.   Oh, what I
I have gone through!"

"No doubt," said Piers gently, "you have lent him
money?"

She reddened again ; her head sank.

"Yes—I have lent him money, when he was in need.   Just
before the death of your father."

"Once only?"

"Once—or twice"—

"To be sure.   Lately, too, I daresay?"

"Yes"—

"Then you quite understand his character?"

"I do now," Mrs. Hannaford replied wretchedly.   "But I
must tell you more.   If it were only a suspicion of my
husband's, I should hardly care at all.   But someone must
have betrayed me to him, and have told deliberate false-
hoods.   I am accused—it was when I was at the seaside
once—and he came to the same hotel—Oh, the shame, the
shame!"

She covered her face with her hands, and turned away.

"Why," cried Piers, in wrath, "that fellow is quite capable
of having betrayed you himself.   I mean, of lying about you
for his own purposes."

"You think he could be so wicked?"

"I don't doubt it for a moment.   He has done his best to
persuade you to ruin yourself for him, and he thinks, no
doubt, that if you are divorced, nothing will stand between
him and you—in other words, your money."

"He said, when I saw him yesterday, that now it had come
to this, I had better take that step at once.   And when I spoke
of my innocence, he asked who would believe it?   He seemed
sorry ; really he did.   Perhaps he is not so bad as one
fears?"

"Where did you see him yesterday?" asked Otway.

"At his lodgings.   I was *obliged* to go and see him as soon
as possible.   I have never been there before.   He behaved

very kindly. He said of course he should declare my innocence"—

"And in the same breath assured you no one would believe it? And advised you to go off with him at once?"

"I know how bad it seems," said Mrs. Hannaford. "And yet, it is all my own fault—my own long folly. Oh, you must wonder why I have brought you here to tell you this! It's because there was no one else I could speak to, as a friend, and I felt I should go mad if I couldn't ask someone's advice. Of course I could go to a lawyer—but I mean someone who would sympathise with me. I am not very strong; you know I have been ill: this blow seems almost more than I can bear; I thought I would ask you if you could suggest anything—if you would see him, and try to arrange something." She looked at Piers distractedly. "Perhaps money would help. My husband has been having money from me; perhaps if we offered him more? Ought I to see him, myself? But there is ill-feeling between us; and I fear he would be glad to injure me, glad!"

"I will see Daniel," said Piers, trying to see hope where reason told him there was none. "With him, at all events, money can do much."

"You will? You think you may be able to help me? I am in such terror when I think of my brother hearing of this. And Irene! Think, if it becomes public—everyone talking about the disgrace—what will Irene do? Just at the time of her marriage!" She held out her hands, pleadingly. "You would be glad to save Irene from such a shame?"

Piers had not yet seen the scandal from this point of view. It came upon him with a shock, and he stood speechless.

"My husband hates them," pursued Mrs. Hannaford, "and you don't know what *his* hatred means. Just for that alone, he will do his worst against me—hoping to throw disgrace on the Derwents."

"I doubt very much," said Piers, who had been thinking hard, "whether, in any event, this would affect the Derwents in people's opinion."

"You don't think so? But do you know Arnold Jacks? I feel sure he is the kind of man who would resent bitterly such a thing as this. He is very proud—proud in just that kind of way—do you understand? Oh, I know it would make trouble between him and Irene."

"In that case," Piers began vehemently, and at once checked himself.

"What were you going to say?"

"Nothing that could help us."

When he raised his eyes again, Mrs. Hannaford was gazing at him with pitiful entreaty.

"For *her* sake," she said, in a low, shaken voice, "you will try to do something?"

"If only I can!"

"Yes! I know you! You are good and generous.—It ought surely to be possible to stop this before it gets talked about? If I were guilty, it would be different. But I have done no wrong; I have only been weak and foolish. I thought of going straight to my brother, but there is the dreadful thought that he might not believe me. It is so hard for a woman accused in this way to seem innocent; men always see the dark side. He has no very good opinion of me, as it is, I know he hasn't. I turned so naturally to you; I felt you would do your utmost for me in my misery.—If only my husband can be brought to see that I am not guilty, that he wouldn't win the suit, then perhaps he would cease from it. I will give all the money I can—all I have!"

Piers stood reflecting.

"Tell me all the details you have learnt," he said. "What evidence do they rely on?"

Her head bowed, her voice broken, she told of place and time and the assertions of so-called witnesses.

"Why has this plot against you been a year in ripening?" asked Otway.

"Perhaps we are wrong in thinking it a plot. My husband may only just have discovered what he thinks my guilt in some chance way. If so, there is hope."

They sat mute for a minute or two.

"If only I can hide this from Olga," said Mrs. Hannaford. "Think how dreadful it is for me, with her! We were going to ask you to spend another evening with us—but how is it possible? If I send you the invitation, will you make an answer excusing yourself—saying you are too busy? To prevent Olga from wondering. How hard, how cruel it is! Just when we had made ourselves a home here, and might have been happy!"

Piers stood up, and tried to speak words of encouragement.

The charge being utterly false, at worst a capable solicitor might succeed in refuting it. He was about to take his leave, when he remembered that he did not know Daniel's address : Mrs. Hannaford gave it.

"I am sorry you went there," he said.

And as he left the room, he saw the woman's eyes follow him with that look of woe which signals a tottering mind.

CHAPTER XXIII

WITHOUT investigating her motives, Irene Derwent deferred as long as possible her meeting with the man to whom she had betrothed herself. Nor did Arnold Jacks evince any serious impatience in this matter. They corresponded in affectionate terms, exchanging letters once a week or so. Arnold, as it chanced, was unusually busy, his particular section of the British Empire supplying sundry problems just now not to be hurriedly dealt with by those in authority; there was much drawing-up of reports, and translating of facts into official language, in Arnold's secretarial department. Of these things he spoke to his bride-elect as freely as discretion allowed; and Irene found his letters interesting.

The ladies in Cheshire were forewarned of the new Irene who was about to visit them; political differences did not at all affect their kindliness; indeed, they saw with satisfaction the girl's keen mood of loyalty to the man of her choice. She brought with her the air of Greater Britain; she spoke much, and well, of the destinies of the Empire.

"I see it all more clearly since this bit of Colonial experience," she said. "Our work in the world is marked out for us; we have no choice, unless we turn cowards. Of course we shall be hated by other countries, more and more. We shall be accused of rapacity, and arrogance, and everything else that's disagreeable in a large way; we can't help that. If we enrich ourselves, that is a legitimate reward for the task we perform. England means liberty and enlightenment; let England spread to the ends of the earth! We mustn't be afraid of greatness! We *can't* stop—still less draw back. Our politics have become our religion. Our rulers have a greater responsibility than was ever known in the world's history—and they will be equal to it!"

The listeners felt that a little clapping of the hands would have been appropriate ; they exchanged a glance, as if consulting each other as to the permissibility of such applause. But Irene's eloquent eyes and glowing colour excited more admiration than criticism ; in their hearts they wished joy to the young life which would go on its way through an ever-changing world long after they and their old-fashioned ideas had passed into silence.

In a laughing moment, Irene told them of the proposal she had received from Trafford Romaine. This betokened her high spirits, and perchance indicated a wish to make it understood that her acceptance of Arnold Jacks was no unconsidered impulse. The ladies were interested, but felt this confidence something of an indiscretion, and did not comment upon it. They hoped she would not be tempted to impart her secret to persons less capable of respecting it.

During these days there came a definite invitation from Mrs. Borisoff, who was staying in Hampshire, at the house of her widowed mother, and Irene gladly accepted it. She wished to see more of Helen Borisoff, whose friendship, she felt, might have significance for her at this juncture of life. The place and its inhabitants, she found on arriving, answered very faithfully to Helen's description ; an old manor-house, beautifully situated, hard by a sleepy village ; its mistress a rather prim woman of sixty, conventional in every thought and act, but too good-natured to be aggressive, and living with her two unmarried daughters, whose sole care was the spiritual and material well-being of the village poor.

"Where I come from, I really don't know," said Helen to her friend. "My father was the staidest of country gentlemen. I'm a sport, plainly. You will see my mother watch me every now and then with apprehension. I fancy it surprises her that I really do behave myself—that I don't even say anything shocking. With you, the dear old lady is simply delighted ; I know she prays that I may not harm you. You are the first respectable acquaintance I have made since my marriage."

In the lovely old garden, in the still meadows, and on the sheep-cropped hillsides, they had many a long talk. Now that Irene was as good as married, Mrs. Borisoff used less reserve in speaking of her private circumstances ; she explained the terms on which she stood with her husband.

"Marriage, my dear girl, is of many kinds ; absurd to speak

of it as one and indivisible. There's the marriage of interest, the marriage of reason, the marriage of love; and each of these classes can be almost infinitely subdivided. For the majority of folk, I'm quite sure it would be better not to choose their own husbands and wives, but to leave it to sensible friends who wish them well. In England, at all events, they *think* they marry for love, but that's mere nonsense. Did you ever know a love match? I never even heard of one, in my little world.—Well," she added, with her roguish smile, "putting yourself out of the question."

Irene's countenance betrayed a passing inquietude. She had an air of reflection; averted her eyes; did not speak.

"The average male or female is *never* in love," pursued Helen. "They are incapable of it. And in this matter I— *moi qui vous parle*—am average. At least, I think I am; all evidence goes to prove it, so far. I married my husband because I thought him the most interesting man I had ever met. That was eight years ago, when I was two-and-twenty. Curiously, I didn't try to persuade myself that I was in love; I take credit for this, my dear! No, it was a marriage of reason. I had money, which Mr. Borisoff had not. He really liked me, and does still. But we are reasonable as ever. If we felt obliged to live always together, we should be very uncomfortable. As it is, I travel for six months when the humour takes me, and it works *à merveille*. Into my husband's life, I don't inquire; I have no right to do so, and I am not by nature a busybody. As for my own affairs, Mr. Borisoff is not uneasy; he has great faith in me — which, speaking frankly, I quite deserve. I am, my dear Irene, a most respectable woman—there comes in my parentage."

"Then," said Irene, looking at her own beautiful finger-nails, "your experience, after all, is disillusion."

"Moderate disillusion," replied the other, with her humorously judicial air. "I am not grievously disappointed. I still find my husband an interesting—a most interesting— man. Both of us being so thoroughly reasonable, our marriage may be called a success."

"Clearly, then, you don't think love a *sine quâ non*?"

"Clearly not. Love has nothing whatever to do with marriage, in the statistical—the ordinary—sense of the term. When I say love, I mean Love — not domestic affection. Marriage is a practical concern of mankind at large; Love is a personal experience of the very few. Think of our common phrases, such as 'choice of a wife'; think of the perfectly sound advice given by sage elders to the young who are thinking of marriage, implying deliberation, care. What have these things to do with Love? You can no more choose to be a lover, than to be a poet. *Nascitur non fit*—oh yes, I know my Latin. Generally, the man or woman born for Love is born for nothing else."

"A deplorable state of things!" exclaimed Irene, laughing.

"Yes—or no. Who knows? Such people ought to die young. But I don't say that it is invariably the case. To be capable of loving, and at the same time to have other faculties, and the will to use them—ah! There's your complete human being."

"I think "— Irene began, and stopped, her voice failing.

"You think, *belle Irène*?"

"Oh, I was going to say that all this seems to me sensible and right. It doesn't disturb me."

"Why should it?"

"I think I will tell you, Helen, that my motive in marrying is the same as yours was."

"I surmised it."

"But, you know, there the similarity will end. It is quite certain "—she laughed—"that I shall have no six-months' vacations. At present, I don't think I shall desire them."

"No. To speak frankly, I augur well of your marriage."

These words affected Irene with a sense of relief. She had imagined that Mrs. Borisoff thought otherwise. A bright smile sunned her countenance; Helen, observing it, smiled too, but more thoughtfully.

"You must bring your husband to see me in Paris some time next year. By the bye, you don't think he will disapprove of me?"

"Do you imagine Mr. Jacks "—

"What were you going to say?"

Irene had stopped as if for want of the right word. She was reflecting.

"It never struck me," she said, "that he would wish to regulate my choice of friends. Yet I suppose it would be within his right?"

"Conventionally speaking, undoubtedly."

"Don't think I am in uncertainty about this particular instance," said Irene. "No, he has already told me that he liked you. But of the general question, I had never thought."

"My dear, who does, or can, think before marriage of all that it involves? After all, the pleasures of life consist so largely in the unexpected."

Irene paced a few yards in silence, and when she spoke again it was of quite another subject.

Whether this sojourn with her experienced and philosophical friend made her better able to face the meeting with Arnold Jacks was not quite certain. At moments she fancied so; she saw her position as wholly reasonable, void of anxiety; she was about to marry the man she liked and respected—safest of all forms of marriage. But there came troublesome moods of misgiving. It did not flatter her self-esteem to think of herself as excluded from the number of those who are capable of love; even in Helen Borisoff's view, the elect, the fortunate. Of love, she had thought more in this last week or two than in all her years gone by. Assuredly, she knew it not, this glory of the poets. Yet she could inspire it in others; at all events, in one, whose rhythmic utterance of the passion ever and again came back to her mind.

A temptation had assailed her (but she resisted it) to repeat those verses of Piers Otway to her friend. And in thinking of them, she half reproached herself for the total silence she had preserved towards their author. Perhaps he was uncertain whether the verses had ever reached her. It seemed unkind. There would have been no harm in letting him know that she had read the lines, and—as poetry—liked them.

Was her temper prosaic? It would at any time have surprised her to be told so. Owing to her father's influence, she had given much time to scientific studies, but she knew herself by no means defective in appreciation of art and literature. By whatever accident, the friends of her earlier years had been notable rather for good sense and good feeling than for æsthetic fervour; the one exception, her cousin Olga, had rather turned her from thoughts about the beautiful, for Olga seemed emotional in excess, and was not without taint of affectation. In Helen Borisoff she knew for the first time a woman who cared supremely for music, poetry, pictures, and who combined with this a vigorous practical intelligence. Helen could burn with enthusiasm, yet never exposed herself to suspicion of weak-mindedness. Posturing was her scorn, but no one spoke more ardently of the things she admired. Her acquaintance with recent literature was wider than that of anyone Irene had known; she talked of it in the most interesting way, giving her friend new lights, inspiring her with a new energy of thought. And Irene was sorry to go away. She vaguely felt that this companionship was of moment in the history of her mind; she wished for a larger opportunity of benefiting by it.

Dr. Derwent and his son were now at Cromer; there Irene was to join them; and thither, presently, would come Arnold Jacks.

On the day of her departure there arose a storm of wind and rain, which grew more violent as she approached the Norfolk coast; and nothing could have pleased her better. Her troubled mood harmonised with the darkened, roaring sea; moreover, this atmospheric disturbance made something to talk about on arriving. She suffered no embarrassment at the meeting with her father and Eustace, who of course awaited her at the station. To their eyes, Irene was in excellent spirits, though rather wearied after the tiresome journey. She said very little about her stay in Hampshire.

The last person in the world with whom Irene would have chosen to converse about her approaching marriage was her excellent brother Eustace; but the young man was not content with offering his good wishes; to her surprise, he took the opportunity of their being alone together on the beach, to speak with most unwonted warmth about Arnold Jacks.

"I really was glad when I heard of it! To tell you the truth, I had hoped for it. If there is a man living whom I respect, it is Arnold. There's no end to his good qualities. A downright good and sensible fellow!"

"Of course I'm very glad you think so, Eustace," replied his sister, stooping to pick up a shell.

"Indeed I do. I've often thought that one's sister's choice in marriage must be a very anxious thing; it would have worried me awfully if I had felt any doubts about the man."

Irene was inclined to laugh.

"It's very good of you," she said.

"But I mean it. Girls haven't quite a fair chance, you know. They can't see much of men."

"If it comes to that," said Irene merrily, "men seem to me in much the same position."

"Oh, it's so different. Girls—women—are good. There's nothing unpleasant to be known about them."

"Upon my word, Eustace! *On n'est pas plus galant!* But I really feel it my duty to warn you against that amiable optimism. If you were so kind as to be uneasy on my account, I shall be still more so on yours. Your position, my dear boy, is a little perilous."

Eustace laughed, not without some amiable confusion. To give himself a countenance, he smote at pebbles with the head of his walking-stick.

"Oh, I shan't marry for ages!"

"That shows rather more prudence than faith in your doctrine."

"Never mind. Our subject is Arnold Jacks. He's a splendid fellow. The best and most sensible fellow I know."

It was not the eulogy most agreeable to Irene in her present state of mind. She hastened to dismiss the topic, but thought with no little surprise and amusement of Eustace's self-revelation. Brothers and sisters seldom know each other; and these two, by virtue of widely differing characteristics, were scarce more than mutually well-disposed strangers.

Less emphatic in commendation, Dr. Derwent appeared not less satisfied with his future son-in-law. Irene's scrutiny, sharpened by intense desire to read her father's mind, could detect no qualification of his contentment. As his habit was, the Doctor, having found an opportunity, broached the subject with humorous abruptness.

"It's no business of mine; I don't wish to be impertinent; but if I *may* be allowed to express approval"—

Irene raised her eyes for a moment, bestowing upon him a look of affection and gratitude.

"He's a thorough Englishman, and that means a good deal in the laudatory sense. The best sort of husband for an English girl, I've no manner of doubt."

Dr. Derwent was not effusive; he had said as much as he cared to say on the more intimate aspect of the matter. But he spoke long and carefully regarding things practical. Irene had his entire confidence; nothing in the state of his affairs

needed to be kept from her knowledge. He spoke of the
duty he owed to his two children respectively, and in sufficient
detail of Arnold Jacks' circumstances. On the death of John
Jacks (which the Doctor suspected was not remote) Arnold
would be a something more than a well-to-do man; his wife, if
she aimed that way, might look for a social position such as
the world envied.

"And on the whole," he added, "as society must have
leaders, I prefer that they should be people with brains as
well as money. The ambition is quite legitimate. Do your
part in civilising the drawing-room, as Arnold conceives he is
doing his on a larger scale. A good and intelligent woman is
no superfluity in the world of wealth nowadays."

Irene tried to believe that this ambition appealed to her.
Nay, at times it certainly did so, for she liked the brilliant and
the commanding. On the other hand, it seemed imperfect as
an ideal of life. In its undercurrents her thought was always
more or less turbid.

A letter from Arnold announced his coming. A day after,
he arrived.

Many times as she had enacted in fancy the scene of their
meeting, Irene found in the reality something quite unlike her
anticipation. Arnold, it was true, behaved much as she
expected; he was perfect in well-bred homage; he said the
right things in the right tone; his face declared a sincere
emotion, yet he restrained himself within due limits of respect.
The result in Irene's mind was disappointment and fear.

He gave her too little; he seemed to ask too much.

The first interview—in a private sitting-room at the hotel
where they were all staying—lasted about half an hour; it
wrought a change in Irene for which she had not at all
prepared herself, though the doubts and misgivings which had
of late beset her pointed darkly to such a revulsion of feeling.
She had not understood; she could not understand, until
enlightened by the very experience. Alone once more, she
sat down all tremulous; pallid as if she had suffered a shock
of fright. An indescribable sense of immodesty troubled her
nerves: she seemed to have lost all self-respect: the thought
of going forth again, of facing her father and brother, was
scarcely to be borne. This acute distress presently gave way
to a dull pain, a sinking at the heart. She felt miserably
alone. She longed for a friend of her own sex, not necessarily

to speak of what she was going through, but for the moral support of a safe companionship. Never had she known such a feeling of isolation, and of over-great responsibility.

A few tears relieved her. Irene was not prone to weeping; only a great crisis of her fate would have brought her to this extremity.

It was over in a quarter of an hour—or seemed so. She had recovered command of her nerves, had subdued the excess of emotion. As for what had happened, that was driven into the background of her mind, to await examination at leisure. She was a new being, but for the present could bear herself in the old way. Before leaving her room, she stood before the looking-glass, and smiled. Oh yes, it would do!

Arnold Jacks was in the state of mind which exhibited him at his very best. An air of discreet triumph sat well on this elegant Englishman; it prompted him to continuous discourse, which did not lack its touch of brilliancy; his features had an uncommon animation, and his slender, well-knit figure—of course clad with perfect seaside propriety—appeared to gain an inch, so gallantly he held himself. He walked the cliffs like one on guard over his country. Without for a moment becoming ridiculous, Arnold, with his first-rate English breeding, could carry off a great deal of radiant self-consciousness.

Side by side, he and Irene looked very well; there was suitability of stature, harmony of years. Arnold's clean-cut visage, manly yet refined, did no discredit to the choice of a girl even so striking in countenance as Irene. They drew the eyes of passers-by. Conscious of this, Irene now and then flinched imperceptibly; but her smile held good, and its happiness flattered the happy man.

Eustace Derwent departed in a day or two, having an invitation to join friends in Scotland. He had vastly enjoyed the privilege of listening to Arnold's talk. Indeed, to his sister's amusement, he plainly sought to model himself on Mr. Jacks, in demeanour, in phraseology, and in sentiments; not without success.

CHAPTER XXIV

ON one of those evenings at the seaside, Dr. Derwent, glancing over the newspapers, came upon a letter signed "Lee Hannaford." It had reference to some current dispute about the merits of a new bullet. Hannaford, writing with authority, criticised the invention; he gave particulars (the result of an experiment on an old horse) as to its mode of penetrating flesh and shattering bone; there was a gusto in his style, that of the true artist in bloodshed. Pointing out the signature to Arnold Jacks, Dr. Derwent asked in a subdued tone, as when one speaks of something shameful:

"Have you seen or heard of him lately?"

"About ten days ago," replied Arnold. "He was at the Hyde Wilsons', and he had the impertinence to congratulate me. He did it, too, before other people, so that I couldn't very well answer as I wished. You are aware, by the bye, that he is doing very well—belongs to a firm of manufacturers of explosives?"

"Indeed?—I wish he would explode his own head off."

The Doctor spoke with most unwonted fierceness. Arnold Jacks, without verbally seconding the wish, showed by an uneasy smile that he would not have mourned the decease of this relative of the Derwents. Mrs. Hannaford's position involved no serious scandal, but Arnold had a strong dislike for any sort of social irregularity; here was the one detail of his future wife's family circumstances which he desired to forget. What made it more annoying than it need have been was his surmise that Lee Hannaford nursed rancour against the Derwents, and would not lose an opportunity of venting it. In the public congratulation of which Arnold spoke, there had been a distinct touch of malice. It was not impossible that the man hinted calumnies with regard to his wife, and, under the circumstances, slander of that kind was the most difficult thing to deal with.

But in Irene's society these unwelcome thoughts were soon dismissed. With the demeanour of his betrothed, Arnold was abundantly satisfied; he saw in it the perfect medium between demonstrativeness and insensibility. Without ever having reflected on the subject, he felt that this was how a girl of entire refinement should behave in a situation demanding supreme delicacy. Irene never seemed in "a coming-on disposition," to use the phrase of a young person who had not the advantage of English social training; it was evidently her wish to behave, as far as possible, with the simplicity of mere friendship. In these days, Mr. Jacks, for the first time, ceased to question himself as to the prudence of the step he had taken. Hitherto he had been often reminded that, socially speaking, he might have made a better marriage; he had felt that Irene conquered somewhat against his will, and that he wooed her without quite meaning to do so. On the cliffs and the sands at Cromer, these indecisions vanished. The girl had never looked to such advantage; he had never been so often apprised of the general admiration she excited. Beyond doubt, she would do him credit—in Arnold's view the first qualification in a wife. She was really very intelligent, could hold her own in any company, and with experience might become a positively brilliant woman.

For caresses, for endearments, the time was not yet; that kind of thing, among self-respecting people of a certain class, came only with the honeymoon. Yet Arnold never for a moment doubted that the girl was very fond of him. Of course it was for his sake that she had refused Trafford Romaine—a most illuminating incident. That she was proud of him, went without saying. He noted with satisfaction how thoroughly she had embraced his political views, what a charming Imperialist she had become. In short, everything promised admirably. At moments, Arnold felt the burning of a lover's impatience.

They parted. The Derwents returned to London; Arnold set off to pay a hasty visit or two in the North. The wedding was to take place a couple of months hence, and the pair would spend their Christmas in Egypt.

A few days after her arrival in Bryanston Square, Irene went to see the Hannafords. She found her aunt in a deplorable state, unable to converse, looking as if on the verge of a serious illness. Olga behaved strangely, like one in harassing trouble of which she might not speak. It was a painful visit, and on her return home Irene talked of it to her father.

"Something wretched is going on of which we don't know," she declared. "Anyone could see it. Olga is keeping some miserable secret, and her mother looks as if she were being driven mad."

"That ruffian, I suppose," said the Doctor. "What can he be doing?"

The next day he saw his sister. He came home with a gloomy countenance, and called Irene into his study.

"You were right. Something very bad indeed is going on, so bad that I hardly like to speak to you about it. But secrecy is impossible; we must use our common sense— Hannaford is bringing a suit for divorce."

Irene was so astonished that she merely gazed at her father, waiting his explanations. Under her eyes Dr. Derwent suffered an increase of embarrassment, which tended to relieve itself in anger.

"It will kill her," he exclaimed, with a nervous gesture. "And then, if justice were done, that scoundrel would be hanged!"

"You mean her husband?"

"Yes. Though I'm not sure that there isn't another who deserves the name.—She wants to see you, Irene, and I think you must go at once. She says she has things to tell you that will make her mind easier. I'm going to send a nurse to be with her: she mustn't be left alone. It's lucky I went to-day. I won't answer for what may happen in four-and-twenty hours. Olga isn't much use, you know, though she's doing what she can."

It was about one o'clock. Saying she would be able to lunch at her aunt's house, Irene forthwith made ready, and drove to Campden Hill. She was led into the drawing-room, and sat there, alone, for five minutes; then Olga entered. The girls advanced to each other with a natural gesture of distress.

"She's asleep, I'm glad to say," Olga whispered, as if still in a sickroom. "I persuaded her to lie down. I don't think she has closed her eyes the last two or three nights. Can you wait? Oh, do, if you can! She does so want to see you."

"But why, dear? Of course I will wait; but why does she ask for *me*?"

Olga related all that had come to pass, in her knowledge. Only by ceaseless importunity had she constrained her mother to reveal the cause of an anguish which could no longer be disguised. The avowal had been made yesterday, not long before Dr. Derwent's coming to the house.

"I wanted to tell you, but she had forbidden me to speak to anyone. What's the use of trying to keep such a thing secret? If uncle had not come, I should have telegraphed for him. Of course he made her tell him, and it has put her at rest for a little; she fell asleep as soon as she lay down. Her dread is that we shan't believe her. She wants, I think, only to declare to you that she has done no wrong."

"As if I could doubt her word!"

Irene tried to shape a question, but could not speak. Her cousin also was mute for a moment. Their eyes met, and fell.

"You remember Mr. Otway's brother?" said Olga, in an unsteady voice, and then ceased.

"He? Daniel Otway?"

Irene had turned pale; she spoke under her breath. At once there recurred to her the unexplained incident at Malvern Station.

"I knew mother was foolish in keeping up an acquaintance with him," Olga answered, with some vehemence. "I detested the man, what I saw of him. And I suspect—of course mother won't say—he has been having money from her."

An exclamation of revolted feeling escaped Irene. She could not speak her thoughts; they were painful almost beyond endurance. She could not even meet her cousin's look.

"It's a hideous thing to talk about," Olga pursued, her head bent and her hands crushing each other, "no wonder it seems to be almost driving her mad. What do you think she did, as soon as she received the notice? She sent for Piers Otway, and told him, and asked him to help her. He came in the afternoon, when I was out. Think how dreadful it must have been for her!"

"How could *he* help her?" asked Irene, in a strangely subdued tone, still without raising her eyes.

"By seeing his brother, she thought, and getting him, perhaps, to persuade my father—how I hate the name!—that there were no grounds for such an action."

"What"—Irene forced each syllable from her lips—"what are the grounds alleged?"

Olga began a reply, but the first word choked her. Her self-command gave way, she sobbed, and turned to hide her face.

"You, too, are being tried beyond your strength," said Irene, whose womanhood fortified itself in these moments of wretched doubt and shame. "Come, we must have some lunch whilst aunt is asleep."

"I want to get it all over—to tell you as much as I know," said the other. "Mother says there is not even an appearance of wrong-doing against her—that she can only be accused by deliberate falsehood. She hasn't told me more than that—and how can I ask? Of course *he* is capable of everything —of any wickedness!"

"You mean Daniel Otway?"

"No—her husband—I will never again call him by the other name."

"Do you know whether Piers Otway has seen his brother?"

"He hadn't up to yesterday, when he sent mother a note, saying that the man was away, and couldn't be heard of."

With an angry effort Olga recovered her self-possession. Apart from the natural shame which afflicted her, she seemed to experience more of indignation and impatience than any other feeling. Growing calmer, she spoke almost with bitterness of her mother's folly.

"I told her once, quite plainly, that Daniel Otway wasn't the kind of man she ought to be friendly with. She was offended: it was one of the reasons why we couldn't go on living together. I believe, if the truth were known, it was worry about him that caused her break-down in health. She's a weak, soft-natured woman, and he—I know very well what *he* is. He and the other one—both Piers Otway's brothers—have always been worthless creatures. She knew it well enough, and yet—! I suppose their mother"—

She broke off in a tone of disgust. Irene, looking at her with more attentiveness, waited for what she would next say.

"Of course you remember," Olga added, after a pause, "that they are only half-brothers to Piers Otway?"

"Of course I do."

"*His* mother must have been a very different woman. You have heard—?"

They exchanged looks. Irene nodded, and averted her eyes, murmuring, " Aunt explained to me, after his father's death."

" One would have supposed," said Olga, " that *they* would turn into the honourable men, and *he* the scamp. Nature doesn't seem to care much about setting us a moral lesson."

And she laughed—a short, bitter laugh. Irene, her brows knit in painful thought, kept silence.

They were going to the dining-room, when a servant made known to them that Mrs. Hannaford was asking for her daughter.

" Do have something to eat," said Olga, " and I'll tell her you are here. You *shall* have lunch first; I insist upon it, and I'll join you in a moment."

In a quarter of an hour, Irene went up to her aunt's room. Mrs. Hannaford was sitting in an easy-chair, placed so that a pale ray of sunshine fell upon her. She rose, feebly, only to fall back again; her hands were held out in pitiful appeal, and tears moistened her cheeks. Beholding this sad picture, Irene forgot the doubt that offended her; she was all soft compassion. The suffering woman clung about her neck, hid her face against her bosom, sobbed and moaned.

They spoke together till dusk. The confession which Mrs. Hannaford made to her niece went further than that elicited from her either by Olga or Dr. Derwent. In broken sentences, in words of shamefaced incoherence, but easily understood, she revealed a passion which had been her torturing secret, and a temptation against which she had struggled year after year. The man was unworthy; she had long known it; she suffered only the more. She had been imprudent, once or twice all but reckless, never what is called guilty. Convinced of the truth of what she heard, Irene drew a long sigh, and became almost cheerful in her ardour of solace and encourage-ment. No one had ever seen the Irene who came forth under this stress of circumstance; no one had ever heard the voice with which she uttered her strong heart. The world? Who cared for the world? Let it clack and grin! They would defend the truth, and quietly wait the issue. No more weakness! Brain and conscience must now play their part.

" But if it should go against me? If I am made free of that man—? "

" Then be free of him !" exclaimed the girl, her eyes flashing through tears. " Be glad !"

"No—no! I am afraid of myself"—

"We will help you. When you are well again, your mind will be stronger to resist. Not *that*—never *that*! You know it is impossible."

"I know. And there is one thing that would really make it so. I haven't told you—another thing I had to say—why I wanted so to see you."

Irene looked kindly into the agitated face.

"It's about Piers Otway. He came to see us here. I had formed a hope"—

"Olga?"

"Yes. Oh, if that could be!"

She caught the girl's hand in her hot palms, and seemed to entreat her for a propitious word. Irene was very still, thinking; and at length she smiled.

"Who can say? Olga is good and clever"—

"It might have been; I know it might. But after this?"

"More likely than not," said Irene, with a half-absent look, "this would help to bring it about."

"Dear, only your marriage could [have changed him—nothing else. Oh, I am sure, nothing else! He has the warmest and truest heart!"

Irene sat with bowed head, her lips compressed; she smiled again, but more faintly. In the silence there sounded a soft tap at the door.

"I will see who it is," said Irene.

Olga stood without, holding a letter. She whispered that the handwriting of the address (to Mrs. Hannaford) was Piers Otway's, and that possibly this meant important news. Irene took the letter, and re-entered the room. It was necessary to light the gas before Mrs. Hannaford could read the sheet that trembled in her hand.

"What I feared! He can do nothing."

She held the letter to Irene, who perused it. Piers began by saying that as result of a note he had posted yesterday, Daniel had this morning called upon him at his office. They had had long talk.

"He declared himself quite overcome by what had happened, and said he had been away from town endeavouring to get at an understanding of the so-called evidence against him. Possibly his inquiries might effect something; as yet they were useless. He was very vague, and did not reassure me; I could not make him answer simple questions. There is no honesty in the man. Unfortunately I have warrant for saying this, on other accounts. Believe me when I tell you that the life he leads makes him unworthy of your lightest thought. He is utterly, hopelessly ignoble. It is a hateful memory that I, who feel for you a deep respect and affection, was the cause of your coming to know him.

"But for the fear of embarrassing you, I should have brought this news, instead of writing it. If you are still keeping your trouble a secret, I beseech you to ease your mind by seeing Dr. Derwent, and telling him everything. It is plain that your defence must at once be put into legal hands. Your brother is a man of the world, and much more than that; he will not, cannot, refuse to believe you, and his practical aid will comfort you in every way. Do not try to hide the thing even from your daughter; she is of an age to share your suffering, and to alleviate it by her affection. Believe me, silence is mistaken delicacy. You are innocent; you are horribly wronged; have the courage of a just cause. See Dr. Derwent at once; I implore you to do so, for your own sake, and for that of all your true friends."

At the end, Irene drew a deep breath.

"He, certainly, is one of them," she said.

"Of my true friends? Indeed, he is."

Again they were interrupted. Olga announced the arrival of the nurse sent by Dr. Derwent to tend the invalid. Thereupon Irene took leave of her aunt, promising to come again on the morrow, and went downstairs, where she exchanged a few words with her cousin. They spoke of Piers Otway's letter.

"Pleasant for us, isn't it?" said Olga, with a dreary smile. "Picture us entertaining friends who call!"

Irene embraced her gently, bade her be hopeful, and said good-bye.

At home again, she remembered that she had an engage-ment to dine out this evening, but the thought was insufferable. Eustace, who was to have accompanied her, must go alone. Having given the necessary orders, she went to her room, meaning to sit there until dinner. But she grew restless and impatient; when the first bell rang, she made a hurried change of dress, and descended to the drawing-room. An evening newspaper failed to hold her

14

attention; with nervous movements, she walked hither and thither. It was a great relief to her when the door opened and her father came in.

Contrary to his custom, the Doctor had not dressed. He bore a wearied countenance, but at sight of Irene tried to smooth away the lines of disgust.

"It was all I could do to get here by dinner-timer. Excuse me, Mam'zelle Wren; they're the clothes of an honest working-man."

The pet syllable (a joke upon her name as translated by Thibaut Rossignol) had not been frequent on her father's lips for the last year or two; he used it only in moments of gaiety or of sadness. Irene did not wish to speak about her aunt just now, and was glad that the announcement of dinner came almost at once. They sat through an unusually silent meal, the few words they exchanged having reference to public affairs. As soon as it was over, Irene asked if she might join her father in the library.

"Yes, come and be smoked," was his answer.

This mood did not surprise her. It was the Doctor's principle to combat anxiety with jests. He filled and lit one of his largest pipes, and smoked for some minutes before speaking. Irene, still nervous, let her eyes wander about the book-covered walls; a flush was on her cheeks, and with one of her hands she grasped the other wrist, as if to restrain herself from involuntary movement.

"The nurse came," she said at length, unable to keep silence longer.

"That's right. An excellent woman; I can trust her."

"Aunt seemed better when I came away."

"I'm glad."

Volleys of tobacco were the only sign of the stress Dr. Derwent suffered. He loathed what seemed to him the sordid tragedy of his sister's life, and he resented as a monstrous thing his daughter's involvement in such an affair. This was the natural man; the scientific observer took another side, urging that life was life and could not be escaped, refine ourselves as we may; also that a sensible girl of mature years would benefit rather than otherwise by being made helpful to a woman caught in the world's snare.

"Whilst I was there," pursued Irene, "there came a letter from Mr. Otway. No, no; not from *him*; from Mr. Piers Otway."

She gave a general idea of its contents, and praised its tone.

"I daresay," threw out her father, almost irritably, "but I shall strongly advise her to have done with all of that name."

"It's true they are of the same family," said Irene, "but that seems a mere accident, when one knows the difference between our friend Mr. Otway and his brothers."

"Maybe; I shall never like the name. Pray don't speak of 'our friend.' In any case, as you see, there must be an end of that."

"I should like you to see his letter, father. Ask aunt to show it you."

The Doctor smoked fiercely, his brows dark. Rarely in her lifetime had Irene seen her father wrathful — save for his outbursts against the evils of the world and the time. To her he had never spoken an angry word. The lowering of his features in this moment caused her a painful flutter at the heart; she became mute, and for a minute or two neither spoke.

"By the bye," said Dr. Derwent suddenly, "it is a most happy thing that your aunt's money was so strictly tied up. No one can be advantaged by her death—except that American hospital. Her scoundrelly acquaintances are aware of that fact, no doubt."

"It's a little hard, isn't it, that Olga would have nothing?"

"In one way, yes. But I'm not sure she isn't safer, so."

Again there fell silence. Again Irene's eyes wandered, and her hands moved nervously.

"There is one thing we must speak of," she said at length. "If the case goes on, Arnold will of course hear of it."

Dr. Derwent looked keenly at her before replying.

"He knows already."

"He knows? How?"

"By common talk in some house he frequents. Agreeable! I saw him this afternoon; he took me aside, and spoke of this. It is his belief that Hannaford himself has set the news going."

Irene seemed about to rise. She sat straight, every nerve tense, her face glowing with indignation.

"What an infamy!"

"Just so. It's the kind of thing we're getting mixed up with."

"How did Arnold speak to you? In what tone?"

"As any decent man would—I can't describe it otherwise.

He said that of course it didn't concern him, except in so far as it was likely to annoy our family. He wanted to know whether you had heard, and—naturally enough—was vexed that you couldn't be kept out of it. He's a man of the world, and knows that, nowadays, a scandal such as this matters very little. Our name will come into it, I fear, but it's all forgotten in a week or two."

They sat still and brooding for a long time. Irene seemed on the point of speaking once or twice, but checked herself. When at length her father's face relaxed into a smile, she rose, said she was weary, and stepped forward to say good-night.

"We'll have no more of this subject, unless compelled," said the Doctor. "It's worse than vivisection."

And he settled to a book—or seemed to do so.

CHAPTER XXV

IRENE passed a restless night. The snatches of unrefreshing sleep which she obtained as the hours dragged towards morning were crowded with tumultuous dreams; she seemed to be at strife with all manner of people, now defending herself vehemently against some formless accusation, now arraigning others with a violence strange to her nature. Worst of all, she was at odds with her father, about she knew not what; she saw his kind face turn cold and hard in reply to a passionate exclamation with which she had assailed him. The wan glimmer of a misty October dawn was very welcome after this pictured darkness. Yet it brought reflections that did not tend to soothe her mind.

Several letters for her lay on the breakfast-table; among them, one from Arnold Jacks, which she opened hurriedly. It proved to be a mere note, saying that at last he had found a house which seemed in every respect suitable, and he wished Irene to go over it with him as soon as possible; he would call for her at three o'clock. "Remember," he added, "you dine with us. We are by ourselves."

She glanced at her father, as if to acquaint him with this news; but the Doctor was deep in a leading-article, and she did not disturb him. Eustace had correspondence of his own which engrossed him. No one seemed disposed for talk this morning.

The letter which most interested her came from Helen Borisoff, who was now at home, in Paris. It was the kind of letter that few people are so fortunate as to receive nowadays, covering three sheets with gaiety and good-nature, with glimpses of interesting social life and many an amusing detail. Mrs. Borisoff was establishing herself for the winter, which promised all sorts of good things yonder on the Seine. She had met most of the friends she cared about, among whom were men and women with far-echoing names. With her husband she was on delightful terms; he had welcomed her charmingly; he wished her to convey his respectful homage to the young English lady with whom his wife had become *liée*, and the hope that at no distant time he might make her acquaintance. After breakfast, Irene lingered over this letter, which brightened her imagination. Paris shone luringly as she read. Had circumstances been different, she would assuredly have spent a month there with Helen.

Well, she was going to Egypt, after—

One glance she gave at Arnold's short note. "My dear Irene"—"In haste, but ever yours." These lines did not tempt her to muse. Yet Arnold was ceaselessly in her mind. She wished to see him, and at the same time feared his coming. As for the house, it occupied her thoughts with only a flitting vagueness. Why so much solicitude about the house? In any decent quarter of London, was not one just as good as another? But for the risk of hurting Arnold, she would have begged him to let her off the inspection, and to manage the business as he thought fit.

A number of small matters claimed her attention during the morning, several of them connected with her marriage. Try as she might, she could not bring herself to a serious occupation with these things; they seemed trivial and tiresome. Her thoughts wandered constantly to the house at Campden Hill, which had a tragic fascination. She had promised to see her aunt to-day, but it would be difficult to find time, unless she could manage to get there between her business with Arnold and the hour of dinner. Olga was to telegraph if anything happened. A chill misgiving took hold upon her as often as she saw her aunt's face, so worn and woe-stricken; and it constantly hovered before her mind's eye.

The revelation made to her yesterday had caused a mental shock greater than she yet realised. That Mrs. Hannaford, a woman whom she had for many years regarded as elderly, should be possessed and overcome by the passion of love, was a thing so strange, so at conflict with her fixed ideas, as to be all but incredible. In her aunt's presence, she scarcely reflected upon it; she saw only a woman bound to her by natural affection, who had fallen into dire misfortune and wretchedness. Little by little, the story grew upon her understanding; the words in which it had been disclosed came back to her, and with a new significance, a pathos hitherto unfelt. She remembered that Olga's mother was not much more than forty years old; that this experience began more than five years ago; that her life had been loveless; that she was imaginative and of emotional temper. To dwell upon these facts was not only to see one person in a new light, but to gain a wider perception of life at large. Irene had a sense of enfranchisement from the immature, the conventional.

She would have liked to be alone, to sit quietly and think. She wanted to review once more, and with fuller self-consciousness, the circumstances which were shaping her future. But there was no leisure for such meditation; the details of life pressed upon her, urged her onward, as with an impatient hand. This sense of constraint became an irritation—due in part to the slight headache, coming and going, which reminded her of her bad night. Among the things she meant to do this morning was the writing of several letters to so-called friends, who had addressed her in the wonted verbiage on the subject of her engagement. Five minutes proved the task impossible. She tore up a futile attempt at civility, and rose from the desk with all her nerves quivering.

"How well I understand," she said to herself, "why men swear!"

At eleven o'clock, unable to endure the house, she dressed for going out, and drove to Mrs. Hannaford's.

Olga was not at home. Before going into her aunt's room, Irene spoke with the nurse, who had no very comforting report to make; Mrs. Hannaford could not sleep, had not closed her eyes for some four-and-twenty hours; Dr. Derwent had looked in this morning, and was to return later with another medical man. The patient longed for her niece's visit; it might do good.

She stayed about an hour, and it was the most painful hour her life had yet known. The first sight of Mrs. Hannaford's face told her how serious this illness was becoming; eyes unnaturally wide, lips which had gone so thin, head constantly moving from side to side as it lay back on the cushion of the sofa, were indications of suffering which made Irene's heart ache. In a faint, unsteady, lamenting voice, the poor woman talked ceaselessly; now of the wrong that was being done her, now of her miseries in married life, now again of her present pain. Once or twice Irene fancied her delirious, for she seemed to speak without consciousness of a hearer. To the inquiry whether it was in her niece's power to be of any service, she answered at first with sorrowful negatives, but said presently that she would like to see Piers Otway; could Irene write to him, and ask him to come?

"He shall come," was the reply.

On going down, Irene met her cousin, just returned. To her she spoke of Mrs. Hannaford's wish.

"I promised he should be sent for. Will you do it, Olga?"

"It is already done," Olga answered. "Did she forget? One of the things I went out for was to telegraph to him."

They gazed at each other with distressful eyes.

"Oh, what does the man deserve who has caused this?" exclaimed Olga, who herself began to look ill. "It's dreadful! I am afraid to go into the room. If I had someone here to live with me!"

Irene's instinct was to offer to come, but she remembered the difficulties. Her duties at home were obstacles sufficient. She had to content herself with promising to call as often as possible.

Returning to Bryanston Square, she thought with annoyance of the possibility that her father and Piers Otway might come face to face in that house. Never till now had she taxed her father with injustice. It seemed to her an intolerable thing that the blameless man should be made to share in obloquy merited by his brother. And what memory was this which awoke in her? Did not she herself once visit upon him a fault in which he had little if any part? She recalled that evening, long ago, at Queen's Gate, when she was offended by the coarse behaviour of Piers Otway's second brother. True, there was something else that moved her censure on that occasion, but she would scarcely have noticed it save for the foolish incident at the door. Fortune was not his friend. She thought of the circumstances of his birth, which had so cruelly wronged him when Jerome Otway died. Now, more likely than not, her father would resent his coming to Mrs. Hannaford's, would see in it something suspicious, a suggestion of base purpose.

"I can't stand that!" Irene exclaimed to herself. "If he is calumniated, I shall defend him, come of it what may!"

At luncheon, Dr. Derwent was grave and disinclined to converse. On learning where Irene had been, he nodded, making no remark. It was a bad sign that his uneasiness could no longer be combated with a dry joke.

As three o'clock drew near, Irene made no preparation for going out. She sat in the drawing-room, unoccupied, and was found thus when Arnold Jacks entered.

"You got my note?" he began, with a slight accent of surprise.

Irene glanced at him, and perceived that he did not wear his wonted countenance. This she had anticipated, with an uneasiness which now hardened in her mind to something like resentment.

"Yes. I hoped you would excuse me. I have a little headache."

"Oh, I'm sorry!"

He was perfectly suave. He looked at her with a good-natured anxiety. Irene tried to smile.

"You won't mind if I leave all that to you? Your judgment is quite enough. If you really like the house, take it at once. I shall be delighted."

"It's rather a responsibility, you know. Suppose we wait till to-morrow?"

Irene's nerves could not endure an argument. She gave a strange laugh, and exclaimed :

"Are you afraid of responsibilities? In this case, you must really face it. Screw up your courage."

Decidedly, Arnold was not himself. He liked an engagement of banter; it amused him to call out Irene's spirit, and to conquer in the end by masculine force in guise of affectionate tolerance. To-day he seemed dull, matter-of-fact, inclined to vexation ; when not speaking, he had a slightly absent air, as if ruminating an unpleasant thought.

"Of course I will do as you wish, Irene. Just let me describe the house "—

She could have screamed with irritation.

"Arnold, I entreat you! The house is nothing to me. I mean, one will do as well as another, if *you* are satisfied."

"So be it. I will never touch on the subject again."

His tone was decisive. Irene knew that he would literally keep his word. This was the side of his character which she liked, which had always impressed her ; and for the moment her nerves were soothed.

"You will forgive me?" she said gently.

"Forgive you for having a headache?—Will it prevent you from coming to us this evening?"

"I should be grateful if you let me choose another day."

He did not stay very long. At leave-taking, he raised her hand to his lips, and Irene felt that he did it gracefully. But when she was alone again, his manner, so slightly yet so noticeably changed, became the harassing subject of her thought. That the change resulted from annoyance at the scandal in her family she could not doubt; such a thing would be hard for Arnold to bear. When were they to speak of it? Speak they must, if the affair went on to publicity. And, considering the natural difficulty Arnold would find in approaching such a subject, ought not she to take some steps of her own initiative?

By evening, she saw the position in a very serious light. She asked herself whether it did not behove her to offer to make an end of their engagement.

"Your aunt has brain fever," said Dr. Derwent, in the library after dinner. And Irene shuddered with dread.

Early next morning she accompanied her father to Mrs. Hannaford's. The Doctor went upstairs; Irene waited in the dining-room, where she was soon joined by Olga. The girl's face was news sufficient; her mother grew worse—had passed a night of delirium. Two nurses were in the house, and the medical man called every few hours. Olga herself looked on the point of collapse; she was haggard with fear; she trembled and wept. In spite of her deep concern and sympathy, Irene's more courageous temper reproved this weakness, wondered at it as unworthy of a grown woman.

"Did Mr. Otway come?" she asked, as soon as it was possible to converse.

"Yes. He was a long time in mother's room, and just before he left her your father came."

"They met?"

"No. Uncle seemed angry when I told him. He said, 'Get rid of him at once!' I suppose he dislikes him because of his brother. It's very unjust."

Irene kept silence.

"He came down—and we talked. I am so glad to have any friend near me! I told him how uncle felt. Of course he will not come again"—

"Why not? This is *your* house, not my father's!"

"But poor mother couldn't see him now—wouldn't know

him. I promised to send him news frequently. I'm going to telegraph this morning."

"Of course," said Irene, with emphasis. "He must understand that *you* have no such feeling"—

"Oh, he knows that! He knows I am grateful to him—very grateful"—

She broke down again, and sobbed. Irene, without speaking, put her arms around the girl and kissed her cheek.

Dr. Derwent and his daughter met again at luncheon. Afterwards, Irene followed into the library.

"I wish to ask you something, father. When you and Arnold spoke about this hateful thing, did you tell him, unmistakably, that aunt was slandered?"

"I told him that I myself had no doubt of it."

"Did he seem—do you think that *he* doubts?"

"Why?"

Irene kept silence, feeling that her impression was too vague to be imparted.

"Try," said her father, "to dismiss the matter from your thoughts. It doesn't concern you. You will never hear an allusion to it from Jacks. Happen what may"—his voice paused, with suggestive emphasis—"you have nothing to do with it. It doesn't affect your position or your future in the least."

As she withdrew, Irene was uneasily conscious of altered relations with her father. The change had begun when she wrote to him announcing her engagement; since, they had never conversed with the former freedom, and the shadow now hanging over them seemed to chill their mutual affection. For the first time, she thought with serious disquiet of the gulf between old and new that would open at her marriage, of all she was losing, of the duties she was about to throw off—duties which appeared so much more real, more sacred, than those she undertook in their place. Her father's widowerhood had made him dependent upon her in a higher degree than either of them quite understood until they had to reflect upon the consequences of parting; and Irene now perceived that she had dismissed this consideration too lightly. She found difficulty in explaining her action, her state of mind, her whole self. Was it really only a few weeks ago? To her present mood, what she had thought and done seemed a result of youth and inexperience, a condition long outlived,

When she had sat alone for half an hour in the drawing-room, Eustace joined her. He said their father had gone out. They talked of indifferent things till bedtime.

In the morning, the servant who came into Irene's room gave her a note addressed in the Doctor's hand. It contained the news that Mrs. Hannaford had died before daybreak. Dr. Derwent himself did not appear till about ten o'clock, when he arrived together with his niece. Olga had been violently hysterical; it seemed the wisest thing to bring her to Bryanston Square; the change of surroundings and Irene's sympathy soon restored her to calm.

At midday a messenger brought Irene a letter from Arnold Jacks. Arnold wrote that he had just heard of her aunt's death: that he was deeply grieved, and hastened to condole with her. He did not come in person, thinking she would prefer to let this sad day pass over before they met, but he would call to-morrow morning. In the meantime, he would be grateful for a line assuring him that she was well.

Having read this, Irene threw it aside as if it had been a tradesman's circular. Not thus should he have written—if write he must, instead of coming. In her state of agitation after the hours spent with Olga, this bald note of sympathy seemed almost an insult; to keep silence as to the real cause of Mrs. Hannaford's death was much the same, she felt, as hinting a doubt of the poor lady's innocence. Arnold Jacks was altogether too decorous. Would it not have been natural for a man in his position to utter at least an indignant word? It might have been as allusive as his fine propriety demanded, but surely the word should have been spoken!

After some delay, she replied in a telegram, merely saying that she was quite well.

Olga, as soon as she felt able, had sat down to write a letter. She begged her cousin to have it posted at once.

"It's to Mr. Otway," she said, in an unsteady voice. And, when the letter had been despatched, she added, "It will be a great blow to him. I had a letter last night asking for news— Oh, I meant to bring it!" she exclaimed, with a momentary return of her distracted manner. "I left it in my room. It will be lost—destroyed!"

Irene quieted her, promising that the letter should be kept safe.

"Perhaps he will call," Olga said presently. "But no, not

so soon. He may have written again. I must have the letter, if there is one. Someone must go over to the house this evening."

Through a great part of the afternoon, she slept, and whilst she was sleeping there arrived for her a telegram, which, Irene did not doubt, came from Piers Otway. It proved to be so, and Olga betrayed nervous tremors after reading the message.

"I shall have a letter in the morning," she said to her cousin, several times; and after that she did not care to talk, but sat for hours busy with her thoughts, which seemed not altogether sad.

At eleven o'clock next morning, Arnold Jacks was announced. Irene, who sat with Olga in the drawing-room, had directed that her visitor should be shown into the library, and there she received him. Arnold stepped eagerly towards her; not smiling, indeed, but with the possibility of a smile manifest in every line of his countenance. There could hardly have been a stronger contrast with his manner of the day before yesterday. For this Irene had looked. Seeing precisely what she expected, her eyes fell; she gave a careless hand; she could not speak.

Arnold talked, talked. He said the proper things, and said them well; to things the reverse of proper, not so much as the faintest reference. This duty discharged, he spoke of the house he had taken; his voice grew animated; at length the latent smile stole out through his eyes and spread to his lips. Irene kept silence. Respecting her natural sadness, the lover made his visit brief, and retired with an air of grave satisfaction.

CHAPTER XXVI

OLGA knew that by her mother's death she became penniless. The income enjoyed by Mrs. Hannaford under the will of her sister in America was only for life : by allowing a third of it to her husband, she had made saving impossible, and, as she left no will, her daughter could expect only such trifles as might legally fall to her share when things were settled. To her surviving parent, the girl was of course no more than a stranger. It surprised no one that Lee Hannaford, informed through the lawyers of what had happened, simply kept silence, leaving his wife's burial to the care of Dr. Derwent.

Three days of gloom went by; the funeral was over; Irene and her cousin sat together in their mourning apparel, not simply possessed by natural grief, but overcome with the nervous exhaustion which results from our habits and customs in the presence of death. Olga had been miserably crying, but was now mute and still; Irene, pale, with an expression of austere thoughtfulness, spoke of the subject they both had in mind.

"There is no necessity to take any step at all—until you are quite yourself again—until you really wish. This is your home; my father would like you to stay."

"I couldn't live here after you are married," replied the other, weakly, despondently.

Irene glanced at her, hung a moment on the edge of speech, then spoke with a self-possession which made her seem many years older than her cousin.

"I had better tell you now, that we may understand each other. I am not going to be married."

To Olga's voiceless astonishment she answered with a pale smile. Grave again, and gentle as she was firm, Irene continued.

"I am going to break my engagement. It has been a

mistake. To-night I shall write a letter to Mr. Jacks, saying that I cannot marry him; when it has been sent, I shall tell my father."

Olga had begun to tremble. Her features were disturbed with an emotion which banished every sign of sorrow; which flushed her cheeks and made her eyes seem hostile in their fixed stare.

"How can you do that?" she asked, in a hard voice. "How is it possible?"

"It seems to me far more possible than the alternative—a life of repentance."

"But—what do you mean, Irene? When everything is settled—when your house is taken—when everyone knows! What do you mean? Why shall you do this?"

The words rushed forth impetuously, quivering on a note of resentment. The flushed cheeks were turning pallid; the girl's breast heaved with indignant passion.

"I can't fully explain it to you, Olga." The speaker's tones sounded very soft and reasonable after that outbreak. "I am doing what many a girl would do, I feel sure, if she could find courage—let us say, if she saw clearly enough. It will cause confusion, ill-feeling, possibly some unhappiness, for a few weeks, for a month or two; then Mr. Jacks will feel grateful to me, and my father will acknowledge I did right; and everybody else who knows anything about it will have found some other subject of conversation."

"You are fond of somebody else?"

It was between an exclamation and an inquiry. Bending forward, Olga awaited the reply as if her life depended upon it.

"I am fond of no one—in that sense."

Irene's look was so fearless, her countenance so tranquil in its candour, that the agitated girl grew quieter.

"It isn't because you are *thinking* of someone else that you can't marry Mr. Jacks?"

"I am thinking simply of myself. I am afraid to marry him. No thought of the kind you mean has entered my head."

"But how will it be explained to everybody?"

"By telling the truth — always the best way out of a difficulty. I shall take all the blame on myself, as I ought."

"And you will live on here, just as usual, seeing people— ?"

"No, I don't think I could do that. Most likely I shall go for a time to Paris."

Olga's relief expressed itself in a sigh.

"In all this," continued Irene, "there's no reason why you shouldn't stay here. Everything, you may be sure, will be settled very quietly. My father is a reasonable man."

After a short reflection, Olga said that she could not yet make up her mind. And therewith ended their dialogue. Each was glad to go apart into privacy, to revolve anxious thoughts, and to seek rest.

That her father was "a reasonable man," Irene had always held a self-evident proposition. She had never, until a few days ago, conceived the possibility of a conflict between his ideas of right and her own. Domestic discord was to her mind a vulgar, no less than an unhappy, state of things. Yet, in the step she was now about to take, could she feel any assurance that Dr. Derwent would afford her the help of his sympathy—or even that he would refrain from censure? Reason itself was on her side; but an otherwise reasonable man might well find difficulty in acknowledging it, under the circumstances.

The letter to Arnold Jacks was already composed; she knew it by heart, and had but to write it out. In the course of a sleepless night, this was done. In the early glimmer of a day of drizzle and fog, the letter went to post.

There needed courage—yes, there needed courage—on a morning such as this, when the skyless atmosphere weighed drearily on heart and mind, when hope had become a far-off thing, banished for long months from a grey, cold world, to go through with the task which Irene had set herself. Could she but have slept, it might have been easier for her; she had to front it with an aching head, with eyes that dazzled, with blood fevered into cowardice.

Dr. Derwent was plainly in no mood for conversation. His voice had been seldom heard during the past week. At the breakfast-table he read his letters, glanced over the paper, exchanged a few sentences with Eustace, said a kind word to Olga; when he rose, one saw that he hoped for a quiet morning in his laboratory.

"Could I see you for half an hour before lunch, father?"

He looked into the speaker's face, surprised at something unusual in her tone, and nodded without smiling.

"When you like."

She stood at the window of the drawing-room, looking over the enclosure in the square, the dreary so-called garden, with its gaunt leafless trees that dripped and oozed. Opposite was the long façade of characterless houses, like to that in which she lived; the steps, the door-columns, the tall narrow windows; above them, murky vapour.

She moved towards the door, hesitated, looked about her with unconsciously appealing eyes. She moved forward again, and on to her purpose.

"Well?" said the Doctor, who stood before a table covered with scientific apparatus. "Is it about Olga?"

"No, dear father. It's about Irene."

He smiled; his face softened to tenderness.

"And what about Mam'zelle Wren? It's hard on Wren, all this worry at such a time."

"If it didn't sound so selfish, I should say it had all happened for my good. I suppose we can't help seeing the world from our own little point of view."

"What follows on this philosophy?"

"Something you won't like to hear, I know; but I beg you to be patient with me. When were you not? I never had such need of your patience and forbearance as now.— Father, I cannot marry Arnold Jacks. And I have told him that I can't."

The Doctor very quietly laid down a microscopic slide. His forehead grew wrinkled; his lips came sharply together; he gazed for a moment at an open volume on a high desk at his side, then said composedly:

"This is your affair, Irene. All I can do is to advise you to be sure of your own mind."

"I *am* sure of it—very sure of it!"

Her voice trembled a little; her hand, resting upon the table, much more.

"You say you have told Jacks?"

"I posted a letter to him this morning."

"With the first announcement of your change of mind?— How do you suppose he will reply?"

"I can't feel sure."

There was silence. The Doctor took up a piece of paper, and began folding and re-folding it, the while he meditated.

"You know, of course," he said at length, "what the world thinks of this sort of behaviour?"

"I know what the world is likely to *say* about it. Unfortunately, the world seldom thinks at all."

"Granted. And we may also assume that no explanation offered by you or Jacks will affect the natural course of gossip. Still, you would wish to justify yourself in the eyes of your friends."

"What I wish before all, of course, is to save Mr. Jacks from any risk of blame. It must be understood that I, and I alone, am responsible for what happens."

"Stick to your philosophy," said her father. "Recognise the fact that you cannot save him from gossip and scandal—that people will credit as much or as little as they like of any explanation put forth. Moreover, bear in mind that this action of yours is defined by a vulgar word, which commonly injures the man more than the woman. In the world's view, it is worse to be made ridiculous than to act cruelly."

A look of pain passed over the girl's face.

"Father, I am not acting cruelly. It is the best thing I can do, for him as well as for myself. On his side, no deep feeling is involved, and as for his vanity—I can't consider that."

"You have come to the conclusion that he is not sufficiently devoted to you?"

"I couldn't have put it in those words, but that is half the truth. The other half is, that I was altogether mistaken in my own feelings.—Father, you are accustomed to deal with life and death. Do you think that fear of gossip, and desire to spare Mr. Jacks a brief mortification, should compel me to surrender all that makes life worth living, and to commit a sin for which there is no forgiveness?"

Her voice, thoroughly under control, its natural music subdued rather than emphasised, lent to these words a deeper meaning than they would have conveyed if uttered with vehemence. They woke in her father's mind a memory of long years ago, recalled the sound of another voice which had the same modulations.

"I find no fault with you," he said gravely. "That you can do such a thing as this proves to me how strongly you feel about it. But it is a serious decision—more serious,

perhaps, than you realise. Things have gone so far. The
mere inconvenience caused will be very great."

"I know it. I have felt tempted to yield to that thought—
to let things slide, as they say. Convenience, I feel sure, is
a greater power on the whole than religion or morals or the
heart. It doesn't weigh with me, because I have had such a
revelation of myself as blinds me to everything else. I *dare*
not go on ! "

"Don't think I claim any authority over you," said the
Doctor. "At your age, my only right as your father is in my
affection, my desire for your welfare. Can you tell me more
plainly how this change has come about ? "

Irene reflected. She had seated herself, and felt more
confidence now that, by bending her head, she could escape
her father's gaze.

"I can tell you one of the things that brought me to a
resolve," she said. "I found that Mr. Jacks was disturbed
by the fear of a public scandal which would touch our name ;
so much disturbed that, on meeting me after aunt's death, he
could hardly conceal his gladness that she was out of the way."

"Are you sure you read him aright ? "

"Very sure."

"It was natural—in Arnold Jacks."

"It was. I had not understood that before."

"His relief may have been as much on your account as
his own."

"I can't feel that," replied Irene. "If it were true, he
could have made me feel it. There would have been something—if only a word—in the letter he wrote me about the
death. I didn't expect him to talk to me about the hateful
things that were going on ; I *did* hope that he would give me
some assurance of his indifference to their effect on people's
minds.—Yet no ; that is not quite true. Even then, I had
got past hoping it. Already I understood him too well."

"Strange ! All this new light came after your engagement ? "

Irene bent her head again, for her cheeks were warm. In
a flash of intellect, she wondered that a man so deep in the
science of life should be so at a loss before elementary facts
of emotional experience. She could only answer by saying
nothing.

Dr. Derwent murmured his next words.

"I, too, have a share in the blame of all this."

" You, father ? "

" I knew the man better than you did, or could.   I shirked a difficult duty.   But one reason why I did so, was that I felt in doubt as to your mind.   The fact that you were my daughter did not alter the fact that you were a woman, and I could not have any assurance that I understood you.   If there had been a question of his life, his intellectual powers, his views—I would have said freely just what I thought.   But there was no need ; no objection rose on that score ; you saw the man, from that point of view, much as I did—only with a little more sympathy.   In other respects, I trusted to what we call women's instinct, women's perceptiveness.   To me, he did not seem your natural mate ; but then I saw with man's eyes ; I was afraid of meddling obtusely."

" Don't reproach yourself, father.   The knowledge I have gained could only have come to me in one way."

" Of course he will turn to me, in appeal against you."

" If so, it will be one more proof how rightly I am acting."

The Doctor smiled, all but laughed.

" Considering how very decent a fellow he is, your mood seems severe, Irene.—Well, you have made up your mind. It's an affair of no small gravity, and we must get through it as best we can.   I have no doubt whatever it's worse for you than for anyone else concerned."

" It is so bad for me, father, that, when I have gone through it, I shall be at the end of my strength.   I shall run away from the after consequences."

" What do you mean ? "

" I shall accept Mrs. Borisoff's invitation, and go to Paris. It is deserting you, but "—

Dr. Derwent wore a doubtful look ; he pondered, and began to pace the floor.

" We must think about that."

Though her own mind was quite made up, Irene did not see fit to say more at this juncture.   She rose.   Her father continued moving hither and thither, his hands behind his back, seemingly oblivious of her presence.   To him, the trouble seemed only just beginning, and he was not at all sure what the end would be.

" Jacks will come this evening, I suppose ? " he threw out, as Irene approached the door.

" Perhaps this afternoon."

He looked at her with sympathy, with apprehension.   Irene, endeavouring to smile in reply, passed from his view.

Olga had gone out, merely saying that she wished to see a friend, and that she might not be back to luncheon.   She did not return.   Father and daughter were alone together at the meal.   Contrary to Irene's expectation, the Doctor had become almost cheerful; he made one or two quiet jokes in the old way, of course on any subject but that which filled their minds, and his behaviour was marked with an unusual gentleness. Irene was so moved by grateful feeling, that now and then she could not trust her voice.

"Let me remind you," he said, observing her lack of appetite, "that an ill-nourished brain can't be depended upon for sanity of argument."

"It aches a little," she replied quietly.

"I was afraid so.   What if you rest to-day, and let me postpone for you that interview—?"

The suggestion was dreadful; she put it quickly aside.   She hoped with all her strength that Arnold Jacks would have received the letter already, and that he would come to see her this afternoon.   To pass another night with her suspense would be a strain scarce endurable.

Fog still hung about the streets, shifting, changing its density, but never allowing a glimpse of sky.   Alone in the drawing-room, Irene longed for the end of so-called day, that she might shut out that spirit-crushing blotch of bare trees and ugly houses.   She thought, of a sudden, how much harder we make life than it need be, by dwelling amid scenes that disgust, in air that lowers vitality.   There fell on her a mood of marvelling at the aims and the satisfactions of mankind.   This hideous oblong, known as Bryanston Square—how did it come to seem a desirable place of abode?   Nay, how was it for a moment tolerable to reasoning men and women?   This whole London now gasping in foul vapours that half obscured, half emphasised its inexpressible monstrosity, its inconceivable abominations—by what blighting of eye and soul did a nation come to accept it as their world-shown pride, their supreme City?   She was lost in a truth-perceiving dream.   Habit and association dropped away; things declared themselves in their actuality; her mind whirled under the sense of human folly, helplessness, endurance.

"Irene"—

A cry escaped her; she started at the sound of her name as if terrified. Arnold Jacks had entered the room, and drawn near to her, whilst she was deep in reverie.

"I am sorry to have alarmed you," he added, smiling tolerantly.

With embarrassment which was almost shame — for she despised womanish nervousness—Irene turned towards the fireplace, where chairs invited them.

"Let us sit down and talk," she said, in a softened voice. "I am so grateful to you for coming at once."

CHAPTER XXVII

HIS manner was that to which she had grown accustomed, or differed so little from it that, in ordinary circumstances, she would have remarked no peculiarity. He might have seemed, perhaps, a trifle less matter-of-fact than usual, slightly more disposed to ironic playfulness. At ease in the soft chair, his legs extended, with feet crossed, he observed Irene from under humorously bent brows; watched her steadily, until he saw that she could bear it no longer. Then he spoke.

"I thought we should get through without it."

"Without what?"

"This little reaction. It comes into the ordinary prognosis, I believe; but we seemed safe. Yet I can't say I'm sorry. It's better, no doubt, to get this over before marriage."

Irene flushed, and for a moment strung herself to the attitude of offended pride. But it passed. She smiled to his smile, and, playing with the tassel of her chair, responded in a serious undertone.

"I hoped my letter could not possibly be misunderstood."

"I understand it perfectly. I am here to talk it over from your own standpoint."

Again he frowned jocosely. His elbows on the chair-arms, he tapped together the points of his fingers, exhibiting nails which were all that they should have been. Out of regard for the Derwents' mourning, he wore a tie of black satin, and his clothes were of dark-grey, a rough material which combined the effects of finish and of carelessness—note of the well-dressed Englishman.

"We cannot talk it over," rejoined Irene. "I have nothing to say—except that I take blame and shame to myself, and that I entreat your forgiveness."

Under his steady eye, his good-humoured, watchful mastery, she was growing restive.

"I was in doubt whether to come to-day," said Jacks, in a reflective tone. "I thought at first of sending a note, and postponing our meeting. I understood so perfectly the state of mind in which you wrote—the natural result of most painful events. The fact is, I am guilty of bad taste in seeming to treat it lightly; you have suffered very much, and won't be yourself for some days. But, after all, it isn't as if one had to do with the ordinary girl. To speak frankly, I thought it was the kindest thing to come—so I came."

Nothing Arnold had ever said to her had so appealed to Irene's respect as this last sentence. It had the ring of entire sincerity; it was quite simply spoken; it soothed her nerves.

"Thank you," she answered, with a grateful look. "You did right. I could not have borne it—if you had just written and put it off. Indeed, I could not have borne it."

Arnold changed his attitude; he bent forward, his arms across his knees, so as to be nearer to her.

"Do you think *I* should have had an easy time?"

"I reproach myself more than I can tell you. But you must understand—you *must* believe that I mean what I am saying!" Her voice began to modulate. "It is not only the troubles we have gone through. I have seen it coming—the moment when I should write that letter. Through cowardice, I have put it off. It was very unjust to you; you have every right to condemn my behaviour; I am unpardonable. And yet I hope—I do so hope—that some day you will pardon me."

In the man's eyes, she had never been so attractive, so desirable, so essentially a woman. The mourning garb became her, for it was moulded upon her figure, and gave effect to the admirably pure tone of her complexion. Her beauty, in losing its perfect healthfulness, gained a new power over the imagination; the heavy eyes suggested one knew not what ideal of painters and poets; the lips were more sensuous since they had lost their mocking smile. All passion of which Arnold Jacks was capable sounded in the voice with which he now spoke.

"I shall never pardon you, because I shall never feel you have injured me. Say to me what you want to say. I will listen. What can I do better than listen to your voice? I won't argue; I won't contradict. Relieve your mind, and let us see what it all comes to in the end."

Irene had a creeping sense of fear. This tone was so unlike what she had expected. Physical weakness threatened a defeat which would have nothing to do with her will. If she yielded now, there would be no recovering her self-respect, no renewal of her struggle for liberty. She wished to rise, to face him upon her feet, yet had not the courage. His manner dictated hers. They were not playing parts on a stage, but civilised persons discussing their difficulties in a soft-carpeted drawing-room. The only thing in her favour was that the afternoon drew on, and the light thickened. Veiled in dusk, she hoped to speak more resolutely.

"Must I repeat my letter?"

"Yes, if you feel sure that it still expresses your mind."

"It does. I made a grave mistake. In accepting your offer of marriage, I was of course honest, but I didn't know what it meant; I didn't understand myself. Of course it's very hard on you that your serious purpose should have for its only result to teach me that I was mistaken. If I didn't know that you have little patience with such words, I should say that it shows something wrong in our social habits.—Yet, that's foolish; you are right, that is quite silly. It isn't our habits that are to blame, but our natures—the very nature of things. I had to engage myself to you before I could know that I ought to have done nothing of the kind."

She paused, suddenly breathless, and a cough seized her.

"You've taken cold," said Jacks, with graceful solicitude.

"No, no! It's nothing."

Dusk crept about the room. The fire was getting rather low.

"Shall I ring for lamps?" asked Arnold, half rising.

Irene wished to say no, but the proprieties were too strong. She allowed him to ring the bell, and, without asking leave, he threw coals upon the fire. For five minutes their dialogue suffered interruption; when it began again, the curtains were drawn, and warm rays succeeded to turbid twilight.

"I had better explain to you," said Arnold, in a tone of delicacy overcome, "this state of mind in which you find yourself. It is perfectly natural; one has heard of it; one sees the causes of it. You are about to take the most important step in your whole life, and, being what you are, a very intelligent and very conscientious girl, you have thought and thought about its gravity until it frightens you. That's the simple explanation of your trouble. In a week—perhaps in a day or two—it will have passed. Just wait. Don't think of it. Put your marriage—put me—quite out of your mind. I won't remind you of my existence for—let us say before next Sunday. Now, is it agreed?"

"I should be dishonest if I pretended to agree."

"But—don't you think you owe it to me to give what I suggest a fair trial?"

The words were trenchant, the tone was studiously soft. Irene strung herself for contest, hoping it would come quickly and undisguised.

"I owe you much. I have done you a great injustice. But waiting will do no good. I know my mind at last. I see what is possible and what impossible."

"Do you imagine, Irene, that I can part with you on these terms? Do you really think I could shake hands, and say good-bye, at this stage of our relations?"

"What can I do?" Her voice, kept low, shook with emotion. "I confess an error—am I to pay for it with my life?"

"I ask you only to be just to yourself as well as to me. Let three days go by, and see me again."

She seemed to reflect upon it. In truth she was debating whether to persevere in honesty, or to spare her nerves with dissimulation. A promise to wait three days would set her free forthwith; the temptation was great. But something in her had more constraining power.

"If I pretended to agree, I should be ashamed of myself. I should have passed from error into baseness. You would have a right to despise me; as it is, you have only a right to be angry."

As though the word acted upon his mood, Arnold sprang forward from the chair, fell upon one knee close beside her, and grasped her hands. Irene instinctively threw herself back, looking frightened; but she did not attempt to rise. His face was hot-coloured, his eyes shone unpleasantly; but before he spoke, his lips parted in a laugh.

"Are you one of the women," he said, "who have to be conquered? I didn't think so. You seemed so reasonable."

"Do you dream of conquering a woman who cannot love you?"

"I refuse to believe it. I recall your own words."

He made a movement to pass one arm about her waist.

"No! After what I have said—!"

Her hands being free, she sprang up and broke away from him. Arnold rose more slowly, his look lowered with indignation. Eyes bent on the ground, hands behind him, he stood mute.

"Must I leave you?" said Irene, when she could steady her voice.

"That is my dismissal?"

"If you cannot listen to me, and believe me—yes."

"All things considered, you are a little severe."

"You put yourself in the wrong. However unjust I have been to you, I can't atone by permitting what you call conquest. No, I assure you, I am *not* one of those women."

His eyes were now fixed upon her; his lips announced a new determination, set as they were in the lines of resentful dignity.

"Let me put the state of things before you," he said in his softest tones, just touched with irony. "The fact of our engagement has been published. Our marriage is looked for by a host of friends and acquaintances, and even by the mere readers of the newspapers. All but at the last moment, on a caprice, an impulse you do not pretend to justify to one's intelligence, you declare it is all at an end. Pray, how do you propose to satisfy natural curiosity about such a strange event?"

"I take all the blame. I make it known that I have behaved—unreasonably; if you will, disgracefully."

"That word," replied Jacks, faintly smiling, "has a meaning in this connection which you would hardly care to reflect upon. Take it that you have said this to your friends: what do *I* say to *mine*?"

Irene could not answer.

"I have a pleasant choice," he pursued. "I can keep silence—which would mean scandal, affecting both of us, according to people's disposition. Or I can say, with simple pathos, 'Miss Derwent begged me to release her.' Neither alternative is agreeable to me. It may be unchivalrous. Possibly another man would beg to be allowed to sacrifice his reputation, to ensure your quiet release. To be frank with you, I value my reputation, I value my chances in life. I have no mind to make myself appear worse than I am."

Irene had sunk into a chair again. As he talked, Jacks moved to a sofa near her, and dropped on to the end of it.

"Surely there is a way," began the girl's voice, profoundly troubled. "We could let it be known, first of all, that the marriage was postponed. Then—there would be less talk afterwards."

He leaned towards her, upon his elbow.

"It interests me—your quiet assumption that my feelings count for nothing."

Irene reddened. She was conscious of having ignored that aspect of the matter, and dreaded to have to speak of it. For the revelation made to her of late taught her that, whatever Arnold Jacks' idea of love might be, it was not hers. Yet perhaps, in his way, he loved her—the way which had found expression a few minutes ago.

"I can only repeat that I am ashamed."

"If you would grant me some explanation," Jacks resumed, with his most positive air, that of the born man of business. "Don't be afraid of hurting my sensibilities. Have I committed myself in any way?"

"It is a change in myself—I was too hasty—I reflected afterwards instead of before"—

"Forgive me if I make the most of that admission. Your hastiness was certainly not my fault. I did not unduly press you; there was no importunity. Such being the case, don't you think I may suggest that you ought to bear the consequences? I can't—I really can't think them so dreadful."

Irene kept silence, her face bent and averted.

"Many a girl has gone through what you feel now, but I doubt whether ever one before acted like this. They kept their word; it was a point of honour."

"I know; it is true." She forced herself to look at him. "And the result was lives of misery—dishonour—tragedies."

"Oh, come now"—

"You *dare* not contradict me!" Her eyes flashed; she let her feeling have its way. "As a man of the world, you know the meaning of such marriages, and what they may, what they do often, come to. A girl hears of such facts— realises them too late. You smile. No, I don't want to talk for effect; it isn't my way. All I mean is that I, like so many girls who have never been in love, accepted an offer of marriage on the wrong grounds, and came to feel my mistake—who knows how?—not long after. What you are asking me to do, is to pay for the innocent error with my life. The price is too great. You speak of your feelings; they are not so strong as to justify such a demand — And there's another thought that surely must have entered your mind. Knowing that I feel it impossible to marry you, how can you still, with any shadow of self-respect, urge me to do so? Is your answer, again, fear of what people will say? That seems to me more than cowardice. How strange that an honourable man doesn't see it so!"

Jacks abandoned his easy posture, sat straight, and fixed upon her the look of masculine disdain.

"I simply don't believe in the impossibility of your becoming my wife."

"Then talk is useless. I can only tell you the truth, and reclaim my liberty."

"It's a question of time. You wouldn't—well, say you couldn't, marry me to-morrow. A month hence you would be willing. Because you suffer from a passing illusion, I am to unsettle all my arrangements, and face an intolerable humiliation. The thing is impossible."

With vast relief Irene heard him return upon this note, and strike it so violently. She felt no more compunction. The man was finally declared to her, and she could hold her own against him. Her headache had grown fierce; her mouth was dry; shudders of hot and cold ran through her. The struggle must end soon.

"I am forgetting hospitality," she said, with sudden return to her ordinary voice. "You would like tea."

Arnold waved his hand contemptuously.

"No?—Then let us understand each other in the fewest possible words."

"Good." He smiled, a smile which seemed to tighten every muscle of his face. "I decline to release you from your promise."

She could meet his gaze, and did so as she answered with cold collectedness:

"I am very sorry. I think it unworthy of you."

"I shall make no change whatever in my arrangements. Our marriage will take place on the day appointed."

"That can hardly be, Mr. Jacks, if the bride is not there."

"Miss Derwent, the bride will be there!"

He was not jesting. All the man's pride rose to assert dominion. The prime characteristic of his nation, that personal arrogance which is the root of English freedom, which accounts for everything best, and everything worst, in the growth of English power, possessed him to the exclusion of all less essential qualities. He was the subduer amazed by improbable defiance. He had never seen himself in such a situation; it was as though a British admiral on his ironclad found himself mocked by some elusive little gunboat, newly invented by the condemned foreigner. His intellect refused to acknowledge the possibility of discomfiture; his soul raged mightily against the hint of bafflement. Humour would not come to his aid; the lighter elements of race were ousted; he was solid insolence, wooden-headed self-will.

Irene had risen.

"I am not feeling quite myself. I have said all there is to be said, and I must beg you to excuse me."

"You should have begun by saying that. It is what I insisted upon."

"Shall we shake hands, Mr. Jacks?"

"To be sure!"

"It is good-bye. You understand me? If, after this, you imagine an engagement between us, you have only yourself to blame."

"I take the responsibility." He released her hand, and made a stiff bow. "In three days, I shall call."

"You will not see me."

"Perhaps not. Then, three days later. Nothing whatever is changed between us. A little discussion of this sort is all to the good. Plainly, you have thought me a much weaker man than I am: when that error of judgment is removed, our relations will be better than ever."

The temptation to say one word more overcame Irene's finer sense of the becoming. Jacks had already taken his hat, and was again bowing, when she spoke.

"You are so sure that your will is stronger than mine?"

"Perfectly sure," he replied, with superb tranquillity.

No one had ever seen, no one again would ever see, that face of high disdainful beauty, pain-stricken on the fair brow, which Irene for a moment turned upon him. As he withdrew, the smile that lurked behind her scorn glimmered forth for an instant, and passed in the falling of a tear.

She went to her room, and lay down. The sleep she had not dared to hope for fell upon her whilst she was trying to set her thoughts in order. She slept until eight o'clock; her headache was gone.

Neither with her father, nor with Olga, did she speak of what had passed.

Before going to bed, she packed carefully a large dress-basket and a travelling-bag, which a servant brought down for her from the box-room. Again she slept, but only for an hour or two, and at seven in the morning she rose.

CHAPTER XXVIII

THE breakfast hour was nine o'clock. Dr. Derwent, as usual, came down a few minutes before, and turned over the letters lying for him on the table. Among them he found an envelope addressed in a hand which looked very much like Irene's; it had not come by post. As he was reading the note it contained, Eustace and Olga Hannaford entered together, talking. He bade them good-morning, and all sat down to table.

"Irene's late," said Eustace presently, glancing at the clock.

The Doctor looked at him, with an odd smile.

"She left Victoria ten minutes ago," he said, "by the Calais-boat express."

Eustace and Olga stared, exclaimed.

"She suddenly made up her mind to accept an invitation from Mrs. Borisoff."

"But—what an extraordinary thing!" pealed Eustace, who was always greatly disturbed by anything out of routine. "She didn't speak of it yesterday!"

Olga gazed at the Doctor. Her wan face had a dawn of brightness.

"How long is she likely to stay, uncle?"

"I haven't the least idea."

"Well, she can't stay long," Eustace exclaimed. "Ah! I have it! Don't you see, Olga? It means Parisian dresses and hats!"

Dr. Derwent exploded in laughter.

"Acute young man! Now the ordinary male might have lost himself for a day in wild conjectures. This points to the woolsack, Olga!"

She laughed, for the first time in many days, and her appetite for breakfast was at once improved.

In his heart, Dr. Derwent did not grieve over the singular

240

events of yesterday and this morning. He had no fault to find with Arnold Jacks, and could cheerfully accept him as a son-in-law ; but it was easy to imagine a husband more suitable for such a girl as Irene. Moreover, he had suspected, since the engagement, that she had not thoroughly known her own mind. But he was far from anticipating such original and decisive action on the girl's part. The thing being done, he could secretly admire it, and the flight to Paris relieved his mind from a prospect of domestic confusion. Just for a moment he questioned himself as to Irene's security, but only to recognise how firm was his confidence in her.

Socially, the position was awkward. He had a letter from Jacks, a sensible and calmly worded letter, saying that Irene was overwrought by recent agitations, that she had spoken of putting an end to their engagement, but that doubtless a few days would see all right again. Arnold must now be apprised of what had happened, and, as all consideration was due to him, the Doctor despatched a telegram asking him to call as soon as he could. This brought Jacks to Bryanston Square at midday, and there was a conversation in the library. Arnold spoke his mind; with civility, but in unmistakable terms, he accused the Doctor of remissness. "Paternal authority," it seemed to him, should have sufficed to prevent what threatened nothing less than a scandal. Irene's father could not share this view; the girl was turned three-and-twenty; there could be no question of dictating to her, and as for expostulation, it had been honestly tried.

"You are aware, I hope," said Jacks stiffly, "that Mrs. Borisoff has not quite an unclouded reputation?"

"I know no harm against her."

"She is as good as parted from her husband, and leads a very dubious wandering life."

"Oh, it's all right. People countenance her who wouldn't do so if there were anything really amiss."

"Well, Dr. Derwent," said the young man, in a conclusive tone, "evidently all is at an end. It remains for us to agree upon the manner of making it known. Should the announcement come from your side or from mine?"

The Doctor reflected.

"You no longer propose to wait the effect of a little time?"

"Emphatically, no. This step of Miss Derwent's puts that out of the question."

16

"I see. — Perhaps you feel that, in justice to yourself, it should be made known that she has done something of which you disapprove?"

Arnold missed the quiet irony of this question.

"Not at all. Our engagement ended yesterday; with to-day's events I have nothing to do."

"That is the generous view," said Dr. Derwent, smiling pleasantly. "Do you know, I fancy we had better each of us tell the story in his own way. It will come to that in the end, won't it? You had a disagreement; you thought better of your proposed union; what more simple? I see no room for scandal."

"Be it so. Have the kindness to acquaint Miss Derwent with what has passed between us."

After dinner that evening, Dr. Derwent related the matter to his son. Eustace was astounded, and presently indignant. It seemed to him inconceivable that Arnold Jacks should have suffered this affront. He would not look at things from his sister's point of view; absurd to attempt a defence of her; really, really, she had put them all into a most painful position! An engagement was an engagement, save in the event of grave culpability on either side. Eustace spoke as a lawyer; his professional instincts were outraged. He should certainly call upon the Jackses and utterly dissociate himself from his sister in this lamentable affair.

"Why, what a shock it will be to Mrs. Jacks!"

"She'll get over it, I fancy," remarked the Doctor drily.

The young barrister withdrew to his room, where he read hard until very late. Eustace was no trifler; he had brains, and saw his way to make use of them to the one end which addressed his imagination, that of social self-advancement. His studies to-night were troubled with a resentful fear lest Irene's "unwomanly" behaviour (a generation ago it would have been "unladylike") should bring the family name into some discredit. Little ejaculations escaped him, such as "Really!" and "Upon my word!" Eustace had never been known to use stronger language.

When his son had retired, Dr. Derwent stepped up to the drawing-room, where Olga Hannaford was sitting. After kindly regretting that she should be alone, he repeated to his niece what he had just told Eustace. Doubtless she would hear very soon from Irene.

"I have already heard something about this," said Olga. "I'm sure she has done right, but no one will ever know what it cost her."

"That's the very point we have all been losing sight of," observed her uncle, gratified. "It would have been a good deal easier, no doubt, to go on to the marriage."

"Easier!" echoed the girl. "She has done the most wonderful thing! I admire her, and envy her strength of character."

The Doctor's eyes had fallen upon that crayon portrait which held the place of honour on the drawing-room walls. Playing with superstition, as does every man capable of high emotional life, he was wont to see in the pictured countenance of his dead wife changes of expression, correspondent with the mood in which he regarded it. At one time the beloved features smiled upon him; at another they were sad, or anxious. To-night, the eyes, the lips were so strongly expressive of gladness that he felt startled as he gazed. A joy from the years gone by suddenly thrilled him. He sat silent, too deeply moved by memories for speech about the present. And when at length he resumed talk with Olga, his voice was very gentle, his words all kindliness. The girl had never known him so sympathetic with her.

On the morrow—it was Saturday—Olga received a letter from Piers Otway, who said that he had something of great importance to speak about, and must see her; could they not meet at the Campden Hill house, it being inadvisable for him to call at Dr. Derwent's? Either this afternoon or to-morrow would do, if Olga would appoint a time.

She telegraphed, appointing this afternoon at three.

Half an hour before that, she entered the house, which was now occupied only by a caretaker. Dr. Derwent was trying to let it furnished for the rest of the short lease. Olga had a fire quickly made in the drawing-room, and ordered tea. She laid aside her outdoor things, viewed herself more than once in a mirror, and moved about restlessly. When there sounded a visitor's knock at the front door, she flushed and was overcome with nervousness; she stepped forward to meet her friend, but could not speak. Otway had taken her hand in both his own; he looked at her with grave kindliness. It was their first meeting since Mrs. Hannaford's death.

"I hesitated about asking you to see me here," he said. "But I thought—I hoped "—

His embarrassment increased, whilst Olga was gaining self-command.

"You were quite right," she said. "I think I had rather see you here than anywhere else. It isn't painful to me—oh, anything but painful!"

They sat down. Piers was holding a large envelope, bulgy with its contents, whatever they were, and sealed; his eyes rested upon it.

"I have to speak of something which at first will sound unwelcome to you; but it is only the preface to what will make you very glad. It is about my brother. I have seen him two or three times this last week on a particular business, in which at length I have succeeded. Here," he touched the envelope, "are all the letters he possessed in your mother's writing."

Olga looked at him in distressful wonder and suspense.

"Not one of them," he pursued, "contains a line that you should not read. They prove absolutely, beyond shadow of doubt, that the charge brought against your mother was false. The dates cover nearly five years—from a simple note of invitation to Ewell—you remember—down to a letter written about three weeks ago. Of course I was obliged to read them through; I knew to begin with what I should find. Now I give them to you. Let Dr. Derwent see them. If any doubt remains in his mind, they will make an end of it."

He put the packet into Olga's hands. She, overcome for the moment by her feelings, looked from it to him, at a loss for words. She was struck with a change in Otway. That he should speak in a grave tone, with an air of sadness, was only natural; but the change went beyond this; he had not his wonted decision in utterance; he paused between sentences, his eyes wandering dreamily; one would have taken him for an older man than he was wont to appear, and of less energy. Thus might he have looked and spoken after some great effort, which left him wearied, almost languid, incapable of strong emotion.

"Why didn't he show these letters before?" she asked, turning over the sealed envelope.

"He had no wish to do so," answered Piers, in an undertone.

"You mean that he would have let anything happen—which he could have prevented?"

"I'm afraid he would."

"But he offered them now?"

"No—or rather yes, he offered them," Piers smiled bitterly. "Not, however, out of wish to do justice."

Olga could not understand. She gazed at him wistfully.

"I bought them," said Piers. "It made the last proof of his baseness."

"You gave money for them? And just that you might give them to me?"

"Wouldn't you have done the same, to clear the memory of someone you loved?"

Olga laid the packet aside; then, with a quick movement, stepped towards him, caught his hand, pressed it to her lips. Piers was taken by surprise, and could not prevent the action; but at once Olga's own hand was prisoned in his; they stood face to face, she blushing painfully, he pale as death, with lips that quivered in their vain effort to speak.

"I shall be grateful to you as long as I live," the girl faltered, turning half away, trying gently to release herself.

Piers kissed her hand, again and again, still speechless. When he allowed her to draw it away, he stood gazing at her like a man bewildered; there was moisture on his forehead; he seemed to struggle for breath.

"Let us sit down again and talk," said Olga, glancing at him.

But he moved towards her, the strangest look in his eyes, the fixed expressionless gaze of a somnambulist.

"Olga"—

"No, no!" she exclaimed, as if suddenly stricken with fear, throwing out her arms to repel him. "You didn't mean that! It is my fault. You never meant that."

"Yes! Give me your hand again!" he said in a thick voice, the blood rushing into his cheeks.

"Not now. You misunderstood me. I oughtn't to have done that. It was because I could find no word to thank you."

She panted the sentences, holding her chair as if to support herself, and with the other hand still motioning him away.

"I misunderstood—?"

"I am ashamed—it was thoughtless—sit down and let us talk as we were doing. Just as friends, it is so much better. We meant nothing else."

It was as if the words fell from her involuntarily : they were babbled, rather than spoken; she half laughed, half cried. And Otway, a mere automaton, dropped upon his chair, gazing at her, trembling.

"I will let my uncle see the letters at once," Olga went on, in confused hurry. "I am sure he will be very grateful to you. But for you, we should never have had this proof. I, of course, did not need it; as if I doubted my mother ! But he—I can't be sure what he still thinks. How kind you have always been to us !"

Piers stood up again, but did not move toward her. She watched him apprehensively. He walked half down the room and back again, then exclaimed, with a wild gesture :

"I never knew what a curse one's name could be ! I used to be proud of it, because it was my father's; now I would gladly take any other."

"Just because of that man ?" Olga protested. "What does it matter ?"

"You know well what it matters," he replied, with an unnatural laugh.

"To me—nothing whatever."

"You try to think not. But the name will be secretly hateful to you as long as you live."

"Oh ! How can you say that ! The name is yours, not his. Think how long we knew you before we heard of him ! I am telling the simple truth. It is you I think of, when "—

He was drawing nearer to her, and again that strange, fixed look came into his eyes.

"I wanted to ask you something," said Olga quickly. "Do sit down—will you? Let us talk as we used to—you remember?"

He obeyed her, but kept his eyes on her face.

"What do you wish to ask, Olga ?"

The name slipped from his tongue; he had not meant to use it, and did not seem conscious of having done so.

"Have you seen old Mr. Jacks lately ?"

"I saw him last night."

"Last night?" Her breath caught. "Had he anything—anything interesting to say ?"

"He is ill. I only sat with him for half an hour. I don't know what it is. It doesn't keep him in bed ; but he lies on a sofa, and looks dreadfully ill, as if he suffered much pain."

" He told you nothing ? "

Their eyes met.

" Nothing that greatly interested me," replied Piers heavily, with the most palpable feint of carelessness. " He mentioned what of course you know, that Arnold Jacks is not going to be married after all."

Olga's head drooped, as she said in a voice barely audible :

" Ah, you knew it."

" What of that ? "

" I see—you knew it "—

" What of that, Olga ? " he repeated impatiently. " I knew it as a bare fact—no explanation. What does it mean ? You know, I suppose ? "

In spite of himself, look and tones betrayed his eagerness for her reply.

" They disagreed about something," said Olga. " I don't know what. I shouldn't wonder if they make it up again."

At this moment the woman in care of the house entered with the tea-tray. To give herself a countenance, Olga spoke of something indifferent, and when they were alone again, their talk avoided the personal matters which had so embarrassed both of them. Olga said presently that she was going to see her friend Miss Bonnicastle to-morrow.

" If I could see only the least chance of supporting myself, I would go to live with her again. She's the most sensible girl I know, and she did me good."

" How, did you good ? "

" She helped me against myself," replied Olga abruptly. " No one else ever did that."

Then she turned again to the safer subjects.

" When shall I see you again ? " Otway inquired, rising after a long silence, during which both had seemed lost in their thoughts.

" Who knows ?—But I will write and tell you what my uncle says about the letters, if he says anything. Again, thank you ! "

She gave her hand frankly. Piers held it, and looked into her face as once before.

" Olga "—

The girl uttered a cry of distress, drew her hand away, and exclaimed in a half-hysterical voice :

" No ! What right have you ? "

" Every right !   Do you know what your mother said to me
—her last words to me— ? "

" You mustn't tell me ! " Her tones were softer. " Not to-day.
If we meet again "—

" Of course we shall meet again ! "

" I don't know.—Yes, yes ; we shall. But you must go
now ; it is time I went home."

He touched her hand again, and left the room without
looking back. Before the door had closed behind him, Olga
ran forward with a stifled cry. The door was shut. She
stood before it with tears in her eyes, her fingers clenched
together on her breast, and sobbed miserably.

For nearly half an hour she sat by the fire, head on hands,
deeply brooding. In the house there was not a sound. All
at once it seemed to her that a voice called, uttering her name ;
she started, her blood chilled with fear. The voice was her
mother's ; she seemed still to hear it, so plainly had it been
audible, coming from she knew not where.

She ran to her hat and jacket, which lay in a corner of the
room, put them on with feverish haste, and fled out into the
street.

CHAPTER XXIX

" I WILL be frank with you, Piers," said Daniel Otway, as he sat by the fireside in his shabby lodgings, his feet on the fender, a cigarette between his fingers. He looked yellow and dried up ; shivered now and then, and had a troublesome cough. " If I could afford to be generous, I would be ; I should enjoy it. It's one of the worst evils of poverty, that a man can seldom obey the promptings of his better self. I can't give you these letters ; can't afford to do so. You have glanced through them ; you see they really are what I said. The question is, what are they worth to you ? "

Piers looked at the threadbare carpet, reflected, spoke.

" I'll give you fifty pounds."

A smile crept from the corner of Daniel's shrivelled lips to his bloodshot eye.

"Why you are so anxious to have them," he said, "I don't know and don't ask. But if they are worth fifty to you, they are worth more. You shall have them for two hundred."

And at this figure the bundle of letters eventually changed hands. It was a serious drain on Piers Otway's resources, but he could not bargain long, the talk sickened him. And when the letters were in his possession, he felt a joy which had no equivalent in terms of cash.

He said to himself that he had bought them for Olga. In a measure, of course, for all who would be relieved by knowing that Mrs. Hannaford had told the truth ; but first and foremost for Olga. On Olga he kept his thoughts. He was persuading himself that in her he saw his heart's desire.

For Piers Otway was one of those men who cannot live without a woman's image to worship. Irene Derwent being now veiled from him, he turned to another beautiful face, in whose eyes the familiar light of friendship seemed to be changing, softening. Ambition had misled him ; not his to triumph on the heights of glorious passion ; for him a humbler happi-

ness, a calmer love. Yet he would not have been Piers
Otway had this mood contented him. On the second day of
his dreaming about Olga, she began to shine before his
imagination in no pale light. He mused upon her features
till they became the ideal beauty; he clad her, body and soul,
in all the riches of love's treasure-house; she was at length his
crowned lady, his perfect vision of delight.

With such thoughts had he sat by Mrs. Hannaford, at the
meeting which was to be their last. He was about to utter
them, when she spoke Olga's name. "In you she will always
have a friend? If the worst happens—?" And when he
asked, "May I hope that she would some day let me be
more than that?" the glow of joy on that stricken face, the
cry of rapture, the hand held to him, stirred him so deeply
that his old love-longing seemed a boyish fantasy. "Oh, you
have made me happy! You have blotted out all my follies
and sufferings!" Then the poor tortured mind lost itself.

This was the second death which had upon Piers Otway
the ageing effect known to all men capable of thoughts about
mortality. The loss of his father marked for him the end of
irresponsible years; he entered upon manhood with that grief
blended of reverence and affection. By the grave of Mrs.
Hannaford (he stood there only after the burial) he was
touched again by the advancing shadow of life's dial, and it
marked the end of youth. For youth is a term relative to
heart and mind. At six-and-twenty many a man has of manhood only the physique; many another is already falling
through experience to a withered age. Piers had the sense of
transition; the middle years were opening before him. The
tears he shed for his friend were due in part to the poignant
perception of utter severance with boyhood. But a few weeks
ago, talking with Mrs. Hannaford, he could revive the spirit
of those old days at Geneva, feel his identity with the Piers
Otway of that time. It would never be within his power
again. He might remember, but memory showed another
than himself.

A note from John Jacks summoned him to Queen's Gate.
Not till afterwards did he understand that Mr. Jacks' real
motive in sending for him was to get light upon the rupture
between Arnold and Miss Derwent. Piers' astonishment at
what he heard caused his friend to quit the subject.

In the night that followed, Piers for the first time in his

life felt the possibility of base action. The experience has come to all men, and, whatever the result, always leaves its mark. Looking at the fact of Irene's broken engagement, he could explain it only in one way; the cause must be Mrs. Hannaford—the doubt as to her behaviour, the threatened scandal. Idle to attempt surmises as to the share of either side in what had come about; the difference had been sufficiently grave to part them. And this parting was to him a joy which shook his whole being. He could have raised a song of exultation.

And in his hands lay complete evidence of the dead woman's guiltlessness. To produce it was possibly to reconcile Arnold Jacks and Irene. Viewed by his excited mind, the possible became certain; he evolved a whole act of drama between those two, turning on prejudices, doubts, scruples natural in their position; he saw the effect of their enlightenment. Was it a tempting thought, that he could give Irene back again into her bridegroom's arms?

It brought sweat to his forehead; it shook him with the fierce torture of a jealous imagination. He fortified base suggestion by the natural revolt of his flesh. Once had he passed through the fire; to suffer that ordeal again was beyond human endurance. Irene was free. He paced the room, repeating wildly that Irene was free. And the mere fact of her freedom proved that she did not love the man—so it seemed to *him*, in his subordination of every motive to that passionate impulse. To him it brought no hope—what of that! Irene did not belong to another man.

The fire needed stirring. As he broke the black surface of coal, a flame shot up, red, lambent, a serpent's tongue. It had a voice; it tempted. He took the packet of letters from the table.

He had not yet read them through; had only tested them here and there under his brother's eye. Yes, they were the letters of a woman who, suffering (as he knew) the strongest temptation to which her nature could be exposed, subdued herself in obedience to what she held the law of duty. He read page after page. Again and again she all but said, " I love you"; again and again she told her tempter that his suit was useless, that she would rather die than yield. Daniel Otway had used every argument to persuade her to defy the world and follow him—easy to understand his motives. One saw that, if she had been alone, she would have done so; but there was her daughter, there was her brother; to them she sacrificed what seemed to her the one chance of happiness left in a wasted life.

Piers interrupted his reading to hear once more the voice that counselled baseness. Whom would it injure, if he destroyed these papers? Certainly not Irene, his first thought, who, he held it proved, was well rescued from a mistaken marriage. Not Dr. Derwent, or Olga, who, he persuaded himself, had already no doubt whatever of Mrs. Hannaford's innocence. Not the poor dead woman herself—

What was this passage on which his eye had fallen? " I have long had a hope that your brother Piers might marry Olga. It would make me very happy; I cannot imagine for her a better husband. It came first into my mind years ago, at Geneva, and I have never lost the wish. Ah! how grateful you would make me, if, forgetting ourselves, you would join me in somehow trying to bring about this happiness for those two! Piers is coming to live in London. Do see as much of him as you can. I think very, very highly of him, and he is almost as dear to me as a son of my own. Speak to him of Olga. Sometimes a suggestion—and you know that I desire only his good."

The voice spoke to him from the grave; it had a sweeter tone than that other. He read on; he came to the last sheet—so sad, so hopeless, that it brought tears to his eyes.

"Cannot you defend me? Cannot you prove the falsehood of that story? Cannot you save me from this bitter disgrace? Oh, who will show the truth and do me justice?"

Could he burn that letter? Could he close his ears against that cry of one driven to death by wrong?

He drew a deep sigh, and looked about him as if waking from a bad dream. Why, he had come near to whole brotherhood with a man as coldly cruel and infamous as any that walked the earth! Destroying these letters, he would have been worse than Daniel.

Straightway he wrote to Olga, requesting the appointment with her. Upon Olga once more he fixed his mind. He resolved that he would not part from her without asking her to be his wife. If he had but done so before hearing that news from John Jacks! Then it seemed to him that Olga was his happiness,

From the house at Campden Hill he came away in a strangely excited mood; glad, sorry; cold, desirous; torn this way and that by conflict of passions and reasons. The only clear thought in his mind was that he had done a great act of justice. How often does it fall to a man to enjoy this privilege? Not once in a lifetime to the multitude; such opportunity is the signal favour of fate. Had he let it pass, Piers felt he must have sunk so in his own esteem, that no light of noble hope would ever again have shone before him. He must have gone plodding the very mire of existence—Daniel's brother, never again anything but Daniel's brother.

Would Dr. Derwent give him a thought of thanks? Would Irene hear how those letters were recovered?

Sunday passed, he knew not well how. He wrote a letter to Olga, but destroyed it. On Monday he was very busy, chiefly at the warehouses of the Commercial Docks; a man of affairs; to look upon, not strikingly different from many another with whom he rubbed shoulders in Fenchurch Street and elsewhere. On Tuesday he had to go to Liverpool, to see an acquaintance of Moncharmont who might perchance be useful to them. The journey, the change, were not unpleasant. He passed the early evening with the man in question, who asked him at what hotel he meant to sleep. Piers named the house he had carelessly chosen, adding that he had not been there yet; his bag was still at the station.

"Don't go there," said his companion. "It's small and uncomfortable and dear. You'll do much better at——."

Without giving a thought to the matter, Otway accepted this advice. He went to the station, withdrew his bag, and bade a cabman drive him to the hotel his acquaintance had named. But no sooner had the cab started than he felt an unaccountable misgiving, an uneasiness as to this change of purpose. Strange as he was to Liverpool, there seemed no reason why he should hesitate so about his hotel; yet the mental disturbance became so strong that, when all but arrived, he stopped the cab and bade his driver take him to the other house, that which he had originally chosen. A downright piece of superstition, he said to himself, with a nervous laugh. He could not remember to have ever behaved so capriciously.

The hotel pleased him. After inspecting his bedroom, he

came down again to smoke and glance over the newspapers; it was about half-past nine. Half a dozen men were in the smoking-room; by ten o'clock there remained, exclusive of Piers, only three, of whom two were discussing politics by the fireside, whilst the third sat apart from them in a deep chair, reading a book. The political talk began to interest Otway; he listened, behind his newspaper. The louder of the disputants was a man of about fifty, dressed like a prosperous merchant; his cheeks were flabby, his chin triple or quadruple, his short neck, always very red, grew crimson as he excited himself. He was talking about the development of markets for British wares, and kept repeating the phrase "trade outlets," as if it had a flavour which he enjoyed. England, he declared, was falling behind in the competition for the world's trade.

"It won't do. Mark my word, if we don't show more spirit, we shall be finding ourselves in Queer Street. Look at China, now! I call it a monstrous thing, perfectly monstrous, the way we're neglecting China."

"My dear sir," said the other, a thin, bilious man, with an undecided manner, "we can't force our goods on a country"—

"What! Why, that's exactly what we *can* do, and ought to do! What we always *have* done, and always *must* do, if we're going to hold our own," vociferated he of the crimson neck. "I was speaking of China, if you hadn't interrupted me. What are the Russians doing? Why, making a railway straight to China! And we look on, as if it didn't matter, when the matter is national life or death. Let me give you some figures. I know what I'm talking about. Are you aware that our trade with China amounts to only half a crown a head of the Chinese population? Half a crown! While with little Japan, our trade comes to something like eighteen shillings a head. Let me tell you that the equivalent of that in China would represent about three hundred and sixty millions per annum!"

He rolled out the figures with gusto culminating in rage. His eyes glared; he snorted defiance, turning from his companion to the two strangers whom he saw seated before him.

"I say that it's our duty to force our trade upon China. It's for China's good—can you deny that? A huge country packed with wretched barbarians! Our trade civilises them—can you deny it? It's our duty, as the leading Power of the world! Hundreds of millions of poor miserable barbarians. And "—he shouted—"what else are the Russians, if you come to that? Can *they* civilise China? A filthy, ignorant nation, frozen into stupidity, and downtrodden by an Autocrat!"

"Well," murmured the diffident objector, "I'm no friend of tyranny; I can't say much for Russia"—

"I should think you couldn't. Who can? A country plunged in the darkness of the Middle Ages! The country of the *knout*! Pah! Who *can* say anything for Russia?"

Vociferating thus, the champion of civilisation fixed his glare upon Otway, who, having laid down the paper, answered this look of challenge with a smile.

"As you seem to appeal to me," sounded in Piers' voice, which was steady and good-humoured, "I'm bound to say that Russia isn't altogether without good points. You spoke of it, by the bye, as the country of the knout; but the knout, as a matter of fact, was abolished long ago.".

"Well, well—yes; yes—one knows all about that," stammered the loud man. "But the country is still ruled in the *spirit* of the knout. It doesn't affect my argument. Take it broadly, on an ethnological basis." He expanded his chest, sticking his thumbs into the armholes of his waistcoat. "The Russians are a Slavonic people, I presume?"

"Largely Slav, yes."

"And pray, sir, what have the Slavs done for the world? What do we owe them? What Slavonic name can anyone mention in the history of progress?"

"Two occur to me," replied Piers, in the same quiet tone, "well worthy of a place in the history of intellectual progress. There was a Pole named Kopernik, known to you, no doubt, as Copernicus, who came before Galileo; and there was a Czech named Huss—John Huss—who came before Luther."

The bilious man was smiling. The fourth person present in the room, who sat with his book at some distance, had turned his eyes upon Otway with a look of peculiar interest.

"You've made a special study, I suppose, of this sort of thing," said the fat-faced politician, with a grin which tried to be civil, conveying, in truth, the radical English contempt for mere intellectual attainment. "You're a supporter of Russia, I suppose?"

"I have no such pretension. Russia interests me, that's all."

"Come now, would you say that in any single point Russia, modern Russia, as we understand the term, had shown the way in *practical* advance?"

All were attentive—the silent man with the book seeming particularly so.

"I should say in one rather important point," Piers replied. "Russia was the first country to abolish capital punishment for ordinary crime."

The assailant showed himself perplexed, incredulous. But this state of mind, lasting only for a moment, gave way to genial bluster.

"Oh, come now! That's a matter of opinion. To let murderers go unhung"—

"As you please. I could mention another interesting fact. Long before England dreamt of the simplest justice for women, it was not an uncommon thing for a Russian peasant, who had appropriated money earned by his wife, to be punished with a flogging by the village commune."

"A flogging! Why, there you are!" cried the other, with hoarse laughter—"What did I say? If it isn't the knout, it's something equivalent. As if we hadn't proved long ago the demoralising effect of corporal chastisement! We should be ashamed, sir, to flog men nowadays in the army or navy. It degrades: we have outgrown it.—No, no, sir, it won't do! I see you have made a special study, and you've mentioned very interesting facts; but you must see that they are wide of the mark—painfully wide of the mark.—I must be thinking of turning in; have to be up at six, worse luck, to catch a train. Good-night, Mr. Simmonds! Good-night to you, sir—good-night!"

He bustled away, humming to himself; and, after musing a little, the bilious man also left the room. Piers thought himself alone, but a sound caused him to turn his head; the person whom he had forgotten, the silent reader, had risen and was moving his way. A tall, slender, graceful man, well dressed, aged about thirty. He approached Otway, came in front of him, looked at him with a smile, and spoke.

"Sir, will you permit me to thank you for what you have said in defence of Russia—my country?"

The English was excellent; almost without foreign accent. Piers stood up, and held out his hand, which was cordially grasped. He looked into a face readily recognisable as that of a Little Russian; a rather attractive face, with fine, dreamy eyes and a mouth expressive of quick sensibility; above the good forehead, waving chestnut hair.

"You have travelled in Russia?" pursued the stranger.

"I lived at Odessa for some years, and I have seen something of other parts."

"You speak the language?"

Piers offered proof of this attainment, by replying in a few Russian sentences. His new acquaintance was delighted, again shook hands, and began to talk in his native tongue. They exchanged personal information. The Russian said that his name was Korolevitch; that he had an estate in the Government of Poltava, where he busied himself with farming, but that for two or three months of each year he travelled. Last winter he had spent in the United States; he was now visiting the great English seaports, merely for the interest of the thing. Otway felt how much less impressive was the account he had to give of himself, but his new friend talked with such perfect simplicity, so entirely as a good-humoured man of the world, that any feeling of subordination was impossible.

"Poltava I know pretty well," he said gaily. "I've been more than once at the July fair, buying wool. At Kharkoff too, on the same business."

They conversed for a couple of hours, at first amusing themselves with the rhetoric and arguments of the red-necked man. Korolevitch was a devoted student of poetry, and discovered not without surprise the Englishman's familiarity with that branch of Russian literature. He heard with great interest the few words Otway let fall about his father, who had known so many Russian exiles. In short, they got along together admirably, and, on parting for the night, promised each other to meet again in London some ten days hence.

When he had entered his bedroom, and turned the key in the lock, Piers stood musing over this event. Of a sudden there came into his mind the inexplicable impulse which brought

him to this hotel, rather than to that recommended by the
Liverpool acquaintance.   An odd incident, indeed.   It helped
a superstitious tendency of Otway's mind, the disposition he
had, spite of obstacle and misfortune, to believe that destiny
was his friend.

CHAPTER XXX

AT home again, Piers wrote to Olga, the greater part of the letter being occupied with an account of what had happened at Liverpool. It was not a love-letter, yet differed in tone from those he had hitherto written her; he spoke with impatience of the circumstances which made it difficult for them to meet, and begged that it might not be long before he saw her again. Olga's reply came quickly; it was frankly intimate, with no suggestion of veiled feeling. Her mother's letters, she said, were in Dr. Derwent's hands. "I told him who had given them to me, and how you obtained them. I doubt whether he will have anything to say to me about them, but that doesn't matter; he knows the truth." As for their meeting, any Sunday afternoon he would find her at Miss Bonnicastle's, in Great Portland Street. "I wish I were living there again," she added. "My uncle is very kind, but I can't feel at home here, and hope I shall not stay very long."

So, on the next Sunday, Piers wended his way to Great Portland Street. Arriving about three o'clock, he found the artist of the posters sitting alone by her fire, legs crossed and cigarette in mouth.

"Ah, Mr. Otway!" she exclaimed, turning her head to see who entered in reply to her cry of "Don't be afraid!" Without rising, she held a hand to him. "I didn't think I should ever see you here again. How are you getting on? Beastly afternoon—come and warm your toes."

The walls were hung with clever brutalities of the usual kind. Piers glanced from them to Miss Bonnicastle, speculating curiously about her. He had no active dislike for this young woman, and felt a certain respect for her talent, but he thought, as before, how impossible it would be ever to regard her as anything but an abnormality. She was not ill-looking, but seemed to have no single characteristic of her sex which appealed to him.

"What do you think of that?" she asked abruptly, handing him an illustrated paper which had lain open on her lap.

The page she indicated was covered with some half-dozen small drawings, exhibiting scenes from a popular café in Paris, done with a good deal of vigour, and some skill in the seizing of facial types.

"Your work?" he asked.

"Mine?" she cried scoffingly. "I could no more do that than swim the Channel. Look at the name, can't you?"

He found it in a corner.

"Kite? Our friend?"

"That's the man. He's been looking up since he went to Paris. Some things of his in a French paper had a lot of praise; nude figures—queer symbolical stuff, they say, but uncommonly well done. I haven't seen them; in London they'd be called indecent, the man said who was telling me about them. Of course that's rot. He'll be here in a few days, Olga says."

"She hears from him?"

"It was a surprise letter; he addressed it to this shop, and I sent it on.—That's only pot-boiling, of course." She snatched back the paper. "But it's good in its way—don't you think?"

"Very good."

"We must see the other things they talk about—the nudes."

There was a knock at the door. "Come along!" cried Miss Bonnicastle, craning back her head to see who would enter. And on the door opening, she uttered an exclamation of surprise.

"Well, this is a day of the unexpected! Didn't know you were in England."

Piers saw a slim, dark, handsome man, who, in his elegant attire, rather reminded one of a fashion-plate; he came briskly forward, smiling as if in extreme delight, and bent over the artist's hand, raising it to his lips.

"Now, *you'd* never do that," said Miss Bonnicastle, addressing Otway, with an air of mock gratification. "This is Mr. Florio, the best-behaved man I know. Signor, you've heard us speak of Mr. Otway. Behold him!"

" Ah ! Mr. Otway, Mr. Otway ! " cried the Italian joyously.
" Permit me the pleasure to · shake hands with you ! One
more English friend ! I collect English friends, as others
collect pictures, *bric-à-brac*, what you will. Indeed, it
is my pride to add to the collection — my privilege, my
honour."

After exchange of urbanities, he turned to the exhibition on
the walls, and exhausted his English in florid eulogy, not a word
of which but sounded perfectly sincere. From this he passed
to a glorification of the art of advertisement. It was the triumph
of our century, the supreme outcome of civilisation ! Otway,
amusedly observant, asked with a smile what progress the art
was making in Italy.

" Progress ! " cried Florio, with indescribable gesture.
" Italy and progress !—Yet," he proceeded, with a change of
voice, " where would Italy be, but for advertisements ? Italy
lives by advertisements. She is the best advertised country in
the world ! Suppose the writers and painters ceased to
advertise Italy ; suppose it were no more talked about ;
suppose foreigners ceased to come ! What would happen to
Italy, I ask you ? "

His face conveyed so wonderfully the suggestion of ravenous
hunger, that Miss Bonnicastle screamed with laughter. Piers
did not laugh, and turned away for a moment.

Soon after, there entered Olga Hannaford. Seeing the two
men, she reddened and looked confused, but Miss Bonnicastle's
noisy greeting relieved her. Her hand was offered first to
Otway, who pressed it without speaking ; their eyes met, and
to Piers it seemed that she made an appeal for his forbearance,
his generosity. The behaviour of the Italian was singular.
Mute and motionless, he gazed at Olga with a wonder
which verged on consternation ; when she turned towards him,
he made a profound bow, as though he met her for the
first time.

" Don't you remember me, Mr. Florio ? " she asked, in an
uncertain voice.

" Oh—indeed—perfectly," was the stammered reply.

He took her fingers with the most delicate respectfulness,
again bowing deeply ; then drew back a little, his eyes
travelling rapidly to the faces of the others, as if seeking
an explanation. Miss Bonnicastle broke the silence, saying
they must have some tea, and calling upon Olga to help

her in preparing it. For a minute or two the men were left alone. Florio, approaching Piers on tiptoe, whispered anxiously:

" Miss Hannaford is in mourning ? "

" Her mother is dead."

With a gesture of desolation, the Italian moved apart, and stood staring absently at a picture on the wall. For the next quarter of an hour, he took scarcely any part in the conversation; his utterances were grave and subdued; repeatedly he glanced at Olga, and, if able to do so unobserved, let his eyes rest upon her with agitated interest. But for the hostess, there would have been no talk at all, and even she fell far short of her wonted vivacity. When things were at their most depressing, someone knocked.

"Who's that, I wonder?" said Miss Bonnicastle. "All right!" she called out. "Come along."

A head appeared; a long, pale, nervous countenance, with eyes that blinked as if in too strong a light. Miss Bonnicastle started up, clamouring an excited welcome. Olga flushed and smiled. It was Kite who advanced into the room; on seeing Olga he stood still, became painfully embarrassed, and could make no answer to the friendly greetings with which Miss Bonnicastle received him. Forced into a chair at length, and sitting sideways, with his long legs intertwisted, and his arms fidgeting about, he made known that he had arrived only this morning from Paris, and meant to stay in London for a month or two—perhaps longer—it depended on circumstances. His health seemed improved, but he talked in the old way, vaguely, languidly. Yes, he had had a little success; but it amounted to nothing; his work — rubbish! rubbish! Thereupon the café sketches in the illustrated papers were shown to Florio, who poured forth exuberant praise. A twinkle of pleasure came into the artist's eyes.

"But the other things we heard about?" said Miss Bonnicastle. "The what-d'ye-call 'ems, the figures "—

Kite shrugged his shoulders, and looked uneasy.

"Oh, pot-boilers! Poor stuff. Happened to catch people's eyes. Who told you about them?"

"Some man—I forget. And what are you doing now?"

" Oh, nothing. A little black-and-white for that thing," he pointed contemptuously to the paper. " Keeps me from idleness."

" Where are you going to live ? "

" I don't know.   I shall find a garret somewhere.   Do you know of one about here ? "

Olga's eyes chanced to meet a glance from Otway.   She moved, hesitated, and rose from her chair.   Kite and the Italian gazed at her, then cast a look at each other, then both looked at Otway, who had at once risen.

" Do you walk home ? " said Piers, stepping towards her.

" I'd better have a cab."

It was said in a quietly decisive tone, and Piers made no reply.   Both took leave with few words.   Olga descended the stairs rapidly, and, without attention to her companion, turned at a hurried pace down the dark street.   They had walked nearly a hundred yards when she turned her head and spoke.

" Can't you suggest some way for me to earn my living?   I mean it.   I must find something."

" Have you spoken to your uncle about it ? " asked Piers mechanically.

" No ; it's difficult.   If I could go to him with something definite."

" Have you spoken to your cousin ? "

Olga delayed an instant, and answered with an embarrassed abruptness.

" She's gone to Paris."

Before Piers could recover from his surprise, she had waved to an empty hansom driving past.

"Think about it," she added, "and write to me.   I must do something.   This life of loneliness and idleness is unbearable."

And Piers thought ; to little purpose, for his mind was once more turned to Irene, and it cost him a painful effort to dwell upon Olga's circumstances.   He postponed writing to her, until shame compelled him, and the letter he at length despatched seemed so empty, so futile, that he could not bear to think of her reading it.   With astonishment he received an answer so gratefully worded that it moved his heart.   She would reflect on the suggestions he had made ; moreover, as he advised, she would take counsel frankly with the Doctor ; and, whatever was decided, he should hear at once.   She counted on him as a friend, a true friend ; in truth, she had no other.   He must continue to write to her, but not often, not more than once a fortnight or so. And let him be assured that she never for a moment forgot her lifelong debt to him.

This last sentence referred, no doubt, to her mother's letters. Dr. Derwent, it seemed, would make no acknowledgment of the service rendered him by a brother of the man whom he must regard as a pitiful scoundrel. How abhorred by him must be the name of Otway!

And could it be less hateful to his daughter, to Irene?

The days passed. A pleasant surprise broke the monotony of work and worry when, one afternoon, the office-boy handed in a card bearing the name Korolevitch. The Russian was spending a week in London, and Otway saw him several times; on one occasion they sat talking together till three in the morning. To Piers this intercourse brought vast mental relief, and gave him an intellectual impulse of which he had serious need in his life of solitude, ever tending to despondency. Korolevitch, on leaving England, volunteered to call upon Moncharmont at Odessa. He had wool to sell, and why not sell it to his friends? But he, as well as Piers, looked for profit of another kind from this happy acquaintance.

It was not long before Otway made another call upon Miss Bonnicastle, and at this time, as he had hoped, he found her alone, working. He led their talk to the subject of Kite.

"You ought to go and see him in his garret," said Miss Bonnicastle. "He'd like you to."

"Tell me, if you know," threw out the other, looking into her broad, good-natured face. "Is he still interested in Miss Hannaford?"

"Why, of course! He's one of the stupids who keep up that kind of thing for a lifetime. But 'he that will not when he may'! Poor silly fellow! How I should enjoy boxing his ears!"

They laughed, but Miss Bonnicastle seemed very much in earnest.

"He's tormenting his silly self," she went on, "because he has been unfaithful to her. There was a girl in Paris. Oh, he tells me everything! We're good friends. The girl over there did him enormous good, that's all I know. It was she that set him to work, and supplied him with his model at the same time! What better could have happened? And now the absurd creature has qualms of conscience!"

"Well," said Piers, smiling uneasily, "it's intelligible."

"Bosh! Don't be silly! A man has his work to do, and he must get what help he can. I shall pack him off back to Paris."

"I'll go and see him, I think.—About the Italian, Florio. Has he also an interest?"

"In Olga? Yes, I fancy he has, but I don't know much about him. He comes and goes, on business. There's a chance, I think, of his dropping in for money before long. He isn't a bad sort—what do you think?"

That same afternoon Piers went in search of Kite's garret. It was a garret literally, furnished with a table and a bed, and little else, but a large fire burned cheerfully, and on the table, beside a drawing-board, stood a bottle of wine. When he had welcomed his visitor, Kite pointed to the bottle.

"I got used to it in Paris," he said, "and it helps me to work. I shan't offer you any, or you might be made ill; the cheapest claret on the market, but it reminds me of — of things."

There rose in Otway's mind a suspicion that, to-day at all events, Kite had found his cheap claret rather too seductive. His face had an unwonted warmth of colour, and his speech an unusual fluency. Presently he opened a portfolio and showed some of the work he had done in Paris: drawings in pen-and-ink, and the published reproductions of others; these latter, he declared, were much spoilt in the process work. The motive was always a nude female figure, of great beauty; the same face, with much variety of expression; for background all manner of fantastic scenes, or rather glimpses and suggestions of a poet's dreamland.

"You see what I mean?" said Kite. "It's simply Woman, as a beautiful thing, as a—a—oh, I can't get it into words. An ideal, you know — something to live for. Put her in a room—it becomes a different thing. Do you feel my meaning? English people wouldn't have these, you know. They don't understand. They call it sensuality."

"Sensuality!" cried Piers, after dreaming for a moment. "Great heavens! then why are human bodies made beautiful?"

The artist gave a strange laugh of gratification.

"There you hit it! Why—why? The work of the Devil, they say."

"The worst of it is," said Piers, "that they're right as regards most men. Beauty, as an inspiration, exists only for the few.

Beauty of any and every kind—it's all the same. There's no safety for the world as we know it, except in utilitarian morals."

Later, when he looked back upon these winter months, Piers could distinguish nothing clearly. It was a time of confused and obscure motives, of oscillation, of dreary conflict, of dull suffering. His correspondence with Olga, his meetings with her, had no issue. He made a thousand resolves; a thousand times he lost them. But for the day's work, which kept him in an even tenor for a certain number of hours, he must have drifted far and perilously.

It was a life of solitude. The people with whom he talked were mere ghosts, intangible, not of his world. Sometimes, amid a crowd of human beings, he was stricken voiceless and motionless: he stared about him, and was bewildered, asking himself what it all meant.

His health was not good; he suffered much from headaches; he fell into languors, lassitude of body and soul. As a result, imagination seemed to be dead in him. The torments of desire were forgotten. When he heard that Irene Derwent had returned to London, the news affected him only with a sort of weary curiosity. Was it true that she would not marry Arnold Jacks? It seemed so. He puzzled over the story, wondered about it; but only his mind was concerned, never his emotions.

Once he was summoned to Queen's Gate. John Jacks lay on a sofa, in his bedroom; he talked as usual, but in a weaker voice, and had the face of a man doomed. Piers saw no one else in the house, and on going away felt that he had been under that roof for the last time.

His mind was oppressed with the thought of death. As happens, probably, to every imaginative man at one time or another, he had a conviction that his own days were drawing to a premature close. Speculation about the future seemed idle; he had come to the end of hopes and fears. Night after night his broken sleep suffered the same dream; he saw Mrs. Hannaford, who stretched her hands to him, and with a face of silent woe seemed to implore his help. Help against Death; and his powerlessness wrung his heart with anguish. Waking, he thought of all the women—beautiful, tender, objects of infinite passion and worship—who even at that moment lay smitten by the great destroyer; the gentle, the loving, racked, disfigured, flung into the horror of the grave. And his being rose in revolt; he strove in silent agony against the dark ruling of the world.

One day there was of tranquil self-possession, of blessed calm. A Sunday in January, when, he knew not how, he found himself amid the Sussex lanes, where he had rambled in the time of harvest. The weather, calm and dry and mild, but without sunshine, soothed his spirit. He walked for hours, and towards nightfall stood upon a wooded hill, gazing westward. An overcast, yet not a gloomy sky; still, soft-dappled; with rifts and shimmerings of pearly blue scattered among multitudinous billows, which here were a dusky yellow, there a deep neutral tint. In the low west, beneath the long dark edge, a soft splendour, figured with airy cloudlets, waited for the invisible descending sun. Moment after moment the rifts grew longer, the tones grew warmer; above began to spread a rosy flush; in front, the glory brightened, touching the cloud-line above it with a tender crimson.

If all days could be like this! One could live so well, he thought, in mere enjoyment of the beauty of earth and sky, all else forgotten. Under this soft-dusking heaven, death was welcome rest, and passion only a tender sadness.

He said to himself that he had grown old in hopeless love— only to doubt in the end whether he had loved at all.

CHAPTER XXXI

THE lad he employed in his office was run over by a cab one slippery day, and all but killed. Piers visited him in the hospital, thus seeing for the first time the interior of one of those houses of pain, which he always disliked even to pass. The experience did not help to brighten his mood; he lacked that fortunate temper of the average man, which embraces as a positive good the less of two evils. The long, grey, low-echoing ward, with its atmosphere of antiseptics; the rows of little white camp-beds, an ominous screen hiding this and that; the bloodless faces, the smothered groan, made a memory that went about with him for many a day.

It strengthened his growing hatred of London, a huge battlefield calling itself the home of civilisation and of peace; battlefield on which the wounds were of soul no less than of body. In these gaunt streets along which he passed at night, how many a sad heart suffered, by the dim glimmer that showed at upper windows, a hopeless solitude amid the innumerable throng! Human cattle, the herd that feed and breed, with them it was well; but the few born to a desire for ever unattainable, the gentle spirits who from their prisoning circumstance looked up and afar, how the heart ached to think of them! Some girl, of delicate instinct, of purpose sweet and pure, wasting her unloved life in toil and want and indignity; some man, whose youth and courage strove against a mean environment, whose eyes grew haggard in the vain search for a companion promised in his dreams; they lived, these two, parted perchance only by the wall of neighbour houses, yet all huge London was between them, and their hands would never touch. Beside this hunger for love, what was the stomach-famine of a multitude that knew no other?

The spring drew nigh, and Otway dreaded its coming. It was the time of his burning torment, of imagination traitor to the worthier mind; it was the time of reverie that rapt him above everything ignoble, only to embitter by contrast the destiny he could not break. He rose now with the early sun ; walked fast and far before the beginning of his day's work, with an aim he knew to be foolish, yet could not abandon. From Guilford Street, along the byways, he crossed Tottenham Court Road, just rattling with its first traffic, crossed Portland Place, still in its soundest sleep, and so onward till he touched Bryanston Square. The trees were misty with half-unfolded leafage ; birds twittered cheerily among the branches ; but Piers heeded not these things. He stood before the high narrow-fronted house, which once he had entered as a guest, where never again would he be suffered to pass the door. Irene was here, he supposed, but could not be sure, for on the rare occasions when he saw Olga Hannaford they did not speak of her cousin. Of the course her life had taken, he knew nothing whatever. Here, in the chill bright morning, he felt more a stranger to Irene than on the day, six years ago, when with foolish timidity he ventured his useless call. She was merely indifferent to him then ; now she shrank from the sound of his name.

On such a morning, a few weeks later, he pursued his walk in the direction of Kensington, and passed along Queen's Gate. It was between seven and eight o'clock. Nearing John Jacks' house, he saw a carriage at the door ; it could of course be only the doctor's, and he became sad in thinking of his kind old friend, for whom the last days of life were made so hard. Just as he was passing, the door opened, and a man, evidently a doctor, came quickly forth. With movement as if he were here for this purpose, Otway ran up the steps ; the servant saw him, and waited with the door still open.

" Will you tell me how Mr. Jacks is ? " he asked.

" I am sorry to say, sir," was the subdued answer, " that Mr. Jacks died at three this morning."

Piers turned away. His eyes dazzled in the sunshine.

The evening papers had the news, with a short memoir— half of which was concerned not with John Jacks, but with his son Arnold.

It seemed to him just possible that he might receive an invitation to attend the funeral ; but nothing of the kind came to him. The slight, he took it for granted, was not social, but personal. His name, of course, was offensive to Arnold

Jacks, and probably to Mrs. John Jacks; only the genial old man had disregarded the scandal shadowing the Otway name.

On the morrow, it was made known that the deceased Member of Parliament would be buried in Yorkshire, in the village churchyard which was on his own estate. And Otway felt glad of this; the sombre and crowded hideousness of a London cemetery was no place of rest for John Jacks.

A fortnight later, at eleven o'clock on Sunday morning, Piers mounted with quick stride the stairs leading to Miss Bonnicastle's abode. The door of her workroom stood ajar; his knock brought no response; after hesitating a little, he pushed the door open, and went in.

Accustomed to the grotesques and vulgarities which generally met his eye upon these walls, he was startled to behold a life-size figure of great beauty, suggesting a study for a serious work of art rather than a design for a street poster. It was a woman, in classic drapery, standing upon the seashore, her head thrown back, her magnificent hair flowing unrestrained, and one of her bare arms raised in a gesture of exultation. As he gazed at the drawing with delight, Miss Bonnicastle appeared from the inner room, dressed for walking.

"What do you think of *that*?" she exclaimed.

"Better than anything you ever did!"

"True enough! That's Kite. Don't you recognise his type?"

"One thinks of Ariadne," said Piers, "but the face won't do for her."

"Yes, it's Ariadne—but I doubt if I shall have the brutality to finish out my idea. She is to have lying on the sand by her a case of Higginson's Hair-wash, stranded from a wreck, and a bottle of it in her hand. See the notion? Her despair consoled by discovery of Higginson!"

They laughed, but Piers broke off in half-serious anger.

"That's damnable! You won't do it. For one thing, the mob wouldn't understand. And in heaven's name do spare the old stories! I'm amazed that Kite should consent to it."

"Poor old fellow!" said Miss Bonnicastle, with an indulgent smile, "he'll do anything a woman asks of him. But I shan't have the heart to spoil it with Higginson; I know I shan't."

"After all," Piers replied, "I don't know why you shouldn't.

What's the use of our scruples? That's the doom of everything beautiful."

"We'll talk about it another time. I can't stop now. I
have an appointment. Stay here if you like, and worship
Ariadne. I shouldn't wonder if Olga looks round this
morning, and it'll disappoint her if there's nobody here."

Piers was embarrassed. He had asked Olga to meet him,
and wondered whether Miss Bonnicastle knew of it. But she
spared him the necessity of any remark by speeding away at
once, bidding him slam the door on the latch when he
departed.

In less than ten minutes, there sounded a knock without,
and Piers threw the door open. It was Olga, breathing
rapidly after her ascent of the stairs, and a startled look in her
eyes as she found herself face to face with Otway. He
explained his being here alone.

"It is kind of you to have come!"

"Oh, I have enjoyed the walk. A delicious morning!
And how happy one feels when the church bells suddenly
stop!"

"I have often known that feeling," said Piers merrily.
"Isn't it wonderful, how London manages to make things
detestable which are pleasant in other places! The bells in
the country!—But sit down. You look tired"—

She seated herself, and her eyes turned to the beautiful
figure on the wall. Piers watched her countenance.

"You have seen it already?" he said.

"A few days ago."

"You know who did it?"

"Mr. Kite, I am told," she answered absently. "And,"
she added, after a pause, "I think he disgraced himself by
lending his art to such a purpose."

Piers said nothing, and looked away to hide his smile of
pleasure.

"I asked you to come," were his next words, "to show you
a letter I have had from John Jacks' solicitors."

Glancing at him with surprise, Olga took the letter he held
out, and read it. In this communication, Piers Otway was
informed that the will of the late Mr. Jacks bequeathed to
him the capital which the testator had invested in the firm of
Moncharmont & Co., and the share in the business which it
represented.

"This is important to you," said the girl, after reflecting for a moment, her eyes down.

"Yes, it is important," Piers answered, in a voice not quite under control. "It means that, if I choose, I can live without working at the business. Just live; no more, at present, though it may mean more in the future. Things have gone well with us, for a beginning; much better than I, at all events, expected. What I should like to do, now, would be to find a man to take my place in London. I know some-one who, just possibly, might be willing—a man at Liverpool."

"Isn't it a risk?" said Olga, regarding him with shame-faced anxiety.

"I don't think so. If *I* could do so well, almost any real man of business would be sure to do better. Moncharmont, you know, is the indispensable member of the firm."

"And—what would you do? Go abroad, I suppose?"

"For a time, at all events. Possibly to Russia—I have a purpose—too vague to speak of yet—I should frighten myself if I spoke of it. But it all depends upon"— He broke off, unable to command his voice. A moment's silence, during which he stared at the woman on the wall, and he could speak again. "I can't go alone. I can't do — can't think of— anything seriously, whilst I am maddened by solitude!"

Olga sat with her head bent. He drew nearer to her.

"It depends upon you. I want you for my companion— for my wife"—

She looked him in the face—a strange, agitated, half-defiant look.

"I don't think that is true! You don't want *me*"—

"You! Yes, you, Olga! And only you!"

"I don't believe it. You mean—any woman." Her voice all but choked. "If that one"—she pointed to the wall— "could step towards you, you would as soon have her. You would *rather*, because she is more beautiful."

"Not in my eyes!" He seized her hand, and said, half laughing, shaken with the moment's fever, "Come and stand beside her, and let me see how the real living woman makes pale the ideal!"

Flushing, trembling at his touch, she rose. Her lips parted; she had all but spoken; when there came a loud knock at the door of the room. Their hands fell, and they gazed at each other in perturbation.

"Silence!" whispered Otway. "No reply!"

He stepped softly to the door; silently he turned the key in the lock. No sooner had he done so, than someone without tried the handle; the door was shaken a little, and there sounded another knock, loud, peremptory. Piers moved to Olga's side, smiled at her reassuringly, tried to take her hand; but, with a frightened glance towards the door, she shrank away.

Two minutes of dead silence; then Otway spoke just above his breath.

"Gone! Didn't you hear the footstep on the stairs?"

Had she just escaped some serious peril, Olga could not have worn a more agitated look. Her hand resisted Otway's approach; she would not seat herself, but moved nervously hither and thither, her eyes constantly turning to the door. It was in vain that Piers laughed at the incident, asking what it could possibly matter to them that some person had wished to see Miss Bonnicastle, and had gone away thinking no one was within; Olga made a show of assenting, she smiled and pretended to recover herself, but was still tremulous and unable to converse.

He took her hands, held them firmly, compelled her to meet his look.

"Let us have an end of this, Olga! Your life is unhappy— let me help you to forget. And help *me*! I want your love. Come to me—we can help each other—put an end to this accursed loneliness, this longing and raging that eats one's heart away!"

She suffered him to hold her close—her head bent back, the eyes half veiled by their lids.

"Give me one day—to think"—

"Not one hour, not one minute! Now!"

"Because you are stronger than I am, that doesn't make me really yours." She spoke in stress of spirit, her eyes wide and fearful. "If I said 'yes,' I might break my promise. I warn you! I can't trust myself—I warn you not to trust me!"

"I will take the risk!"

"I have warned you.—Yes, yes! I will try!—Let me go now, and stay here till I have gone. I *must* go now!" She shook with hysterical passion. "Else I take back my promise!—I will see you in two days; not here; I will think of some place."

18

She drew towards the exit, and when her one hand was on the key, Piers, with sudden self-subdual, spoke.

"You have promised!"

"Yes, I will write very soon."

With a look of gratitude, a smile all but of tenderness, she passed from his sight.

On the pavement, she looked this way and that. Fifty yards away, on the other side of the street, a well-dressed man stood supporting himself on his umbrella, as if he had been long waiting; though to her shortness of sight the figure was featureless, Olga trembled as she perceived it, and started at a rapid walk towards the cab-stand at the top of the street. Instantly, the man made after her, almost running. He caught her up before she could approach the vehicles.

"So you were there! Something told me you were there!"

"What do you mean, Mr. Florio?"

The man was raging with jealous anger; trying to smile, he showed his teeth in a mere grin, and sputtered his words.

"The door was shut with the key! Why was that?"

"You mustn't speak to me in this way," said Olga, with troubled remonstrance rather than indignation. "When I visit my friend, we don't always care to be disturbed"—

"Ha! Your friend — Miss Bonnicastle — was *not* there! I have seen her in Oxford Street! She has said no one was there this morning, but I doubted—I came!"

Whilst speaking, he kept a look turned in the direction of the house from which Olga had come. And of a sudden his eyes lit with fierce emotion.

"See! Something told me! *That* is your friend!"

Piers Otway had come out. Olga could not have recognised him at this distance, but she knew the Italian's eyes would not be deceived. Instantly she took to flight, along a cross-street leading eastward. Florio kept at her side, and neither spoke until breathlessness stopped her as she entered Fitzroy Square.

"You are safe," said her pursuer, or companion. "He is gone the other way.—Ah! you are pale! You are suffering! Why did you run—run—run? There was no need."

His voice had turned soothing, caressing; his eyes melted in compassion as they bent upon her.

"I have given you no right to hunt me like this," said Olga, panting, timid, her look raised for a moment to his.

"I take the right," he laughed musically. "It is the right of the man who loves you."

She cast a frightened glance about the square, which was almost deserted, and began to walk slowly on.

"Why was the door shut with the key?" asked Florio, his head near to hers. "I thought I would break it open! And I wish I had done so," he added, suddenly fierce again.

"I have given you no right," stammered Olga, who seemed to suffer under a sort of fascination, which dulled her mind.

"I take it!—Has *he* a right? Tell me that! You are not good to me; you are not honest to me; you deceive—deceive! Why was the door shut with the key? I am astonished! I did not think this was done in England—a lady—a young lady!"

"Oh, what do you mean?" Olga exclaimed, with a face of misery. "There was no harm. It wasn't *I* who wished it to be locked!"

Florio gazed at her long and searchingly, till the blood burned in her face.

"Enough!" he said with decision, waving his arm. "I have learnt something. One always learns something new in England. The English are wonderful — yes, they are wonderful. *Basta!* and *addio!*"

He raised his hat, turned, moved away. As if drawn irresistibly, Olga followed. Head down, arms hanging in the limpness of shame, she followed, but without drawing nearer. At the corner of the square, Florio, as if accidentally, turned his head; in an instant, he stood before her.

"Then you do not wish good-bye?"

"You are very cruel! How can I let you think such things? You *know* it's false!"

"But there must be explanation!"

"I can easily explain. But not here—one can't talk in the street"—

"Naturally!—Listen! It is twelve o'clock. You go home; you eat; you repose. At three o'clock, I pay you a visit. Why not? You said it yourself the other day, but I could not decide. Now I have decided. I pay you a visit; you receive me privately—can you not? We talk, and all is settled!"

Olga thought for a moment, and assented. A few minutes afterwards, she was rolling in a cab towards Bryanston Square.

On Monday evening, Piers received a note from Olga. It ran thus :

"I warned you not to trust me. It is all over now; I have, in your own words, 'put an end to it.' We could have given no happiness to each other. Miss Bonnicastle will explain. Good-bye!"

He went at once to Great Portland Street. Miss Bonnicastle knew nothing, but looked anxious when she had seen the note and heard its explanation.

"We must wait till the morning," she said. "Don't worry. It's just what one might have expected."

Don't worry! Piers had no wink of sleep that night. At post-time in the morning, he was at Miss Bonnicastle's, but no news arrived. He went to business; the day passed without news; he returned to Great Portland Street, and there waited for the last postal delivery. It brought the expected letter; Olga announced her marriage that morning to Mr. Florio.

"It's better than I feared," said Miss Bonnicastle. "Now go home to bed, and sleep like a philosopher."

Good advice, but not of much profit to one racked and distraught with amorous frenzy, with disappointment sharp as death. Through the warm spring night, Piers raved and agonised. The business hour found him lying upon his bed, sunk in dreamless sleep.

CHAPTER XXXII

A GAIN it was springtime—the spring of 1894. Two years had gone by since that April night when Piers Otway suffered things unspeakable in flesh and spirit, thinking that for him the heavens had no more radiance, life no morrow. The memory was faint; he found it hard to imagine that the loss of a woman he did not love could so have afflicted him. Olga Hannaford—Mrs. Florio—was matter for a smile; he hoped that he might some day meet her again, and take her hand with the old friendliness, and wish her well.

He had spent the winter in St. Petersburg, and was making arrangements for a visit to England, when one morning there came to him a letter which made his eyes sparkle and his heart beat high with joy. In the afternoon, having given more than wonted care to his dress, he set forth from the lodging he occupied at the lower end of the Nevski Prospect, and walked to the Hôtel de France, near the Winter Palace, where he inquired for Mrs. Borisoff. After a little delay, he was conducted to a private sitting-room, where again he waited. On a table lay two periodicals, at which he glanced, recognising with a smile recent numbers of the *Nineteenth Century* and the *Vyestnik Evropy*.

There entered a lady with a bright English face, a lady in the years between youth and middle age, frank, gracious, her look of interest speaking a compliment which Otway found more than agreeable.

"I have kept you waiting," she said, in a tone that dispensed with formalities, "because I was on the point of going out when they brought your card"—

"Oh, I am sorry"—

"But I am not. Instead of twaddle and boredom round somebody or other's samovar, I am going to have honest talk under the chaperonage of an English teapot—my own teapot, which I carry everywhere. But don't be afraid; I shall not give you English tea. What a shame that I have been here for two months without our meeting! I have talked about you—wanted to know you. Look!"

She pointed to the periodicals which Piers had already noticed.

"No," she went on, checking him as he was about to sit down, "*that* is your chair. If you sat on the other, you would be polite and grave and—like everybody else; I know the influence of chairs. That is the chair my husband selects when he wishes to make me understand some point of etiquette. Miss Derwent warned you, no doubt, of my shortcomings in etiquette?"

"All she said to me," replied Piers, laughing, "was that you are very much her friend."

"Well, that is true, I hope.—Tell me, please; is the article in the *Vyestnik* your own Russian?"

"Not entirely. I have a friend named Korolevitch, who went through it for me."

"Korolevitch? I seem to know that name. Is he, by chance, connected with some religious movement, some heresy?"

"I was going to say I am sorry he is; yet I can't be sorry for what honours the man. He has joined the Dukhobortsi; has sold his large estate, and is devoting all the money to their cause. I'm afraid he'll go to some new-world colony, and I shall see little of him henceforth. A great loss to me."

Mrs. Borisoff kept her eyes upon him as he spoke, seeming to reflect rather than to listen.

"I ought to tell you," she said, "that I don't know Russian. Irene—Miss Derwent almost shamed me into working at it; but I am so lazy—ah, so lazy! You are aware, of course, that Miss Derwent has learnt it?"

"Has learnt Russian?" exclaimed Piers. "I didn't know —I had no idea"—

"Wonderful girl! I suppose she thinks it a trifle."

"It's so long," said Otway, "since I had any news of Miss Derwent. I can hardly consider myself one of her friends,—at least, I shouldn't have ventured to do so until this morning, when I was surprised and delighted to have a letter from her about that *Nineteenth Century* article, sent through the publishers. She spoke of you, and asked me to call—saying she had written an introduction of me by the same post."

Mrs. Borisoff smiled oddly.

"Oh yes; it came. She didn't speak of the *Vyestnik*?"

"No."

"Yet she has read it—I happen to know. I'm sorry I can't. Tell me about it, will you?"

The Russian article was called "New Womanhood in England." It began with a good-tempered notice of certain novels then popular, and passed on to speculations regarding the new ideals of life set before English women. Piers spoke of it as a mere bit of apprentice work, meant rather to amuse than as a serious essay.

"At all events, it's a success," said his listener. "One hears of it in every drawing-room. Wonderful thing—you don't sneer at women. I'm told you are almost on our side—if not quite. I've heard a passage read into French — the woman of the twentieth century. I rather liked it."

"Not altogether?" said Otway, with humorous diffidence.

"Oh! A woman never quite likes an ideal of womanhood which doesn't quite fit her notion of herself.—But let us speak of the other thing, in the *Nineteenth Century*—'The Pilgrimage to Kief.' For life, colour, sympathy, I think it altogether wonderful. I have heard Russians say that they couldn't have believed a foreigner had written it."

"That's the best praise of all."

"You mean to go on with this kind of thing? You might become a sort of interpreter of the two nations to each other. An original idea. The everyday thing is to exasperate Briton against Russ, and Russ against Briton, with every sort of cheap joke and stale falsehood. All the same, Mr. Otway, I'm bound to confess to you that I don't like Russia."

"No more do I," returned Piers, in an undertone. "But that only means, I don't like the worst features of the Middle Ages. The Russian-speaking cosmopolitan whom you and I know isn't Russia; he belongs to the Western Europe of to-day, his country represents Western Europe of some centuries ago. Not strictly that, of course; we must allow for race; but it's how one has to think of Russia."

Again Mrs. Borisoff scrutinised him as he spoke, averting her eyes at length with an absent smile.

"Here comes my tutelary teapot," she said, as a pretty maid-servant entered with a tray. "A phrase I got from Irene, by the bye—from Miss Derwent, who laughs at my carrying the thing about in my luggage. She has clever little phrases of that sort, as you know."

"Yes," fell from Piers, dreamily. "But it's so long since I heard her talk."

When he had received his cup of tea, and sipped from it, he asked with a serious look :

"Will you tell me about her ? "

"Of course I will. But you must first tell me about yourself. You were in business in London, I believe ? "

"For about a year. Then I found myself with enough to live upon, and came back to Russia. I had lived at Odessa "—

"You may presuppose a knowledge of what came before," interrupted Mrs. Borisoff, with a friendly nod.

"I lived for several months with Korolevitch, on his estate near Poltava. We used to talk—heavens ! how we talked ! Sometimes eight hours at a stretch. I learnt a great deal. Then I wandered up and down Russia, still learning."

"Writing, too ? "

"The time hadn't come for writing. Korolevitch gave me no end of useful introductions. I've had great luck on my travels."

"Pray, when did you make your studies of English women ? "

Piers tried to laugh ; declared he did not know.

"I shouldn't wonder if you generalise from one or two ? " said his hostess, letting her eyelids droop as she observed him lazily. "Do you know Russian women as well ? "

By begging for another cup of tea, and adding a remark on some other subject, Piers evaded this question.

"And what are you going to do ? " asked Mrs. Borisoff. "Stay here, and write more articles ? "

"I'm going to England in a few days, for the summer."

"That's what I think I shall do. But I don't know what part to go to. Advise me, can you ? Seaside—no ; I don't like the seaside. Do you notice how people—our kind of people, I mean—are losing their taste for it in England ? It's partly, I suppose, because of the excursion train. One doesn't grudge the crowd its excursion train, but it's so much nicer to imagine their blessedness than to see it.—Or are you for the other point of view ? "

Otway gave an expressive look.

"That's right. Oh, the sham philanthropic talk that goes on in England! How it relieves one to say flatly that one does *not* love the multitude!—No seaside, then. Lakes—no; Wales—no; Highlands—no. Isn't there some part of England one would like if one discovered it?"

"Do you want solitude?" asked Piers, becoming more interested.

"Solitude? H'm!" She handed a box of cigarettes, and herself took one. "Yes, solitude. I shall try to get Miss Derwent to come for a time. New Forest—no. Please, please, do suggest! I'm nervous; your silence teases me."

"Do you know the Yorkshire dales?" asked Otway, watching her as she watched a nice little ring of white smoke from the end of her cigarette.

"No! That's an idea. It's your own country, isn't it?"

"But—how do you know that?"

"Dreamt it."

"I wasn't born there, but lived there as a child, and later a little. You might do worse than the dales, if you like that kind of country. Wensleydale, for instance. There's an old Castle, and a very interesting one, part of it habitable, where you can get quarters."

"A Castle? Superb!"

"Where Queen Mary was imprisoned for a time, till she made an escape"—

"Magnificent! Can I have the whole Castle to myself?"

"The furnished part of it, unless someone else has got it already for this summer. There's a family, the caretakers, always in possession—if things are still as they used to be."

"Write for me at once, will you? Write immediately! There is paper on the desk."

Piers obeyed. Whilst he sat penning the letter, Mrs. Borisoff lighted a second cigarette, her face touched with a roguish smile. She studied Otway's profile for a moment; became grave; fell into a mood of abstraction, which shadowed her features with weariness and melancholy. Turning suddenly to put a question, Piers saw the change in her look, and was so surprised that he forgot what he was going to say.

"Finished?" she asked, moving nervously in her chair.

When the letter was written, Mrs. Borisoff resumed talk in the same tone as before.

"You have heard of Dr. Derwent's discoveries about diphtheria?—That's the kind of thing one envies, don't you think? After all, what can we poor creatures do in this world, but try to ease each other's pain? The man who succeeds in *that* is the man I honour."

"I too," said Piers. "But he is lost sight of, nowadays, in comparison with the man who invents a new gun or a new bullet."

"Yes—the beasts!" exclaimed Mrs. Borisoff, with a laugh. "What a world! I'm always glad I have no children. —But you wanted to speak, not about Dr. Derwent, but Dr. Derwent's daughter."

Piers bent forward, resting his chin on his hand.

"Tell me about her—will you?"

"There's not much to tell. You knew about the broken-off marriage?"

"I knew it *was* broken off."

"Why, that's all anyone knows, except the two persons concerned. It isn't our business. The world talks far too much about such things—don't you think? When we are civilised, there'll be no such thing as public weddings, and talk about anyone's domestic concerns will be the grossest impertinence.—That's an *obiter dictum*. I was going to say that Irene lives with her father down in Kent. They left Bryanston Square half a year after the affair. They wander about the Continent together, now and then. I like that chumming of father and daughter; it speaks well for both."

"When did you see her last?"

"About Christmas. We went to a concert together. That's one of the things Irene is going in for—music. When I first knew her, she didn't seem to care much about it, though she played fairly well."

"I never heard her play," fell from Piers, in an undertone.

"No; she only did to please her father now and then. It's a mental and moral advance, her new love of music. I notice that she talks much less about science, much more about the things one really likes—I speak for myself. Well, it's just possible I have had a little influence there. I confess my inability to chat about either physic or physics. It's weak, of course, but I have no place in your new world of women."

"You mistake, I think," said Piers. "That ideal has

nothing to do with any particular study. It supposes intelligence, that's all."

" So much the better. You must write about it in English; then we'll debate. By the bye, if I go to your Castle, you must come down to show me the country."

" I should like to."

" Oh, that's part of the plan. If we don't get the Castle, you must find some other place for me. I leave it in your hands—with an apology for my impudence."

After a pause, during which each of them mused smiling, they began to talk of their departure for England. Otway would go direct, in a few days' time; Mrs. Borisoff had to travel a long way round, first of all accompanying her husband to the Crimea, on a visit to relatives. She mentioned her London hotel, and an approximate date when she might be heard of there.

" Get the Castle if you possibly can," were her words as they parted. " I have set my heart on the Castle."

" So have I," said Piers, avoiding her look.

And Mrs. Borisoff laughed.

CHAPTER XXXIII

ONCE in the two years' interval he had paid a short visit to England. He came on disagreeable business—to see his brother Daniel, who had fallen into the hands of the police on an infamous charge, and only by the exertions of clever counsel (feed by Piers) received the benefit of a doubt and escaped punishment. Daniel had already written him several begging letters, and, when detected in what looked like crime, declared that poverty and ill-health were his excuse. He was a broken man. Surmising his hidden life, Piers wondered at the pass a man can be brought to, in our society, by his primitive instincts; instincts which may lead, when they are impetuous, either to grimiest degradation or loftiest attainment. To save him, if possible, from the worst extremities, Piers granted him a certain small income, to be paid weekly, and therewith bade him final adieu.

The firm of Moncharmont & Co. grew in moderate prosperity. Its London representative was a far better man, from the commercial point of view, than Piers Otway, and on visiting the new offices—which he did very soon after reaching London, in the spring of 1894—Piers marvelled how the enterprise had escaped shipwreck during those twelve months which were so black in his memory with storm and stress. The worst twelvemonth of his life!—with the possible exception of that which he spent part at Ewell, part at Odessa.

Since, he had sailed in no smooth water; had seen no haven. But at least he sailed onward, which gave him courage. Was courage to be now illumined with hope? He tried to keep that thought away from him; he durst not foster it. Among the papers he brought with him to England was a letter, which, having laid it aside, he never dared to open again. He knew it by heart—unfortunately for his peace.

He returned to another London than that he had known,

a London which smiled welcome. It was his duty, no less than his pleasure, to call upon certain people for whom he had letters of introduction from friends in Russia, and their doors opened wide to him. Upon formalities followed kindness; the season was beginning, and at his modest lodgings arrived cards, notes, bidding to ceremonies greater and less; one or two of these summonses bore names which might have stirred envy in the sons of fashion.

Solus feci! He allowed himself a little pride. His doing, it was true, had as yet been nothing much to the eye of the world; but he had made friends under circumstances not very favourable, friends among the intelligent and the powerful. That gift, it seemed, was his, if no other—the ability to make himself liked, respected. He, by law the son of nobody, had begun to approve himself true son of the father he loved and honoured.

His habits were vigorous. Rising very early, he walked across the Park, and had a swim in the Serpentine. The hours of the solid day he spent, for the most part, in study at the British Museum. Then, if he had no engagement, he generally got by train well out of town, and walked in sweet air until nightfall; or, if weather were bad, he granted himself the luxury of horse-hire, and rode—rode, teeth set against wind and rain. This earned him sleep—his daily prayer to the gods.

At the date appointed, he went in search of Mrs. Borisoff, who welcomed him cordially. Her first inquiry was whether he had got the Castle.

"I have got it," Piers replied, and entered into particulars. They talked about it like children anticipating a holiday. Mrs. Borisoff then questioned him about his doings since he had been in England. On his mentioning a certain great lady, a Russian, with whom he was to dine, next week, his friend replied with a laugh, which she refused to explain.

"When can you spend an evening here? I don't mean a dinner. I'll give you something to eat, but it doesn't count; you come to talk, as I know you can, though you didn't let me suspect it at Petersburg. I shall have one or two others, old chums, not respectable people. Name your own day."

When the evening came, Piers entered Mrs. Borisoff's drawing-room with trepidation. He glanced at the guest who had already arrived—a lady unknown to him. When again the door opened, he looked, trembling. His fearful hope ended only in a headache, but he talked, as was expected of him, and the hostess smiled approval.

"These friends of yours," he said aside to her, before leaving, "are nice people to know. But"—

And he broke off, meeting her eyes.

"I don't understand," said his hostess, with a perplexed look.

"Then I daren't try to make you."

A few days after, at the great house of the great Russian lady, he ascended the stairs without a tremor, glanced round the room with indifference. No one would be there whom he could not face calmly. Brilliant women awed him a little at first, but it was not till afterwards, in the broken night following such occasions as this, that they had power over his imagination; then he saw them, drawn upon darkness, their beauty without that halo of worldly grandeur which would not allow him to forget the gulf between them. The hostess herself shone by quality of intellect rather than by charm of feature; she greeted him with subtlest flattery, a word or two of simple friendliness in her own language, and was presenting him to her husband, when, from the doorway, sounded a name which made Otway's heart leap, and left him tongue-tied.

"Mrs. Borisoff and Miss Derwent."

He turned, but with eyes downcast: for a moment he durst not raise them. He moved, insensibly, a few steps backward, shadowed himself behind two men who were conversing together. And at length he looked.

With thrill of marvelling and rapture, with chill of self-abasement. When, years ago, he saw Irene in the dress of ceremony, she seemed to him peerlessly radiant; but it was the beauty and the dignity of one still girlish. What he now beheld was the exquisite fulfilment of that bright promise. He had not erred in worship; she who had ever been to him the light of life, the beacon of his passionate soul, shone before him supreme among women. What head so noble in its unconscious royalty! What form so faultless in its mould and bearing! He heard her speak — the graceful nothings of introduction and recognition; it was Irene's voice toned to a fuller music. Then her face dazzled, grew distant; he turned away to command himself.

Mrs. Borisoff spoke beside him.

" Have you no good-evening for me ? "

" So this was what you meant ? "

" You have a way of speaking in riddles."

" And you—a way of acting divinely. Tell me," his voice sank, and his words were hurried. " May I go up to her as any acquaintance would? May I presume that she knows me ? "

" You mean Miss Derwent? But—why not? I don't understand you."

" No—I forget—it seems to you absurd. Of course—she wrote and introduced me to you "—

" You are amusing—which is more than can be said of everyone."

She bent her head, and turned to speak with someone else. Piers, with what courage he knew not, stepped across the carpet to where Miss Derwent was sitting. She saw his approach, and held her hand to him as if they had met only the other day. That her complexion was a little warmer than its wont, Piers had no power of perceiving ; he saw only her eyes, soft-shining as they rose to his, in their depths an infinite gentleness.

" How glad I am that you got my letter just before leaving Petersburg ! "

" How kind of you to introduce me to Mrs. Borisoff ! "

" I thought you would soon be friends."

It was all they could say. At this moment, the host murmured his request that Otway would take down Mrs. Borisoff ; the hostess led up someone to be introduced to Miss Derwent. Then the procession began.

Piers was both disappointed and relieved. To have felt the touch upon his arm of Irene's hand would have been a delight unutterable, yet to desire it was presumption. He was not worthy of that companionship ; it would have been unjust to Irene to oblige her to sit by him through the dinner, with the inevitable thoughts rising in her mind. Better to see her from a distance—though it was hard when she smiled at the distinguished and clever-looking man who talked, talked. It cost him, at first, no small effort to pay becoming attention to Mrs. Borisoff ; the lady on his other hand, a brilliant beauty, moved him to a feeling almost hostile—he knew not why. But as the dinner progressed, as the kindly vintage circled in his blood, he felt the stirrings of a deep joy. By his own

effort he had won reception into Irene's world. It was something; it was much—remembering all that had gone before.

He spoke softly to his partner.

"I am going to drink a silent health—that of my friend
Korolevitch. To him I owe everything."

"I don't believe *that*, but I will drink it too—I was speaking
of him to Miss Derwent. She wants to know all about the
Dukhobortsi. Instruct her, afterwards, if you get a chance.
Do you think her altered?"

"No—yes!"

"By the bye, how long is it really since you first knew her?"

"Eight years—just eight years."

"You speak as if it were eighty."

"Why, so it seems, when I look back. I was a boy, and
had the strangest notions of the world."

"You shall tell me all about that some day," said Mrs.
Borisoff, glancing at him. "At the Castle, perhaps"—

"Oh yes! At the Castle!"

When the company divided, and Piers had watched Irene
pass out of sight, he sat down with a tired indifference.
But his host drew him into conversation on Russian subjects,
and, as had happened before now in gatherings of this kind,
Otway presently found himself amid attentive listeners, whilst
he talked of things that interested him. At such moments
he had an irreflective courage, which prompted him to utter
what he thought without regard to anything but the common
civilities of life. His opinions might excite surprise; but they
did not give offence; for they seemed impersonal, the natural
outcome of honest and capable observation, with never a touch
of national prejudice or individual conceit. It was well,
perhaps, for the young man's natural modesty, that he did not
hear certain remarks afterwards exchanged between the more
intelligent of his hearers.

When they passed to the drawing-room, the piano was
sounding there. It stopped; the player rose, and moved
away, but not before Piers had seen that it was Irene. He felt
robbed of a delight. Oh, to hear Irene play!

Better was in store for him. With a boldness natural to the
hour, he drew nearer, nearer, watching his opportunity. The
chair by Irene's side became vacant; he stepped forward, and
was met with a frank countenance, which invited him to take
the coveted place. Miss Derwent spoke at once of her interest

in the Russian sectaries with whom—she had heard—Otway was well acquainted, the people called Dukhobortsi, who held the carrying of arms a sin, and suffered persecution because of their conscientious refusal to perform military service. Piers spoke with enthusiasm of these people.

"They uphold the ideal above all necessary to our time. We ought to be rapidly outgrowing warfare; isn't that the obvious next step in civilisation? It seems a commonplace that everyone should look to that end, and strive for it. Yet we're going back—there's a military reaction—fighting is glorified by everyone who has a loud voice, and in no country more than in England. I wish you could hear a Russian friend of mine speak about it, a rich man who has just given up everything to join the Dukhobortsi. I never knew before what religious passion meant. And it seems to me that this is the world's only hope—peace made a religion. The forms don't matter; only let the supreme end be peace. It is what people have talked so much about—the religion of the future."

His tones moved the listener, as appeared in her look and attitude.

"Surely all the best in every country lean to it," she said.

"Of course! That's our hope—but at the same time the pitiful thing; for the best hold back, keep silence, as if their quiet contempt could prevail against this activity of the reckless and the foolish."

"One can't *make* a religion," said Irene sadly. "It is just this religious spirit which has decayed throughout our world. Christianity turns to ritualism. And science—we were told, you know, that science would be religion enough."

"There's the pity—the failure of science as a civilising force. I know," added Piers quickly, "that there are men whose spirit, whose work, doesn't share in that failure; they are the men—the very few—who are above self-interest. But science, on the whole, has come to mean money-making and weapon-making. It leads the international struggle; it is judged by its value to the capitalist and the soldier."

"Isn't this perhaps a stage of evolution that the world must live through—to its extreme results?"

"Very likely. The signs are bad enough."

"You haven't yourself that enthusiastic hope?"

"I try to hope," said Piers, in a low, unsteady voice, his eyes falling timidly before her glance. "But what you said is

19

so true—one can't create the spirit of religion. If one hasn't it "— He broke off, and added with a smile, " I think I have a certain amount of enthusiasm. But when one has seen a good deal of the world, it's so very easy to feel discouraged. Think how much sheer barbarism there is around us, from the brutal savage of the gutter to the cunning savage of the Stock Exchange ! "

Irene had a gleam in her eyes ; she nodded appreciation.

" If," he went on vigorously, " if one could make the multitude really understand — understand to the point of action—how enormously its interest is peace ! "

" More hope that way, I'm afraid," said Irene," than through idealisms."

" Yes, yes. If it comes at all, it'll be by the way of self-interest. And really it looks as if the military tyrants might overreach themselves here and there. Italy, for instance. Think of Italy, crushed and cursed by a blood-tax that the people themselves see to be futile. One enters into the spirit of the men who freed Italy from foreigners—it was glorious ; but how much more glorious to excite a rebellion there against her own rulers ! Shouldn't you enjoy doing that ? "

At times, there is no subtler compliment to a woman than to address her as if she were a man. It must be done involuntarily, as was the case with this utterance of Otway's. Irene rewarded him with a look such as he had never had from her, the look of rejoicing comradeship.

" Indeed I should ! Italy is becoming a misery to those who love her. Is no plot going on? Couldn't one start a conspiracy against that infamous misgovernment ? "

" There's an arch-plotter at work. His name is Hunger. Let us be glad that Italy can't enrich herself by manufactures. Who knows? The revolution against militarism may begin there, as that against feudalism did in France. Talk of enthusiasm ! How should we feel if we read in the paper some morning that the Italian people had formed into an army of peace—refusing to pay another centesimo for warfare ? "

" The next boat for Calais ! The next train for Rome ! "

Their eyes met, interchanging gleams of laughter.

" Oh, but the crowd, the crowd ! " sighed Piers. " What is bad enough to say of it ? Who shall draw its picture with long enough ears ? "

" It has another aspect, you know,"

"It has. At its best, a smiling simpleton; at its worst, a murderous maniac."

"You are not exactly a socialist," remarked Irene, with that smile which, linking past and present, blended in Otway's heart old love and new—her smile of friendly irony.

"Socialism? I seldom think of it; which means, that I have no faith in it.—When we came in, you were playing."

"I miss the connection," said Irene, with a puzzled air.

"Forgive me. I am fond of music, and it has been in my mind all the time—the hope that you would play again."

"Oh, that was merely the slow music, as one might say, of the drawing-room mysteries—an obligato in the after-dinner harmony. I play only to amuse myself—or when it is a painful duty."

Piers was warned by his tactful conscience that he had held Miss Derwent quite long enough in talk. A movement in their neighbourhood gave miserable opportunity; he resigned his seat to another expectant, and did his best to converse with someone else.

Her voice went with him as he walked homeward across the Park, under a fleecy sky silvered with moonlight; the voice which now and again brought back so vividly their first meeting at Ewell. He lived through it all again, the tremors, the wild hopes, the black despair of eight years ago. How she encountered him on the stairs, talked of his long hours of study, and prophesied—with that indescribable blending of gravity and jest, still her characteristic—that he would come to grief over his examination. Irene! Irene! Did she dream what was in his mind and heart? The long, long love, his very life through all labours and cares and casualties—did she suspect it, imagine it? If she had received his foolish verses (he grew hot to think of them), there must have been at least a moment when she knew that he worshipped her, and does such knowledge ever fade from a woman's memory?

Irene! Irene! Was she brought nearer to him by her own experience of heart-trouble? That she had suffered, he could not doubt; impossible for her to have given her consent to marriage unless she believed herself in love with the man who wooed her. It could have been no trifling episode in her life, whatever the story; Irene was not of the women who yield their hands in jest, in pique, in light-hearted ignorance. The change visible in her was more, he fancied, than could be

due to the mere lapse of time; during her silences, she had
the look of one familiar with mental conflict, perhaps of one
whose pride had suffered an injury.   The one or two glances
which he ventured whilst she was talking with the man who
succeeded to his place beside her, perceived a graver countenance, a reserve such as she had not used with him; and of
this insubstantial solace he made a sort of hope which winged
the sleepless hours till daybreak.

He had permission to call upon Mrs. Borisoff at times alien
to polite routine.   Thus, when nearly a week had passed, he
sought her company at midday, and found her idling over a
book, her seat by a window which viewed the Thames, and the
broad Embankment with its plane trees, and London beyond
the water, picturesque in squalid hugeness through summer
haze and the sagging smoke of chimneys numberless.   She
gave a languid hand, pointed to a chair, gazed at him with
embarrassing fixity.

"I don't know about the Castle," were her first words.
"Perhaps I shall give it up."

"You are not serious?"

Piers spoke and looked in dismay; and still she kept her
heavy eyes on him.

"What does it matter to *you*?" she asked carelessly.

"I counted on—on showing you the dales"—

Mrs. Borisoff nodded twice or thrice, and laughed, then
pointed to the prospect through the window.

"This is more interesting.   Imagine historians living a
thousand years hence—what would they give to see what we
see now!"

"Oh, one often has that thought.   It's about the best way
of making ordinary life endurable."

They watched the steamers and barges, silent for a minute
or two.

"So you had rather I didn't give up the Castle?"

"I should be horribly disappointed."

"Yes—no doubt you would.   Why did you come to see
me to-day?   No, no, no!   The real reason."

"I wanted to talk about Miss Derwent," Piers answered,
bracing himself to frankness.

Mrs. Borisoff's lips contracted, in something which was
not quite a smile, but which became a smile before she
spoke.

"If you hadn't told the truth, Mr. Otway, I would have sent you about your business. Well, talk of her; I am ready."

"But certainly not if it wearies you"—

"Talk! talk!"

"I'll begin with a question. Does Miss Derwent go much into society?"

"No; not very much. And it's only the last few months that she has been seen at all in London—I mean, since the affair that people talked about."

"Did they talk—disagreeably?"

"Gossip—chatter—half malicious without malicious intention —don't you know the way of the sweet creatures? I would tell you more if I could. The simple truth is that Irene has never spoken to me about it—never once. When it happened, she came suddenly to Paris, to a hotel, and from there wrote me a letter, just saying that her marriage was off; no word of explanation. Of course I fetched her at once to my house, and from that moment to this I have heard not one reference from her to the matter. You would like to know something about the hero? He has been away a good deal—building up the Empire, as they say; which means, of course, looking after his own and other people's dividends."

"Thank you. Now let us talk about the Castle."

But Mrs. Borisoff was not in a good humour to-day, and Piers very soon took his leave. Her hand felt rather hot; he noticed this particularly, as she let it lie in his longer than usual—part of her absent-mindedness.

Piers had often resented, as a weakness, his susceptibility to the influence of others' moods; he did so to-day, when, having gone to Mrs. Borisoff in an unusually cheerful frame of mind, he came away languid and despondent. But his scheme of life permitted no such idle brooding as used to waste his days; self-discipline sent him to his work, as usual, through the afternoon, and in the evening he walked ten miles.

The weather was brilliant. As he stood, far away in rural stillness, watching a noble sunset, he repeated to himself words which had of late become his motto, "Enjoy now! This moment will never come again." But the intellectual resolve was one thing, the moral aptitude another. He did not enjoy; how many hours in all his life had brought him real enjoyment? Idle to repeat and repeat that life was the passing minute, which must be seized, made the most of; he could not live in the present; life was to him for ever a thing postponed. "I will live—I will enjoy—some day!" As likely as not that day would never dawn.

Was it true, as admonishing reason sometimes whispered, that happiness cometh not by observation, that the only true content is in the moments which we pass without self-consciousness? Is all attainment followed by disillusion? A man aware of his health is on the verge of malady. Were he to possess his desire, to exclaim, "I am happy," would the Fates chastise his presumption?

That way lay asceticism, which his soul abhorred. On, rather, following the great illusion, if this it were! "The crown of life"—philosophise as he might, that word had still its meaning, still its inspiration. Let the present pass untasted; he preferred his dream of a day to come.

Next morning, very unexpectedly, he received a note from Mrs. Borisoff, inviting him to dine with her a few days hence. About her company she said nothing, and Piers went, uncertain whether it was a dinner *tête-à-tête* or with other guests. When he entered the room, the first face he beheld was Irene's.

It was a very small party, and the hostess wore her gayest countenance. A delightful evening, from the social point of view; for Piers Otway a time of self-forgetfulness in the pleasures of sight and hearing. He could have little private talk with Irene; she did not talk much with anyone; but he saw her, he heard her voice, he lived in the glory of her presence. Moreover, she consented to play. Of her skill as a pianist, Otway could not judge; what he heard was Music, music absolute, the very music of the spheres. When it ceased, Mrs. Borisoff chanced to look at him; he was startlingly pale, his eyes wide as if in vision more than mortal.

"I leave town to-morrow," said his hostess, as he took leave. "Some friends are going with me. You shall hear how we get on at the Castle."

Perhaps her look was meant to supplement this bare news. It seemed to offer reassurance. Did she understand his look of entreaty in reply?

Music breathed about him in the lonely hours. It exalted his passion, lulled the pains of desire, held the flesh subservient to spirit. What is love, says the physiologist, but ravening sex? If so, in Piers Otway's breast the primal instinct had undergone strange transformation.   How wrought?—he asked himself.   To what destiny did it correspond, this winged love soaring into the infinite?   This rapture of devotion, this utter humbling of self, this ardour of the poet-soul singing a fellow-creature to the heaven of heavens—by what alchemy comes it forth from blood and tissue?   Nature has no need of such lyric life; her purpose is well achieved by humbler instrumentality.   Romantic lovers are not the ancestry of noblest lines.

And if—as might well be—his love were defeated, fruitless, what end in the vast maze of things would his anguish serve?

CHAPTER XXXIV

AFTER his day's work, he had spent an hour among the pictures at Burlington House. He was lingering before an exquisite landscape, unwilling to change this atmosphere of calm for the roaring street, when a voice timidly addressed him :

"Mr. Otway!"

How altered! The face was much, much older, and in some indeterminable way had lost its finer suggestions. At her best, Olga Hannaford had a distinction of feature, a singularity of emotional expression, which made her beautiful ; in Olga Florio the lines of visage were far less subtle, and classed her under an inferior type. Transition from maidenhood to what is called the matronly had been too rapid ; it was emphasised by her costume, which cried aloud in its excess of modish splendour.

"How glad I am to see you again!" she sighed tremorously, pressing his hand with fervour, gazing at him with furtive directness. "Are you living in England now?"

Piers gave an account of himself. He was a little embarrassed, but quite unagitated. A sense of pity averted his eyes after the first wondering look.

"Will you—may I venture—can you spare the time to come and have tea with me? My carriage is waiting—I am quite alone—I only looked in for a few minutes, to rest my mind after a lunch with, oh, such tiresome people!"

His impulse was to refuse, at all costs to refuse. The voice, the glance, the phrases jarred upon him, shocked him. Already he had begun "I am afraid"— when a hurried, vehement whisper broke upon his excuse.

"Don't be unkind to me! I beg you to come! I entreat you!"

"I will come with pleasure," he said in a loud voice of ordinary civility.

At once she turned, and he followed. Without speaking, they descended the great staircase; a brougham drove up; they rolled away westward. Never had Piers felt such thorough moral discomfort; the heavily perfumed air of the carriage depressed and all but nauseated him; the inevitable touch of Olga's garments made him shrink. She had begun to talk, and talked incessantly throughout the homeward drive; not much of herself, or of him, but about the pleasures and excitements of the idle-busy world. It was meant, he supposed, to convey to him an idea of her prosperous and fashionable life. Her husband, she let fall, was for the moment in Italy; affairs of importance sometimes required his presence there; but they both preferred England. The intellectual atmosphere of London—where else could one live on so high a level?

The carriage stopped in a street beyond Edgware Road, at a house of more modest appearance than Otway had looked for. Just as they alighted, a nursemaid with a perambulator was approaching the door; Piers caught sight of a very pale little face shadowed by the hood, but his companion, without heeding, ran up the steps, and knocked violently. They entered.

Still the oppressive atmosphere of perfumes. Left for a few minutes in a little drawing-room, or boudoir, Piers stood marvelling at the ingenuity which had packed so much furniture and *bric-à-brac*, so many pictures, so much drapery, into so small a space. He longed to throw open the window; he could not sit still in this odour-laden hothouse, where the very flowers were burdensome by excess. When Olga reappeared, she was gorgeous in flowing tea-gown; her tawny hair hung low in artful profusion; her neck and arms were bare, her feet brilliantly slippered.

"Ah! How good, how good, it is to sit down and talk to you once more!—Do you like my room?"

"You have made yourself very comfortable," replied Otway, striking a note as much as possible in contrast to that of his hostess. "Some of these drawings are your own work, no doubt?"

"Yes, some of them," she answered languidly. "Do you remember that pastel? Ah, surely you do—from the old days at Ewell!"

"Of course!—That is a portrait of your husband?" he added, indicating a head on a little easel.

"Yes—idealised!"

She laughed, and put the subject away. Then tea was brought in, and after pouring it, Olga grew silent. Resolute to talk, Piers had the utmost difficulty in finding topics, but he kept up an everyday sort of chat, postponing as long as possible the conversation foreboded by his companion's face. When he was weary, Olga's opportunity came.

"There is something I *must* say to you"—

Her arms hung lax, her head drooped forward, she looked at him from under her brows.

"I have suffered so much—oh, I have suffered! I have longed for this moment. Will you say—that you forgive me?"

"My dear Mrs. Florio"— Piers began with good-natured expostulation, a sort of forced bluffness; but she would not hear him.

"Not that name! Not from *you*. There's no harm; you won't—you can't misunderstand me, such old friends as we are. I want you to call me by my own name, and to make me feel that we are friends still—that you can really forgive me."

"There is nothing in the world to forgive," he insisted, in the same tone. "Of course we are friends! How could we be anything else?"

"I behaved infamously to you! I can't think how I had the heart to do it!"

Piers was tortured with nervousness. Had her voice and manner declared insincerity, posing, anything of that kind, he would have found the situation much more endurable; but Olga had tears in her eyes, and not the tears of an actress; her tones had recovered something of their old quality, and reminded him painfully of the time when Mrs. Hannaford was dying. She held a hand to him, her pale face besought his compassion.

"Come now, let us talk in the old way, as you wish," he said, just pressing her fingers. "Of course I felt it—but then I was myself altogether to blame. I importuned you for what you couldn't give. Remembering that, wasn't your action the most sensible, and really the kindest?"

"I don't know," Olga murmured, in a voice just audible.

"Of course it was! There now, we've done with all that. Tell me more about your life this last year or two. You are such a brilliant person. I felt rather overcome"—

"Nonsense!' But Olga brightened a little. "What of your own brilliancy? I read somewhere that you are a famous man in Russia"—

Piers laughed, spontaneously this time, and, finding it a way of escape, gossiped about his own achievements with mirthful exaggeration.

"Do you see the Derwents?" Mrs. Florio asked of a sudden, with a sidelong look.

So vexed was Otway at the embarrassment he could not wholly hide, and which delayed his answer that he spoke the truth with excessive bluntness.

"I have met Miss Derwent in society."

"I don't often see them," said Olga, in a tone of weariness. "I suppose we belong to different worlds."

At the earliest possible moment, Piers rose with decision. He felt that he had not pleased Mrs. Florio, that perhaps he had offended her, and in leaving her he tried to atone for involuntary unkindness.

"But we shall see each other again, of course!" she exclaimed, retaining his hand. "You will come again soon?"

"Certainly I will."

"And your address—let me have your address"—

He breathed deeply in the open air. Glancing back at the house when he had crossed the street, he saw a white hand waved to him at a window; it hurried his step.

On the following day, Mrs. Florio visited her friend Miss Bonnicastle, who had some time since exchanged the old quarters in Great Portland Street for a house in Pimlico, where there was a larger studio (workshop, as she preferred to call it), hung about with her own and other people's designs. The artist of the poster was full as ever of vitality and of good-nature, but her humour had not quite the old spice; a stickler for decorum would have said that she was decidedly improved, that she had grown more womanly; and something of this change appeared also in her work, which tended now to the graceful rather than the grotesque. She received her fashionable visitant with off-hand friendliness, not altogether with cordiality.

"Oh, I've something to show you. Do you know that name?"

Olga took a business-card, and read upon it : " Alexander Otway, Dramatic & Musical Agent."

" It's his brother," she said, in a voice of quiet surprise.

"I thought so. The man called yesterday — wants a fetching thing to boom an Irish girl at the halls. There's her photo."

It represented a piquant person in short skirts; a face neither very pretty nor very young, but likely to be deemed attractive by the public in question. They amused themselves over it for a moment.

" He used to be a journalist," said Olga. " Does he seem to be doing well ? "

" Couldn't say. A great talker, and a furious Jingo."

" Jingo ? "

"This woman is to sing a song of his composition, all about the Empire. Not the hall; the British. Glorifies the Flag, that blessed rag—a rhyme I suggested to him, and asked him to pay me for. It's a taking tune, and we shall have it everywhere, no doubt. He sang a verse—I wish you could have heard him. A queer fish ! "

Olga walked about, seeming to inspect the pictures, but in reality much occupied with her thoughts.

" Well," she said presently, " I only looked in, dear, to say how-do-you-do."

Miss Bonnicastle was drawing ; she turned, as if to shake hands, but looked her friend in the face with a peculiar expression, far more earnest than was commonly seen in her.

" You called on Kite yesterday morning."

Olga, with slight confusion, admitted that she had been to see the artist. For some weeks Kite had suffered from an ailment which confined him to the house; he could not walk, and indeed could do nothing but lie and read, or talk of what he would do, when he recovered his health. Cheap claret having lost its inspiring force, the poor fellow had turned to more potent beverages, and would ere now have sunk into inscrutable deeps but for Miss Bonnicastle, who interested herself in his welfare. Olga, after losing sight of him for nearly two years, by chance discovered his whereabouts and his circumstances, and twice in the past week had paid him a visit.

" I wanted to tell you," pursued Miss Bonnicastle, in a

steady, matter-of-fact voice, "that he's going to have a room in this house, and be looked after."

"Indeed?"

There was a touch of malice in Olga's surprise. She held herself rather stiffly.

"It's just as well to be straightforward," continued the other. "I should like to say that it'll be very much better if you don't come to see him at all."

Olga was now very dignified indeed.

"Oh, pray say no more! I quite understand—quite!"

"I shouldn't have said it at all," rejoined Miss Bonnicastle, "if I could have trusted your—discretion. The fact is, I found I couldn't."

"Really!" exclaimed Olga, red with anger. "You might spare me insults!"

"Come, come! We're not going to fly at each other, Olga. I intended no insult; but, whilst we're about it, do take advice from one who means it well. Sentiment is all right, but sentimentality is all wrong. Do get rid of it, there's a good girl. You're meant for something better."

Olga made a great sweep of the floor with her skirts, and vanished in a whirl of perfume.

She drove straight to the address which she had seen on Alexander Otway's card. It was in a decently sordid street south of the river; in a window on the ground floor hung an announcement of Alexander's name and business. As Olga stood at the door, there came out, showily dressed for walking, a person in whom she at once recognised the original of the portrait at Miss Bonnicastle's. It was no other than Mrs. Otway, the "Biddy" whose simple singing had so pleased her brother-in-law years ago.

"Is it the agent you want to see?" she asked, in her tongue of County Wexford. "The door to the right."

Alexander jumped up, all smiles at sight of so grand a lady. He had grown very obese, and very red about the neck; his linen might have been considerably cleaner, and his coat better brushed. But he seemed in excellent spirits, and glowed when his visitor began by saying that she wished to speak in confidence of a delicate matter.

"Mr. Otway, you have an elder brother, his name Daniel."

The listener's countenance fell.

"Madam, I'm sorry to say I have."

" He has written to me, more than once, a begging letter.
My name doesn't matter; I'll only say that he used to know
me slightly long ago.   I wish to ask you whether he is really
in want."

Alexander hesitated, with much screwing of the features.

"Well, he may be, now and then," was his reply at length.
" I have helped him, but, to tell the truth, it's not much good.
So far as I know, he has no regular supplies—but it's his own
fault."

"Exactly."   Olga evidently approached a point still more
delicate.   "I presume he has worn out the patience of *both*
brothers?"

"Ah!"   The agent shook his head.   "I'm sorry to say
that the *other's* patience—I see you know something of our
family circumstances—never allowed itself to be tried.   He's
very well off, I believe, but he'll do nothing for poor Dan,
and never would.   I'm bound to admit Dan has his faults,
but still"—

His brows expressed sorrow rather than anger on the subject
of his hard-fisted relative.

" Do you happen to know anything," pursued Olga, lowering
her voice, " of a transaction about certain—certain letters,
which were given up by Daniel Otway?"

"Why—yes.   I've heard something about that affair."

" Those letters, I always understood, were purchased from
him at a considerable price."

" That's true," replied Alexander, smiling familiarly as he
leaned across the table.   " But the considerable price was
never paid—not one penny of it."

Olga's face changed.   She had a wondering, lost, pained
look.

" Mr. Otway, are you *sure* of that?"

"Well, pretty sure.   Dan has talked of it more than once,
and I don't think he could talk as he does if there wasn't a
real grievance.   I'm very much afraid he was cheated.   Perhaps I oughtn't to use that word; I daresay Dan had no right
to ask money for the letters at all.   But there was a bargain,
and I'm afraid it wasn't honourably kept on the other side."

Olga reflected for a moment, and rose, saying that she
was obliged, that this ended her business.   Alexander's
curiosity sought to prolong the conversation, but in vain.   He
then threw out a word concerning his professional interests;

would the lady permit him to bespeak her countenance for a new singer, an Irish girl of great talent, who would be coming out very shortly?

"She has a magnificent song, madam! The very spirit of Patriotism—stirring, stirring! Let me offer you one of her photos. Miss Ennis Corthy — you'll soon see the announcements."

Olga drove away in a troubled dream.

CHAPTER XXXV

"THE 13th will suit admirably," wrote Helen Borisoff. "That morning my guests leave, and we shall be quiet —except for the popping of guns round about. Which reminds me that my big, healthy Englishman of a cousin (him you met in town) will be down here to slaughter little birds in aristocratic company, and may most likely look in to tell us of his bags. I will meet you at the station."

So Irene, alone, journeyed from King's Cross into the North Riding. At evening, the sun golden amid long lazy clouds that had spent their showers, she saw wide Wensleydale, its closing hills higher to north and south as the train drew onward, green slopes of meadow and woodland rising to the bent and the heather. At a village station appeared the welcoming face of her friend Helen. A countryman with his homely gig drove them up the hillside, the sweet air singing about them from moorland heights, the long dale spreading in grander prospect as they ascended, then hidden as they dropped into a wooded glen, where the horse splashed through a broad beck and the wheels jolted over boulders of limestone. Out again into the sunset, and at a turn of the climbing road stood up before them the grey old Castle, in its shadow the church and the hamlet, and all around the glory of rolling hills.

Of the four great towers, one lay a shattered ruin, one only remained habitable. Above the rooms occupied by Mrs. Borisoff and her guests was that which had imprisoned the Queen of Scots; a chamber of bare stone, with high embrasure narrowing to the slit of window which admitted daylight, and, if one climbed the sill, gave a glimpse of far mountains. Down below, deep under the roots of the tower, was the Castle's dungeon, black and deadly. Early on the morrow Helen led her friend to see these things. Then they climbed to the battlements, where the sun shone hot, and Helen pointed out

THE CROWN OF LIFE 305

the features of the vast landscape, naming heights, and little dales which pour their tributaries into the Ure, and villages lying amid the rich pasture.

"And yonder is Hawes," said Irene, pointing to the head of the dale.

"Yes; too far to see."

They did not exchange a look. Irene spoke at once of something else.

There came to lunch Mrs. Borisoff's cousin, a grouse-guest at a house some miles away. He arrived on horseback, and his approach was watched with interest by two pairs of eyes from the Castle windows. Mr. March looked well in the saddle, for he was a strong, comely man of about thirty, who lived mostly under the open sky. Irene had met him only once, and that in a drawing-room; she saw him now to greater advantage, heard him talk freely of things he under-stood and enjoyed, and on the whole did not dislike him. With Helen he was a favourite; she affected to make fun of him, but had confessed to Irene that she respected him more than any other of her county-family kinsfolk. As he talked of his two days' shooting, he seemed to become aware that Miss Derwent had no profound interest in this subject, and there fell from him an unexpected apology.

"Of course it isn't a very noble kind of sport," he said, with a laugh. "One is invited—one takes it in the course of things. I prefer the big game, where there's a chance of having to shoot for your life."

"I suppose one *must* shoot something," remarked Irene, as if musing a commonplace.

March took it with good-nature, like a man who cannot remember whether that point of view ever occurred to him, but who is quite willing to think about it. Indeed, he seemed more than willing to give attention to anything Miss Derwent chose to say: something of this inclination had appeared even at their first meeting, and to-day it was more marked. He showed reluctance when the hour obliged him to remount his horse. Mrs. Borisoff's hope that she might see him again before he left this part of the country received a prompt and cheerful reply.

Later that afternoon, the two friends climbed the great hillside above the Castle, and rambled far over the moorland, to a windy height where they looked into deep wild Swaledale.

20

Their talk was only of the scenes around them, until, on their way back, they approached a line of three-walled shelters, built of rough stone, about the height of a man. In reply to Irene's question, Helen explained the use of these structures; she did so in an off-hand way, with the proper terms, and would have passed on, but Irene stood gazing.

"What! They lie in ambush here, whilst men drive the birds towards them, to be shot?"

"It's sport," rejoined the other indifferently.

"I see. And here are the old cartridges." A heap of them lay close by amid the ling. "I don't wonder that Mr. March seemed a little ashamed of himself."

"But surely you knew all about this sort of thing!" said Mrs. Borisoff, with a little laugh of impatience.

"No, I didn't."

She had picked up one of the cartridge-cases, and, after examining it, her eyes wandered about the vast-rolling moor. The wind sang low; the clouds sailed across the mighty dome of heaven; not a human dwelling was visible, and not a sound broke upon nature's infinite calm.

"It amazes me," Irene continued, subduing her voice. "Incredible that men can come up here just to bang guns and see beautiful birds fall dead! One would think that what they *saw* here would stop their hands—that this silence would fill their minds and hearts, and make it impossible!"

Her voice had never trembled with such emotion in Helen's hearing. It was not Irene's habit to speak in this way; she had the native reticence of English women, preferring to keep silence when she felt strongly, or to disguise her feeling with irony and jest. But the hour and the place overcame her; a noble passion shone in her clear eyes, and thrilled in her utterance.

"What barbarians!"

"Yet you know they are nothing of the kind," objected Helen. "At least, not all of them."

"Mr. March?—You called him, yourself, a fine barbarian, quoting from Matthew Arnold. I never before understood how true that description was."

"I assure you, it doesn't apply to him, whatever I may have said in joke. This shooting is the tradition of a certain class. It's one of the ways in which great, strong men get their necessary exercise. Some of them feel, at moments, just as you do, I've no doubt; but there they are, a lot of them together, and a man can't make himself ridiculous, you know."

"You're not like yourself in this, Helen," said Irene. "You're not speaking as you think. Another time, you'll confess it's abominable savagery, with not one good word to be said for it. And more contemptible than I ever suspected! I'm so glad I've seen this. It helps to clear my thoughts about—about things in general."

She flung away the little yellow cylinder—flung it far from her with disgust, and, as if to forget it, plucked as she walked on a spray of heath, which glowed with its purple bells among the redder ling. Helen's countenance was shadowed. She spoke no more for several minutes.

When two days had passed, March again came riding up to the Castle, and lunched with the ladies. Irene was secretly vexed. At breakfast she had suggested a whole day's excursion, which her friend persuaded her to postpone; the reason must have been Helen's private knowledge that Mr. March was coming. In consequence, the lunch fell short of perfect cheerfulness. For reasons of her own, Irene was just a little formal in her behaviour to the guest; she did not talk so well as usual, and bore herself as a girl must who wishes, without unpleasantness, to check a man's significant approaches.

In the hot afternoon, chairs were taken out into the shadow of the Castle walls, and there the three sat conversing. Some-one drew near, a man, whom the careless glance of Helen's cousin took for a casual tourist about to view the ruins. Helen herself, and in the same moment, Irene, recognised Piers Otway. It seemed as though Mrs. Borisoff would not rise to welcome him; her smile was dubious, half surprised. She cast a glance at Irene, whose face was set in the austerest self-control, and thereupon not only stood up, but stepped forward with cordial greeting.

"So you have really come! Delighted to see you! Are you walking—as you said?"

"Too hot!" Piers replied, with a laugh. "I spent yesterday at York, and came on in a cowardly way by train."

He was shaking hands with Irene, who dropped a word or two of mere courtesy. In introducing him to March, Mrs. Borisoff said, "An old friend of ours," which caused her stalwart cousin to survey the dark, slimly-built man very attentively.

"We'll get you a chair, Mr. Otway"—

"No, no! Let me sit or lie here on the grass. It's all I feel fit for after the climb."

He threw himself down, nearer to Helen than to her friend, and the talk became livelier than before his arrival. Irene emerged from the taciturnity into which she had more and more withdrawn, and March, not an unobservant man, evidently noted this, and reflected upon it. He had at first regarded the new-comer with a civil aloofness, as one not of his world; presently, he seemed to ask himself to what world the singular being might belong—a man who knew how to behave himself, and whose talk implied more than common *savoir-vivre*, yet who differed in such noticeable points from an Englishman of the leisured class.

Helen was in a mischievous mood. She broached the subject of grouse, addressing to Otway an ambiguous remark which led March to ask, with veiled surprise, whether he was a sportsman.

"Mr. Otway's taste is for bigger game," she exclaimed, before Piers could reply. "He lives in hope of potting Russians on the Indian frontier."

"Well, I can sympathise with him in that," said the large-limbed man, puzzled but smiling. "He'll probably have a chance before very long."

No sooner had he spoken than a scarlet confusion glowed upon his face. In speculating about Otway, he had for the moment forgotten his cousin's name.

"I *beg* your pardon, Helen!—What an idiot I am! Of course you were joking, and I"—

"Don't, don't, don't apologise, Edward! Tell truth and shame—your Russian relatives! I like you all the better for it."

"Thank you," he answered. "And after all, there's no harm in a little fighting. It's better to fight and have done with it than keeping on plotting between compliments. Nations are just like schoolboys, you know; there has to be a round now and then; it settles things, and is good for the blood."

Otway was biting a blade of grass; he smiled and said nothing. Mrs. Borisoff glanced from him to Irene, who also was smiling, but looked half vexed.

THE CROWN OF LIFE

THE CROWN OF LIFE   309

"How can it be good, for health or anything else?" Miss Derwent asked suddenly, turning to the speaker.

"Oh, we couldn't do without fighting. It's in human nature."

"In uncivilised human nature, yes."

"But really, you know," urged March, with good-natured deference, "it wouldn't do to civilise away pluck—courage—heroism—whatever one likes to call it."

"Of course it wouldn't. But what has pluck or heroism to do with bloodshed? How can anyone imagine that courage is only shown in fighting? I don't happen to have been in a battle, but one knows very well how easy it must be for any coward or brute, excited to madness, to become what's called a hero. Heroism is noble courage in ordinary life. Are you serious in thinking that life offers no opportunities for it?"

"Well—it's not quite the same thing"—

"Happily, not! It's a vastly better thing. Every day some braver deed is done by plain men and women—yes, women, if you please—than was ever known on the battlefield. One only hears of them now and then. On the railway—on the sea—in the hospital—in burning houses—in accidents of road and street—are there no opportunities for courage? In the commonest everyday home life, doesn't any man or woman have endless chances of being brave or a coward? And this is civilised courage, not the fury of a bull at a red rag."

Piers Otway had ceased to nibble his blade of grass; his eyes were fixed on Irene. When she had made a sudden end of speaking, when she smiled her apology for the fervour forbidden in polite converse, he still gazed at her, self-oblivious. Helen Borisoff watched him, askance.

"Let us go in and have some tea," she said, rising abruptly.

Soon after, March said good-bye, a definite good-bye; he was going to another part of England. With all the grace of his caste he withdrew from a circle, in which, temptations notwithstanding, he had not felt quite at ease. Riding down the dale through a sunny shower, he was refreshed and himself again.

"Where do you put up to-night?" asked Helen of Otway, turning to him, when the other man had gone, with a brusque familiarity.

"At the inn down in Redmire."

"And what do you do to-morrow?"

"Go to see the falls at Aysgarth, for one thing. There's been rain up on the hills ; the river will be grand."

"Perhaps we shall be there."

When Piers had left them, Helen said to her friend :

"I wanted to ask him to stay and dine—but I didn't know whether you would like it."

"I ?   I am not the hostess."

"No, but you have humours, Irene. One has to be careful."

Irene knitted her brows, and stood for a moment with face half averted.

"If I cause this sort of embarrassment," she said frankly, "I think I oughtn't to stay."

"It's easily put right, my dear girl.   Answer me a simple question.   If I lead Mr. Otway to suppose that his company for a few days is not disagreeable to us, shall I worry you, or not ?"

"Not in the least," was the equally direct answer.

"That's better.   We've always got along so well, you know, that it's annoying to feel there's something not quite understood between us.—Then I shall send a note down to the inn where he's staying, to appoint a meeting at Aysgarth to-morrow. And I shall ask him to come here for the rest of the day, if he chooses."

At nightfall, the rain-clouds spread from the hills of Westmorland, and there were some hours of downpour. This did not look hopeful for the morrow, but, on the other hand, it promised a finer sight at the falls, if by chance the weather grew tolerable. The sun rose amid dropping vapours, and at breakfast-time had not yet conquered the day, but a steady brightening soon put an end to doubt. The friends prepared to set forth.

As they were entering the carriage there arrived the postman, with letters for both, which they read driving down to the dale. One of Irene's correspondents was her brother, and the contents of Eustace's letter so astonished her that she sat for a time absorbed in thought.

"No bad news, I hope?" said Helen, who had glanced quickly over a few lines from her husband, now at Ostend.

"No, but startling.   You may as well read the letter."

It was written in Eustace Derwent's best style ; really a very good letter, both as to composition and in the matter of feeling. After duly preparing his sister for what might come as a shock, he made known to her that he was about to marry Mrs. John Jacks, the widow of the late Member of Parliament. "I can quite imagine," he proceeded, "that this may trouble your mind by exciting unpleasant memories, and perhaps may make you apprehensive of disagreeable things in the future. Pray have no such uneasiness. Only this morning I had a long talk with Arnold Jacks, who was very friendly, and indeed could not have behaved better. He spoke of you, and quite in the proper way; I was to remember him very kindly to you, if I thought the remembrance would not be unwelcome. As for my dear Marian, you will find her everything that a sister should be." Followed sundry details and promise of more information when they met again in town.

"Describe her to me," said Helen, who had a slight acquaintance with Irene's brother.

"One word does it — irreproachable. A couple of years older than Eustace, I think; John Jacks was more than twice her age, so it's only fair. The dear boy will probably give up his profession, and become an ornament of society, a model of all the proprieties. Wonderful! I shan't realise it for a few days."

As they drove on to the bridge at Aysgarth, Piers Otway stood there awaiting them. They exchanged few words; the picture before their eyes, and the wild music that filled the air, imposed silence. Headlong between its high banks plunged the swollen torrent, the roaring spate; brown from its washing of the peaty moorland, and churned into flying flakes of foam. Over the worn ledges, at other times a succession of little waterfalls, rolled in resistless fury a mighty cataract; at great rocks in mid-channel it leapt with surges like those of an angry sea. The spectacle was fascinating in its grandeur, appalling in its violence; with the broad leafage of the glen arched over it in warm, still sunshine, wondrously beautiful.

They wandered some way by the river banks; then drove to other spots of which Otway spoke, lunched at a village inn, and by four o'clock returned all together to the Castle. After tea, Piers found himself alone with Irene. Mrs. Borisoff had left the room whilst he was speaking, and so silently that for a moment he was not aware of her withdrawal. Alone with Irene, for the first time since he had known her; even at

Ewell, long ago, they had never been together without companionship. There fell a silence. Piers could not lift his eyes to the face which had all day been before him, the face which seemed more than ever beautiful amid nature's beauties. He wished to thank her for the letter she had written him to St. Petersburg, but was fearful of seeming to make too much of this mark of kindness. Irene herself resumed the conversation.

"You will continue to write for the reviews, I hope?"

"I shall try to," he answered softly.

"Your Russian must be very idiomatic. I found it hard in places."

Overcome with delight, he looked at her and bent towards her.

"Mrs. Borisoff told me you had learnt. I know what that means—learning Russian in England, out of books. I began to do it at Ewell—do you remember?"

"Yes, I remember very well. Have you written anything besides these two articles?"

"Written—yes, but not published. I have written all sorts of things." His voice shook. "Even—verse."

He repented the word as soon as it was uttered. Again his eyes could not move towards hers.

"I know you have," said Irene, in the voice of one who smiles.

"I have never been sure that you knew it—that you received those verses."

"To tell you the truth, I didn't know how to acknowledge them. I never received the dedication of a poem, before or since, and in my awkwardness I put off my thanks till it was too late to send them. But I remember the lines; I think they were beautiful. Shall you ever include them in a volume?"

"I wrote no more, I am no poet. Yet if you had given a word of praise"— he laughed, as one does when emotion is too strong—"I should have written on and on, with a glorious belief in myself."

"Perhaps it was as well, then, that I said nothing. Poetry must come of itself, without praise—don't you think?"

"Yes, I lived it—or tried to live it—instead of putting it into metre."

"That's exactly what I once heard my father say about himself. And he called it consuming his own smoke."

Piers could not but join in her quiet laugh, yet he had never felt a moment less opportune for laughter. As if to prove that she purposely changed the note of their dialogue, Irene reached a volume from the table, and said in the most matter-of-fact voice :

"Here's a passage of Tolstoi that I can't make out. Be my professor, please. First of all, let me hear you read it aloud, for the accent."

The lesson continued till Helen entered the room again. Irene so willed it.

CHAPTER XXXVI

SHE sat by her open window, which looked over the dale to the long high ridge of moors, softly drawn against a moonlit sky. Far below sounded the rushing Ure, and at moments there came upon the fitful breeze a deeper music, that of the falls at Aysgarth, miles away. It was an hour since she had bidden good-night to Helen, and two hours or more since all else in the Castle and in the cottages had been still and dark. She loved this profound quiet, this solitude guarded by the eternal powers of nature. She loved the memories and imaginings borne upon the stillness of these grey old towers.

The fortress of warrior-lords, the prison of a queen, the Royalist refuge—fallen now into such placid dreaminess of age. Into the dark chamber above, desolate, legend-haunted, perchance in some moment of the night there fell through the narrow window-niche a pale moonbeam, touching the floor, the walls of stone; such light in gloom as may have touched the face of Mary herself, wakeful with her recollections and her fears. Musing it in her fancy, Irene thought of love and death.

Had it come to her at length, that love which was so strange and distant when, in ignorance, she believed it her companion? Verses in her mind, verses that would never be forgotten, however lightly she held them, sang and rang to a new melody. They were not poetry—said he who wrote them. Yet they were truth, sweetly and nobly uttered. The false, the trivial, does not so cling to memory, year after year.

They had helped her to know him, these rhyming lines, or so she fancied. They shaped in her mind, slowly, insensibly, an image of the man, throughout the lapse of time when she neither saw him nor heard of him. Whether a true image how should she assure herself? She only knew that no feature of it seemed alien when compared with the impression of those two last days. Yet the picture was an ideal; the very man she could honour, love; he and no other. Did she perilously deceive herself in thinking that this ideal and the man who spoke with her, were one?

It had grown without her knowledge, apart from her will, this conception of Piers Otway. The first half-consciousness of such a thought came to her when she heard from Olga of those letters, obtained by him for a price, and given to the kinsfolk of the dead woman. An interested generosity? She had repelled the suggestion as unworthy, ignoble. Whether the giver was ever thanked, she did not know. Dr. Derwent kept cold silence on the subject, after once mentioning it to her in formal words. Thanks, undoubtedly, were due to him. To-night it pained her keenly to think that perhaps her father had said nothing.

She began to study Russian, and in secret; her impulse dark, or so obscurely hinted that it caused her no more than a moment's reverie. Looking back, she saw but one explanation of the energy, the zeal which had carried her through these labours. It shone clear on the day when a letter from Helen Borisoff told her that an article in a Russian review, just published, bore the name of Piers Otway. Thence onward, she was frank with herself. She recognised the meaning of the intellectual process which had tended to harmonise her life with that she imagined for her ideal man. There came a prompting of emotion, and she wrote the letter which Piers received.

All things were made new to her; above all, her own self. She was acting in a way which was no result of balanced purpose, yet, as she perfectly understood, involved her in the gravest responsibilities. She had no longer the excuse which palliated her conduct eight years ago; that heedlessness was innocent indeed compared with the blame she would now incur, if she excited a vain hope merely to prove her feelings, to read another chapter of life. Solemnly in this charmed stillness of midnight, she searched her heart. It did not fail under question.

A morning sleep held her so much later than usual that, before she had left her chamber, letters were brought to the door by the child who waited upon her. On one envelope she saw the Doctor's handwriting; on the other that of her cousin, Mrs. Florio. Surprised to hear from Olga, with whom she had had very little communication for a year or two, she opened that letter first.

"Dear Irene," it began, "something has lately come to my knowledge which I think I am only doing a duty in acquainting you with. It is very unpleasant, but not the first unpleasant piece of news that you and I have shared together. You remember all about Piers Otway and those letters of my poor mother's, which he said he bought for us from his horrid brother? Well, I find that he did *not* buy them—at all events that he never paid for them. Daniel Otway is now broken-down in health, and depends on help from the other brother, Alexander, who has gone in for some sort of music-hall business! Not only did Piers *cheat* him out of the money promised for the letters (I fear there's no other word for it), but he has utterly refused to give the man a farthing—though in good circumstances, I hear. This is all very disagreeable, and I don't like to talk about it, but as I hear Piers Otway has been seeing you, it's better you should know." She added "very kind regards," and signed herself "yours affectionately." Then came a postscript. "Mrs. A. Otway is actually on the music-hall stage herself, in short skirts!"

The paper shook in Irene's hand. She turned sick with fear and misery.

Mechanically the other letter was torn open. Dr. Derwent wrote about Eustace's engagement. It did not exactly surprise him; he had observed significant things. Nor did it exactly displease him, for since talking with Eustace and with Marian Jacks (the widow), he suspected that the match was remarkable for its fitness. Mrs. Jacks had a large fortune—well, one could resign oneself to that. "After all, Mam'zelle Wren, there's nothing to be uneasy about. Arnold Jacks is sure to marry very soon (a dowager duchess, I should say), and on that score there'll be no awkwardness. When the Wren makes a nest for herself, I shall convert this house into a big laboratory, and be at home only to bacteria."

But the Doctor, too, had a postscriptum. "Olga has been writing to me, sheer scandal, something about the letters you wot of having been obtained in a dishonest way. I won't say I believe it, or that I disbelieve it. I mention the thing only to suggest that perhaps I was right in not making any acknowledgment of that obligation. I felt that silence was the wise as well as the dignified thing—though someone disagreed with me."

When Irene entered the sitting-room, her friend had long since breakfasted.

"What's the matter?" Helen asked, seeing so pale and troubled a countenance.

"Nothing much; I overtired myself yesterday. I must keep quiet for a little."

Mrs. Borisoff herself was in no talkative frame of mind. She, too, an observer might have imagined, had some care or worry. The two very soon parted; Irene going back to her room, Helen out into the sunshine.

A malicious letter this of Olga's; the kind of letter which Irene had not thought her capable of penning. Could there be any substantial reason for such hostile feeling? Oh, how one's mind opened itself to dark suspicion, when once an evil whisper had been admitted!

She would not believe that story of duplicity, of baseness. Her very soul rejected it, declared it impossible, the basest calumny. Yet how it hurt! How it humiliated! Chiefly, perhaps, because of the evil art with which Olga had reminded her of Piers Otway's disreputable kinsmen. Could the two elder brothers be so worthless, and the younger an honest, brave man, a man without reproach—her ideal?

Irene clutched at the recollection which till now she had preferred to banish from her mind. Piers was not born of the same mother, might he not inherit his father's finer qualities, and, together with them, something noble from the woman whom his father loved? Could she but know that history! The woman was a law-breaker; respectability gave her hard names; but Irene used her own judgment in such matters, and asked only for knowledge of facts. She had as good as forgotten the irregularity of Piers Otway's birth. Whom, indeed, did it or could it concern? Her father, least of all men, would dwell upon it as a subject of reproach. But her father was very capable of pointing to Daniel and to Alexander, with a shake of the head. He had a prejudice against Piers—this letter reminded her of it only too well. It might be feared that he was rather glad than otherwise of the "sheer scandal" Olga had conveyed to him.

Confident in his love of her, which would tell ill on the side of his reasonableness, his justice, she had not, during these crucial days, thought much about her father. She saw his face now, if she spoke to him of Piers. Dr. Derwent, like all men of brains, had a good deal of the aristocratic temper; he scorned the vulgarity of the vulgar; he turned in angry

impatience from such sorry creatures as those two men; and
often lashed with his contempt the ignoble amusements
of the crowd. Olga doubtless had told him of the singer in
short skirts—

She shed a few tears. The very meanness of the injury
done her at this crisis of emotion heightened its cruelty.

Piers might come to the Castle this morning. Now and
then she glanced from her window, if perchance she should
see him approaching; but all she saw was a group of holiday-
makers, the happily infrequent tourists who cared to turn from
the beaten track up the dale to visit the Castle. She did not
know whether Helen was at home, or had rambled away. If
Piers came, and his call was announced to her, could she go
forth and see him?

Not to do so, would be unjust, both to herself and to him.
The relations between them demanded, of all things, honesty
and courage. No little courage, it was true; for she must
speak to him plainly of things from which she shrank even in
communing with herself.

Yet she had done as hard a thing as this. Harder, perhaps,
that interview with Arnold Jacks which set her free. Honesty
and courage—clearness of sight and strength of purpose where
all but every girl would have drifted dumbly the common way
—had saved her life from the worst disaster: saved, too, the
man whom her weakness would have wronged. Had she not
learnt the lesson which life sets before all, but which only a
few can grasp and profit by?

Towards midday she left her room, and went in search of
Helen; not finding her within doors, she stepped out on to the
sward, and strolled in the neighbourhood of the Castle. A
child whom she knew approached her.

"Have you seen Mrs. Borisoff?" she asked.

"She's down at the beck, with the gentleman," answered
the little girl, pointing with a smile to the deep, leaf-hidden
glen half a mile away.

Irene lingered for a few minutes and went in again.

At luncheon-time Helen had not returned. The meal was
delayed for her, more than a quarter of an hour. When at
length she entered, Irene saw she had been hastening; but
Helen's features seemed to betray some other cause of
discomposure than mere unpunctuality. Having glanced at
her once or twice, Irene kept an averted face. Neither spoke

as they sat down to table; only when they had begun the meal did Helen ask whether her friend felt better. The reply was a brief affirmative. For the rest of the time they talked a little, absently, about trivialities; then they parted; without any arrangement for the afternoon.

Irene's mind was in that state of perilous commotion which invests with dire significance any event not at once intelligible. Alone in her chamber, she sat brooding with tragic countenance. How could Helen's behaviour be explained? If she had met Piers Otway and spent part of the morning with him, why did she keep silence about it? Why was she so late in coming home, and what had heightened her colour, given that peculiar shiftiness to her eyes?

She rose, went to Helen's door, and knocked.

"May I come in?"

"Of course.—I have a letter to write by post-time."

"I won't keep you long," said Irene, standing before her friend's chair, and regarding her with grave earnestness. "Did Mr. Otway call this morning?"

"He was coming; I met him outside, and told him you weren't very well. And"—she hesitated, but went on with a harder voice and a careless smile—"we had a walk up the glen. It's very lovely, the higher part. You must go. Ask him to take you."

"I don't understand you," said Irene coldly. "Why should I ask Mr. Otway to take me?"

"I beg your pardon. You are become so critical of words. and phrases. To take *us*, I'll say."

"That wouldn't be a very agreeable walk, Helen, whilst you are in this strange mood. What does it all mean? I never foresaw the possibility of misunderstandings such as this between us. Is it I who am to blame, or you? Have I offended you?"

"No, dear," was the dreamy response.

"Then why do you seem to wish to quarrel with me?"

Helen had the look of one who strugglingly overcomes a paroxysm of anger. She stood up.

"Would you leave me alone for a little, Irene? I'm not quite able to talk. I think we've both of us been doing too much—overtaxing ourselves. It has got on my nerves."

"Yes, I will go," was the answer, spoken very quietly. "And to-morrow morning I will return to London."

She moved away.

"Irene!"

"Yes—?"

"I have something to tell you before you go." Helen spoke with a set face, forcing herself to meet her friend's eyes. "Mr. Otway wants an opportunity of talking with you, alone. He hoped for it this morning. As he couldn't see you, he talked about you to me—you being the only subject he could talk about. I promised to be out of the way if he came this afternoon."

"Thank you—but why didn't you tell me this before?"

"Because, as I said, things have got rather on my nerves." She took a step forward. "Will you overlook it—forget about it? Of course I should have told you before he came."

"It's strange that there should be anything to overlook or forget between *us*," said Irene, with wide pathetic eyes.

"There isn't really! It's not you and I that have got muddled—only things, circumstances. If you had been a little more chummy with me. There's a time for silence, but also a time for talking."

"Dear, there are things one *can't* talk about, because one doesn't know what to say, even to oneself."

"I know! I know it!" replied Helen, with emphasis.

And she came still nearer, with hand held out.

"All nerves, Irene! Neuralgia of—of the common sense, my dear!"

They parted with a laugh and a quick clasp of hands.

CHAPTER XXXVII

FOR half an hour Irene sat idle. She was waiting, and could do nothing but wait. Then the uncertainty as to how long this suspense might hold her grew insufferable; she was afraid, too, of seeing Helen again, and having to talk, when talk would be misery. A thought grew out of her unrest — a thought clear-shining amid the tumult of turbid emotions. She would go forth to meet him. He should see that she came with that purpose—that she put away all trivialities of prescription and of pride. If he were worthy, only the more would he esteem her. If she deluded herself— it lay in the course of Fate.

His way up from Redmire was by the road along which she had driven on the evening of her arrival, the road that dipped into a wooded glen, where a stream tumbled amid rocks and boulders, over smooth-worn slabs and shining pebbles, from the moor down to the river of the dale. He might not come this way. She hoped—she trusted Destiny.

She stood by the crossing of the beck. The flood of yesterday had fallen; the water was again shallow at this spot, but nearly all the stepping-stones had been swept away. For help at such times, a crazy little wooden bridge spanned the current a few yards above. Irene brushed through the long grass and the bracken, mounted on to the bridge, and, leaning over the old bough which formed a rail, let the voice of the beck soothe her impatience.

Here one might linger for hours, in perfect solitude; very rarely in the day was this happy stillness broken by a footfall, a voice, or the rumbling of a peasant's cart. A bird twittered, a breeze whispered in the branches; ever and ever the water kept its hushing note.

But now someone was coming. Not with audible footstep; not down the road at which Irene frequently glanced; the intruder approached from the lower part of the glen, along the beck-side, now walking in soft herbage, now striding from stone to stone, sometimes lifting the bough of a hazel or a rowan that hung athwart his path. He drew near to the crossing. He saw the figure on the bridge, and for a moment stood at gaze.

Irene was aware of someone regarding her. She moved. He stood below, the ripple-edge of the water touching his foot. Upon his upturned face, dark eyes wide in joy and admiration, firm lips wistfully subduing their smile, the golden sunlight shimmered through overhanging foliage. She spoke.

"Everything around is beautiful, but this most of all."

"There is nothing more beautiful," he answered, "in all the dales."

The words had come to her easily and naturally, after so much trouble as to what the first words should be. His look was enough. She scorned her distrust, scorned the malicious gossip that had excited it. Her mind passed into consonance with the still, warm hour, with the loveliness of all about her.

"I haven't been that way yet." She pointed up the glen. "Will you come?"

"Gladly! I was here with Mrs. Borisoff this morning, and wished so much you had been with us."

Irene stepped from the bridge down to the beck-side. The briefest shadow of annoyance had caused her to turn her face away; there followed contentment that he spoke of the morning, at once and so frankly. She was able to talk without restraint, uttering her delight at each new picture as they went along. They walked very slowly, ever turning to admire, stopping to call each other's attention with glowing words. At a certain point, they were obliged to cross the water, their progress on this side barred by natural obstacles. It was a crossing of some little difficulty for Irene, the stones being rugged, and rather far apart; Piers guided her, and at the worst spot held out his hand.

"Jump! I won't let you fall."

She sprang with a happy girlish laugh to his side, and withdrew her hand very gently.

"Here is a good place to rest," she said, seating herself on a boulder. And Piers sat down at a little distance.

The bed of the torrent was full of great stones, very white, rounded and smoothed by the immemorial flow, by their tumbling and grinding in time of spate; they formed innumerable little cataracts, with here and there a broad plunge of foam-streaked water, perilously swift and deep. By the bank, the current spread into a large, still pool, of colour a rich brown where the sunshine touched it, and darkly green where it lay beneath spreading branches; everywhere limpid, showing the pebbles or the sand in its cool depths. Infinite were the varyings of light and shade, from a dazzling gleam on the middle water, to the dense obscurity of leafy nooks. On either hand was a wood, thick with undergrowth; great pines, spruces and larches, red-berried rowans, crowding on the steep sides of the ravine; trees of noble stature, shadowing fern and flower, towering against the sunny blue. Just below the spot where Piers and Irene rested, a great lichened hazel stretched itself all across the beck; in the upward direction a narrowing vista, filled with every tint of leafage, rose to the brown of the moor and the azure of the sky. All about grew tall, fruiting grasses, and many a bright flower; clusters of pink willow-weed, patches of yellow ragwort, the perfumed meadowsweet, and, amid bracken and bramble, the purple shining of a great campanula.

On the open moor, the sun blazed with parching heat; here was freshness as of spring, the waft of cool airs, the scent of verdure moistened at the root.

"Once upon a time," said Otway, when both had been listening to their thoughts, "I fancied myself as unlucky a man as walked the earth. I've got over that."

Irene did not look at him; she waited for the something else which his voice promised.

"Think of my good fortune in meeting you this afternoon. If I had gone to the Castle another way, I should have missed you; yet I all but did go by the fields. And there was nothing I desired so much as to see you somewhere—by yourself."

The slight failing of his voice at the end helped Irene to speak collectedly.

"Chance was in my favour, too. I came down to the beck, hoping I might meet you."

She saw his hand move, the fingers clutch together. Before he could say anything, she continued.

"I want to tell you of an ill-natured story that has reached my ears. Not to discuss it; I know it is untrue. Your two brothers—do you know that they speak spitefully of you?"

"I didn't know it. I don't think I have given them cause."

"I'm very sure you haven't. But I want you to know about it, and I shall tell you the facts.—After the death of my aunt, Mrs. Hannaford, you got from the hands of Daniel Otway a packet of her letters; he bargained with you, and you paid his price, wishing those letters to be seen by my father and my cousin Olga, whose minds they would set at rest. Now, Daniel Otway is telling people that you never paid the sum you promised him, and that, being in poverty, he vainly applies to you for help."

She saw his hand grasp a twig that hung near him, and drag it rudely down; she did not look at his face.

"I should have thought," Piers answered, with grave composure, "that nothing Daniel Otway said could concern me. I see it isn't so. It must have troubled you, for you to speak of it."

"It has; I thought about it. I rejected it as a falsehood."

"There's a double falsehood. I paid him the price he asked, on the day he asked it, and I have since"—he checked himself—"I have not refused him help in his poverty."

Irene's heart glowed within her. Even thus, and not otherwise, would she have desired him to refute the slander. It was a test she had promised herself; she could have laughed for joy. Her voice betrayed this glad emotion.

"Let him say what he will; it doesn't matter now. But how comes it that he is poor?"

"That I should like to know." Piers threw a pebble into the still, brown water near him. "Five years ago, he came into a substantial sum of money. I suppose—it went very quickly. Daniel is not exactly a prudent man."

"I imagine not," remarked Irene, allowing herself a glimpse of his countenance, which she found to be less calm than his tone. "Let us have done with him.—Five years ago," she added, with soft accents, "some of that money ought to have been yours, and you received nothing."

"Nothing was legally due to me," he answered, in a voice lower than hers.

"That I know. I mention it—you will forgive me?—because I have sometimes feared that you might explain to yourself wrongly my failure to reply when you sent me those verses, long ago. I have thought, lately, that you might suppose I knew certain facts at that time. I didn't; I only learnt them afterwards. At no time would it have made any difference."

Piers could not speak.

"Look!" said Irene, in a whisper, pointing.

A great dragon-fly, a flash of blue, had dropped on to the surface of the pool, and lay floating. As they watched, it rose, to drop again upon a small stone amid a shallow current; half in, half out of, the sunny water, it basked.

"Oh, how lovely everything is!" exclaimed Irene, in a voice that quivered low. "How perfect a day!"

"It was weather like this when I first saw you," said Piers. "Earlier, but just as bright. My memory of you has always lived in sunshine. I saw you first from my window; you were standing in the garden at Ewell; I heard your voice. Do you remember telling the story of Thibaut Rossignol?"

"Oh yes, yes!"

"Is he still with your father?"

"Thibaut? Why, Thibaut is an institution. I can't imagine our house without him. Do you know that he always calls me Mademoiselle Irène?"

"Your name is beautiful in any language. I wonder how many times I have repeated it to myself? And thought, too, so often of its meaning; longed, for *that*—and how vainly!"

"Say the name—now," she faltered.

"Irene!—Irene!"

"Why, you make music of it! I never knew how musical it sounded.—Hush! Look at that thing of light and air!"

The dragon-fly had flashed past them. This way and that it darted above the shining water, then dropped once more, to float, to sail idly with its gossamer wings.

Piers stole nearer. He sat on a stone by her side.

"Irene!"

"Yes. I like the name when you say it."

"May I touch your hand?"

Still gazing at the dragon-fly, as if careless of what she did, she held her hand to him. Piers folded it in both his own.

"May I hold it as long as I live?"

"Is that a new thought of yours?" she asked, in a voice that shook as it tried to suggest laughter in her mind.

"The newest! The most daring and the most glorious I ever had."

"Why, then I have been mistaken," she said softly, for an instant meeting his eyes. "I fancied I owed you something for a wrong I did, without meaning it, more than eight years gone by."

"That thought had come to you?" Piers exclaimed, with eyes gleaming.

"Indeed it had. I shall be more than half sorry if I have to lose it."

"How foolish I was! What wild, monstrous folly! How could you have dreamt for a moment that such a one as I was could dare to love you?—Irene, you did me no wrong. You gave me the ideal of my life—something I should never lose from my heart and mind—something to live towards! Not a hope; hope would have been madness. I have loved you without hope; loved you because I had found the only one I could love—the one I must love—on and on to the end."

She laid her free hand upon his that clasped the other, and bowed him to her reasoning mood.

"Let me speak of other things—that have to be made plain between you and me. First of all, a piece of news. I have just heard that my brother is going to marry Mrs. John Jacks."

Piers was mute with astonishment. It was so long since he had seen Mrs. Jacks, and he pictured her as a woman much older than Eustace Derwent. His clearest recollection of her was that remark she made at the luncheon-table about the Irish, that they were so "sentimental"; it had blurred her beauty and her youth in his remembrance.

"Yes, Eustace is going to marry her; and I shouldn't wonder if the marriage turns out well. It leads to the disagreeable thing I have to talk about.—You know that I engaged myself to Arnold Jacks. I did so freely, thinking I did right. When the time of the marriage drew near, I had learnt that I had done *wrong*. Not that I wished to be the wife of anyone else. I loved nobody; I did not love the man I was pretending to. As soon as I knew that—what was I to do? To marry him was a crime—no less a crime for its being committed every day. I took my courage in both hands. I told him I did not love him, I would not marry him. And—I ran away."

The memory made her bosom heave, her cheeks flush.

"Magnificent!" commented the listener, with a happy smile.

"Ah! but I didn't do it very well. I treated him badly—yes, inconsiderately, selfishly. The thing had to be done—but there were ways of doing it. Unfortunately I had got to resent my captivity, and I spoke to him as if *he* were to blame. From the point of view of delicacy, perhaps he was; he should have released me at once, and that he wouldn't. But I was too little regardful of what it meant to him—above all, to his pride. I have so often reproached myself. I do it now for the last time. There!" She picked up a pebble to fling away. "It is gone! We speak of the thing no more."

A change was coming upon the glen. The sun had passed; it shone now only on the tree-tops. But the sky above was blue and warm as ever.

"Another thing," she pursued, more gravely. "My father"—

Piers waited a moment, then said with eyes downcast:

"He does not think well of me?"

"That is my grief, and my trouble. However, not a serious trouble. Of you, personally, he has no dislike; it was quite the opposite when he met you; when you dined at our house — you remember? He said things of you I am not going to repeat, sir. It was only after the disaster which involved your name. Then he grew prejudiced."

"Who can wonder?"

"It will pass over. My father is no stage-tyrant. If *he* is not open to reason, what man living is? And no man has a tenderer heart. He was all kindness and forbearance and understanding when I did a thing which might well have made him angry. Some day you shall see the letter he wrote me, when I had run away to Paris. In it, he spoke, as never to me before, of his own marriage — of his love for my mother. Every word remains in my memory, but I can't trust my voice to repeat them, and perhaps I ought not—even to you."

"May I go to him, and speak for myself?"

"Yes—but not till I have seen him."

"Can't I spare you that?" said Piers, in a voice which, for the first time, sounded his triumphant manhood. "Do you think I fear a meeting with your father, or doubt of its result? If I had gone merely on my own account, to try to remove his prejudice and win his regard, it would have been a different thing; indeed, I could never have done that; I felt too keenly his reasons for disliking me. But now! In what man's presence should I shrink, and feel myself unworthy? You have put such words into my heart as will gain my cause for me the moment they are spoken. I have no false shame—no misgivings. I shall speak the truth of myself and you, and your father will hear me."

Irene listened with the love-light in her hazel eyes; the face she turned upon him brought back a ray of sunshine to the slowly shadowing glen.

"I will think till to-morrow," she said. "Come to the Castle to-morrow morning, and I shall have settled many things. But now we must go; Helen will wonder what has become of me; I didn't tell her I was going out."

He bent over her hand; she did not withdraw it from him as they walked through the bracken, and beneath the green boughs, and picked their way over the white stones of the rushing beck.

At the road, they parted.

An hour after sunset, Piers was climbing the hillside towards the Castle, now a looming shape against a sky still duskily purpled from the west. He climbed slowly, doubting at each step whether to go nearer, or to wave his hand and turn. Still, he approached. In the cottages a few lights were seen; but no one moved; there was no voice. His own footstep on the sward fell soundless.

He stood before the tower which was inhabited, and looked at the dim-lighted windows. To the entrance led a long flight of steps, and, as he gazed through the gloom, he seemed to discern a figure standing there, before the door-way. He was not mistaken; the figure moved, descended. Motionless, he saw it turn towards him. Then he knew the step, the form; he sprang forward.

" Irene ! "

"You have come to say good-night? See how our thoughts chime; I guessed you would."

Her voice had a soft, caressing tremor; her hand sought his.

"Irene! You have given me a new life, a new soul!"

Her lips were near as she answered him.

"Rest from your sorrows, my dearest.   I love you!
I love you!"

He was alone again in the darkness, on the hillside.   He
heard the voice of the far-off river, and to his rapturous
mood it sounded as a moaning, brought a sudden sadness.
All at once, he thought amid his triumph of those unhappy
ones whom the glory of love would never bless; those, men
and women, born to a vain longing such as he had known,
doomed to the dread solitude from which he by miracle
had been saved.   His heart swelled, and his eyes were hot
with tears.

But as he went down to the dale, the calm of the silent
hour crept over him.   He whispered the beloved name, and
it gave him peace; such peace as follows upon the hallowing
of a profound passion, justified of reason, and proof under
the hand of time.

THE END

Notes

1. *Gissing; The Critical Heritage,* ed. Pierre Coustillas and Colin Partridge (London, 1972), p. 353. Without going as far as D. H. Lawrence in defiance of the proprieties, Gissing was among the writers who wanted to reassert the rights of the body in love and its expression in art. In *The Commonplace Book* he says: 'Imagine the future historian writing in wonderment of the absurd reticence with which our novelists treat sexual objects, and comparing this with their licence to describe in detail the most hideous of murders' *George Gissing's Commonplace Book,* ed. Jacob Korg (New York, 1962), p. 44.

2. The terms 'rampant militarism' are those used by Gissing himself to describe the situation in Germany. They are taken from a letter to Bertz of 10 February 1898 quoted by Jacob Korg in his *George Gissing: A Critical Biography,* p. 224; this shows, of course, that Gissing's criticism was not particularly aimed at Britain but at any form of imperialism.

3. The Dukhobortsi (see notes to the text) were helped by Leo Tolstoy, himself a preacher of non-violence. Gissing sent him a copy of *The Crown of Life.*

4. *The Private Papers of Henry Maitland,* Morley Roberts, (London, 1958), p. 94.

5. Particularly interesting is 'Tyrtaeus', an article he wrote for *Review of the Week,* 4 November 1899, and reprinted in *The Gissing Newsletter,* July 1974.

6. *Letters of George Gissing to Members of his Family,* collected and arranged by Algernon and Ellen Gissing (London, 1972), p. 367.

7. *The Private Papers of Henry Ryecroft* (Spring, XVI).

Notes to the Text

Page 4, line 5:
Per Bacco— Line 18: *Benissimo.* Gissing, like his hero, was well acquainted with the French and German languages. Moreover he had started learning Italian in 1885 with a view to reading the *Divina Commedia.*

Page 4, lines 5-7:
I couldn't follow it myself: but I, like our fat friend, am little better than one of the wicked. A reference to Falstaff in *King Henry IV* Part I, I, i, 105, who says: 'Now am I, if a man should speak truly, little better than one of the wicked.'

Page 4, line 13:
Was soll es bedeuten? From the opening line of Heinrich Heine's famous poem *'Lorelei' ('Ich weiss nicht, was soll es bedeuten').*

Page 5, line 18:
A l'heure qu'il est: under present circumstances.

Page 7, line 22:
The People's Charter. Chartism is widely considered as the first organized political movement of the working class. Its programme, published in 1883 as The People's Charter, was repeatedly presented to Parliament through petitions and refused, The movement collapsed after 1848.

Page 11, line 10:
A Home Ruler. In 1881 Gladstone had granted the three 'Fs' claimed by Parnell. The next step for the Irish was to obtain 'Home Rule', that is political autonomy. Converted to that idea, Gladstone tried to pass the Bill through Parliament. It was rejected on 8 June 1886 by 343 votes to 313. It was followed by the secession of the 'Liberal Unionists' led by Joseph Chamberlain.

Page 11, line 31:
You help me to realise Horatius Cocles. Publius Horatius Cocles, a Roman who, for a time, all alone, opposed the army of Porsena, king of Etruria. He is described in Macaulay's *Lays of Ancient Rome.*

Page 20, line 23:
His reverence for the great Master who ruled (at Balliol): a reference to Benjamin Jowett (1817-93), who became Master of Balliol in 1870.

Page 35, line 15:
To follow Knowledge like a sinking star. Tennyson, *Ulysses,* line 31.

Page 38, lines 3-4:
His special weakness, originally amiable, had become an enthralling vice. The phrase 'an amiable weakness' comes from Fielding, *Tom Jones,* Book X, Chapter VIII.

Page 38, line 4:
The soul of goodness in the man was corrupted. Perhaps a reference to Shakespeare, *King Henry V,* IV, i, 4: 'There is some soul of goodness in things evil/Would men observingly distil it out.'

Page 39, line 15:
Emollit mores. From Ovid: *Epistulae ex Ponto,* II, ix, 47: 'Adde quod ingenuas didicisse fideliter artes/*Emollit mores* nec sinit esse feros'.

Page 47, line 7:
A small Indian rug being displayed as a thing of beauty. The first line, of course, of Keats's *Endymion.*

Page 47, line 41:
Ecce signum! Occurs in Shakespeare, *King Henry IV,* Part I, II, iv, 190. It is, however, a fairly common expression.

Page 48, line 20:
— *the blind Fury with the abhorred shears.* Milton, *'Lycidas'* line 75.

Page 48, line 38:
The pale cast of thought. Shakespeare, *Hamlet,* III, i, 85.

Page 51, line 30:
Glorious war. Perhaps from Shakespeare, *Othello,* III, iii, 355; 'Pride, pomp, and circumstance of glorious war'.

Page 56, line 40:
Their ways are not mine; let them not be yours. From Isaiah, 55:8: 'For my thoughts are not your thoughts, neither are your ways, saith the Lord'.

Page 58, lines 27-8:
They drove in a cab to festive regions, and as one to the manner born, 'and to the manner born' occurs in Shakespeare, *Hamlet,* I, iv, 14.

Page 59, line 30;
'*Haply the Queen Moon is on her throne, clustered around with all her starry fays.'* Keats, 'Ode to a *Nightingale',* stanza IV, ii, 6-7.

Page 64, line 26:
A sounding cataract. Perhaps a reference to Wordsworth, '*Lines composed a few miles above Tintern Abbey',* line 76: 'The sounding cataract/Haunted me like a passion'.

Page 68, lines 9-10:
Jerome was drawn to her, wooed her, and won her love. Perhaps an echo of *King Richard III, I, ii, 229.* 'Was ever woman in this humour woo'd./Was ever woman in this humour won?'

Page 69, line 11:
In a youthful poem (Jerome Otway) *had sung of Love as 'the crown of life'.* This, together with the quotation from Victor Hugo on p. 104, *('L'amour c'est la couronne,/Laisse-toi couronner')* explains the title of this novel. The phrase 'the crown of life' had, however, been in Gissing's mind for a good many years. In *A Life's Morning,* published eleven years before *The Crown of Life,* he spoke of ideal love as 'that bliss which was the crown of life' (Ch. XI) and again in Ch. XVII of the same novel: 'the ideal which saw the crown of life in passion triumphant'. The expression 'the crown of life' may be of biblical origin (James 1:12 and Rev. 2:10). Besides in *The Tempest,* Gonzalo says: 'Look down you gods,/And on this couple drop a blessed crown!' (V, i, 20 1-2).

Page 69, line 15:
The few chosen, where all are called. 'For many are called, but few are chosen' (Matthew, 22: 14).

Page 69, line 20:
On the heights of noble life, a face shines before them, the face of one who murmurs 'Guardami ben!' Is this a misprint? In Dante's *Purgatorio* (Canto XXX, line 73) the poet meets his beloved, who addresses him with the words: '*Guardaci ben! Ben son, ben son Beatrice'.* This is quoted from the edition by John D. Sinclair, who translates: 'Look at me well; I am , I am indeed Beatrice.' It might be added that in *A Life's Morning* (Ch. II) Mr Athel, on meeting Beatrice Redwing, exclaims: '*Guardami ben: ben son, ben son Beatrice!'* Or is the misprint in Sinclair's book?

Page 70, line 13:
Li ruscelletti che de' verdi colli/Del Casentin discendon giuso in Arno.

Dante, *Inferno,* Canto XXX, lines 64-5, Sinclair translates: 'The little stream that from the green hills of the Casentino flows down to the Arno'.

Page 72, line 4:
'Con l'animo che vince ogni battaglia,/Se col suo grave corpo non s'accascia.' Dante, *Inferno,* Canto XXIV, ii, 53-4. Sinclair translates: 'with the soul, which conquers in every battle if it sink not with its body's weight'.

Page 74, line 8:
The English way of mirth between man and maid: 'the way of a man with a maid' (Proverbs 30: 19).

Page 76, line 8:
There's a quotation from Virgil. Irene must have been thinking of the *Aeneid,* VI, 851: *'Tu regere imperio populos, Romane, memento/(Hae tibi erunt artes), pacisque imponere morem,/Parcere subjectis et debellare superbos.'*

Page 77, line 32:
The pink of modern maidenhood, fancy free: 'In maiden meditation, fancy-free', Shakespeare, *A Midsummer Night's Dream,* II, i, 164.

Page 80, line 31:
We may really become a mere nation of shopkeepers: a very common phrase, of course, usually ascribed to Napoleon. Other sources, however, have been suggested, Adam Smith in *The Wealth of Nations,* for instance.

Page 80, line 36:
'We are told,' said Irene, *'that England must expand.'* There may be an allusion here to a book by Sir John Seeley, called *The Expansion of England in the Eighteenth Century,* 1883, in which imperialism is described as the ideal for the British nation to accept.

page 82, line 32:
In corpore vili: the complete version of this condemnation of vivisection is *'Fiat experimentum in corpore vili'.*

Page 86, line 28:
He suffered from the death of old friends, especially that of John Bright. Bright died in 1889.

Page 98, line 3:
The wonted tenor of her life: 'the noiseless tenor of their way' occurs in Gray: 'Elegy Written in a Country Churchyard', XIX.

Page 98, line 9:
'Blessings in disguise'. This expression probably comes from the poet James Hervey (1714-58). It is, however, an expression in everyday use.

Page 104, line 35:
Les Chants du Crépuscule by Victor Hugo, published in 1835.

Page 110, line 25:
De mortuis. Ascribed to Chilo, but a common tag, of course.

Page, 111, line 17:
I should quote Bumble about the law. In *Oliver Twist* Ch. 51, Mr Bumble
says: 'If the law supposes that, . . . the law is a ass— a idiot.'

Page, 117, line 8:
Solvitur quaerendo: 'Solvitur ambulando', which is proverbial, seems to be
more usual.

Page 122, last line:
Airy nothings: Shakespeare speaks of 'airy nothings' in *A Midsummer
Night's Dream,* V, i, 16.

Page 132, line 30:
To display advertisements. This kind of conversation exposing the vulgarity
of the age of commercialism reminds one of the scenes in *In The Year of
Jubilee* in which Luckworth Crewe, another mouthpiece of the commercial
spirit, speaks in similar terms to Nancy Lord.

Page 140, line 14:
When you come in we'll put the kettle on, and all have tea. There may be
an allusion to the raven in Dickens, *Barnaby Rudge,* which cries 'Polly put
the kettle on, we'll all have tea' (Ch. 17).

Page 141, line 26:
Avos: although Piers Otway knew Russian well he was wrong about *avos.*
It does not mean 'fire away' but 'perhaps'.

Page 158, line 12:
'When the next great war comes, newspapers will be the chief cause of it.'
Attacks on newspapers are very common in Gissing, for instance in
Ryecroft, Summer VI and VII.

Page 166, line 26:
He loved the name for its meaning. Peace! The Greek form of Irene,
eirènè actually means 'peace' derived from the Greek *eirènikos.* The
adjective 'irenic' means: 'conducive to or operating toward peace or
conciliations. This is a particularly significant illustration of the importance
granted by Gissing to the names and Christian names of his characters.
They generally have a symbolic value related either to their temper or to a
theme, or to both. Think for instance of Jerome Otway's three sons, who
were named after his favourite writer or political leaders. Moreover, the

passage is a remarkable illustration of the parallel existing between Piers's personal quest for Peace on the personal and international level: both will only be found in love.

Page 168, line1:
The transcendent mood of Browning's ideal lover. Probably a reference to 'The Statue and the Bust', in which the reunion of two lovers is deferred year after year, until they realize they have been dreaming.

Page 168, line 19:
'*The intelligence of the heart*' This heralds the passage in *Henry Ryecroft*, alluded to in the introduction: 'Foolishly arrogant I was; I used to judge the worth of a person by his intellectual power and attainment. I could see no good where there was no logic, no charm where there was no learning. Now I think that one has to distinguish between two forms of intelligence, that of the brain and that of the heart, and I have come to regard the second as by far the more important.' *(Henry Ryecroft*, Spring XVI). Gissing has gone a long way since he made Godwin Peak say: 'I hate low, uneducated people! I hate them worse than the filthiest vermin!' *Born in Exile*, Gollancz Classics, p. 47.

Page 169, line 18:
Custom's tyranny. In *Othello*, I. iii. 230, Shakespeare speaks of the 'tyrant custom'. There may be no connection, however.

Page 170, line 15:
The chances of life. In *The Book of Common Prayer* (Holy Communion, Collects after the Offertory) we read: 'All the changes and chances of this mortal life'.

Page 174, end:
The quotation from Meredith is the eleventh and final stanza of 'The Last Contention'.

Page 179, end:
Pride in their port. The quotation from Goldsmith comes from 'The Traveller', line 327.

Page 180, line 16:
Johnson defined Patriotism . . . as the last refuge of a scoundrel. From Boswell's *Life* (7 April 1775).

Page 182, line 25:
Again we meet in a London Street—which is rhyme and sounds like Browning, doesn't it? Is this an actual quotation? Or has it been merely made up by Daniel Otway? The rhythm is suggestive of Browning's 'Waring'.

Page 183, line 16:
Lend me your ears. Shakespeare, *Julius Caesar,* III, ii, 79.

Page 183, lines 31-20:
Pray, your exquisite reason? 'I have no exquisite reason for it, but I have reason good enough' Shakespeare, *Twelfth Night,* II, iii, 159.

Page 186, end:
'Quand on perd, par triste occurrence'. Alfred de Musset also supplied the motto for *Isabel Clarendon.* In a letter to Ellen Gissing, Musset is referred to in a list of 'really great men'. On the other hand, in his *Commonplace Book* Gissing complained of the ineptitude of the (French) language for poetry (45). Apart from quotations from Victor Hugo and Alfred de Musset there is some more evidence of French (linguistic) influence in *The Crown of Life* (not surprising as it was written shortly after the first meeting with Gabrielle Fleury). On p. 170 we find *'borner la carrière à ses émotions* and on p. 199 *'On n'est pas plus galant!'* The Derwent family has a French servant (Thibaut Rossignol) and Piers Otway is associated with a French-speaking Swiss (Moncharmont). Cf. also: 'Take the best type of Frenchman, for instance, Is he necessarily fatuous in his criticism of us? (p. 76).

Page 196, line 6:
Nascitur non fit— 'Nascimur poetae, fimus oratores' is attributed to Cicero.

Page 204, line 21:
'And then, if justice were done, that scoundrel would be hanged'. The use of *hanged* is rather interesting. In his *Commonplace Book* (6), Gissing remarked that *he was hung* sounds 'ghastly' and 'he was hanged' 'rather humorous'.

Page 256, line 11:
To abolish capital punishment. The death-penalty problem is dealt with at greater length in *The Commonplace Book,* pp. 24-5.

Page 271, line 23:
The bells in the country! Remarks on church bells are extremely frequent in Gissing's work.

Page 278, line 23:
He has joined the Dukhobortsi. The Dukhobortsi were members of a religious sect founded in the Ukraine in the second half of the eighteenth century. They rejected official dogma and hierarchy, and believed in inner revelation. God's word is in every man and he must try to listen to it; this inner message is eternal Christ. Their religious radicalism was coupled with political radicalism. Their resistance to secular authorities took the form of a refusal to do military service and to pay taxes. They were often

persecuted and exiled to the Caucasus. Eventually the Russian government allowed them to emigrate to Cyprus and especially to Canada. They were helped in their attempt to leave Russia and to gather the necessary money by Quakers and Tolstoy, who wrote a number of 'pot-boilers' for that reason. Their emigration started in 1898 and ended in 1899.

Page 280, line 36:
'Seaside—no; I don't like the seaside.' Interesting to compare with Ryecroft's remarks on the seaside.

Page 285, line 9:
Solus feci! A fairly common tag, of unknown origin.

Page 308, line 32:
Tell truth and shame—your Russian relatives. There are two sources for this quotation: Ben Johnson, *Tale of a Tub,* II, I. 'Hark you, John Clay, if you have/Done any such thing, tell troth and shame the devil.' Shakespeare, *King Henry IV* III, i, 62, 'O, while you live, tell truth, and shame the devil.'

Page 320, line 19:
There's a time for silence, but also a time for talking. Echoes the famous enumeration in Ch. 3 of Ecclesiastes.

Bibliography

I—**Articles and reviews dealing with the first edition (* indicates a reprint in** *Gissing: The Critical Heritage)*
Academy, 28 October 1899, p. 485
New Age, 2 November 1899, p. 132 (Socius)
Spectator, 4 November 1899, pp. 661-2 (C. L. Graves)
Review of the Week, 4 November 1899, pp. 16-17 (Morley Roberts)*
Publisher's Circular, 4 November 1899, p. 498
New York Tribune Illustrated Supplement, 5 November 1899, p. 13*
St James's Gazette, 7 November 1899, p. 12*
Manchester Guardian, 7 November 1899, p. 4
Globe, 8 November 1899, p. 4
Scotsman, 9 November 1899, p. 3
Daily Chronicle, 10 November 1899, p. 4
Literature, 11 November 1899, pp. 470-1*
Speaker, 11 November 1899, p. 153
Pall Mall Gazette, 11 November 1899, p. 4
Morning Post, 16 November 1899, p. 3
Literary World (London), 17 November 1899, p. 377
Daily News, 17 November 1899, p. 9
Glasgow Herald, 17 November 1899, p. 4
Athenaeum, 18 November 1899, p. 683
World, (London), 22 November 1899, p. 31
Public Opinion (New York), 30 November 1899, p. 697
Author, 1 December 1899, p. 164
Saturday Review, 2 December 1899, p. 712
Outlook (London), 9 December 1899, p. 626
Queen, 9 December 1899, p. 1006 (M.C.B.)
New York Times Saturday Review of Books and Arts, 23 December 1899, p. 898 (William L. Alden)
Westminster Gazette, 30 December 1899, p. 3

Bookman (London), December 1899, p. 89
Guardian (London), 17 January 1900, p. 103
Critic (New York), January 1900, p. 91
Book Lover (Melbourne), January 1900, p. 2 (H. H. Champion)*
Mercure de France, February 1900, p. 551 (Henry-D. Davray)

II — Books and articles containing material on *The Crown of Life*
Anon., 'An Idealistic Realist', *Atlantic Monthly*, February 1904, pp. 280-2*
Bateson, Margaret (Mrs. W. E. Heitland), 'Mr George Gissing', *Guardian* (London), 6 January 1904, pp.34-5
Coustillas, P. (ed.), *Collected Articles on George Gissing* (1968)
Coustillas, P. and Partridge, C. (ed.), *Gissing: The Critical Heritage* (1972). Contains reviews of *The Crown of Life* and a number of articles in which the novel is discussed
Coustillas, P. (ed.), *The Letters of George Gissing to Gabrielle Fleury* (1964)
Davies, Oswald H., *George Gissing. A Study in Literary Leanings* (1966; reprinted by Kohler & Coombes, Dorking 1975 with an introduction by P. Coustillas)
Donnelly, Mabel Collins, *George Gissing, Grave Comedian* (1954)
Gissing, Algernon and Ellen (eds.), *Letters of George Gissing to Members of his Family* (1927)
Gordan, John D., *George Gissing 1857-1903. An Exhibition from the Berg Collection* (1954)
Green, Roger Lancelyn (ed.), *Kipling: The Critical Heritage* (1971)
Korg, Jacob, *George Gissing. A Critical Biography* (1963)
McKay, Ruth Capers, *George Gissing and his Critic Frank Swinnerton* (1933)
More, Paul Elmer, introduction to *The Private Papers of Henry Ryecroft* (Modern Library, 1918)
Poole, Adrian, *Gissing in Context* (1975)
Roberts, Morley, *The Private Life of Henry Maitland* (1912; new editions, 1923 and 1958)
Spiers, J. and Coustillas, P., *The Rediscovery of George Gissing* (1971)
Swinnerton, Frank, *George Gissing, a Critical Study* (1912; new editions, 1923 and 1966)
Tindall, Gillian, *The Born Exile: George Gissing* (1974)
Wolff, Joseph J., *George Gissing: An Annotated Bibliography of Writings about Him* (1974)
Young, Arthur (ed.), *The Letters of George Gissing to Eduard Bertz* (1961)

III — Other related material
Allen, Walter, *The English Novel* (1954)
Baker, Ernest A., *The History of the English Novel*, vol. IX (1936)
Ford, Boris (ed.), *From Dickens to Hardy* (1958)
Funke, Elizabeth, *Die Diskussion über den Burenkrieg in Politik und Presse der Deutschen Schweiz* (Zürich, 1974)

Korg, Jacob (ed.), *George Gissing's Commonplace Book* (1962)

Kruger, Rayne, *Goodbye Dolly Gray: The Story of the Boer War* (London, 1961)

Lehmann, Joseph H., *The First Boer War* (London, 1972)

More, Paul Elmer, 'George Gissing', *Shelburne Essays* (Fifth Series), 1908, pp. 45-65

Murray, John Middleton, 'George Gissing, in *Katherine Mansfield and Other Literary Studies* (1959)

Oprsal, Pavel, *Die Russische Sekte der Douchoboren, 1886-1908 Groningen* (Offsetdrukkerij Fa. Veenstra Visser, Leyde, 1967)

Pollard, Arthur (ed.), *The Victorians* (1970)

Woodcock, George and Avakumovic, Ivan. *The Doukhobors* (London, 1968)

Young, W. T., *Cambridge History of English Literature, vol. XIII, ch. XIV* (1916)